ENDURING
DARKNESS

ALSO BY RAVEN WOOD

To see the most recently updated list of books by Raven Wood, please visit: www.authorravenwood.com

CONTENT WARNINGS

Enduring Darkness is a bully romance intended for mature readers. It contains violence and graphic sexual content. If you have specific triggers, you can find the full list of content warnings at: www.authorravenwood.com/content-warnings

ENDURING DARKNESS

RAVEN WOOD

For everyone who has a secret knife kink

ALINA

When people think you're made of glass, the last place you should be is probably a university for assassins. And to be fair, I can't really argue with that logic. But it was the only way that I could carve out some freedom for myself.

"Alina! We're leaving."

I heave a sigh.

Carve out some freedom, yes. But with massive emphasis on *some*.

The door to my bedroom vibrates in its hinges as a fist pounds impatiently on it.

"Alina. Now."

"Yes," I reply, not bothering to hide the irritation in my tone. "I heard you the first time, Mikhail."

Brushing my hands down my shirt, I walk over to the door and open it.

My eldest brother, Mikhail, is standing right on the other side, his blue eyes locked on me and his pale brows raised expectantly. I'm half a second away from snapping at him that

I'm actually ready with two minutes to spare, but I manage to suppress the impulse.

Pissing off Mikhail is a bad idea. Especially today. Since he is the eldest, he is in charge of the rest of us Petrovs here at Blackwater University. And if he decides to start limiting my already limited freedom here, all of this will have been for nothing. Not to mention that we're about to head back to our family home in the city for a *family meeting* where we will discuss whether I should stay at Blackwater or not, which is a meeting I'm dreading terribly.

So instead of taking that out on Mikhail, I drop my gaze. "I'm sorry."

His voice softens as he replies, "It's alright. You do actually have one minute to spare."

I look up to find him smiling at me. It's a smile that few other people ever get to see. Mikhail is one of the best hitmen in the senior year, and most people give him, and our entire family, a wide berth. Especially now that there are five of us on campus. No one wants to risk angering the Petrov family. Well, except for the Hunters, of course.

"Mikhail! Alina!" Anton calls from downstairs. "Are you coming or what? The twins are threatening to drive if you don't get down here soon."

"Over my dead body," Mikhail replies. "Which is exactly the state we will all end up in if either of them is driving."

My twin cousins, Maksim and Konstantin, let out a terrifyingly synchronized evil laugh from somewhere below.

Mikhail shakes his head in exasperation before jerking his chin at me. We start down towards the front door.

We're renting one of the freestanding houses in the residential area of Blackwater University. All students live here, so the entire area is filled with houses as well as larger buildings that contain apartments or dorm rooms. While I would have preferred to rent a place of my own instead of sharing it with my two brothers and my two cousins, I have to admit that our house is beautiful.

The floor and walls are made of pale wood, there are white marble countertops in the kitchen, and arched windows to let in the light. Around the house is a small lawn with some bushes and trees that provide privacy from our neighboring houses as well as from the main road.

I glance out the window and towards the car out by the curb as Mikhail and I reach the hallway where Anton and the twins are waiting. Dread rolls through my stomach again.

"Ready?" Anton asks.

"Yes," I reply, keeping my voice casual.

Anton's gray eyes search my face for a long second. He can probably tell that I'm nervous. But thankfully, he doesn't comment on it.

"Alright, then let's go," Konstantin says.

After slapping his brother on the arm, he throws open the door and strolls out. Maksim follows him. Mikhail heaves a sigh and shakes his head once more before he and Anton walk out as well. I pause for a second, getting that awful dread back under control, before doing the same.

The front door lets out a click as I lock it. My brothers and cousins are already halfway down the stone path that cuts through the lawn and leads to the street, but I don't hurry to catch up with them. Instead, I study them as I walk.

To the east, the sun is just barely rising, tinting the sky and the rest of the world with a bit of red. The faint light plays over the four men walking ahead of me. I look like them, and at the same time, I look nothing like them.

Konstantin and Maksim are not identical twins, so they're

easy to tell apart. But both of them have brown hair and brown eyes. Anton has that same hair color too, courtesy of our father and theirs, who are brothers. But Anton got our mother's gray eyes. I did as well. I got her blonde hair too. As did Mikhail.

But that's where the similarities end.

All of them are tall, athletic, and powerful.

And I'm... not.

"I'm telling you, I'm riding shotgun," Konstantin declares when I at last catch up with the four of them where they have stopped close to the car.

"The hell you are," Maksim retorts.

"*I'm* riding shotgun," Anton interjects.

"Oh really?" Konstantin replies. "And why is that?"

"Because it's *my* brother's car."

"Are we really having this conversation?" Mikhail interrupts, shooting the three of them an incredulous look. "What are you? Five years old?"

"We're—"

Everyone abruptly stops speaking as the sound of voices suddenly comes from around the corner. We all whirl around to face the three men who have just appeared on the street a short distance from us.

My heart leaps into my throat.

The Hunters.

I've seen them before, of course. But because we decided that I should avoid being seen in public together with my brothers and cousins, the Hunters haven't known who I am. Since I don't want to be dragged into their war with my family, I had planned to keep it that way.

Irritation fights with the stunned shock inside me.

What are these three psychos even doing walking through

the residential area at the crack of dawn on a bloody Saturday?

I flick a glance towards my brothers.

The temperature seems to plummet several degrees as their gazes lock on the Hunter brothers.

God damn it. This is not happening. Not today of all days.

I quickly shift my gaze back to the Hunters, trying to read their mood while my heart pounds in my chest.

Rico, the guy in the middle, stares at me in surprise. As if he is shocked that there is a fifth Petrov on campus that he didn't know about. Which is probably the case. Then his gaze turns assessing.

Bitterness churns in my stomach because I know what he sees. A skinny girl who barely reaches their collarbones. None of the lean muscles that practically all other first-years have. No athletic body. No threat whatsoever. I'm twenty years old, but all anyone ever sees when they look at me is a breakable little girl.

Rico and his brothers look anything but breakable. All three of them are tall and muscular. Even bigger than my brothers. And they have an almost tangible air of lethal power radiating off them.

Though Rico is handsome, almost to the point of being pretty, with his brown hair that curls softly and brown eyes that glitter almost gold in the light from the rising sun, there is no mistaking the quiet authority in his gaze. One word from him, and I'm sure the grass itself would bow down.

According to rumors, he was the one who somehow managed to keep their eldest brother, Eli, in check when he was still at Blackwater. I've only heard about Eli from my brothers, since he graduated this summer before I enrolled, but apparently he's an absolute maniac with very little impulse control who put a gun to Anton's head and almost cut out Mikhail's eye last year. Thank God he's not here right now at least. If he was, Mikhail would probably already have attacked.

I shift my gaze to the broad-shouldered guy on Rico's left.

Jace, the youngest of them, somehow always manages to look like he has just rolled out of bed. But despite his effortlessly messy brown hair, the sight of him makes alarm bells chime in my head. Because he looks like someone who could burn the world down just because he was bored.

But the worst one of all is Kaden.

I slide my gaze to the man standing on Rico's other side.

And my heart stops.

Kaden Hunter is staring straight at me.

As opposed to Jace and Rico, whose brown hair curls softly, Kaden's hair is black and straight. Severe. Everything about him is severe. From the sharp cut of his cheekbones to the lethal muscles his body is carved from to his cold dark brown eyes. Ice seeps through my veins at the way those emotionless eyes bore into mine, making my pulse flutter nervously.

Almost every time I see Kaden, he is twirling a knife in his hand. He was when he rounded the corner, but he's not anymore. Now, he's just standing there, completely still, while staring at me. Like a predator sizing up its prey. And all I can do is to just stare back at him with wide eyes while my heart thunders in my chest, because I suddenly get the feeling that if I so much as breathe right now, he's going to attack.

"Alina, get to the car," Mikhail snaps from right next to me.

But I can't take my eyes off Kaden. Because if I do, I just know that something bad is going to happen.

A slow smile, the smile of a true psychopath, spreads across Kaden's lips. It sends a flicker of fear through my body.

"What's this, Mikhail?" Kaden says, though his dark eyes remain locked on me. "You have a little sister? You've been holding out on me."

Mikhail immediately takes a step forward, angling his body so that he is shielding me. Cold hatred drips from his voice as he growls, "If you come within six feet of her, I'll kill you."

That sadistic smile on Kaden's mouth widens.

It makes Anton and the twins shift closer to me as well.

I flick a quick glance at them before meeting Kaden's stare again.

Surprise shoots through me.

Kaden isn't looking at me the way Rico did. He isn't looking at me as if I'm breakable. He's looking at me as if he wants to see just how much I can take before he breaks me. A subtle difference. But a difference nonetheless. And the realization sends a bolt of electricity through my spine.

However, before I can decipher that emotion, Kaden takes a step forward.

My brothers react immediately. Lurching forward, they try to trap Kaden between them. But before they can, Rico darts forward and slams a fist into Anton's side. I jerk back as Mikhail aims a hard kick towards Kaden while my cousins engage Jace.

The sounds of punches and kicks echo through the temperate morning air as they fight. And all I can do is to stand there uselessly and watch. Frustration wells up inside me because I desperately want to help. But I know that if I do, I will only get in the way.

I'm not a fighter. I didn't enroll at this university to

become an assassin. The only reason I'm here is because I managed to convince my father that it would be better if I had some basic training before he married me off to someone he wanted an alliance with. That way, it would be more difficult for my future husband and his family to take advantage of our family. Or that's what I told him at least.

But I'm not here to train. I'm here because I desperately wanted out of an arranged engagement before it was too late. I'm here because I want a few years of freedom before I'm forced into another arranged marriage. Because I know that no matter how much I beg, my father won't break off my next engagement as well. The next match he makes for me will be non-negotiable.

So all I can do while my brothers and cousins fight is to watch. As useless as the glass figurine that everyone always treats me as.

Panic pulses through my body as Kaden suddenly feints a strike to Mikhail's left but instead dives to the right. Towards *me*. I try to scramble backwards, but Kaden grabs my arm before I can get away.

His fingers dig into my upper arm as he yanks me towards him.

Air escapes my lungs in a huff as my back slams into his hard chest.

A moment later, the cold edge of a knife appears across my throat.

All around us, the fight comes to a halt.

My heart is beating so wildly that I'm sure Kaden can feel it.

"One more step, and I'll slit her throat," the psycho behind me announces.

From two steps away, Mikhail is staring at the two of us with a mix of horror, panic, and hatred in his blue eyes.

"You move one muscle, and we'll break his arm," Maksim retorts.

I snap my gaze towards my cousin. Hope surges in my chest. Anton and Rico are standing a few steps from us, and from each other, but the twins have now managed to get Jace down on one knee after he decided to leave himself wide open for Maksim in order to stop Konstantin from reaching Rico a minute ago. Konstantin now instead has a hand on the back of Jace's neck, forcing him to stay down, while Maksim is pushing his arm up at an angle that looks very painful.

Deafening silence hangs over the empty street like a crackling lightning storm.

Kaden's grip on my arm tightens.

"If you don't tell your cousins to get their fucking hands off *my* little brother, you're about to watch your sister bleed out on the street," Kaden declares in a voice so cold that I swear I can see ice spreading across his knife.

My pulse thrums in my ears but I remain perfectly still, because I can tell by the tone of his voice that he means every word. Unless my cousins release Jace, he will slit my throat.

Rage crackles across Mikhail's face, but there is an undercurrent of panic in his voice as he replies, "If you don't get your fucking knife away from my little sister, I'll—"

"I said, lower his fucking arm!" Kaden cuts him off.

I suppress a startled breath as he suddenly yanks his knife high up, pressing the flat of the blade hard underneath my chin and forcing me to tilt my head back until my throat is completely exposed.

"Now!" Kaden finishes, the command slicing through the air and vibrating against my skin.

My cousins shoot a worried glance at Mikhail, who jerks his chin down in confirmation. They all seem to realize just how serious Kaden is.

Maksim lowers Jace's arm, but they don't release him. However, before Kaden can follow through on his threat anyway, Rico speaks up.

"We trade back, and then call it a day," he says.

"Agreed," Anton immediately replies.

Relief flows through me.

Mikhail snaps his gaze to Anton, displeasure flickering in his blue eyes, because we all know that it's Mikhail who calls the shots. But Anton just stares back at him. Our eldest brother doesn't like to lose. Even a tie is considered a loss in his book. And especially against the Hunter family.

However, Mikhail knows that Anton is right. Unless they're willing to spill blood, namely mine, this confrontation has to end like this.

Mikhail forces out a long breath. "Fine."

They all turn to Kaden.

Because my head is tilted so far back, I can see the cruel smile that lurks on his lips.

"I'll release her," Kaden promises. "In exchange for my brother. And a name."

Mikhail's gaze sharpens. "What?"

With his blade still firmly underneath my chin, Kaden looks down at me. "What's your name, little doe?"

My heart does a strange flip at the way he rolls the question over his tongue.

"You fucking—" Mikhail begins.

I cut him off before he can say something that will restart this whole battle again.

"Alina," I reply. With the back of my head pressed against

his muscled chest, I hold Kaden's dark eyes with a steady gaze. And I make damn sure that there is no fear in my voice or in my eyes as I repeat, "My name is Alina."

His cold eyes light up, and he smiles even wider.

Alarm shoots up my spine, and I suddenly feel as if I have made a huge mistake. I shouldn't have masked my fear. I should've let my voice tremble. I should've let him know just how fast my pulse flutters when he holds a knife to my throat.

However, before I can do anything to remedy it, Kaden abruptly removes his blade and shoves me towards Mikhail. I stumble, almost slamming into my brother's chest before his hands appear on my arms instead. My left one still aches slightly from Kaden's iron grip, but I make sure not to show it.

A few steps from us, my cousins have released Jace and backed away.

For a few seconds, the only sound is the rapid hammering of my heart.

Then Mikhail jerks his chin. "Get in the car."

We all obey immediately.

Konstantin holds the back door open for me while Anton climbs into the passenger seat and Maksim rounds the car. I slide into the middle of the backseat. The twins take up position on either side of me.

Once we're all in the car, I glance back towards Mikhail.

My eldest brother spits on the ground before Kaden's feet. Closing my eyes for a second, I resist the urge to groan. I watch intently as Mikhail turns his back on the three psychos and starts towards the driver's seat. Kaden looks like he wants to attack again, but he thankfully doesn't.

Then his cold eyes slide to me.

I snap my gaze back to the windshield ahead while my heart jerks in my chest.

Mikhail reaches the car a second later.

After slamming the door shut, he starts the car and revs the engine angrily before driving off.

"That's it," he announces. "You will not be staying at Blackwater."

"What?" Dread and panic surge through me, and I sit up straight, trying to catch his eyes in the rearview mirror. "Of course I am! You—"

"Did you not just see what happened back there?" Mikhail cuts me off while keeping his eyes on the road.

"That only happened because of *your* war with them," I protest. "It has nothing to do with me."

"It has everything to do with you when Kaden fucking Hunter puts a knife to your throat."

"But he only did that because I was with *you*. If I stay out of his way, something like this won't happen again."

"Of course it will. You—"

"How do you think Dad will react if I tell him that you let Kaden put a blade to my throat?" I interrupt, letting the fear whirling inside me infuse my voice with steel.

Silence descends on the car. Anton shifts uncomfortably in the passenger seat ahead, and the twins suddenly become solely focused on staring out at the fields that flash past outside the windows.

At long last, Mikhail meets my eyes in the rearview mirror.

I never stand up to Mikhail. I never even disobey him. And I never, ever, threaten him.

But I'm desperate now.

"I will be staying at Blackwater," I declare, keeping my

voice strong. "I will stay at least this year. And you will help me convince Mom and Dad of that at this family meeting. And in exchange, we will all pretend that what happened this morning never happened."

Mikhail holds my gaze in the mirror for another second before looking back at the road. The silence in the car is so thick that I can almost feel it pressing against my skin.

I know that Mikhail is under a lot of pressure. That he is desperate to prove himself to our father. To prove that he is worthy of being the heir to the feared Petrov family. Our great assassin family that always competes for the best hitman contracts along with legendary families like the Hunters and the Smiths.

If our father learns that my brothers had let someone from the Hunters, who he hates more than any of the other families, put a knife to my throat, he would see it as an unacceptable and humiliating failure. I know that it's cruel to threaten Mikhail with that, but I can't let him take away the only scrap of freedom I will ever have.

My heart slams against my ribs as Mikhail continues driving in silence for a few more seconds. His jaw clenches. Around us, Anton and our cousins are making sure to look at anything but us.

"Fine," Mikhail grinds out at last.

Relief floods my chest.

"Thank you," I say, softening my voice.

He jerks his chin down in a curt nod. "But if things escalate, we will have this conversation again, Alina." His commanding eyes meet mine in the mirror. "Understood?"

I drop my gaze. "Yes."

"Good."

I can almost feel his anger simmer in the air at the fact that

I practically blackmailed him into this, but the guilt from that still can't overshadow the relief that sparkles inside my whole soul. I will be staying at Blackwater. I will have at least one year of freedom.

Now, all I need to do is to stay as far away from Kaden Hunter as possible.

2

KADEN

My already bad mood is worsening with every second in this fucking house. I don't know what the hell Rico was thinking, dragging us here. I don't want to go to a fucking party. I want to cut someone open and watch the life bleed out of their eyes. Preferably the disrespectful little shit known as Mikhail Petrov who dared to spit on the ground before my feet this morning. Though, his sister would make a nice substitute as well.

I flick my gaze back and forth across the room yet again. But unfortunately, the skinny blonde that I threatened this morning is not here.

Lots of other people *are*, though.

This whole living room is packed with drunk obnoxious people. In fact, this whole house is. Loud music thumps from several rooms and thuds come from upstairs where people must be either dancing or fucking. Or both.

Behind me and to the left, a group of people are playing some kind of drinking game around the massive dining room table. Several other groups are clustered together, drinking and talking by the wall. Others are dancing on the floor where there is room. The armchairs and the couch opposite ours are all occupied as well. And because of the loud music, everyone is yelling in order to be heard over the noise as they try to talk about their fucking inconsequential matters.

I flick a glance at Rico, who is sitting on my left. He is leaning one elbow on the armrest, his chin resting in his palm, as he stares unseeing at the wall on the other side of the room. That lost and almost rootless look that I often see in his eyes is present now too. I want to be angry at him for dragging me to this damn party, but I can't. I hate it when he looks like that, because I know that there is nothing I can do to help him.

After scanning the room again, I shift my gaze to my little brother. Jace is supposed to be sitting on my right, but he alternates between sitting, standing, and leaning to kiss the random girl beside him so often that I'm sure the dark blue couch we're occupying will be suffering from whiplash injuries before the night is over.

Jace's chaotic and restless nature has gotten worse in the past year. And I'm pretty sure that I know why. But I can't confront him about it, because I know that he will just get angry and deny it, and then everything will go to hell.

I suppress the urge to heave an annoyed sigh and instead go back to scanning the room for any sign of the Russians.

All around me, people dance and laugh and flirt. And all of them, even my brothers, wear their emotions plain as day on their faces. It must be exhausting. Feeling so much all the time must be absolutely exhausting. I don't get the point of it at all.

Though I have to admit, I do love watching some emotions flood people's faces. Namely, fear and desperation. I don't even need air. I could survive solely on breathing in that delicious fear that people exude when they tremble and beg at my feet.

"She's here," Rico blurts out, sitting upright in a flash.

I snap my gaze back and forth across the sea of people again. Confusion pulls at my brows when I don't see Alina anywhere.

"Isabella is here," Rico says, his eyes locked on the empty doorway that leads into the hallway beyond.

Of course. He wasn't looking for the little Russian. He was looking for his own nemesis.

The couch groans as Rico shoves to his feet and starts towards the hallway. "But she was leaving. I'm going to confront her."

I wave my hand in silent acknowledgement as he hurries across the room.

Next to me, the girl who was sitting on the armrest beside Jace slides down onto his lap instead and rolls her hips. She looks incredibly similar to the other random girl that he fucked last weekend. Though, to be fair, that might be because I don't care enough to remember their faces. I know that Jace will get bored of her and pick someone else in a few days. He always does.

The girl moans as Jace kisses her throat.

I give my brother a shove. "Get a fucking room before I cut out both her tongue and yours."

Jace flips me off without taking his mouth off her throat. But then he does stand up and pulls the girl by the hand towards where the stairs to the bedrooms are located. He flashes me a grin and then winks before disappearing around the corner. I shake my head.

Alone on the couch with nothing but loud annoying people around me, I decide that I've had enough. I rise to my feet as well and turn towards the glass doors on the other side of the room. They're partly open to let in some fresh air and cool down the increasingly warm room. I slide out a knife and start towards them.

While twirling the knife in my hand, I stalk across the room. The crowd parts before me. I don't know if it's out of respect for my last name and my family's connection to the Morelli mafia family, or if it's simply out of fear of being cut by my spinning blade. And I don't really care. The end result is the same. They know their place and move out of my fucking way.

Temperate night air washes over me as I shove the glass doors open fully and stride out onto the lawn.

To my great annoyance, it's also crowded with people.

I'm just about to simply stalk back home when a voice stops me. Or rather, a *name*.

"Alina," a female voice calls. "You're here! I saw you and your brothers and cousins drive away together this morning when I went for my run, so I was worried you'd be gone all weekend."

All of my senses sharpen as I turn towards the source of the voice. It belongs to Carla, the first-year who lives in this house. Or at least one of the first-years who live here. Her dark curls are pulled up in an elaborate style, and her gold-shimmering dress glitters as she hugs a smaller figure.

Anticipation ripples through me as I study that smaller figure.

Alina Petrov.

She's here.

"Oh, no, it was just a short family meeting," Alina says as she steps back after Carla's hug. "I wouldn't miss this party for anything."

"Good." Carla grins and jerks her chin towards the still open glass doors. "Now, go on in and start getting drunk. You have some catching up to do."

While staying out of Alina's direct line of sight, I study her as she says something else to Carla and then laughs before heading towards the doors. Her long blonde hair ripples as she walks. It falls almost all the way down to the small of her back like a smooth waterfall. Which is a great length for a variety of... restraining methods.

She's wearing a pale blue dress that ends halfway down her thighs, leaving her slim legs and arms on display. I slide my gaze to her delicate wrists and ankles. She would look fantastic in some metal shackles. In rope too. But most of all, those big doe eyes of hers would look incredible brimming with fear.

Making a split-second decision, I walk over to the back of the house to check if it's as crowded as the front. It's not. Only one couple is making out in the shadows of the corner.

I hurry back to the front and grab the first person I come across.

"Hey, what the hell?" The guy I grabbed, a blond second-year who slurs a little when he talks, spins towards me. He glares down at my hand around his arm before looking up to meet my gaze. His eyes go wide and color drains from his face. "Oh. Fuck. Hunter."

"You see that skinny blonde who walked inside a minute ago?" I demand.

His gaze flicks down to the knife I'm still twirling in my hand for a second before returning to my face. "The one who was talking to Carla?"

"Yes."

"Yeah, I saw her."

"Go in there and tell her that Carla needs her help with something out back."

"Wh—"

"Now."

"Alright. Alright." He swallows and casts another wary glance down at my knife before backing away.

I release his arm but watch to make sure that he follows my orders and goes inside. He does.

Once he's out of sight, I move towards the back of the house again. The two people in the corner are still making out. I stride towards them.

"Take a hike," I order.

They jerk back from each other and turn towards me. One look is enough to make them straighten their clothes and hurry away. I move so that I'm standing on the other side of the back door. And then I wait.

Alina appears only a minute later.

Her pale hair shines like silver in the moonlight as she sticks her head out and squints into the darkness. "Carla?"

Thumping music and the sounds of talking drift out into the night from inside as Alina pushes the door open wider and steps out onto the small patio. There is a red plastic cup in her hand.

I wait for the door to fall shut again before taking a step out of the shadows.

"Carla?" Alina says. "Are you here? David said you needed help."

"I'm afraid David lied," I say.

She whips around so fast that she drops her cup. It hits the ground with a thud and tips over. Pink liquid spills across the stones, forming a small puddle.

"You," she breathes as her wide gray eyes meet mine.

While taking a step back, her gaze quickly sweeps over our darkened surroundings as if looking for a way to escape. I have no intention of letting that happen, so I move forward. She instinctively backs up again as I advance on her.

"Where's Carla?" she demands, her voice surprisingly strong.

"No idea. I only used her name as a way to lure you here. And it worked." I cock my head. "Are you and Carla friends?"

She opens her mouth to reply, but then hesitation blows across her delicate features. I continue backing her towards the wall. Her gaze darts around the area again, and she licks her lips. But she doesn't answer my question. As if she's not sure which answer would endanger her more. Or maybe endanger Carla.

Smart. I didn't expect her to be able to consider consequences in such a way while she's in the middle of being threatened.

"Look, I have no issues with you," she begins instead. "Your conflict is with my brothers and my cousins. I have nothing to do with it, so there is no reason for you to—"

"You're a Petrov. That's reason enough."

"I'm—" Her words are cut off as her back suddenly connects with the wall.

She casts a panicked look over her shoulder, as if she hadn't realized that I had been backing her into a corner. Literally.

I keep moving, advancing on her until she's forced to press herself hard against the wall. While still twirling the knife in my hand, I rake my gaze over her body.

Fuck, she really is tiny.

She barely reaches my collarbones, and she's so delicately built that I could snap her neck with one hand.

Her chest rises and falls with rapid breaths, each one making her tits brush against my stomach. She flicks another quick glance down at the blade in my hand, but she says nothing.

Impressive. I had expected her to start babbling like most people do when they're frightened.

Raising the knife, I trail it gently along her jaw. She flinches at the first kiss of steel, but then remains perfectly still.

"Are you afraid, little doe?" I taunt.

"No," she replies, her voice steady.

A vicious smile spreads across my lips.

Because she *is* afraid. There is no mistake about it. I can see it pulsing in her eyes. Can feel it vibrating in the air between us. And it's absolutely intoxicating.

I draw in a deep breath, breathing it in like the sweetest perfume.

With that sadistic grin still on my mouth, I trace the point of the blade down along the slender column of her throat. "No?"

Her chest rises and falls even more rapidly. I can almost see her pulse fluttering under her skin.

My cock hardens. Fuck, she's gorgeous when she's afraid.

Leaning forward, I place my lips next to her ear and draw in another deep breath. She smells like waterlilies. I tilt my head so that I'm sure my breath will caress the shell of her ear when I speak.

"If you answer truthfully, I will let you go," I whisper.

She sucks in a shuddering breath, and a shiver rolls down her spine.

"So I will ask again," I continue. "Are you afraid, little doe?"

For a few seconds, only the faint thumping of music from

inside breaks the silence.

Then she breathes a single shaky word. "Yes."

The smile on my mouth widens. Drawing back, I meet her gaze again. "Good. You should be."

She stares up at me with those wide eyes. My cock is painfully hard. I have never gotten this much pleasure from such a simple threat before. There is something special about this little Russian, and all I want to do is to put her on her knees and make her grovel. To show her what it means to be truly afraid and desperate. But a deal is a deal.

Removing the knife from her throat, I take several steps back and instead raise my other arm to motion towards the door. She doesn't move. Only remains there, pressed against the wall as she eyes me warily. I simply keep watching her as well.

I have given her an out. If she wants it, she's going to have to be brave enough to take it.

After another second of studying me, as if trying to read the nonexistent emotions in my eyes, she edges away from the wall. I remain motionless. Her eyes stay on mine the whole time as she slowly skirts around me and then backs towards the door. I turn so that I can keep her in my field of vision.

Once she reaches the door, she yanks it open.

Loud music once more pulses through the air, spilling into the night. But I know that Alina can hear me when I give her some parting words.

"I'll see you soon, little doe."

Her eyes snap to me for a second. And then she's gone, pulling the door shut behind her.

A cold laugh spills from my lips.

"Very soon," I add.

But only the darkness hears me this time.

3

ALINA

Every nerve in my body is on high alert as I walk through the gray concrete corridors of Blackwater University. When I reach a corner, I cast a quick glance around it before continuing into the next hallway.

God fucking damn Kaden Hunter.

He has made me so paranoid that I now feel the need to check around every corner to make sure that he isn't lurking there, waiting to ambush me. First at Carla's party, and then he showed up again just two days ago. In *class*. He and his damn brothers waltzed right into our hand-to-hand combat class, and our instructor just let them.

Rico targeted some other girl, whose name I think is Isabella, and Jace beat the crap out of Maksim. Presumably as revenge for almost breaking his arm last Saturday. And Kaden… Well, he naturally came after me.

A shiver rolls down my spine as I remember the psychopath smile that curled his lips when he put me on my back over and over again. God, I wish I could've surprised him with some secret ninja move or something. But I'm not a fighter. So instead of taking down that smirking son of a bitch, I constantly found myself on the ground with his muscular body pinning me to the floor and forcing me to tap out.

Another shudder courses through my body at the memory of how it felt to have Kaden straddling my hips. Though this time, the shudder is not entirely out of fear and revulsion.

Shoving that other emotion far into the deepest pits of my mind, I glance around the next corner to make sure that my thoughts haven't somehow managed to summon the devil himself.

A derisive laugh comes from behind me. "What are you doing?"

Embarrassment heats my cheeks, but I keep my voice neutral as I turn around to face the two girls that I know I will find behind me.

Jane, the girl who spoke, arches an eyebrow at me while Leslie, the brown-haired girl next to her, flashes me a mocking smile. Both of them are first-years as well, and ever since they realized just how unskilled I am, they have been bullying me. Not the kind of violent physical things that Kaden inflicts on his victims, but rather the vicious psychological stuff that I'm pretty sure only girls excel at.

Since the best way to deal with that is to appear unaffected, I simply flick my hair back behind my shoulder in a nonchalant move and reply, "Checking for enemies, obviously." I raise my eyebrows as if in shock. "Wait, don't tell me you missed that part of Professor Lawson's class?"

Jane just scoffs but there is a flicker of hesitation in Leslie's eyes, as if she's worried that she did miss something in that class. I almost laugh. God, they're so easy to fool.

I flash Leslie a small smirk.

Anger flits across her face when she realizes that I was just messing with her.

But before she can comment, Jane, who apparently hasn't noticed our little exchange, speaks up again. "I wasn't aware that you were paying attention in any of our classes. Let alone professor Lawson's." Her blue eyes shine with contempt. "We all know that you're not here to become an assassin. So stop wasting everyone's time and just drop out already."

"Not only time," Leslie interjects before I can retort.

Jane turns to frown at her. "What?"

Leslie keeps her eyes on me. "You're a waste of *space* too," she says, her voice laced with sweet malice as she enunciates every word. "You know that, right?"

I make a show of looking down at my body before giving her a slow once-over. "Given that I take up about half the space you do, I would argue otherwise."

Rage flashes in her eyes as she takes a step forward. But before she can do anything else, a voice comes from our lecture hall a short distance away.

"Door closes in thirty seconds," our professor warns. "Anyone who is late will spend the entire night cleaning the floor in my office."

Leslie and Jane shoot me looks dripping with poison before starting towards the door. Since I have no intention of cleaning any floors, I hurry into the lecture hall as well.

It's a circular space, built like an amphitheater with rows that slope down towards the stage at the bottom. Jane and Leslie stride down the steps and join the rest of their posse while I pick a seat in one of the rows at the back instead.

As much as I hate them and their dirty looks and vicious words, they're partly right. I'm not here to be a hitman, so I am technically wasting our professors' time a little bit. But this is the only place where I can enjoy a scrap of freedom, so I will not be leaving Blackwater until someone forces me to.

"Alright," our professor begins.

I tune him out since I don't really need to pass this course, and instead pull out my phone. Last night, I tried to find Kaden on social media so that I could learn something about his habits. And how to avoid running into him. But he doesn't have an account. It shouldn't have been that much of a surprise, given his future line of work. But still. It would have been nice to stalk him the way he seems to stalk me.

My phone vibrates faintly and a text lights up my screen.

I roll my eyes and heave a soft sigh.

Speaking of stalkers…

With annoyance swirling inside me, I open the text.

Eric Wilson: *Alina. Please stop ignoring my texts. I know that you read them. Can we just talk?*

For a few seconds, I consider ignoring this text as well. But then I blow out a long breath and type a reply.

Me: *There is nothing to talk about. Our engagement has been called off. It was simply a business deal between our fathers. Nothing more.*

Eric Wilson: *That's what we need to talk about. You can't just call off our engagement like that.*

With a third sigh in as many minutes, I exit the app, lock the screen, and shove my phone back into my pocket. Eric Wilson. That man does not take no for an answer. In fact, I'm pretty sure that this is the first time in his entire life that someone has told him no.

The Wilson family is very rich because if their successful perfume empire, and they have lots of connections in the business world. That's why Dad wanted me to marry the Wilson heir. If we're married, all of those high-paying conglomerates and powerful business people would go to our family if they needed to rid themselves of some competition.

However, Eric treated me more like a glass figurine to be put on a shelf like a trophy than an actual person. So I begged Dad to end the engagement by convincing him that any rich and influential family would only take advantage of us if I wasn't properly prepared before entering the marriage. And by convincing him that there are much better heirs out there than Eric Wilson. Thankfully, he agreed.

So now, I have at least an entire year of freedom before—

I flinch, my churning mind going completely silent, as I feel the cold kiss of steel against my throat.

Being careful not to move my head, I glance down to find someone holding a knife across my throat from behind my back. No, not *someone*. I know exactly who it is.

"Hello, little doe," Kaden whispers in my ear.

A shiver rolls through my body as his warm breath dances over my skin.

Since he is sitting behind me, I can't see his face. But I swear I can hear the smirk in his voice.

I flick a glance at the other students closest to us. They all watch us discreetly, but no one intervenes. I shift my gaze to the professor, but he is currently answering questions from a guy at the front of the room, so he must not have noticed what is happening yet.

"So rude." Kaden lightly scrapes his blade over my skin as he moves it higher up my throat. "Aren't you going to greet me?"

"Hello, Kaden," I force out between clenched teeth while my heart thunders in my chest.

His nose brushes against my neck, sending a ripple down my spine, as he draws in a deep breath. "That's better."

I shoot pointed stares at the people around me, silently telling them to do something. They all just snap their attention back to the stage.

"What are you doing here?" I grind out.

He tuts softly. "And you're back to being rude."

"You can't just keep showing up like this while I have class. You—"

"Let's go."

His knife disappears from my throat.

A second later, he reaches down over the back of my seat and grabs my arm. With a firm yank, he pulls me to my feet and starts walking towards the door. There is a row of seats between us, forming a flimsy barrier, which should have worked in my favor. But it really doesn't matter. I try to dig my heels into the floor and grab the seats I pass with my other hand, but I'm no match for Kaden's strength, so he simply keeps towing me towards the steps and the waiting door.

I cast a desperate look at the professor, who has now finally noticed us since we're standing up. In fact, everyone is watching us now. We were split into several groups today, so my cousins aren't here. But I stare at the professor pleadingly, hoping that he will intervene.

He shifts his gaze to Kaden for a second.

Then he goes back to teaching.

My heart sinks as Kaden marches me up the steps and then walks us out the door.

The corridor beyond is empty now, since everyone else is already in class. I try to yank my arm out of Kaden's grip as he starts down the hall, but his hand is like a steel band around my upper arm.

"You can't just drag me out of class like this," I protest.

Kaden gives me a sideways look as he continues walking

me through the corridors while lazily twirling the knife in his other hand at the same time. "You keep saying that. *You can't do this. You can't do that.* For a minute there, I thought you might actually be smart. But it looks like you need a more practical demonstration."

My heart rate kicks up. I desperately sweep my gaze around the area, but only empty concrete corridors stare back at us. I try to calm my racing heart as Kaden drags me into the stairwell and starts hauling me up the stairs.

"If my brothers see you manhandling me like this, they will kill you," I say.

His cold dark eyes slide to me, his gaze sharpening. "Was that a threat?"

But before I can reply, Kaden kicks open the door at the top of the stairs and practically throws me through it. I stumble across the threshold and out onto the rooftop. Winds whip through my hair, making it stream behind me like a rippling curtain. While rubbing my arm where Kaden was holding me, I straighten and turn to look around me.

This section of the roof is rather small. There is nothing on it except a couple of glass jars filled with cigarette butts. Not even a railing. It's just a flat concrete patch and a very steep drop on all three sides.

A thud echoes into the warm afternoon air.

I snap my gaze back to the door, which is now closed. It's also blocked by Kaden.

My heart skips a beat.

Light from the golden sun glitters in his dark eyes, and though *my* hair is whipping in the wind, his lies perfectly styled with not a strand out of place. His lethal muscles flex underneath his shirt as he rolls back his broad shoulders while he still continues to effortlessly spin the knife in his hand.

He dominates the space so thoroughly that the rooftop suddenly feels even smaller.

I flick a glance around me again before returning my attention to the dangerous man before me. My mouth suddenly feels very dry. I swallow and edge a step backwards as the reality of my situation becomes clear.

"I said, was that a threat?" Kaden asks, picking up our conversation from earlier.

I quickly shake my head. "No."

That sadistic smile curls his lips again. As if he is enjoying the fear he no doubt sees in my eyes. He takes a step forward.

Alarm flares up my spine, and I edge another step back. "Kaden, please."

His eyes glint. "That's better."

But he still continues advancing on me. My gaze darts desperately around the rooftop, looking for a way out that doesn't involve falling off the edge and plummeting a hundred feet down to the asphalt below. But unless I can get past him and get to the door behind him, I'm trapped here.

Panic crackles through me. If I'm going to make a move, I need to do it now.

Darting to the side, I try to sprint past him.

His hand shoots out and locks around my throat. I jerk to a stop as my escape comes to an abrupt halt. With my heart pounding in my chest, I raise my panicked gaze to Kaden's face.

He smiles like the fucking villain he is.

The muscles in his forearm shift as he flexes his fingers around my throat and then uses his grip to move me back so that I'm standing right in front of him again.

Then he starts backing me towards the edge.

Terror floods my veins.

While digging my heels into the concrete roof, I raise my hands and try to pry his fingers from my throat. It's no use. In the face of his overwhelming strength, I'm completely helpless.

My stomach drops as my heels reach the edge of the roof. But Kaden doesn't stop. He takes one more step, forcing me to arch my back so that half of my body is now hanging over the edge. My feet are still on the roof, but the rest of me isn't.

I immediately stop trying to pry his fingers from my throat and instead wrap both my hands around his toned forearm, because his grip on my throat is now the only thing keeping me from falling off the roof. Wind whips through my hair.

With my pulse pounding in my ears, I stare into Kaden's dark eyes.

He looks like a prince of hell.

Lethally handsome.

Sharp and severe and cold as ice.

Impassive as a god.

And my undoing.

"Please," I beg.

"Do you see how easy this was?" Kaden pushes forward, forcing me to bend my body even farther out over the edge of the roof. "Do you see how easy it is for me to get to you?"

I tighten my grip on his forearm as panic surges through me. "Yes. Yes, I see it."

"At Carla's party. In the sparring room. In the middle of a crowded lecture hall." His intense eyes sear into mine. "No one dares to stop me. Do you know what that means?"

"Yes. No." Fear is scrambling my brain, and I can't figure out what the right answer is, so instead I repeat, "Please."

He leans closer. "It means that when I tell you to do something, you obey."

"Yes. Yes, I understand. Please."

"And don't even think about telling your brothers and cousins about what I do to you."

I wouldn't have done that anyway, because then they would just have taken away my freedom. But I don't want to tell Kaden that, so I just reply, "I won't. I promise."

For another few seconds, he just continues watching me in silence. My heart hammers against my ribs. I draw in sharp, shallow breaths as winds tug at my clothes and whirl through my hair, making it brush against my lower back.

Then a satisfied smirk spreads across Kaden's mouth. "Good."

Relief crashes over me as he takes a couple of steps back, pulling my body back with him. Once I'm standing upright on the roof again, he releases my throat. I draw in a shuddering breath and glance down at the edge of the roof that is still right behind me.

"Now beg."

I snap my gaze back up to Kaden. Because he is standing so close, and because I barely reach his collarbones, I have to crane my neck to meet his eyes. Anticipation glitters in those dark depths.

"What?" is all I manage to say.

Kaden stops twirling his knife and instead uses it to point at the ground before his feet. "Beg."

Confusion whirls through me as I blink at the ground before staring up at him again. "For what?"

An annoyed sigh escapes his lips, and his body shifts as if

he is about to take a step forward. Alarm spikes through me because I suddenly get the feeling that he's about to push me off the roof.

I immediately drop to my knees. "Please."

Kaden stops moving.

"Please, I'm begging you." I don't even know what it is that I'm begging for, but if he wants me to grovel, I'll grovel.

Light dances in those usually so emotionless eyes of his, and a satisfied smirk curves his lips. And because I'm almost eye level with his crotch, I also notice how his cock is now straining against his dark pants.

My heart flips.

He's getting off on this?

God, he really is a psychopath, isn't he?

Kaden arches a dark brow at me. "You call this begging?"

I bow my head and drop my gaze to his boots. "Please, Kaden. I'll do anything you want."

Cold steel appears against my skin as Kaden places the flat of his blade underneath my chin and uses it to tilt my head back up.

The smile on his face as he looks down at me, full of wicked anticipation, makes my heart stop.

"Yes, you will," he promises.

Then he turns around and walks away.

4

KADEN

hwack. I watch as my throwing knife sinks into the target across the grass. The sky is growing darker as the sun slips below the horizon. I know that I should probably go back inside soon, but my mind is still churning. So I draw another blade and throw it at the target.

The image of Alina's big gray eyes as she stared back at me in fear and begged me for mercy drifts across my vision again. My cock hardens. I throw another knife.

I have tormented a lot of people over the years. And I always get a rush of pleasure from watching their fear and humiliation. From watching the desperation that floods their features when they realize that they are entirely at my mercy. But nothing like this.

What I feel when I watch all of those emotions on Alina's face is like nothing I have ever felt. It's absolutely addictive. No one has ever made me crave it like this before.

Sliding out another knife, I hurl it at the target. It lands with a *thwack* that echoes across our silent lawn. Behind me, lights are on in the house I share with Rico and Jace. I know that they're in there somewhere, but I just need a few more minutes to myself. To relish in the rush I still feel whenever I think about what happened on that rooftop yesterday.

Normally, the only feelings that I want to see on other people's faces are fear, desperation, and humiliation. But Alina is somehow different. Watching the emotions on her face is absolutely mesmerizing. And I want to see them all.

I want to draw *every* emotion from her pretty little body.

And I will.

I will make her feel *everything*, and I won't stop until she is reduced to a broken sobbing mess. Then I will dump her back on her brothers' doorstep. And then they will know that I am the one who ruined her.

I start in surprise as something hard taps my shoulder. Spinning around, I reach for my knives only to realize that I have already thrown them all. But it's not Mikhail Petrov, or any of his annoying relatives, that I come face to face with.

Standing two steps away, still pointing a bat at my shoulder, is Jace.

"Distracted much?" he says, raising his eyebrows at me.

I draw my eyebrows down and glare at him. "No."

"Uh-huh." He snorts and gives me a knowing look while using his damn bat to motion between us and the back door he walked out of without me realizing it. "Then how come I could just sneak up on you like this?"

He's right, of course. I was distracted. By thoughts of that little Russian. And I didn't hear Jace open the door and I didn't hear him walk across the grass and all the way up to me. I didn't even feel his presence right behind my back until he tapped me on the shoulder with his damn bat.

But there is no way in hell I'll ever admit that to him. If I do, his already massive ego will grow so large that it won't fit through the door.

"Because I let you," I reply, and flash him a smirk. "Because you're not a threat."

A wicked grin spreads across his own mouth as he points his bat straight at my chest. "Says the unarmed man to the guy with the bat."

"I've already told you. I don't need a weapon to beat you, little brother."

"Hard to beat me when you can't even get within four feet of me."

Grinning at me, he moves until the top of his bat almost brushes against my chest.

I level a dark look at him. "Touch me with that bat. I fucking dare you."

The grin stays on his face, and I can almost see the flames of chaos burn in his eyes. He gets restless easily. These last couple of years more than ever. And if he doesn't have an outlet for it, he will start spiraling. So I sometimes deliberately provoke fights with him just so that he can get it out of his system.

Standing there on the grass, I wait to see if he will go for it. He doesn't.

Instead, he rolls his eyes and spins the bat around so that it's resting against his shoulder instead. "God, you're so dramatic."

I blow out a calculated sigh as if I'm annoyed, and then shake my head as I walk away to retrieve my knives.

"Here I was, trying to be nice," Jace says from where he's still waiting for me on the grass. "And you respond by threatening me. Someone really needs to teach you some manners, brother."

"Keep talking and I'll be the one teaching you some manners."

He snorts. "Come try it. Anyway, I just came out here to tell you that I'm gonna go up and throw a bat at Rico."

My brows furrow in genuine confusion. Yanking out my final knife, I slide it back in its sheath before turning around to face Jace again. "And why, exactly, are you going to throw a bat at Rico?"

"Because he's moping."

Protectiveness surges up inside me, and my voice turns serious as I reply, "Rico is moping? Why?"

"I think he's hit a wall with Isabella."

Nodding, I start back towards him. "I'll come with you."

"I have another bat in the kitchen," Jace says as we walk back to the door. "In case you want to throw one at him too."

"I'm fine."

"Just offering."

Closing the door behind us, I follow Jace towards Rico's bedroom while I shove aside all my thoughts of Alina for now, so that I can focus on helping Rico instead.

I don't understand the point of all the emotions that people always wear on their faces like colorful banners, broadcasting their mood. And I barely have any emotions myself. But I do know one thing.

I don't like seeing my brothers hurt.

5

ALINA

My cousins told me to wait for their sections to finish as well so that we could head to lunch together, but just standing out in the open like this feels like a really bad idea.

Just like most days, our massive class of first-years was split into smaller groups today so that we could fit into the various training areas. Mine ended up finishing twenty minutes early because one of my classmates accidentally shot another student in the leg. Though given the looks they've been giving each other all week, I'm not sure how *accidental* it really was.

Warm winds blow across the parking lot, wrapping around my body like silk. I take a deep breath. Because of the forest close to our secluded campus, the air smells of stone and pine trees out here. It should be a calming scent. However, I feel anything but calm as I stand there outside, waiting for my cousins.

The massive buildings that make up Blackwater University loom around me. Sunlight glints in the windows. Worry prickles my skin. I cast a few quick glances up at the windows, because I can't help but feel as if a certain knife-wielding psycho is up there, watching me.

Standing out here alone like this? I might as well be inviting him to come and torment me.

I snap my gaze back down to the doors and shake my head as I make a decision. Better to wait inside the cafeteria than to stay out here like a damn sitting duck.

Pulling open the heavy doors, I leave the sunlit parking lot behind and walk into the gray concrete halls of Blackwater University. Thankfully, they're completely empty since all other classes still have another fifteen minutes to go. But I make my way to the canteen quickly, just in case.

When I reach it, I find only the other people from my group inside. They're spread out across several tables, some eating together while others appear to be waiting for their friends from the other sections.

I head over to the counter and grab a tray. They're serving cod and potatoes today, which isn't exactly my favorite. But regardless of what's on the menu, the meals are somehow always perfectly cooked and seasoned. For a university for hitmen, I have to admit that they do serve surprisingly good food.

With my tray of steaming food in hand, I head over to a table to wait for my cousins and brothers. The other people scattered across the vast cafeteria talk quietly, their murmuring and the hum of the air conditioner the only sounds that break the stillness.

I've only just picked up my utensils when I can feel the change in the air.

Closing my eyes briefly, I pray that I'm wrong.

But it makes no difference, because when I open my eyes, I

still find my own personal tormentor walking across the room. He must have seen me from the windows when I was standing outside, and decided to leave class early. I *knew* that standing out in the open like that was a dumb fucking move.

Some of the other students pause their conversations to watch when they realize that Kaden is heading straight for me. I glance at them. They look more eager for a show than inclined to help. Guess I'm on my own. Again.

As usual, Kaden is nonchalantly twirling a knife in his hand as he saunters towards me. There's a faint smirk lurking on his lips and a glint in his dark eyes, which is something that I've started to see more often these past couple of days. The sight of it sends a ripple through me, and I suddenly think that I might actually have preferred it when his eyes were completely emotionless instead of full of wicked anticipation like this.

Setting down my utensils, I consider whether to stay or just cut and run. But given the difference in height and physique, I don't think I'd even make it halfway to the door. So in the end, I just sit there, watching as Kaden closes the final distance.

He stops on the other side of the table.

For a while, nothing happens. We just hold each other's gaze in silence while the rest of the cafeteria watches us with bated breath.

A faint smile briefly blows across Kaden's features, as if he finds our little staring contest amusing. I might not be able to run or fight him, but I sure as hell won't be the one speaking first. *He* came to *me*, so if he wants something, he's going to have to spell it out.

"Bring me my lunch," he orders, and the absolute command in his voice cuts through the air like a blade.

It makes my heart lurch and my thighs clench, but all I do is to raise my eyebrows and reply, "Excuse me?"

He stops twirling his knife. My pulse flutters, and I can almost feel the sudden tension in the air crackling like lightning bolts. But I keep my chin up and just stare back at him expectantly. All around us, the room is deadly silent.

Kaden narrows his eyes, and threats bleed into his voice as he says, "Don't make me repeat myself."

"Or what?" I retort before I can stop myself.

He leans forward. I instinctively jerk back, which I realize was a mistake because it makes his eyes glint with satisfaction.

Bracing his palms on the table, he leans over it so that his lethally handsome face is closer to mine. That psychopath smile of his plays over his lips as he cocks his head.

"Are you sure you want to find out, little doe?"

My heart is suddenly racing, and I find myself drawing in shallow breaths while several answers to that question swirl in my head. Most of them very stupid.

I glance down at the knife still in Kaden's hand, now pinned between his palm and the metal tabletop, and I remember the way my pulse jumped when he placed that against my throat the other day. My thighs clench again.

Fuck, what am I doing? There is only one answer to that question. There has to be.

I drop my gaze. "No."

Even though I'm no longer looking at his face, I can hear the smirk in his voice when he replies, "Then get to it."

Metal scrapes against concrete as I push the chair back and stand up. It's shockingly loud in the still unnaturally silent room.

I cast a quick glance towards the doors, hoping against hope that my brothers or cousins will walk through. But there are still a few minutes left of class, so I know that no one is coming to save me.

After grabbing another tray, I place a plate of cod and potatoes on it, along with utensils and a glass of water. Then I turn around and look for the dictatorial psycho.

He is sitting at the same table that the Hunter brothers always occupy, but he is not facing the table. Instead, he has moved his chair so that he is facing the empty space beside the table. And he is watching me with an unreadable mask on his face. The other people in the cafeteria have started eating again, but they're still watching the show in silence.

Keeping my spine straight, I walk up to Kaden's table and set the tray down in front of him a bit more forcefully than strictly necessary, rattling the utensils.

Kaden flicks a disinterested glance at it before meeting my gaze again.

"No," he says.

My brows furrow in genuine confusion.

"Offer it to me," he elaborates.

Irritation flickers through me. He must somehow be able to read that on my face, because his gaze sharpens. He has slid his knife back into its sheath, but I have no doubt that he is about to pull it out again if I don't get a move on, so I blow out a sharp breath and pick up the tray again. Lifting it from the table, I hold it out to him instead.

He gives me a highly unimpressed once-over.

My fingers tighten on the tray, and I clench my jaw in annoyance.

"What?" I ask, barely managing to keep from growling the word.

Kaden leans back in his chair and spreads his legs, the

picture of a smug prince of hell lounging on his throne. Then he shoots a pointed look at the floor.

I blink, my gaze darting between his face, the concrete floor, and the other people in the cafeteria.

No way. He's not going to make me kneel on the floor between his legs *with people watching*.

I snap my gaze back up to his face.

He arches an expectant brow.

Fuck.

I briefly consider whether shoving the plate in his face would work, but quickly decide against it. If I do that, he would probably kill me right here in the canteen. Witnesses be damned.

Kaden clicks his tongue. And it's incredible how such a faint sound can convey so much disappointment. My pulse speeds up.

Since I don't want to find out what Kaden does when he is disappointed, I quickly start lowering myself to my knees while desperately trying to ignore the fact that people are staring. It's terribly difficult, though, because whispers suddenly buzz through the whole room.

Humiliation washes over me, making my cheeks heat.

But at least it's only the people from my group and not the entire school here to witness this.

Still, best get this over and done with quickly.

Once I'm kneeling between Kaden's spread legs, I hold up the tray to him.

He makes no move to take it. Only holds my gaze with that commanding stare of his. Power and utter dominance seem to pulse from his entire body as he stares me down like the merciless demon that he is. The sheer power difference between us right now is so vast that I might as well be bowing before my master.

That's when I realize that *that* is of course what he is waiting for.

While still holding up the tray like an offering, I break eye contact and bow my head so that I'm looking down at the floor instead.

For another few seconds, nothing happens.

Then, at long last, Kaden takes the tray from me. Keeping my eyes on the ground, I slowly lower my hands and rest them in my lap.

A faint thud sounds as Kaden sets the tray down on the table beside him.

My heart patters against my ribs, and embarrassment still radiates from my cheeks.

I suck in a startled breath as soft fingers suddenly appear on my skin.

Kaden draws his fingers along my jaw, surprisingly gently, before taking my chin between his thumb and forefinger. A sigh that almost sounds like a moan escapes his lips as he tilts my head back up so that I meet his gaze.

"Do you have any idea how good you look on your knees between my legs?" he says, his voice dark and rough.

Heat sears my cheeks, but for an entirely different reason this time. My core tightens, and I draw in an unsteady breath.

Then anger floods my system at that absolutely ridiculous reaction.

Latching on to that anger, I glare up at Kaden and instead demand, "Are you done?"

His fingers tighten on my jaw, and his gaze hardens. "I will give you one chance to amend that question."

My heart lurches at the quick switch in his eyes between

searing heat and cold threats. I swallow, my anger quickly dying in the freezing depths of his eyes.

"May I please go back to my table?" I amend.

His grip loosens, and he strokes the side of my jaw with his thumb while a satisfied smile plays over his mouth. "That's better."

He gives me another once-over, this time looking very pleased, and then lets his hand drop. Without another word, he jerks his chin in dismissal and turns back to the table.

I glower at the rude dismissal but quickly climb to my feet and hurry away before he changes his mind. The other people from my group watch me as I walk back to the table. I make sure not to look them in the eye as a fresh wave of embarrassment washes over me. And as I slide back into my seat, I thank God that Leslie and Jane at least weren't here to see this.

Loud voices suddenly boom from the door. After the long silence, it startles practically everyone in the room. Everyone except Kaden, who is now eating his food with his back to me. I glare at him for another second before shifting my attention to the voices by the door.

A few moments later, other students from different groups and years stream into the cafeteria.

I look back down at my plate. My food has now gone cold, but I'm not really hungry anymore so I just end up picking at it.

After a couple of minutes, my cousins appear in my field of vision. They drop down in the chairs opposite mine and raise their eyebrows at me.

"Why didn't you wait for us?" Konstantin asks.

"I felt like a sitting duck, standing out there alone," I reply honestly.

Maksim tilts his head to the side. "Good point."

Before they can question me further, my brothers reach us as well. They take the chairs on either side of me. All around us, the cafeteria is now buzzing with chatter and laughter and clinking utensils.

"You okay?" Anton asks, glancing at me from the corner of his eye as he picks up his knife and fork.

"Of course," I lie, very convincingly too, while I watch the other two Hunter brothers saunter up to join Kaden at his table.

"Your food looks cold," Mikhail comments as he narrows his eyes at me.

However, before he can say anything else, one of the first-years from my group approaches our table.

Dread surges through my stomach like ice water.

Mikhail shoots the guy a hard look, which makes him raise his hands in an appeasing gesture. But he keeps moving until he is standing next to my brother. With his back to the Hunters, he leans down and whispers something to Mikhail.

Rage and disbelief flash across Mikhail's face as he snaps his gaze to me.

For the second time today, I consider whether I would be able to get away if I just cut and run right now.

The guy from my group gives my brother a nod and then quickly walks away while glancing over his shoulder to make sure that the Hunters didn't notice that he just ratted Kaden out.

"Is it true?" Mikhail growls at me in Russian.

Anton and the twins abruptly stop eating and look between me and him.

"Is what true?" Anton asks, also in Russian.

Mikhail, sticking to that same language so that no one will

be able to eavesdrop, gives them a brief but unfortunately very accurate summary of what happened in here before they all arrived.

Anton gapes at him for a second.

Then clothes rustle as all four of them turn to stare at me.

"Well?" Mikhail prompts, his voice tight with anger.

I squirm in my seat, caught between not wanting to admit it but knowing that they won't believe me if I deny it.

"Yes," I admit at last.

Long vicious curses cut through the air. A few people from the tables closest to ours turn to look. They don't need to speak Russian to understand the sentiment behind what was just said.

"But it's fine," I try to assure my brothers and cousins. "He didn't hurt me. And he just did it to get a reaction out of *you*."

But none of them are listening.

Instead, all four of them are staring at Kaden like they want to bathe in his blood.

At the Hunters' table, Jace says something to Kaden, who is still eating nonchalantly as if my entire family isn't plotting his murder right now.

After Jace says something else, Kaden looks up from his plate and sets down his utensils. Then he twists so that he is facing our table fully. I can almost feel the hatred that is radiating from my brothers intensify until it's vibrating in the air.

Kaden locks eyes with me, and a sadistic smile slowly spreads across his lips.

My heart jerks in my chest and heat floods my cheeks once more.

I quickly drop my gaze to the table.

Around me, my family shifts slightly in their seats so that

they're leaning closer to me. As if that can protect me from the psychopath a few tables away.

Mikhail is gripping his utensils so hard that his knuckles have turned white. I glance up in time to see him raise his knife and point it at Kaden in a very clear threat. Kaden only continues to watch us all with that spine-chilling glint in his eyes.

Then he raises his broad shoulders in a lazy shrug that seems to be directed more at something his brother said than at us, and turns back to the table. Picking up his knife and fork, he continues eating as if nothing has happened.

"I am going to fucking kill him," Mikhail growls, in English this time.

"Please just let it be," I argue. "This is what he wanted. He did it just to get a reaction from you."

"Exactly," Anton interjects. "Which is why we can't let him get away with it. He will just keep coming at you if we do."

"No, he only did it because he was given a random opportunity," I lie. "I was here early and so was he. It was just an improvised reaction to a spontaneous opportunity."

But even as the words leave my mouth, I know that every single one is a lie. There is nothing improvised or spontaneous about Kaden Hunter. Everything he does, he does for a reason.

"It doesn't—" Mikhail begins.

"Isabella," Rico suddenly calls across the cafeteria.

We all turn to stare at him and the athletic brown-haired girl standing frozen on the floor halfway across the room. It's the same girl that Rico targeted when Kaden came to humiliate me in the sparring room. I frown as I watch her approach their table.

Since most of the cafeteria missed the show that Kaden

gave them earlier, they watch eagerly now to see if Rico is going to do something interesting to that girl Isabella.

Disappointed sighs sound from several tables when nothing happens. She just sits down to eat with them as if they're friends.

"That," Mikhail suddenly says. "*That* is how we'll take revenge."

"What?" Anton asks.

Then we all follow his gaze, which is now locked on Isabella.

Dread curls inside my stomach.

God damn it.

This is not going to end well.

6

KADEN

nticipation crackles through my body like an electric current. I can practically feel it shooting through my body with every step I take towards the Petrovs' house. It has been a long time since I felt this excited about anything. But ever since I met Alina, I have suddenly gotten a lot of things to be excited about.

After my little game in the cafeteria today, Mikhail and his weak brother and idiot cousins decided to take revenge. Namely by attacking Isabella.

Given how Rico feels about her, that naturally turned out to be a massive fucking mistake.

But one good thing came out of it.

Leverage.

Since Rico loves to execute brutal power plays just as much as the rest of us, he managed to get that stubborn bastard Mikhail to grovel.

And I filmed it all.

With an uncharacteristically broad grin on my face, I slide my phone out of my pocket and pull up the video again while

I continue towards the Petrov residence. Smug victory swirls inside me as I watch it over and over again.

But it's not only for my personal enjoyment. I have a mission to accomplish tonight. Two, actually.

As I reach the Petrovs' front door, I keep the phone in my hand and ring the doorbell.

The moment someone begins pushing down the handle, I hit play and hold up the screen so that it's facing the door.

"*Kneel*," Rico's commanding voice comes from the recording.

Since I have this entire video memorized, I know that, on the screen, I'm just now lifting the phone and holding it so that it's filming Mikhail.

In front of me, the white-painted front door opens to reveal none other than my little doe.

Alina jerks back, more in surprise than fear, and blinks at me in genuine shock. As if she didn't think that I would ever dare to simply stroll up to their front door and ring the doorbell.

"*Beg*," Rico orders on the video.

Alina's eyes dart to the screen, and then grow impossibly wider when she sees that it's a video of her brother kneeling on the ground.

"What's going on?" Konstantin calls from somewhere inside the house.

On the video, Mikhail presses out, "*Please.*"

"*Better*," Rico demands, his voice as commanding on the video as it was in real life.

"*Please, Hunter. I'm begging you.*"

"*For what?*"

"*Mercy.*"

Alina stares at the screen in stunned silence while four people scramble into the hallway behind her.

Konstantin, Maksim, Anton, and Mikhail arrive right in time to hear Mikhail's voice on the video say, *"Please. I'm begging for mercy for my brother."*

Rage pulses across all of their faces as they barrel towards me.

Pausing the video, I flash them a vicious smirk.

Alina leaps out of the way with a yelp as they reach us.

Then a jolt pulses through my face as Mikhail drives his fist into the side of my jaw with enough force to snap my head to the side.

I saw it coming but didn't bother blocking. Pain doesn't really faze me anyway.

Instead, I keep a tight grip on my phone as Mikhail grabs me by the collar and hauls me into their hallway. A *bang* sounds as Anton slams the front door shut while Mikhail practically throws me at his cousins.

Yet again, I don't bother doing anything about it. Because I know that I am the one who holds the real power here.

The twins grab me, locking their arms around my shoulders and throat to keep me trapped as Anton snatches the phone from my hand and Mikhail punches me in the stomach. I clench my stomach muscles beforehand so that I'll keep the air in my lungs.

A snarl rips out of Mikhail's throat when he doesn't hear the huff of pain that he expected.

He slams his fist into the side of my mouth instead, making the edge of my lip split.

I flash him a cocky, blood-soaked smile before sliding my gaze to Anton. "How's your arm, little Petrov?"

Mikhail drives his fist into my stomach again.

Letting the pain just fade through my body, I simply shift my attention back to Mikhail.

"Aww, are you upset that I didn't ask how you are too? Let me remedy that," I say, making my voice drip with sarcasm. Then I fix him with a mocking look. "How are your knees doing after all of the groveling you did this afternoon?"

His fist cracks into my jaw again, snapping my head to the side.

"I will fucking kill you, you slimy son of a bitch," Mikhail growls at me.

From where she is still standing by the now closed door, Alina stares at the five of us with wide gray eyes. I give her a blood-soaked smile before slowly turning my head back so that I'm facing Mikhail. His cousins tighten their grip on me.

"Is that really how you want to start this negotiation?" I ask, locking eyes with Mikhail.

"This isn't a negotiation," he snarls. "This is an execution."

"Seeing as I'm the one with the leverage, I highly doubt that."

Anton shoots me a mocking look from where he is standing next to his brother, and then wiggles the phone he took from me. "You mean this?"

"Yes." I slide my gaze back to Mikhail. "If I release that video, it will spread through the entire criminal underworld within a matter of hours. Who do you think will hire you then, Petrov? After they've seen you kneel and grovel like a little bitch? Like *our* little bitch."

Fury flares in Mikhail's blue eyes, burning like hellfire. Squeezing his hands into fists, he jerks his chin at his cousins before stalking down the hall. The twins drag me with them as they follow, hauling me into their elegant white kitchen. I let them.

"Releasing that video will be difficult without your phone," Anton points out as he follows behind us.

They walk me over to their marble-topped kitchen island when Mikhail snaps his fingers and points to it. Then he turns to grab something from another counter.

The distinct ringing of steel fills the air as Mikhail slides out a meat cleaver before turning back to me. Konstantin and Maksim adjust their grip and then move my arms so that they're holding my hands and forearms on the counter.

Fury still burns in Mikhail's eyes as he flashes me a grin tinted with a bit of insanity. "And it will be very difficult to release the video without hands."

I snicker, which only seems to make Mikhail even more furious.

"Wait," a soft but very distressed voice calls from the doorway. "This is too far. Please, Mikhail, you're taking this too far."

Surprise flickers through my chest as I turn my head to look at Alina, who is shaking her head at her brothers. My little doe is... trying to save me? Now *that* I didn't see coming.

"Are you worried about me, little doe?" I tease.

Her gaze snaps to me, and she crosses her arms over her chest in a way that manages to look both stubborn and cute at the same time. "No." She shoots me a glare. "I'm worried about your psycho brothers hurting my brothers in retaliation."

A slow smile, one that is more threat than anything else, spreads across my lips. "Would you look at that? There is at least one intelligent person here who is capable of analyzing actions and consequences. Maybe there's hope for your family yet."

Alina blinks and then frowns, as if she's not sure whether to be flattered or insulted.

"You—" Mikhail begins, but I cut him off.

"Just because *you* are incapable of thinking more than one step ahead at a time doesn't mean the rest of us are," I say as I turn back to face him. "I have already uploaded the video. It's set to auto release. So unless I walk out of here in the next..." I make a show of turning to look at the clock above the stove, "ten minutes, the video will be released and everyone will know what a pathetic little bitch you are."

Deafening silence descends over the pristine kitchen.

Mikhail flexes his fingers repeatedly on the handle of the meat cleaver, and he clenches his jaw so hard that I'm certain he's about to dislocate it.

I just hold his stare with a smirk on my face, daring him to do it.

Another snarl rips from his throat.

Then he tosses the meat cleaver down into the sink behind him with an angry clanking sound, and then jerks his chin at his cousins. They immediately release me and step back.

Straightening from the countertop, I roll my shoulders back while running my tongue over my split lip. It has already started to knit itself together and is no longer bleeding. But based on the metallic taste in my mouth, I'm pretty sure there is still blood on my teeth. I leave it there as I turn back to Mikhail.

"And now you've finally caught up with the reality of your situation," I taunt. "I knew you would get there in the end."

"What the fuck do you want, Hunter?" he snaps back, but then he betrays himself when his gaze darts to the clock.

"If you hadn't wasted so much time trying to threaten me, we wouldn't be on such a tight schedule now, would we?"

He bares his teeth at me, but all he says is, "Just spit it out."

Turning slowly, I look straight at Alina.

She sucks in a gasp.

I can almost see the charged tension crackling through the room like lightning bolts as the other four Petrovs notice my gaze. They instinctively shift their positions as if to defend her.

A cold laugh escapes my throat because I now know that my plan to ruin her before dumping her back on their doorstep is going to fucking break this family. But I'm not here for that tonight.

"Stay away from my brothers," I say as I turn back to face Mikhail.

Confusion flits across his features. Across all of their faces, in fact. As if their minds are trying to catch up with the direction that this negotiation has just taken. Which was of course entirely intentional.

Using their moment of disorientation, I reach into my pocket and slide out a small listening device that will be able to pick up any conversation they might have inside this kitchen. Then I nonchalantly lean forward over the kitchen island while attaching the bug underneath the edge of the countertop. It's not the best location ever, but given that this is where they brought me, it'll have to do.

"Did you hear me?" I prompt.

"Your brothers?" Mikhail says. "You're not here for…?"

"Alina?" I straighten from the counter again and shrug. "No."

I cast her a highly dismissive look over my shoulder. She draws back slightly, looking hurt. *Good.* She will be more than hurt when I'm done with her. She will be utterly broken.

Locking eyes with Mikhail once more, I repeat. "Stay the

fuck away from my brothers. This is between you and me. If you try to attack them or hurt them or involve them in this war in any way, I will release that video. Am I making myself clear?"

"Then you stay the hell away from my family too," he counters.

I snicker and give him a contemptuous once-over. "Oh Petrov, don't you know? You need leverage in order to blackmail someone. I have it, and you don't. Which means that my family is off limits while yours is…" I slide my gaze to Alina while a cruel smirk curls my lips, "fair game."

"If you hurt her, I will—"

"What?" I snap, my voice hardening and cracking through the air like a whip. "You'll do *what* exactly?" With that merciless expression on my face, I shoot a pointed look up at the clock above the stove. "You have five minutes left before the video is released."

His gaze darts up to it as well, and dread flickers in his blue eyes.

"What's it gonna be, Petrov?" I mock, echoing the exact phrase Rico used when he forced Mikhail into groveling in the first place.

He tears his gaze from the clock and looks from face to face. Or at least he looks at his little brother and his cousins. All three of them nod as if they want him to take the deal. Mikhail flexes his hand repeatedly and clenches his jaw.

"Either you leave my brothers alone and I keep the video to myself," I say. "Or I'll ruin your future before you even graduate."

His chest heaves with angry breaths. The clock ticks loudly into the deafening silence. By the doorway, Alina casts worried glances between the five of us.

"Fine," Mikhail presses out at last.

"Fine what?" I demand.

"Your brothers are off limits." He practically growls the words.

A cold smile stretches my lips. "Wise choice."

Pushing off from the counter, I saunter up to Anton and pluck my phone from his fingers. He watches me with furious gray eyes. So similar and yet so different from Alina's.

"Make sure you keep your little brother and cousins in line too," I say as I start towards the door. "Because if anything, and I mean *anything*, happens to my brothers, accidentally or otherwise..." Lifting my hand, I wiggle the phone in the air above my shoulder as I continue towards the hallway. "This goes viral."

I can practically hear Mikhail's teeth cracking from how hard he must be clenching his jaw, but I don't turn to look.

Instead, I glance down at Alina as I pass her on my way out.

She watches me with a mixture of anger, fear, and... something else. Something I can't quite identify.

I give her one last blood-soaked smile. "Watch your back, little doe."

7

ALINA

Frustrated voices spill out over the threshold and drift into the warm evening air as I open our front door. I sigh as I walk inside and close the door behind me. Angry tension has been pulsing between the walls of our house at all times ever since Kaden Hunter showed up three days ago to deliver his ultimatum.

"Something needs to be done," Mikhail snaps from somewhere inside our kitchen. Even from out here in the hallway, I can hear the strain in his voice. "If he releases that video, I will be…"

He trails off, but we all know how that sentence ends. *Ruined*. If Kaden releases that video, Mikhail will be ruined.

"I'm sorry," Anton says, sounding miserable.

"It's not your fault," Mikhail replies.

I slowly set down my bag on the floor, careful not to make any sound.

"Yes, it is," Anton protests. "If I hadn't let Rico grab me, you'd never had to—"

"No," Mikhail interrupts. "Don't think like that. This is no one's fault but the fucking Hunters."

I start through the hallway and towards the staircase on silent feet. When Mikhail is worried, he's more likely to start restricting my freedom. Which is why I want to make it to my room without him noticing me.

The pale floorboard beneath me lets out a startled creak as I step on it.

"Alina?" Mikhail immediately calls.

I freeze and then shoot an irritated glare down at the offending floorboard.

A moment later, my eldest brother appears in the doorway to the kitchen. Crossing his arms, he gives me a look that makes me squirm.

"Where have you been?" he demands.

Clearing my throat, I brush my hands down over my violet summer dress while trying, and failing, to look unaffected. "I told you this morning that I was going to a friend's house after class."

"Who?"

"Carla."

It's the truth. Carla and the rest of her housemates were hosting a watch party for the new season of a show that I love as well. When I mentioned that in passing yesterday, she invited me to join them.

Mikhail studies me through narrowed eyes for another few seconds. But he must be able to see that I'm telling the truth because he gives me a nod. Uncrossing his arms, he blows out a long breath and rakes a hand through his blond hair.

"Right," he says, and gives me a tired smile. "Sorry. I forgot about that."

"It's alright," I reply while starting towards the stairs again. "I'll just head up to my room and go to bed now."

He nods. For a moment, he just remains standing there, looking worried and exhausted. Then he returns to the kitchen.

"We need to find a way to delete that video," Mikhail says, presumably to Anton, and a deep sigh full of worry and tension rips from his lungs. "That video is like a fucking sword hanging over my head. I can't concentrate on anything."

I pause with my foot on the first step.

My heart aches at the desperation in my brother's tone. I glance back towards the kitchen, and then up towards where my room is.

Easing my foot off the step, I start edging backwards instead.

And then I sneak back to the front door and slip out into the dark evening.

My heart pounds like a battle drum in my chest as I climb in through the upstairs window of Kaden's bedroom. I know that it's his bedroom because I spent a solid hour hiding in the bushes and watching their house.

Rico's car wasn't in front of the house, so he is apparently spending his evening somewhere else, but Jace and Kaden were moving around inside the house for an hour before they headed out and left in Jace's car. That's when I made my move.

I might be a terrible assassin-in-training in most other aspects, but sneaking in and out of places is something I excel at. With my father and brothers and cousins watching my every move, I learned very early that I needed to develop that skill in order to carve out any freedom at all for myself.

Now, as I straighten on the floor of Kaden's dark bedroom, I'm incredibly thankful for that skill. Because I'm going to use it to delete that video and take away the damning sword that Kaden is holding over my brother's head.

Since Kaden's room faces the back of the house and not the street where the cars are, I know that no one will notice if I turn on the lights, so I carefully move towards the switch by the closed door and flip it.

Bright light floods the room.

A jolt shoots through me as I take in the space around me.

Just like the outside of the house, the walls are made of dark wood. So is the floor. And most of the furniture. I study the way he has decorated his room.

I don't know what I was expecting, but I'm somehow simultaneously stunned and not at all surprised.

It's tidy, organized, and meticulous.

There is a large double bed by the wall to my left. It's made to perfection, the black bedclothes so smooth that I could've bounced a quarter off it. The closet and the set of drawers beside it are closed, but the desk is just as spotless as the bed. There is not a lot of stuff on the tabletop, but what's there is structured so that everything has its place.

But in contrast to that tidy perfection are the handful of oddities throughout the room.

A metal hook has been set into the ceiling, but there is nothing hanging from it. The bed has been fitted with some kind of metal frame on top of the normal one. Some metal rings have also been set into the floor and walls.

I frown at the strange choice of décor.

Then I shake my head. I'm not here to sightsee. I'm here to find the video, delete it, and get the hell out before the psycho returns.

Since the desk seems like the most logical place to start, I hurry over to it and start pulling out the drawers. The phone that Kaden brought with him to blackmail Mikhail three days ago was not the one he usually carries, which means that he must be keeping that extra phone in here somewhere.

I scowl as the drawers only reveal neat stacks of papers and notebooks. After quickly lifting them to check that there is nothing underneath, I move on to the drawers on the other side. They reveal nothing incriminating either.

Straightening, I walk over to the closet and throw open the door. Impeccable shirts are hanging in there in neat rows. Most of them are in black, dark gray, or dark blue, and they're organized after function. T-shirts on one side. Thin long-sleeved shirts after that. Then dress shirts. And so on.

I'm struck by an absolutely ridiculous impulse to reach in and wrinkle all of his shirts and switch them all around until it's nothing but a chaotic jumble. But I manage to suppress it. I'm not here to mess with Kaden. I'm here to remove his leverage.

So I leave the shirts in peace and close the door before opening the tall cabinet next to it.

My stomach lurches.

Standing there with my hand still on the now open cabinet door, I just gape at the things I find inside.

Handcuffs and spreader bars and coils of rope. Riding crops and canes and paddles. Blindfolds and noise-cancelling headphones and an entire assortment of different gags. And sex toys.

With my jaw still on the floor, I simply stare at the massive stash for another few seconds. Then I glance towards the hook in the ceiling and the extra metal frame on the bed and the other oddities, and suddenly, I realize exactly what they're for.

Heat floods my cheeks, and my belly, as I run my gaze over Kaden's secret equipment again. A very inconvenient throbbing sensation starts in my clit.

I slam the cabinet door shut.

Nope.

Not doing this.

Not doing this at all.

If I can't find the phone anywhere else, I will go back and search through that cabinet. But only as a last resort.

While trying to block out the images that flashed through my mind earlier, I shake my head and brush my hands down my dress as I stride towards another cabinet. This one is not as tall as the one full of kinky sex stuff, but it's wider.

I open it.

Metal gleams in the bright light from the lamp in the ceiling as the doors swing open.

Yet again, I find myself staring.

Rows of knives line the shelves of the cabinet. Some are arranged in what almost looks like display cases while others rest on small racks. Raising my hand, I gently draw my fingers over the gleaming hilts.

My pulse thrums in my ears.

And because of what I saw in that other cabinet, my thoughts spiral down into all kinds of unacceptable places as I stare at those glittering knives. I curl my fingers around the hilt of a blade and lift it off its rack while my pulse jumps at the memory of how it felt when Kaden pressed one like it against my throat.

"Don't touch that."

I gasp.

Alarm crackles through me, and I whip around so fast that I drop the knife in my haste. It clatters to the floor a short distance from me.

My stomach bottoms out and fear washes through me, drowning my insides in cold water, as I come face to face with the source of the voice.

Kaden Hunter is standing halfway across the room, staring at me. Tension pulses around his lethal body, and the expression on his face makes my blood freeze solid.

There is no smirk on his mouth. No scheming glint in his eyes. No taunting arch of his eyebrows.

His dark eyes are as cold and bottomless as the arctic sea, and his mouth is a severe slash across his face.

Panic shoots up my spine.

Oh God, he's going to kill me.

"Do you have any idea what I do to people who touch my things?" he demands, threats dripping like poison from his every word. His harsh stare slides to the blades in the open cabinet behind me before he locks eyes with me again. "Let alone my *knives?*"

Shallow breaths saw through my throat.

In hindsight, I should probably have realized it. With a room this meticulous, he just had to be one of those people who hate it when others touch his stuff. And he does seem to have an unhealthy relationship with his knives in particular.

Fuck, I need to get out of here.

My gaze darts towards the window that I climbed in through. It's too far for me to reach now that Kaden is in the room. As is the door, which he is blocking with his tall and muscular body. I flick a glance down at the knife I dropped.

Kaden notices, and the expression on his face darkens.

"I will give you one chance to choose your next course of action." His eyes bore into me as he slides out two throwing knives. Hellfire burns like cold flames in those dark depths. "Depending on what you choose, this night will go very differently for you."

I suck in a small shuddering breath. Oh God, he's furious. He's not playing around this time. He's absolutely *furious*, and if I don't do something, he is actually going to kill me for touching his knives.

With growing panic clanging inside my skull, I glance between the window, the door, and the knife again. But I know that none of those options will end well for me.

Fuck. What does he want? What can I do to—

Realization strikes like a lightning bolt. The rooftop. The video of Mikhail. I know exactly what Kaden Hunter wants. What he seems to crave more than anything. And what might just placate him and stop him from slitting my throat right now.

Groveling. He wants people to kneel and beg.

So I do.

Dropping to my knees, I press my palms to the floor before me and bow my head. "Please. Mercy. I'm begging you."

Only a dead silent room answers me. But I don't dare to raise my head, so I remain like that. My heart hammers against my ribs.

Kaden lets the silence stretch for another few seconds. Then he snaps his fingers.

"Look at me," he commands.

With my pulse thrumming in my ears, I slowly raise my gaze to his.

A satisfied smirk curls his lips, and his eyes light up with malice. But some of that terrible danger that radiated from him before has eased now. "Good choice."

I let out a tiny breath, full of shuddering relief. But it's short-lived as Kaden continues speaking.

"Tell you what," he begins, that wickedness still gleaming in his eyes. "Since you chose the only acceptable course of action, I will give you a chance that I have never given anyone else before." Challenge creeps into his tone. "If you can take your punishment without making any noise, I'll let you live."

My heart leaps into my throat. Punishment? Let me live?

But I'm in no position to argue, so I just nod quickly.

A smug huff of laughter escapes his throat.

"Take off your clothes," he says as he starts towards that tall cabinet.

Fear, combined with a very strange thrill, races down my spine. After getting to my feet, I grab the hem of my summer dress and pull it over my head. It flutters down and lands on the floor in a pile of pale violet fabric.

Metal clanks from where Kaden is standing in front of the now open cabinet, but because his muscular body is blocking the view, I can't see what he's doing.

I glance down at my underwear, and hesitation whirls through me. He said *take off your clothes*. Does that mean all of them? My gaze darts back to Kaden, and I make a split-second decision.

Right as he turns back towards me, I toss my final remaining garments onto the floor as well.

Heat sears my cheeks as Kaden stops and rakes his gaze over my now completely naked body. Then he smiles.

"Look at you," he says, sounding pleased. "Capable of following orders."

My clit throbs when his gaze drinks in my body as he

looks me up and down again. No one has ever looked at me like that before. As if my body is a work of art. Something to be appreciated. And not as something that's just a liability that will break at the first hint of pressure.

He walks back to the middle of the room and then twitches two fingers at me in silent command. I move closer.

"Just so you know," he begins. "If I had turned around and found you still in your underwear, I would've doubled your punishment. But it looks like I was right about you. You are an intelligent one."

The combined threat and praise does strange things to my chest.

But before I can figure out how to reply, a dull thud sounds as Kaden drops a spreader bar on the floor. It has two metallic arches at the edges, where I presume the ankles go. But there are also two smaller ones in the middle of the flat bar.

"On your knees," Kaden orders.

I lower myself to my knees before him. A half smirk tugs at the corner of his lips as he watches me for a second before he walks around so that he is standing behind me instead.

Lightning skitters across my skin as his strong hand suddenly appear on my ankle. I shift my body as he moves my legs until my ankles are positioned in the correct slots. Then he places his boot against my shoulder blades and shoves my upper body towards the floor. My heart thuds in my chest, and that strange throbbing sensation is back in my pussy.

Still on my knees, I'm now bent over so that my forehead is resting on the smooth wooden floor.

"Slide your arms between your legs and towards me," Kaden commands from behind me as he removes his boot from my back.

I move my hands from where I was resting them on the floor beside my head and instead slide them underneath me and between my legs until my hands are sticking out behind me instead.

Kaden grabs my wrists and places them into the metal hoops in the middle of the spreader bar. Then he folds over the top piece and locks it.

My heart jerks in my chest.

I'm now trapped like this. Naked and on my knees, doubled over with my legs spread, my ass in the air, and my forehead pressed against the floor while my wrists are shackled to the same spreader bar as my ankles.

I have never felt so humiliated and so turned on at the same time.

In this position, I can't really see anything except the floor beneath me. My pulse flutters like an erratic butterfly as I hear Kaden return to the cabinet and pull something out before walking back to me.

"Remember," he warns. "Not a single sound."

I try to nod but it's very difficult in my current predicament.

Every nerve inside my body is on high alert. I drag in shuddering breaths as I try to brace myself for whatever is about to happen. I can almost hear the blood rushing in my ears.

But everything else is still and silent.

The dreadful anticipation of not knowing what's coming, or when it's coming, is wreaking havoc inside me. I shift slightly on my knees, trying to adjust my position.

I can feel Kaden looming over me, power and dominance radiating from his body and pulsing through the room.

God, what is he doing? Why isn't he—

Pain pulses through my ass.

It takes all of my considerable self-control not to cry out, both in surprise and pain.

Clamping my jaw shut, I grit my teeth as what feels like some kind of thin wooden cane connects with my bare ass again.

A cane. The psycho is fucking *caning* me.

I wiggle my ass to try to relieve some of the ache.

Kaden snaps the cane against the back of my thighs.

Again, I bite back a groan before it can escape my lips as pain blossoms on my skin.

Pressing my forehead against the floor, I keep my mouth firmly shut as Kaden keeps going. He alternates between my ass and the back of my thighs, but always randomly. And sometimes he waits longer before striking while other times he brings the cane down quickly again. All of it makes it impossible to predict where and when the cane is coming.

But I never make a sound.

What most people fail to realize is that I have the patience and self-control of a fucking god. I have spent my entire life sitting prettily and quietly and biting my tongue while my father or brothers or cousins make decisions for me. This is no different.

I knew that no matter what Kaden did to me, I would be able to keep my mouth shut.

However, what I didn't expect was how turned on I would be by this.

Everyone always treats me with silk gloves, like a glass figurine that they're afraid will break if they were to just handle it normally.

And here is Kaden, challenging me to stay quiet while he spanks me with a cane.

It makes me feel strong and powerful in a way that I hadn't expected.

Kaden brings his cane down on my aching ass again. And it's then that I realize with shocking clarity that it's not a cry of pain that I'm stifling in my throat.

It's a moan of dark pleasure.

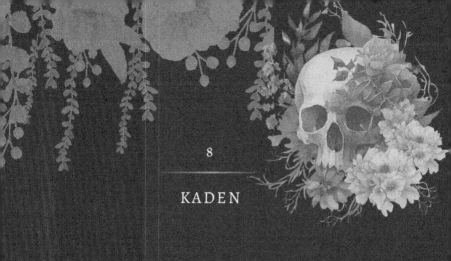

8

KADEN

Something flickered inside me last night. And it's flickering inside me again now as I watch Alina walk across the cafeteria and towards the counter to get some food. It almost feels like… an emotion. An emotion that I can't quite identify.

I hadn't actually expected her to pull it off.

When I saw her touching my knives, I was about five seconds away from slitting her throat. Because no one touches my things. Especially not my knives. They're mine. And no one touches what belongs to me.

Last year, I even came close to skinning Eli's girlfriend alive because she stole one of my blades.

So when I saw Alina picking one up, every territorial and highly possessive part of me was screaming at me to kill her.

But then she got down on her knees and begged for mercy.

My cock hardens at just the memory of it.

It was the only thing that she could have possibly done to save herself, and she managed to figure it out. That impressed me. More than I will ever admit. And it also made that terrible cold fury fade away.

I wasn't going to tell her that, though. So I told her that I would let her live only if she managed to stay silent during her entire punishment.

And for the second time that night, my little doe managed to shock me. Because I really, *really*, hadn't expected her to pull it off.

Sliding my hand over my lap, I discreetly adjust myself as my cock hardens even more at just the thought of what she looked like back then. Naked and trapped in a spreader bar with her ass in the air. I liked the sight of that. But I found myself liking her stubborn strength even more.

Not a lot of people could have endured that little caning session without so much as a whimper.

That odd thing flickers in my chest again.

I need to find out what it is. And what's causing it.

"Man, you really *are* obsessed, aren't you?"

Snapping my gaze away from where Alina is putting a plate of food on her tray, I lock eyes with Jace and then draw my eyebrows down in a warning scowl. "Watch your mouth, little brother."

A wide grin full of challenge spreads across his lips. "Or what?"

"Oh, come on," Rico groans from the chair next to me. Heaving a deep sigh, he fixes Jace with an exasperated stare. "We agreed not to antagonize each other in public. Not while we're in the middle of dealing with both the Petrovs and Isabella at the same time."

Jace frowns in confusion. "No, we didn't."

"We literally talked about it this morning. At breakfast."

"Oh." Jace chuckles and rakes his hand through his messy

brown curls before shrugging. "Well, I wasn't really paying attention."

"Of course you weren't, Golden."

Narrowing his eyes, he yanks his fork up and points it threateningly at Rico. "Don't call me that."

"I'll stop calling you that as soon as you develop an attention span longer than five seconds."

"Five seconds?" Jace gasps dramatically and presses his hand against his chest in a show of shock. "I'll have you know that my current record is actually eight seconds."

A surprised laugh escapes Rico's throat.

Jace grins at him before lifting his shoulders in a nonchalant shrug. "It was when I mopped the floor with Kaden at that video game the other week."

While they were bickering, my gaze had wandered back to Alina as she walked towards the table where the rest of her family are seated, but now I snap it back to my annoying little brother.

"You didn't mop the floor with me," I declare, scowling at him.

"Yeah, I did." His brown eyes glitter as he flashes me a mischievous smile. "Which is why you had to make dinner that night." He cocks his head, looking contemplative. "Though sadly without a pretty little apron on."

Narrowing my eyes, I stare him down. "I will fucking stab you."

He just grins wider.

Next to me, Rico groans and rubs his temples in exasperation.

While he launches into another lecture about why we shouldn't mess with each other in public right now, I slide my gaze back to Alina. She has reached the table now. I watch intently as she sets her tray down next to Konstantin's and pulls out the chair.

Then she pauses.

For a second, she looks down at that chair in dread. Anton says something from her right, and she quickly wipes the expression from her face and sits down.

A sadistic smile spreads across my mouth as she winces when her ass touches the chair, betraying that she's still sore from when I caned her last night.

Anticipation rushes through me.

I had planned to let her cool off for a few days before I went back to tormenting her, but how can I when she looks like that?

Besides, I still need to figure out what that strange flicker in my chest was. And the only way I can do that is by setting up another scene like that with Alina.

Jace snaps his fingers in front of my face. "Are you even listening?"

My hand shoots up, trying to grab his annoying fingers, but he manages to yank them back before I can.

"I need to go," I announce, pushing my chair back and standing up.

Rico studies my face. "Why?"

"There's something I need to take care of before afternoon classes start."

Before either of them can ask anything else, I turn around and stalk away.

"Like I said." Jace chuckles from back at the table. "Obsessed."

I have half a mind to turn around and throw a couple of knives at him, but I manage to resist the temptation.

Besides, he's wrong. I'm not obsessed with Alina. I can

stop at any time.

I just don't want to.

While most of the other students are still eating lunch, I head up to the instructors' offices on the floor above. I have Alina's schedule memorized, so I know exactly which class she has this afternoon.

Once I reach the correct office, I open the door and stride inside without knocking.

"Students who barge into my office without knocking will find themselves..." Mr. Brown begins in a sharp voice. Then he trails off when he realizes who I am. A small sigh of annoyance slips past his lips, and he gives me a tight smile. "Hunter. What can I do for you?"

Because our family is connected, both by money and by blood, to the Morelli family, most students at Blackwater University take great care not to cross us. Since the Morelli family is the biggest and most influential mafia family in this entire state, everyone dreams of landing a permanent contract with them, which is why they don't want to risk pissing off the Morelli family's closest allies.

However, the patriarch Federico Morelli himself has also informed the entire staff at Blackwater that Eli, Rico, Jace, and I are beyond reproach. Which is why the teachers let us do practically whatever we want. They might hate it, but no one disobeys a direct order from Federico Morelli, so they still do what everyone else does when they're faced with our demands. They bow down and obey.

"Tell Alina Petrov that she needs to stay for a while after your class this afternoon," I order.

Suspicion swirls in his eyes. "Why?"

I just stare him down in silence.

He blows out another irritated breath. "Fine. I'll tell her to stay after class. I assume you want *me* to leave though?"

"Correct. And leave the supplies."

It looks like he wants to protest, but in the end, he just jerks his chin down in a nod.

"Good." Turning around, I start back towards the door. "And don't linger afterwards."

Without waiting for his reply, which I know will never be anything other than what I want to hear, I stride back into the corridor.

Dark anticipation crackles through my soul.

If Alina thought last night was humiliating, she has no idea what awaits her this afternoon.

9

ALINA

Confusion pulls at my brows as I scan the large but relatively empty space. The rest of the first-years around me do the same as we all file in through the door.

Just like most of Blackwater University, the walls and floor are made of simple gray concrete. No decorations or unnecessary ornaments. Only bright lights in the ceiling. It was built to be practical. Not beautiful.

There are no tables or chairs in the room. Only a freestanding wooden wall that is easily three times my height. Two ropes hang down the face of it. I slide my gaze to the open boxes on the floor beside it and find even more rope. About half of them are already tied into various knots.

My confusion deepens. Are we really learning how to tie knots? What is this? The boy scouts?

"Welcome," Mr. Brown says as we all stop close to where he is standing by the wooden wall. His shrewd brown eyes skate across our faces before he smiles knowingly. "I always like to start my class with a little competition. To get the energy going, so to speak."

Excitement ripples through several parts of our group. My cousins, who are both in the same group as me this afternoon, rub their hands together and grin. I, on the other hand, am just praying that he won't pick me.

"You," he says, and points at the twins. "How about a little competition between brothers?" Turning, he gestures towards the wooden wall and the two ropes hanging from it. "The first one to reach the top wins."

The moment he has finished speaking, Maksim and Konstantin take off like missiles. Sprinting to the wall, they leap up and grab the rope in both hands as they start climbing.

I gasp as Konstantin's rope suddenly gives out halfway.

He plummets back to the floor, landing with a grunt, while Maksim scrambles up the final distance and slaps his palm onto the top of the wall.

"Ha!" he calls, and turns to grin over his shoulder. Then he sees Konstantin on the ground, and worry blows across his face instead. "You okay?"

Before Konstantin can reply, Mr. Brown starts clapping his hands slowly as if applauding a job well done.

Even more confusion spreads across the whole room, and several people glance at one another.

"Congratulations," Mr. Brown says, and points up at Maksim. "You have just successfully assassinated your target." Lowering his arm, he points towards Konstantin. "While you just fell a hundred feet down the side of the building and died."

"It wasn't my fault," Konstantin protests. With a scowl, he stabs a hand towards the rope he was climbing, which is now lying on the floor. "The rope came free and—"

"Exactly," Mr. Brown interrupts. He pauses for a few seconds to sweep his gaze over all of us. Then he raises a finger in the air. "The rope came free."

Only the faint thuds that Maksim produces as he climbs back down break the confused silence in the room. He drops down next to Konstantin and gives him a quick once-over, to which Konstantin nods, as if confirming that he's fine.

"How many of you walked through that door, took one look at the knots I had laid out, and thought '*what is this, the boy scouts?*' while rolling your eyes?" Mr. Brown asks, breaking the silence.

Embarrassment flashes through me, because that is exactly what I thought. And based on the way half of the other first-years awkwardly shift on their feet, I was not the only one.

"Learning how to tie proper knots might not feel as badass as shooting a gun or wielding a knife," Mr. Brown continues. "But the knowledge will mean the difference between life and death for you all the same. Now, let's get started."

As far as introductions go, I have to admit that this was an incredibly effective one. When Mr. Brown begins showing the different knots and explains what to use them for and how to tie them, everyone watches intently. A lot more attentively than they probably would have without that little demonstration at the beginning.

I try my best throughout the whole class, but I don't really stress over the fact that I can't get the knots right, because I'm not going to become a hitman anyway. Mr. Brown must feel my slight disinterest because he drifts over several times and stares down at me disapprovingly where I sit on the floor and try to replicate the knot he showed.

My ass is still sore from Kaden's punishment yesterday, so

I try to sit on my hip as much as possible, which isn't exactly helping my rope tying efforts either.

The twins cast me questioning glances from a short distance away, silently asking if I want them to help me. I shake my head at them and keep trying.

However, once class is finished and Mr. Brown has dismissed everyone, I suddenly wish that I had tried at least a little harder, because he calls my name before I can leave.

"Miss Petrov."

God, I can hear the disapproval in his voice. Bracing myself, I turn back to face him. "Yes, sir?"

"I'm going to need you to stay after class," he announces.

My chest falls, and I stifle a sigh. Great. I'm at a freaking university for assassins, and I still somehow managed to get detention.

"Should we…?" Maksim asks quietly from where he and Konstantin are waiting for me.

I shake my head. "No. I'll see you back at the house."

They glance between me and our instructor for another second before giving me a slow nod. Then they walk out the door, leaving me alone with the disappointed professor.

He stands there with his arms crossed, staring me down in silence for an uncomfortably long time before he finally blows out a long breath.

"Wait here," he says. "I'll be right back."

Then, without another word, he strides out the door as well and closes it behind him.

Once I'm certain that I'm alone, I run a hand over my face and groan. This was not how I wanted to spend the rest of my afternoon.

After pulling off my hair tie, I rake my hands through my hair and then tie it up into a bun instead. I glance down at my white t-shirt and short blue skirt. In hindsight, this probably wasn't the best attire to wear to class. But my ass and the back of my thighs ached so much this morning that I couldn't bring myself to put on pants. And since I'm not here to become an assassin, I picked comfort over professionalism. However, now I can't help but feel as if that was just one more thing that made Mr. Brown hate me.

The door opens behind me. Turning, I already have an apology ready.

"I'm sorry, sir," I begin. "I should have—"

"Sir? My, my, how polite you've become ever since I took a cane to your perfect little ass."

My heart stops as I come face to face with Kaden Hunter. A smirk plays over his lips as he saunters across the floor. I instinctively take a step back.

"You," I blurt out while my pulse kicks up a notch.

Kaden keeps advancing on me, power and utter control rolling off his honed body with every step. "Me."

"You shouldn't be here." My gaze darts between his face and the now closed door behind him. "Mr. Brown will return any second."

His cold smirk only widens. "No, he won't."

"Yes, he said…" Trailing off, I finally realize what's going on. "You set this up."

Kaden gives me a quick rise and fall of his eyebrows in mocking confirmation.

"Fuck," I curse under my breath.

My legs bump against a box full of ropes, and I suddenly realize that I've continued to back away. Shit. I need to get to the door. Not let him back me farther away from it.

Coming to a halt, I quickly scan the room while trying to

formulate some kind of plan. Kaden continues closing the distance between us.

Since there is nothing in the room that can help me, I do the only thing I can do. I make a break for the door.

My stomach lurches as Kaden wraps an arm around my waist and yanks me off my feet before I can pass him.

It only takes him another few seconds to twist me around, shove me down chest first on the floor and settle his weight on my back.

I press my palms against the cold floor, trying to use my arms for leverage to push myself up. But with Kaden's powerful frame straddling me, I can't get my chest more than one inch off the floor. Clenching my jaw in annoyance, I twist my head to glare at him over my shoulder. But he's facing the other way, so all I can see is his muscular back.

"How's your ass?" Kaden asks, and even though I can't see his face, I can hear the fucking smirk in his voice.

Since I have no intention of gracing that question with a reply, I just turn my head back so that I'm staring towards the door that I can no longer reach.

I gasp, and pain flashes through my ass as Kaden gives it a firm slap.

"When I ask you a question, you answer," Kaden declares, his voice merciless. "Understood?"

"Yes," I grind out.

"Good."

He gently draws his palm over the spot where he spanked me. It soothes the ache and sends a ripple through my belly.

While I'm still busy trying to separate the emotions that flashed through me, Kaden leans sideways and pulls out several lengths of rope from the box next to us.

"Wait," I protest. "What are you—"

But my question gets cut off because I have to bite back a moan when Kaden suddenly leans forward over my legs, making his hard cock press against the top of my ass. I'm still so stunned by my body's reaction to this absolute psycho that I barely feel him wrap a hand around my ankle. It's only when he bends my leg so that my calf is pressed against the back of my thigh that my mind finally catches up with what's going on.

"No, don't—"

"You still haven't answered my question," Kaden interrupts while he starts tying my leg in place like that with a length of rope.

While bucking my hips, I desperately try to pull my leg back, but my calf is firmly trapped against the back of my thigh by that rope now.

"Answer, or I'll spank you again," Kaden warns as he reaches for my other ankle.

I give up on trying to free my left leg and instead concentrate on trying to keep Kaden from grabbing my right one as well. Shifting it sideways, I blindly try to move it out of his reach.

His palm connects with my ass again.

I bite back something between a moan, a groan, and a snarl.

"It's sore," I snap in response to his question before he can do that again.

His hard cock brushes over my ass as he leans forward once more and grabs my right ankle. Another highly inconvenient ripple rolls through me.

"Good," Kaden replies as he bends that leg into the same position as the other one. "That should teach you never to touch my things again."

"Asshole," I mutter into the concrete floor.

He tightens the rope around my right leg, trapping it in place with my calf pressed against the back of my thigh. "What was that?"

"Nothing." It comes out sounding more childish and sullen than I would've preferred.

"That's right."

His weight disappears from my back. I immediately try to push myself up using my hands again, but he just twists around so that he is facing my head instead and plants his palm between my shoulder blades.

"Stay down," he orders as he shoves my chest back down to the floor.

Then he sits down on my ass instead.

A jolt shoots through my confused body as his hard cock now presses against it from a different angle when he leans forward.

Before I can get my mind back on track, he grabs my arms and moves them behind my back. I growl silent curses at him in Russian as he first ties my elbows together behind my back and then ties my wrists as well.

While he works, I try to yank my arms back. But I'm so ridiculously outmatched against this damn man that it doesn't accomplish a single thing. He simply holds my arms with one hand and ties them together with his other. As if I'm nothing but a doll that he plays with.

Resting my forehead against the cold floor, I try to sooth the heat of both embarrassment and... something else... that sears my cheeks.

Once he's done, he also wraps a length of rope that has one knot on it around my waist and down my stomach between my legs before tying it to my hands behind my back. It doesn't really restrict me all that much, at least not compared to the other ropes around my limbs, but I'm not about to point that out. Especially not when I'm already this fucked.

Both of my legs are tied with my calves pressing against the back of my thighs, and my arms are trapped behind my back with ropes securing both my elbows and wrists. I can't stand up. I can't even sit up. All I can do is wiggle on the floor.

Kaden draws his fingers over the back of my neck, which makes goosebumps break out all over my skin. Then he at last stands up.

I once more try to break the ropes restraining me with sheer force, but it doesn't work. I'm completely and utterly trapped.

"Do you have any idea how beautiful you are when you're tied up and completely at my mercy?" Kaden says, his voice coming out darker and a bit rougher than before.

Once again, those two very conflicting emotions heat my cheeks.

I know that, logically, I should only be embarrassed and scared right now. But for some reason, being intimately tied up like this by Kaden has also inexplicably turned me on.

"No," I reply, remembering his earlier warning that he would spank me if I didn't answer his questions.

Kaden chuckles, but it's more of a satisfied sound than a mocking one. "Quick learner. I can't believe your family has kept such an asset hidden away all this time."

My heart swells at the unexpected praise. Asset? He thinks I'm an asset to my family?

However, before I can do something as stupid as to cherish that comment, I remember that this is an enemy. Kaden Hunter is an enemy.

"What do you want, Kaden?" I ask, heaving a deep sigh.

"Who says I want anything?"

"You never do anything without a reason, and I doubt you went through all of this trouble just to tie me up and leave."

Silence falls over the large concrete room.

Panic flutters behind my ribs. Wait, *is* that what he's going to do? Tie me up and then leave? Twisting my head and craning my neck, I try to look up at where he is towering over my bound body. But I can't see his face.

My heart patters in my chest.

He's not going to just walk away and leave me like this. Is he?

"Kaden," I begin when the silence continues to stretch. Even I can hear the desperation leaking into my voice.

"Yes, little doe?"

"Please don't leave me here like this."

"You truly do know how to pick your battles," Kaden says, sounding a little impressed. "When to stand your ground because you have a chance to win. And when to beg for mercy instead of spewing useless bluster in the face of certain defeat." He clicks his tongue. "If only the rest of your family possessed the same intellect too."

Since I'm not sure how to respond to that, I say nothing.

"How about this?" Kaden continues. "Since you responded so well to my last challenge, I will give you another one. If you can make it to the door, I will untie you."

I snap my gaze towards the door. When I'm tied like this, the distance feels impossibly vast.

"Done," I say, because I know that it's the only deal I will get from this domineering bastard.

One of those cold, smug chuckles that can barely be classified as a laugh escapes his wicked lips.

I just clench my jaw and start trying to crawl across the floor.

Lightning shoots through my veins at the first movement.

Sucking in a gasp, I suppress a shiver of pleasure while my mind desperately tries to figure out what the hell happened.

I move again.

Another ripple of pleasure goes through my core.

My eyes widen, because I suddenly understand what's causing it.

That rope that Kaden wrapped around my waist and pulled between my legs before tying it to my wrists had one knot on it. Just one. And the rope also wasn't really restricting me in any way. I thought it was odd but didn't bother asking about it. Now I understand why he did it.

That merciless fucking bastard.

Every time I move my arms, which I have to do in order to crawl forward, I pull at the rope between my legs. And that damn knot in it rubs right against my clit every time. Since I'm wearing a skirt, the only fabric between the knot and my pussy is my thin underwear. I might as well be naked.

"Problem?" Kaden taunts, smug amusement pulsing from his voice.

"No," I growl back.

He just lets out another one of those self-satisfied chuckles.

I start forward again.

The rope grinds against my clit, sending flickers of electricity through my veins. I grit my teeth and try to block it out.

Pleasure pulses through me as I crawl another step forward. Kaden follows next to me. I can feel him raking his gaze over my body, watching my reactions, which isn't exactly helping me keep my head cool.

That damn knot rubs against my clit yet again, and I have to bite my tongue to stop a moan from slipping past my lips. I crawl another step forward.

Embarrassment and pent-up need swirl inside me, making heat radiate from my cheeks.

I wiggle forward, and then have to close my eyes and breathe slowly through my nose as another flash of pleasure shoots up my spine.

"Giving up?" Kaden mocks.

"No," I snap.

Steeling myself, I move forward again.

But with every excruciating inch forward, that throbbing tension inside me grows stronger and stronger.

While biting back another moan, I crawl forward and stare towards the door. I've only made it halfway there. God damn it. How am I supposed to make it all the way over there without... *coming.*

Heat sears my cheeks just at the thought of it. I can't have an orgasm here. Not like this. Kaden would never let me forget it.

"The next time you stop, I will interpret that as you giving up," Kaden informs me. "So unless you want to spend the night tied up in this room, start moving and *keep* moving towards the door until you reach it."

I try to glare at him, but since I can only see halfway up his legs, it's not very effective.

After drawing in a bracing breath, I start moving again.

My clit throbs every time the knot rubs over it, and without those small breaks to recover, the tension thrumming inside me reaches unbearable levels.

A pitiful whimper spills from my lips.

While dragging in shuddering breaths, I desperately try to hold off the orgasm as I crawl towards the door.

Pleasure shoots through me with every jerk of my wrists.

I grit my teeth.

My clit throbs.

Tension pulses inside me like a storm.

I crawl forward again.

Release crackles through me.

The orgasm I have been trying so desperately to hold off washes through my body like a raging flood. I gasp as the pleasure sweeps through me with such intensity that my whole body trembles on the floor.

Kaden immediately crouches down in front of me. I shift my head, trying to hide my face. But he grabs my chin and mercilessly tilts my head back so that I'm staring straight up at him.

Moans and whimpers drip from my lips as I come hard enough to soak my panties. Above me, Kaden studies every inch of my face as if it's the most fascinating thing he has ever seen.

Pleasure continues flickering through my veins for another few seconds.

Then it dies out, and I'm left an embarrassed wet mess who's tied up on the floor with my enemy's hand around my jaw and his intense dark eyes boring into mine.

My chest heaves.

I drag in a shuddering breath and glance towards the door. I didn't make it. And Kaden told me that if I stopped moving...

Oh God. He's going to leave me here now. Tied up and drenched in my own cum. If someone else, especially one of my brothers or cousins, finds me like this, I'm going to locate the nearest gun and shoot myself in the head so that I won't have to live down that embarrassment.

Crouching before me, Kaden still studies me with that astonished expression in his eyes. It sends a surprised jolt through me. I once more try to lower my head so that he can't see my face and my very flushed cheeks, but his hand around my jaw keeps me firmly in place.

"You didn't make it to the door," he says, his voice sounding oddly hoarse.

Dread crashes over me because this is it. This is the moment he stands up and walks out the door, leaving me here.

"Please," I beg. Because against the power he holds over me right now, begging is all I can do.

His gaze drifts over my body before returning to my face again. "But I think you might just have earned your freedom anyway."

Hope surges inside me.

Kaden releases my jaw and stands up again. I twist my head and watch has he walks around me and then crouches down next to my legs instead.

My heart leaps as he slides out a knife and spins it once in his hand.

I suck in a sharp breath as he places the point of the blade against my hip. But all he does is to carefully trace the knife downwards.

A dark thrill races down my spine as he draws the knife along the curve of my ass like a caress. My heart is beating so hard against my ribs that I swear I can hear it through the floor. New sparks of fire surge to life in my lower belly as

Kaden traces his blade along the curve of my ass on the other side as well.

As if he can hear my heart pounding too, he glances at me from the corner of his eye while a faint smirk lurks on his lips.

Then he swiftly and efficiently shifts his knife down and cuts the ropes binding my legs. I stretch them out while he moves on to the ropes around my waist, wrists, and elbows.

Relief washes through my limbs as Kaden frees the rest of my body.

I roll my shoulders and wrists while he gets to his feet. Once I've gotten the slight prickling sensation out of my arms and legs, I stand up as well.

Kaden remains where he is, towering over me from just half a stride away. I resist the impulse to take a step back. Instead, I watch him nonchalantly twirl the knife in his hand for a few seconds before I drag my gaze up to his face.

That mesmerized expression from earlier is gone now. He no longer looks at me as if he finds me fascinating. Instead, he watches me with that customary cold, arrogant expression that makes him look like a prince of hell.

A cruel smirk tilts his lips as he shoots a pointed look down at my pussy. "I would suggest telling your brothers that you spilled some water on yourself."

My gaze snaps down to my skirt. Mortification crashes over me when I find a darker blue spot at the front of my skirt, evidence of my very untimely orgasm. I quickly twist my skirt so that the wet spot is instead located at my hip.

The flat of his blade appears underneath my chin, and he uses it to tilt my head back up.

"Because you remember what I told you would happen if

you tell them what I do to you, don't you?" Keeping the blade underneath my chin, he arches an eyebrow in warning.

I glare up at him. "Yes."

"Fascinating." But there is none of that genuine astonishment on his face this time. Only vicious mocking. "That you can still manage to glare up at me so defiantly only a minute after you've made a complete mess of yourself on the floor before my feet."

Embarrassment warms my cheeks, staining them red.

Kaden smirks and leans down until his lips almost brush against mine. "Much better."

My heart skips a beat at the sudden nearness of his mouth. But before I can do anything about it, he pulls back and removes his knife from my chin. Then he gives me one last knowing once-over before turning and striding away.

And as I stand there and watch the muscles ripple underneath his dark shirt as he walks away while spinning that knife in his hand, I realize with shock and horror that my clit has started to throb again.

What the hell is wrong with me?

10

KADEN

I could clean and reassemble a sniper rifle in my sleep. Which is fortunate, because ever since I left Alina in that room two days ago, all I have been able to think about is her. So as I sit there at the kitchen table in our house, I let my hands just go through the practiced movements while my mind yet again replays that memory.

Alina's beautiful face flashes before my eyes. I wish I had filmed it, because I want to preserve that image forever. How her eyes widened and her mouth dropped open slightly. How her slim body trembled on the floor as the orgasm swept through her. Those cute little moans and whimpers that spilled from her perfect lips. The pleasure that pulsed across her whole face and made her big gray eyes glitter.

I have never seen anything so... *perfect* in my entire life.

The moment that her orgasm ended, I immediately wanted to draw another one from her body just so that I could see it again. I feel like an addict. One hit, and I'm already craving my next fix so badly that my cock threatens to harden just at the thought of watching Alina climax like that again.

"Kaden."

Blocking out all of those images, I make sure to keep my features a blank mask as I look up from the sniper rifle to meet my older brother's gaze.

Eli is sitting across from me at the kitchen table, cleaning a sniper rifle of his own.

He got the strangest coloring of us all. His hair is straight and black like mine. But as opposed to my dark brown eyes, his are almost golden in color.

My gaze drifts over the scar that cuts through Eli's eyebrow and ends at the top of his cheek. It's just one of many scars he received back then, but it still makes my blood boil every time. If I could have just gotten my hands on the people who did that to him, I would've showed them exactly what I do to people who hurt my brothers. But they are long dead now, which is a mercy they didn't deserve. They suffered before they died, yes. But not nearly enough.

"What?" I challenge as Eli raises his eyebrows at me in silent question.

"What's going on?" he demands.

I scowl at him. "I don't know what you're talking about."

"Just because the rest of the world can't read your emotions doesn't mean that *I* can't see when you're trying to hide shit behind that blank mask of yours."

Drawing my eyebrows down, I glower at him. I pride myself on being the one who can read everyone's emotions easily. But apparently, my infuriating brothers have learned to at least partly do the same to me.

"It's nothing," I say, and give him a nonchalant shrug.

His golden eyes narrow. "I can always torture it out of you."

"Uhm," Jace calls over his shoulder from where he is sitting on the couch, cleaning his own sniper rifle at the coffee table. "Have you forgotten that Kaden is our resident torturer?"

I smirk at Eli and raise my eyebrows expectantly.

"Don't forget who brought the sniper rifles," Eli warns, fixing me with a threatening look. "I'm the one who's graduated, which means that I'm the one who has access to unlimited weapons and tools."

"I don't need unlimited weapons and tools to torture someone."

Jace lets out something between a chuckle and a snort.

But before Eli can retort, Rico walks into our combined kitchen and living room. "How's it going?"

"Apart from Eli and Kaden threatening to torture each other?" Jace replies from the cream-colored couch. "Splendid."

Rico levels a disapproving look on me and Eli. "You're threatening to torture each other?"

"Yes," Eli and I reply in unison as if that's the most natural thing in the world.

A laugh escapes Eli's lips, and a small smile tugs at the corner of mine.

"Fucking hell," Rico sighs, and shakes his head at us. "Then at least make sure you're done well before tomorrow."

That sobers everyone up.

We're going to help Rico confront Isabella tomorrow. It's why Eli is here even though he has already graduated from Blackwater. We needed access to sniper rifles without alerting anyone on campus, and without asking Mr. Morelli, so Rico called Eli. Our eldest brother might act all arrogant and bossy, but he dropped everything the moment Rico called and showed up with guns in a matter of hours.

Eli, Rico, Jace, and I might give each other shit for various things more often than not, but we have each other's backs without question every day of the week.

"Everything will be fine tomorrow," Eli says, holding Rico's gaze. "It will all work out."

Rico rakes a hand through his wavy brown hair in a clear show of nerves, but his voice is steady as he says, "Yeah." Before any of us can reply, he strides around the kitchen island and towards the fridge. "Look, I need something to do with my hands right now, so I'm going to make dinner."

"Oh!" Jace exclaims as he turns to grin at Rico. "Can you make that pasta thing you did last week?"

While the two of them start discussing food instead, Eli turns back to me and fixes me with a pointed stare.

I blow out an annoyed sigh, because I know that he won't be letting this go.

"I'm just… confused," I begin.

"By what?"

"You know how I get off on fear and pain and tears?"

"Yeah?" Eli replies, and there is absolutely no judgement in his tone whatsoever.

That's another thing I like about my brothers. None of them judge. Because we're all a bit fucked in the head. Eli and I even more than Rico and Jace. So I know that Eli understands my dark cravings more than anyone.

"Well," I continue. "A couple of days ago, I watched a girl climax and… I liked it."

"You liked watching her come?"

"Yeah." Drawing my eyebrows down, I blow out an irritated sigh. "And that's the thing that confuses me. I've never gotten pleasure from seeing a woman come before. Only from their fear and helplessness."

A wistful smile blows across Eli's face. "I know the feeling. I never craved watching someone come until I met Raina."

"And that's just the problem. I crave it. I need to see it again. Like a fucking addict. It's infuriating."

Eli cocks his head, and uneasiness slithers around my spine at the calculating look in his eyes when he watches me. Fuck, I shouldn't have said anything. Now he will jump to the wrong conclusions.

"Like I said, I've only felt that with Raina," he says, confirming my fear that he is indeed jumping to the conclusion that I somehow care about Alina in any way. Which is absolutely ridiculous. Eli looks me up and down. "Who is this girl?"

"No one," I reply, and make an effort to roll my eyes as if he is being stupid. "Just forget it."

"It's Alina Petrov," Jace calls from the couch. "Mikhail and Anton's little sister."

I snap my gaze to him, my hand already reaching for a knife, as I growl, "I will fucking kill you."

Jace, who has apparently finished well before us, snatches up his sniper rifle and levels it at me. Before my hand has even closed around the hilt of a knife, a red dot appears on my chest as Jace holds the weapon steady.

He grins at me. "As always, you're welcome to try."

From across the table, Eli chuckles and gives Jace an approving nod. I shoot our older brother a dark look.

A *bang* sounds behind me as Rico slams something down on the counter hard enough to make the dark wooden cabinets rattle.

"What the fuck did I just say?" he snaps at us.

Behind the rifle, Jace flashes him a sheepish smile. "Sorry, Mom."

Rico stares Jace down until he lowers his weapon. While Rico is busy muttering curses under his breath, I shoot Jace a look that promises vengeance. He just grins wider, challenge dancing in his eyes like golden sparkles.

"You're sleeping with the enemy?"

My gaze snaps back to Eli, who is staring at me from across the table. *Ah, crap.*

"No," I retort. "I'm tormenting her."

Eli arches an eyebrow. "Then how did you watch her come?"

"I tied her up and put a crotch rope on her and then told her to crawl."

For a few seconds, Eli only blinks at me. Then a smirk curves his mouth. "Fuck, that's hot. I might do that to Raina when I get home."

Smug satisfaction ripples through me. But all I say is, "Yeah. So like I said, I'm not fucking her."

"Yet," Jace says.

Slamming the sniper rifle down on the kitchen table, I yank out a throwing knife and spin towards him. "I swear, one more fucking word out of your mouth and I will put a knife through your eyeball."

With that need for chaos burning in his eyes, he opens his mouth.

However, before he can say anything, Rico speaks up. "If you say one more thing to piss him off, I won't make you that pasta dish."

Jace flicks a glance towards him. Apparently, Rico must have a dead serious expression on his face, because Jace groans in annoyance and then closes his mouth again.

From across the table, Eli sets his sniper rifle down as well before meeting my gaze. "Look, am I happy that you're fucking a Petrov? No."

"I told you, I'm not fucking her," I bite out, but Eli just keeps talking as if I hadn't interrupted.

"But am I going to give you shit about it? No." He chuckles and shakes his head. "I was fucking Raina last year and she poisoned me and blew up my car."

Chopping sounds come from the cutting board by the kitchen island as Rico adds, "Yeah, and don't look at me. I fucked Isabella just last night and tomorrow I'm going to put a gun to her head."

"So we're the last people who should be lecturing you on sleeping with the enemy," Eli picks up with a casual shrug. "You want my advice?"

I hate asking people for help, so I don't manage an answer. But Eli knows me well enough to understand that I want to hear his advice even if I'm too proud to admit it, so he just keeps speaking as if it was a rhetorical question.

"Take what you want." There is a ruthless glint in his eyes as he holds my gaze. "You're a Hunter. We don't wait for things to come to us. We do whatever the hell we want and decimate anyone standing in our way."

A slow smile spreads across my lips. Fuck, I have missed Eli. Rico and Jace are dangerous in their own right, but Eli is in a league of his own when it comes to being brutal and merciless.

With that wicked smile still on my lips, I give our unhinged older brother a slow nod.

Do whatever the hell I want and decimate anyone standing in my way.

Now *that* sounds like a plan.

11

ALINA

The ache from Kaden's caning faded days ago, but now all of my muscles are sore for a different reason. Namely, that godawful obstacle course that our instructor forced us to go through today.

Stretching out my arms in front of me, I try to ease the ache in my muscles as I follow the rest of the girls in my group into the women's locker room. My gaze drifts towards the shower room that is connected to the changing area while I let my arms drop back down again. All I want to do is to just sit down on the floor and let warm water wash over me. And wash away all the damn mud that I'm covered in too.

I stagger a surprised step to the side when someone bumps her shoulder against mine. Finding my balance again, I glance up to see Carla. Just like me and everyone else, she's covered in mud. But there is a spring in her step, and a warm sparkle in her brown eyes.

"Chin up," she says with a smile. "You did your best. That's all that matters."

An embarrassed smile blows across my face. "Thanks."

The truth is that I was absolutely terrible. Again. I finished last every time, which meant that during the team challenge, we would've lost if Carla hadn't been so incredibly skilled that she managed to make up the time difference.

From somewhere behind me, I can feel Leslie and Jane stare daggers at me. But Carla is one of the top people in our year so far, so they are apparently too scared to say anything in front of her.

"Remember," Carla continues as she opens her locker and starts pulling out her towel and shower supplies. "Physical strength is not the only thing that's important. We're all skilled at different things."

I rub a hand over the back of my neck, which only serves to dislodge bits of dried mud and make them fall into the back of my t-shirt. "Thanks. Though I'm not sure I'm skilled at anything at all."

While stripping out of her clothes, she gives me a pointed look. "Girl, I've seen your scores on the theoretical tests. You're smart. Don't let anyone tell you otherwise."

My heart clenches and my throat closes up with a sudden immense gratitude. After the humiliating experience of failing that badly at the obstacle course in front of everyone, I really needed to hear that.

But before I can press out a choked *thank you*, Carla flashes me one of her brilliant smiles and starts towards the shower room. I swallow against the lump in my throat and give her a nod before I open my own locker.

The moment Carla is gone, two shadows creep up on me from both sides. I can feel them looming, but I ignore them as I start pulling out my own towel.

"We almost lost today because of you," Jane says from my left.

"Yeah, but we didn't," I reply without turning to look.

"That's not the point," Leslie adds from my other side.

I just continue pulling out my shampoo and conditioner from my bag inside the locker. Tension crackles through the air around me, but I keep pretending that they're not there.

A *bang* echoes through the room as Jane slams my locker closed.

"Look at me when I talk to you," she snaps.

Heaving a deep sigh, I turn to face the two of them. They stand with their arms crossed, looking down at me as if I'm something that they've just scraped off the bottom of their shoes. However, their *mean girls* vibe is somewhat diminished by the fact that both of them are also covered in mud.

"I'm going to say what everyone else here is thinking," Leslie begins, locking blue eyes full of contempt on me. "You are a waste of space."

I arch an eyebrow at her. "Yeah, I think you've actually already said that."

"You don't deserve to be here."

Rolling my eyes, I blow out an irritated sigh and just start to move past them.

Jane plants a hand against my chest and shoves me back against my locker. "And where do you think you're going?"

"To shower," I reply.

"Oh, I don't think so." Her mouth twists into a mocking smile. "If you're at the bottom of the food chain, you wait for everyone else to shower first."

I briefly consider protesting, but I know how to pick my battles. And this one isn't worth it.

"Fine," I say.

They smirk at me as they walk away while I toss my towel down on the bench and then sit down to wait.

From the other side of the room, the sound of splashing water drifts through the air. I try not to think about how nice it must feel to already be standing there under the warm rushing water while I sit there on the hard wooden bench, still covered in dried mud. Once we're down to half of the group, I strip out of my dirty clothes and wrap the towel around myself in preparation.

By the time it's finally my turn, there are only three other students left in the shower room and four others who are putting on fresh clothes in the locker room. Carla has already left, of course. But Leslie and Jane are among the four people still left in the locker room, and they flash me smug smiles when I walk past. I ignore them and instead hang up my towel on one of the metal hooks in the shower room.

Then I step underneath one of the showerheads that are set into the wall and turn it on. Warm water washes over me.

I wash the mud from my hair and body, and then I do what I had planned to do the moment I walked across the threshold. I sit down on the floor and let the warm water soothe the ache in my muscles.

Even though I don't want to admit it, these constant reminders that I'm not good enough are starting to take their toll on me. I wish Jane and Leslie would just leave me alone. If they didn't take every opportunity to crush my confidence, it would be so much easier to deal with the fact that I truly do suck at most things here at Blackwater.

Tilting my head back, I let the warm water splash down over my face.

And besides, I already have one bully. Isn't that enough? And not just any bully. Kaden Hunter. The worst psycho on campus. Why do I have to deal with both him and petty mean girls like Leslie and Jane. It's not fair.

A sigh escapes my lungs.

But then again, life isn't fair. So why do I expect it to be?

Shaking my head, I decide that my pity party has gone on long enough. I need to get changed and head back to our house before my brothers send out a search party.

I push up from the floor and turn off the shower. Unsurprisingly, everyone else has already finished and left. After squeezing the water from my hair, I start towards the hook where I hung my towel.

Surprise flashes through me.

Trailing to a halt, I stare at the empty towel rack for a few seconds.

Then an exasperated sigh rips from my chest. Someone accidentally took *my* towel too. Great.

With water still dripping from my body, I walk back into the locker room.

It's as deserted as the shower room, but the air is now warm and moist from the prolonged use of the showers. Faint scents of perfume also linger in the air.

Stopping in front of my locker, I open the small metal door.

I blink at it.

Empty.

With confusion pulling at my brows, I shake my head at myself and close the door again. I must have opened the wrong one. Moving sideways, I open the locker next to it.

Also empty.

I open the one on the other side.

Empty as well.

Dread curls around my spine like a cold snake.

Someone didn't *accidentally* take my towel too. They did it on purpose. And they took all of my clothes, even the muddy ones, as well.

With my heart pattering in my chest, I start down the row of lockers, yanking up each one. But they're all empty.

Those smug smiles on Jane and Leslie's lips when I walked into the shower room flash over and over through my mind.

That's why they wanted me to shower last. So that they could steal my clothes and my towel, and to make sure that there was no one else left to help me.

I cast a panicked look around the room. But I've checked all the lockers, and there is nothing here. Not even a forgotten scrap of fabric that I can use.

And my phone was in my bag, so I can't call anyone for help either.

Which means that I will need to walk *naked* across campus until I get to my car or find where they dumped my bag or until someone sees me and takes pity on me.

Fuck, fuck, fuck.

This is worse than anything Kaden could've done. At least he mostly just humiliates me in private. I will never be able to live down the embarrassment of walking naked across campus. This—

My spinning thoughts are interrupted when the door to the locker room is abruptly yanked open.

Relief flutters behind my ribs. But it quickly withers and dies when a familiar voice cuts through the air.

"Are you hiding from me, little doe?"

I suck in a sharp breath as Kaden stalks across the threshold. He is wearing a tight-fitting black t-shirt that shows off every ridge of his sharp muscles, and the holsters around his thighs and hips are as usual filled with knives. Light from the fluorescents falls across his sharp cheekbones, but there is an impatient expression on his devastatingly handsome features.

With my pulse now thundering in my ears, I hurry around the row of lockers so that he won't be able to see me.

Somewhere on the other side, the door falls shut again with a click. For a few seconds, Kaden's footsteps is the only sound in the room. I move when he does, making sure to always stay on the other side of the metal barrier that is now the only thing shielding me from him.

Kaden circles the rows of lockers.

Then he stops.

I do as well.

My heart is pounding in my chest, which makes it hard to hear, but I strain my ears and listen for the sound of his footfalls. They don't start up again.

"There you are."

I almost jump out of my skin.

Whirling around, I find Kaden standing just a few steps away, blocking the way out between the lockers. God damn it. Someone as large as him should not be able to move that quietly.

There is a sadistic smile playing over Kaden's wicked lips as he advances on me. "Were you trying to hide from me, little doe?"

While covering my private parts with my hands, I back away and shake my head. "No."

"Then why are you still here? I was waiting for you outside, but you never showed up."

"I, uhm…"

My back bumps into the cold concrete wall behind me. I cast a quick look over my shoulder in surprise, but there is no more room to back away. I'm trapped between two rows of lockers and the wall behind my back.

Kaden closes the distance between us until he is standing only a single stride away. His lethal body exudes power as he towers over me. My heart thunders in my chest.

He narrows his eyes and flicks a glance up and down my body. "Why are you still naked?"

Keeping my mouth firmly closed, I just swallow nervously while holding his gaze. I don't want to have to admit to Kaden, of all people, that some girls stole my clothes. He already thinks that I'm just a plaything, and for some reason, I just can't bear the thought of him finding out that other people treat me like that too.

"Answer," he orders, his voice tight, and the sheer command in it pulses through my very soul.

I raise my chin. "It's none of your business."

His hand shoots up.

A jolt pulses through me as his hand locks around my throat. While pinning me to the wall, he moves impossibly closer. I suck in an unsteady breath while my heart hammers against my ribs.

"Remember what I told you on the rooftop." He leans down until I can feel his breath dance over my lips with every word, but his eyes are merciless as they remain locked on mine. "When I give you an order, you obey."

I can barely breathe. Not because of his hand around my throat. But rather because I feel like I'm drowning in him. In his intoxicating scent. In his dark voice. In his intense eyes. In his commanding hand on my body. In the sheer dominance that seems to roll off his shoulders like black smoke. And most of all, in the closeness of those dangerous lips.

Right before I can do something absolutely insane, Kaden

pulls back again. I drag in a shuddering breath to clear my head. But his hand stays around my throat, pinning me to the wall, as he levels a commanding stare on me.

"So, let's try this again," he says. "Why are you still naked?"

"Some girls in my class pulled a prank on me," I reply. It wasn't exactly a prank, but it's true enough that I don't think Kaden will spot the lie. "They took my towel and my clothes while I was showering."

His eyes flash.

The sight of it stuns me enough that I draw back in shock and blink at him. But that flash is gone so quickly that, only a second later, I begin doubting if I even saw it at all. It must have just been the fluorescents, because when he speaks, his voice is calm almost to the point of sounding disinterested.

"And why would they do that?"

"Because I'm terrible and I'm not even here to become an assassin," I reply honestly.

His eyes narrow slightly. "Then why are you here?"

I press my lips together.

He tightens his grip on my throat, displeasure flitting across his features. "Do not make me ask you again."

Frustration rips through me, and I throw my arms out in annoyance as I glare up at the demanding psycho. "Because I wanted freedom!"

"From what?"

"From everything!" My chest is suddenly heaving with anger and pent-up frustration, but I'm too annoyed at Kaden, for forcing me to tell him this, to care. "From my life. From my family. From the future that is looming over my head like an executioner's axe. Everyone treats me like a glass figurine to be put on a shelf. So I'm here because I just wanted to live for a few years without being suffocated by that feeling."

The words just tumbled out of me like a flood. Once I had started speaking, I couldn't stop. But now that they're out, I regret every single word.

Kaden cocks his head, studying me with a pensive expression on his stupidly stunning face.

Embarrassment washes over me.

I shouldn't have told him that. I didn't want him to know that, and now he's just going to use it against me.

Letting my arms drop to my sides, I slump back against the wall and close my eyes while I wait for him to start tormenting me again.

Kaden removes his hand from my throat, but I don't bother opening my eyes. I'm so physically outmatched against him that I couldn't win even if I tried. He can do whatever he wants to me, and there is nothing I can do to stop him, so I just stand there and wait for the axe to fall.

Fabric rustles.

Then something soft is pressed against my skin.

I snap my eyes open and blink down at my chest.

"Take it," Kaden orders.

Confusion whirls through me.

For another few seconds, I just stare at the bundle of black fabric that Kaden is holding against my chest. Then I drag my gaze up to him.

Lightning crackles through my veins.

Kaden is standing before me... shirtless.

My mouth drops open slightly as I stare at him.

It's the first time I have seen him half-naked like this. And God above, he is a freaking work of art.

His body is muscular, but without being bulky. It's all sharp abs and firm pectorals and an absolutely sinful V that disappears down his pants.

Heat pools at my core as I imagine what it would feel like to trace my fingers over his warm skin and honed muscles and then follow that V down to where—

"Take it," Kaden orders again. "And put it on."

I snap back to reality.

My gaze darts between his naked chest and the bundle of black fabric that he is still pressing against my skin.

And the realization of what's going on makes another wave of shock clang through my soul.

I curl my fingers into the soft fabric while my mind still repeats the same stunned realization over and over again. *Kaden is giving me his own shirt.*

The moment I have a grip on the shirt, Kaden pulls his hand back.

For another second, I just gape at him in silence.

But then he shoots me a pointed look filled with ruthless authority, and I quickly scramble to put the shirt on.

My heart stops beating and thunders out of control at the same time as I pull the shirt over my head and let it fall down around my body. It's still warm from when he was wearing it. And it smells like him.

I suddenly feel like I'm drowning again. But this time, I don't think I mind it.

Because of our size difference, his t-shirt is so large that it falls all the way to my knees. It's practically a dress, and it covers up my nakedness completely.

After brushing my hands down the soft fabric, I slowly raise my head again and meet Kaden's gaze. But as those usually so cold eyes of his meet mine, I can't think of a single thing to say.

There is a strange fire burning in Kaden's eyes for a few

seconds as he stares between my face and his shirt that I'm wearing.

Then it disappears in a flash, and that lethal ice returns to his expression.

Closing the distance between us again, he takes my chin in a punishing grip and tilts my head up so that he can lock ruthless eyes on me.

"This means nothing," he says, his voice low and deadly. "It just means that you owe me now."

Before I can think of a reply, he releases my chin with a snap of his wrist that forces me to twist my head to the side. And when I turn my head back, he is already stalking away.

I watch his naked back and the way the muscles shift underneath his skin as he raises his arm to shove the door open before disappearing out into the corridor.

Confusion and disbelief ring inside my head like giant bells.

Kaden's intoxicating scent fills my lungs with every breath.

I look down at the shirt, *his* shirt, while his parting words echo inside my skull.

This means nothing.

12

KADEN

Restless energy bounces around inside me. Which just makes me even more irritated. Because I don't get restless. That's Jace's thing. Me? I'm patient. Methodical. In full control of my emotions.

And yet, right now I feel like I want to crawl out of my own skin.

Rico is with Isabella in the bedroom that he has kept her in this past week. I can hear their voices from out in the hall, and it only makes the restlessness inside me worse, so I stalk down the stairs and into the kitchen instead.

Which turns out to be a gigantic fucking mistake because Jace is sitting on the couch in our combined kitchen and living room. Though *sitting* is probably not the right word. He alternates between playing his first-person shooter game on the TV, checking his phone, standing up to grab the bottle of whiskey on the table before him, drinking from the glass he fills, spinning one of his bats randomly in the air, and raking his fingers through his hair. All within the span of less than a minute.

I can practically feel the restless energy radiating from his body. It's so intense that it almost makes the air physically vibrate. And it fuels the chaos in my own soul until I want to hurl a knife through the nearest window just so that I can hear the glass shatter.

Ever since I found Alina naked and stranded in that locker room, I've felt off-kilter. I should have applauded the girls who pulled that prank on her, but instead, I felt only rage. I can't block out the image of how vulnerable she looked when I found her. And I can't seem to forget just how fucking perfect she looked when she was wearing nothing but *my* shirt. I also can't get her words out of my head. Can't block out the frustration and desperation in her eyes when she told me that she doesn't have any freedom.

I can't even imagine what that must be like. I have always just done whatever the hell I want, and God help anyone who tries to stop me. But it sounds like Alina has never been able to make her own choices. It must be awful.

Stunned shock pulses through me.

Did I just... *empathize* with someone?

I scowl as I yank open the fridge. No, I didn't empathize with her. I can't. Because I don't have those kinds of emotions. I was just *analyzing* her state of mind. Yes, that's it. I was analyzing it because there was one thing she said that I related to.

She said that people treat her like a glass figurine. I know what that's like. Though, not in the way she meant it. For me, it's more like people are afraid that my mind will break. That if they say the wrong thing, the last of my humanity will shatter and I will turn into a raging psycho who slaughters everything and everyone around me. And by *they*, I mean my parents. My mother in particular.

"Kaden," Jace says from the couch, pulling me back to reality.

I realize that I'm still standing there with the fridge open, just staring into it. Drawing my eyebrows down in another scowl, I throw the door shut again. Jars and containers clink and rattle inside from the force of it.

"You okay?" Jace asks in a casual voice.

He has twisted around on the couch so that he is facing me. And though the expression on his face is as casual as his tone, I know him well enough to see the concern in his eyes.

I fucking hate it. *I* am the cold and stable rock that can whether all of *their* emotional outbursts. Not the other way around.

"I'm heading out," I declare as I stalk back towards the doorway.

"Do you want me to—"

"No."

Before he can say anything else, I'm down the hallway and out the front door.

I just want to hurt someone. I *need* to hurt someone. I need to see the fear in someone's eyes and know that I hold their life in my hands.

And I know exactly who.

Mikhail Petrov.

If he hadn't been such an insufferable little bitch, I would never have targeted Alina. And if I hadn't targeted Alina, I would never have started to understand how she feels. Because I. Don't. Do. Feelings.

So now, Mikhail Petrov is going to pay for the events that he set in motion.

Striding through the residential area, I storm up to the

Petrovs' front door and pound my fist against it. It's shoved open only a few seconds later by Anton.

"Mikhail, where have you…" he trails off, his gray eyes going wide as he realizes who I am.

My eyes narrow. So, he was expecting Mikhail. Then that means that Mikhail isn't here. Oh well. I suppose his little brother will have to do.

I slam my fist into his jaw.

His head snaps to the side, and he staggers backwards from the blow.

Stalking into the hallway after him, I raise my foot and plant it against his stomach before shoving him backwards. He still hadn't even recovered from my first strike, so the kick sends him sprawling down on the floor. Air escapes his lungs in a huff as his back hits the pale wooden floorboards.

He tries to roll away, but I'm already moving.

Alarm crackles across his face as I drop down on top of his chest, trapping him against the floor. He swings his fist at my face, but I block it with my forearm. The impact vibrates through my bones, but I can barely feel it. I shove his arm to the side and slam my other fist into his jaw.

His cheek hits the floor as his head snaps to the side.

Using his moment of disorientation, I yank out a knife and drive it towards his throat.

Both of his hands fly up and grab my wrist, trying to stop me from sinking that blade into his windpipe.

Terror floods his face.

The sight of it feeds my soul and partly calms the storm that is tearing through it.

Using my free hand, I yank one of his away from my wrist. With the resistance cut in half, my knife immediately moves closer to his throat.

Fear and panic flash like lightning strikes across Anton's face, and he thrashes wildly underneath me. But it's no use. I'm both bigger and stronger than him.

The point of my knife touches Anton's throat.

He immediately stops struggling. Lying there motionless underneath me, he stares up at me while his chest heaves in panic.

"I can end you right here, little Petrov," I say, threats dripping like poison from my every word.

Anton stares up at me, but he says nothing.

It doesn't matter. I drink in the fear that he can't hide and savor the knowledge that I hold his entire existence in the palm of my hand.

One more inch, and he will die right here on the floor like the useless piece of trash that he is.

That terrible storm inside me urges me to do it. To kill him. To watch him bleed out and see the life fade from his eyes.

My fingers flex on the hilt of my knife.

One push. Just one push.

"STOP!"

The feminine voice cuts through the whirling cloud of rage and frustration and restlessness in my mind.

Looking up, I find Alina on her knees next to us. Her big gray eyes are wide with fear and desperation, and they're lined with tears.

"Stop," she says again. Her hand shakes as she reaches towards my arm. "Please, stop."

I look back down at Anton. He just continues holding my gaze, and he still hasn't begged for his life, which I have to admit buys him a measure of respect.

Alina's hand appears on my forearm. It's so small

compared to mine, and yet it makes more of an impact than mine ever could.

Clarity floods my system again.

It's immediately followed by panic and rage.

I almost killed Anton Petrov. The war between our families doesn't exactly have any rules, but if I *killed* one of them, I would've launched us all into a blood feud. Break them? Sure. But kill them? That's off the table. And I know that. I have always known that. So why did I almost cross that line now?

"Please, Kaden," Alina says.

I slide my gaze to her again, and then abruptly push to my feet.

On the floor, Anton drags in a deep breath and then scrambles to his feet as well. Alina does too.

"Go wait in the kitchen," she says, and shoots Anton a commanding look.

He seems as surprised by it as I am.

"Now," she snaps. "I will escort Kaden to the door."

After glancing between the two of us, Anton runs a hand over his throat and then backs towards the kitchen. Alina sweeps out an arm, motioning for me to follow her to the door. Still gripping the knife in my hand, I walk the handful of steps towards the still open door.

My head is clear now, but I can't let her know that I was out of my mind when I showed up, so I keep an air of thrumming violence around me as I move.

Once we reach the door, I spin abruptly and shove her up against the wall. With my palm pressed against her chest, I pin her to the pale wood panels and lean closer.

"You're racking up quite the debt, little doe," I growl,

keeping that unhinged tone in my voice. "You owe me for your brother's life now too."

Raising her chin, she stares up at me defiantly. "What do you want?"

I lean forward and place my lips next to her ear so that her brother won't be able to overhear. "Come to the small training room on the west side tonight. Midnight. Or I will come back here and finish what I started."

She draws in a shaky breath, and I can feel her heart beat faster underneath my palm. But her voice is steady as she replies, "Done."

I step back and let my hand drop from her chest. She remains standing by the wall, watching me with those intelligent eyes that haunt me every second of the day.

All sorts of really bad ideas flash through my mind.

With a snarl, I manage to shove down the impulse to act out every single one of them.

Instead, I turn and stalk out the door.

But with every step, lingering panic clangs through me.

I never lose control like this. That's Eli's thing. He is the one with no impulse control. I plan my moves strategically. I don't just show up at someone's door and start beating the crap out of them without a plan.

And yet, that is exactly what I just did.

All because I can't get Alina Petrov out of my head.

What the hell is this girl doing to me?

13

ALINA

Nervous energy flits through my stomach like erratic butterflies. It's mixed with something that feels suspiciously like excitement. Which is ridiculous. I shouldn't be excited about sneaking out to meet the school's number one psycho Kaden Hunter in the middle of the night. I should be angry at him for almost killing my brother earlier tonight.

But I'm not angry. I'm more... stunned. And almost a little proud. Because Kaden listened to me. No one ever listens to me. But when I told Kaden to stop, he stopped. And when I told him to leave, he left. That was a surprised that I'm still not entirely sure how to interpret.

Light spills out from underneath the door to the small training room on the west side of Blackwater University.

My pulse speeds up as I push down the handle and open the door.

A jolt shoots through me when I find Kaden standing in the middle of the room, looking straight at me as I cross the threshold. I trail to a halt a few steps into the room while the door falls shut behind me again.

It's a rather small space. Like most of Blackwater, the walls are made of gray concrete and there are no unnecessary decorations in the room. But this room has wooden floorboards instead of a simple concrete floor. There are some padded mats stacked in one of the corners, and four punching bags hang from hooks in the ceiling along one of the walls. I sweep my gaze over them before shifting my attention back to Kaden.

He looks much more in control now than he did back at our house earlier. He is wearing the same black t-shirt and dark pants as before. But chaotic restlessness no longer swirls in his eyes, and his black hair now lies perfectly styled instead of looking like he has been running his fingers through it repeatedly. It should feel reassuring, but I know better than that. This calm and cold version, lethal like a shard of ice, is the most dangerous one.

Standing with his hands clasped behind his back, he looks like a ruthless commander waiting for his opponent to kneel at his feet and offer unconditional surrender. My survival instincts are telling me to do just that. But my stubbornness and pride keep me standing there, my chin raised and my eyes firmly locked on his.

"Punctual too," he says, a faint smirk ghosting across his lips. "Why *have* your brothers been hiding you away all this time?"

"They haven't been hiding me," I retort, crossing my arms over my chest. "I just didn't want to get involved in all of your drama."

"And yet, here you are."

"And yet, here I am."

Raising a hand, he twitches two fingers at me, silently ordering me to approach him. His eyes gleam, as if he is waiting to see if I'm going to disobey his presumptuous command.

He really should've learned by now that I'm too smart to fight battles that I can't win.

With my eyes locked on his, I walk across the floor until I'm standing so close that I can almost feel the warmth radiating from his powerful body. His completely intoxicating scent fills my lungs with every breath. It makes my head spin, and I have to drag in a steadying breath before I crane my neck to look up at him.

Light glitters in his normally so blank eyes as he watches me. He slides his fingers along my shoulder and then up my throat before placing two of them underneath my chin, tilting my head farther back. Leaning down, he slants his lips over mine, just shy of touching.

"The things I will do to you," he breathes against my mouth.

A shudder courses through my body and my spine tingles.

Logically, I know that it's probably a threat more than anything else. But I still can't stop my toes from curling at the dark promise in his voice.

Then he lets his hand drop and takes a step back. It's so abrupt that I almost topple forwards at the sudden loss of his nearness.

"Strip," he commands.

Giving my head a quick shake, I try my best to clear it before I reach down and grab the hem of my shirt. While I start stripping out of my clothes, I can't help but think about the fact that this is the third time Kaden has seen me completely naked. Which is a lot, considering that he is an enemy.

But as I straighten again after removing all of my clothes, I can't bring myself to feel embarrassed about it. Because Kaden is once again raking his gaze over my naked body with such heat that it feels like fire licking my skin.

My gaze drops to his hands.

God, what would it feel like to have those strong hands roaming all over my body instead of just his fiery gaze?

Metallic clattering fills the room, shattering my ridiculous train of thought and yanking me back to reality. I glance down to see that Kaden has tossed a pair of handcuffs onto the floor before my feet.

"Put them on," Kaden orders, authority dripping from his dark voice. "Behind your back."

I lower myself to my knees and reach for the handcuffs. They clink faintly as I pick them up and then straighten again before maneuvering them behind my back. The metal is cold against my wrists as I snap them shut.

Kaden, who was just standing there watching me, takes a step forward.

My heart flips when he moves so close that his stomach brushes against my chest, and then reaches his arms around me.

Clicks sound as he simply tightens the handcuffs around my wrists.

My mind, which was going down all sorts of insane roads, scrambles to catch up.

From barely a breath away, Kaden smirks at me, as if he knows exactly what I was thinking. I glare back at him. A soft chuckle escapes his throat.

Taking a step back, he turns and then walks over to one of

the punching bags by the wall. I turn as well, watching him with raised eyebrows.

I blink as he grabs one of those massive bags and lifts it off the hook before tossing it aside. It hits the floor with a loud thud. I stare at him. The bastard doesn't even have the decency to look winded after picking up such a ridiculously heavy object.

"Get over here," he says.

While glowering at his annoyingly muscular body, I walk across the wooden floorboards until I'm standing in the spot that he indicated. He doesn't even watch to see if I obey. Instead, he simply crouches down and starts pulling something out of his black duffel bag.

My eyes widen as he pulls out a spreader bar.

With my heart now thundering in my chest, I stand there and watch as Kaden straightens and moves back to me instead. Amusement tugs at the corner of his lips, as if he can hear my heart pounding.

Stopping in front of me, he crouches down while still holding the spreader bar.

My heart jerks. Because God damn, I like the sight of him on his knees before me.

A shiver rolls down my spine as Kaden draws his hand over the inside of my thigh and then down my leg until he reaches my ankle. Electricity skitters across my skin at his featherlight touch. I shift my stance slightly as he then locks my ankle into one side of the spreader bar.

Then he twists and grabs my other ankle.

With effortless power, he moves my leg to the side, widening my stance, until my ankle reaches the other shackle. Then he locks that one as well.

I'm left standing there with my wrists handcuffed behind

my back and my legs spread wide and trapped in that metal rod.

Kaden straightens again.

Wickedness glints in his eyes as he looks me up and down. It makes my pulse race and my stomach lurch, but I manage to keep my features blank as I hold his gaze.

The corner of his mouth tilts upwards, as if he can see right through me.

I lick my lips.

"Worried?" he taunts.

"No."

"Liar."

"Maybe if you actually did something that makes me worry, I would be," I retort in a mocking tone.

I regret it the second that the words are out of my mouth.

Kaden's gaze sharpens, and he wraps his hand around my jaw. "You're going to regret that you said that."

I know, I almost reply.

Releasing my chin, he walks back to his duffel bag again and pulls out a metal chain. I swallow, my eyes tracking his movements as he returns. My skin prickles with both anticipation and worry as he fastens the chain to my handcuffs.

Metallic rattling fills the dead silent training room as Kaden slings the other end over the hook that the punching bag used to hang from. Then he starts pulling.

I suck in a gasp as my hands are forced upwards into the air behind my back.

Kaden keeps pulling on the chain until I have to bend over to prevent my shoulders from being dislocated by the unnatural angle of my arms. When I'm leaning forwards in that way, I'm not in any danger of actually hurting anything in my arms or shoulders, but there is a constant strain on my muscles.

"Kaden," I say, my voice coming out more uncertain than I would've liked.

Completely naked, slightly bent over with my legs shackled and spread wide, and my arms forced up behind me like this, I suddenly feel very vulnerable.

"Yes, little doe?" Kaden replies as he saunters back to his duffel bag again.

Several sentences are right there on my tongue. Each one more pitiful than the last. I force myself to swallow them and instead say, "So, what challenge do you have for me this time?"

Only silence answers me while Kaden rummages around in his duffel bag. Once he has found what he's looking for, he straightens and then strides back to me. Because of the angle, I can't see what he's holding until he stops right in front of me.

Shock pulses through my soul.

For a few seconds, all I can do is to stare at the sleek black vibrator that Kaden is holding. It's one of those handheld wand things.

Jerking my head back, I stare up at him with wide eyes.

"No challenge today," Kaden says. Anticipation and cold amusement dance across his face. "I already know that you will lose. Today, I'm just going to see how long it takes for you to start begging me."

My heart pounds in my chest. "Begging you for what?"

He draws his free hand up my throat and then takes a firm grip on my jaw, holding my head up like that so that we can meet each other's gaze. My muscles ache at the conflicting angles that my poor body is now bent into.

A slow smile spreads across Kaden's dangerously

handsome face as he turns on the vibrator and at last replies, "Begging me to let you come."

"I will not be—"

My retort is cut off by a gasp as Kaden presses the vibrating head of the wand straight against my clit. I squirm, trying to move away, but Kaden's firm hand around my jaw and the chain pulling my arms up behind my back keep me trapped in place.

Irregular vibrations pulse through my clit.

I bite my lip hard as a moan threatens to spill from my mouth.

Shifting my stance, I try to close my legs to stop the sweet torture. But the spreader bar keeps my pussy mercilessly exposed to Kaden.

Tension starts building inside me.

Kaden shifts the position of the vibrator slightly.

I suck in a sharp breath as it hits the perfect spot, and I yank futilely against my restraints. With his other hand still gripping my jaw, Kaden studies every flicker of emotion on my face.

My pussy throbs as the vibrations keep coming.

The tension trapped inside me grows.

A pitiful moan slips past my lips.

Kaden smiles like the fucking villain that he is.

I try to throw my head from side to side, but he just tightens his fingers on my jaw.

Pent-up need swirls inside me.

The vibrator sends demanding pulses through my clit, pushing me farther and farther towards that sweet release. My heart hammers in my chest as I careen towards the edge. One more pulse. One more second. And then—

Kaden yanks the vibrator away from my pussy.

The loss of it is so jarring that I gasp. I blink repeatedly to clear my spinning head from the anticipated release that never came.

Once my vision is clear, I find Kaden grinning down at me.

"That's one." He arches an expectant brow. "Should we try again?"

Before I can reply, he presses the vibrator back against my aching clit.

A low moan escapes me. I try to lower my head so that Kaden can't see the pleasure that must be returning to my eyes now that the vibrations are back, but I can't because he keeps his grip on my chin as he studies my face.

My shoulders ache, and I try to shift my position again to ease the strain on my muscles. All that does is to bring my pussy more firmly onto the vibrator.

I squeeze my eyes shut in embarrassment as another desperate moan drips from my lips.

"Eyes on me." The force of his command cuts through the room like a knife.

Obeying his order, I meet his demanding stare again. My heart does a backflip at the incredible hunger I find in his eyes when they once more lock on mine.

My mouth drops open in surprise. But right then, the vibrator sends a strong pulse through my clit, and another gasp rips from my mouth instead.

Kaden keeps his instrument of torture right where it is.

That terrible tension inside me skyrockets again. I wiggle and jerk in my restraints as the edge of an orgasm draws closer. Pent-up release whirls through me until I feel like I'm coming apart at the seams.

Just a little bit more. Just—

The vibrations stop.

"No!" The word tears out of my chest like a bullet.

Kaden's eyes glitter with vicious glee as he stares down at me.

Snapping my mouth shut, I glare up at him in what I hope is stubborn defiance. He lets out a low chuckle.

"Two," he says.

Then he brings the vibrator back to my pussy.

I only make it to six before he has turned me into a sobbing mess of need.

"No," I plead, breaking down at last.

Tears line my eyes as I stare up at the demon before me, because I'm going to die if he brings me to the edge a seventh time without letting me come.

My arms and shoulders ache from the restrictive position he has kept me in, but I barely feel it. All I can feel is that terrible tension that is trapped inside me like a crackling lightning storm. I need release. I need it more than I need air or water or my stubborn pride.

"Please," I beg, desperation bleeding from my voice and radiating from my entire face. "Please, let me come. You have to let me come."

He tightens his grip on my jaw and cocks his head. "I *have to?*"

"Kaden." I try to stomp my foot in frustration, but it's difficult with the spreader bar still locked to my ankles.

Arching a dark brow, he fixes me with a pointed stare as he spins the vibrator in his hand like it's one of his knives. "Is that really the tone you want to be taking with me right now?"

"Please—"

"Maybe we should see if we can make it to ten?"

"No!" A broken sob rips from my throat and I yank against

my restraints again while staring up at him with pleading eyes. "You win! I submit. I surrender. Please, just please, let me come."

He holds my gaze with merciless eyes as he stares me down like a god. Like my own personal god who holds my fate in the palm of his ruthless hand. And in that moment, I know that I will do whatever he wants. If he tells me to crawl and lick his boots, that's what I will do. As long as he finally lets me come, I will do anything he says.

God, this man wields power and control the same way that he wields his blades. With utter precision and terrifying dominance. And it's so fucking hot that I can barely breathe.

"Beg me for permission to come," he orders.

"Please, Kaden," I gasp out. "I'm begging you for permission to come."

A wide smile curls his lips.

He turns the vibrator on again.

For another few seconds, that low buzzing sound is the only thing breaking the silence.

Then he brings it to my clit, and a sobbing moan spills out of my mouth instead. My body practically melts as that pulsing sensation returns.

"Six," Kaden says while the vibrations start building up the tension inside me again. "I have to say, I am impressed."

Only a whimper answers him as I soar towards the edge of that orgasm yet again.

Kaden looks me up and down, his gaze searing into my skin and making me tumble faster towards the edge of release.

"You might look weak and breakable," he muses as he returns his gaze to mine. "But you're a resilient one, aren't you?"

His strange praise and approval send a flutter through my soul.

I drag in unsteady breaths as the whirling tension inside me reaches unbearable levels again. If he's going to deny me another orgasm, he will do it any second now. Fear and desperation and shameless pleading fill my eyes as I look up at him, silently begging him not to do it.

A pleased smirk blows across his sharp features.

And the vibrator stays in place.

My pussy aches with pent-up need as I reach the very edge again.

Strong pulses vibrate against my clit.

The edge is right there. I—

Release explodes through me.

I gasp, and my body jerks in my restraints, making the chain rattle, as a violent orgasm sweeps through me.

Kaden keeps the vibrator against my clit, intensifying the release, and I come so hard that stars flash before my eyes.

Moans drip from my lips like honey and my legs shake uncontrollably as pleasure crashes through my whole body. It's more intense, more intoxicating, than anything I have ever experienced before.

And if this addictively dangerous man could accomplish *that* with just a vibrator, then I can't help but wonder what he could do to me if he ever fucked me properly.

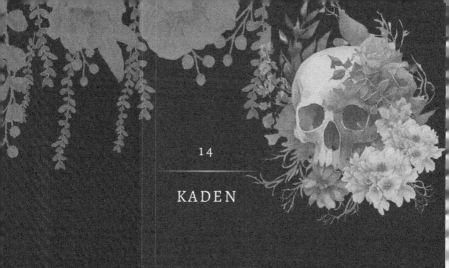

14

KADEN

"Kaden." My mother's voice cuts through the memories playing over and over again inside my head. "What are you thinking about?"

I'm thinking about when I tied up Alina a week ago and edged her over and over again until she broke down sobbing and begged me to let her come. I'm thinking about the flickers of pleasure that burst like starlight behind her eyes right before she comes. I'm thinking about those tiny little whimpers that spill from her lips when she's near the edge. I'm thinking about how her small body trembles before a waiting orgasm. I'm thinking about how she gasps and how her eyes go wide when she finally falls over the edge. And I'm thinking about the pleasure that radiates from her eyes, bright as sunlight, when she comes, and how the sight of it makes my heart skip a beat.

I made Alina come two more times, just so that I could commit every one of those extraordinary details to memory, before I finally released her from the handcuffs and spreader bar and allowed her to leave. Though at that point, her body was so utterly spent that she could no longer walk, so I ended up having to carry her to my car and then drive her back to her house.

But I naturally can't tell my mother any of that, so I just look up from my plate and give her a reassuring smile that I know from experience that she believes. "Nothing. Just school stuff."

At the head of the table, my father nods, completely believing that fake smile as well.

"Of course," he says, and flashes our mother, who sits opposite him, a proud smile. "Kaden has always been the most diligent about his education out of all of our boys."

"Hey," Jace protests from where he sits directly across from me. "You're our parents, you're not supposed to play favorites."

Our father levels such a disapproving look on Jace that he actually shrinks in his seat.

Jonathan Hunter is a man who commands respect just by walking into a room. Eli, Jace, and I all got our impressive build from him. He is tall and broad-shouldered, with straight brown hair and blue eyes so sharp that they could cut steel. That, combined with the fact that he is a legendary hitman, makes people incredibly careful not to cross him. And he raised us with the same arrogant the-world-belongs-to-me attitude that he also has, so he really shouldn't be so surprised when we exhibit those same traits.

"You, young man," Jonathan says, his sharp eyes locked firmly on Jace. "Will be no son of mine if you continue to neglect your studies at Blackwater."

"I'm not neglecting them," Jace retorts with a sullen glower.

"If the—"

"Jonathan, please," our mother interrupts. From where she sits at the end of the table on my left, she reaches forward and places one hand on my forearm and the other on Jace's in a comforting gesture. "Must we argue like this when we finally have all four of our boys here with us for the first time in ages?"

Light from the candles that have been placed along the polished oak table glitter in her warm brown eyes as she bats her long lashes at her husband. Sofia Morelli might not be a leader in the Morelli mafia family, since she is only one of the daughters of one of Federico's sisters, but she still knows exactly how to get people to do what she wants.

And our father has never been able to deny her anything, so he heaves a deep sigh and leans back in his chair again.

"Of course not, Sofia," he says. "You're right. Let's not argue."

On my right, Eli flicks a discreet glance towards the hand she still has on my arm, and amusement tugs at his lips. I consider sliding out a knife and stabbing it into my troublesome older brother's thigh, but decide against it. It would leave red bloodstains on the white napkins that our mother has placed beside our plates, and she would not like that.

From the ornate wooden chair opposite Eli, Rico shoots me a warning look as if he could tell what I had been about to do. Eli just grins wider, which means that he knew as well.

Fucking hell.

My parents might buy my fake smiles and pretend politeness, but my brothers know the real me.

"Excellent," our mother says as she sits back in her chair as well and pushes her wavy black hair back behind her shoulders. "Then it's settled. No arguing." She turns to Rico.

"You said that there was something you wanted to tell us. Do you want to do that now while we wait for dessert or should we talk about that after we have finished eating?"

The moment that Sofia's eyes are focused on Rico, our father snaps his commanding gaze back to Jace. Unspoken threats pulse through the air as he stares my younger brother down. The meaning is clear. *Get your fucking shit together or I will beat your ass like I did Eli's when I found out that he was skipping class his first year at Blackwater.*

Jace quickly drops his gaze.

I watch the silent exchange, feeling strange emotions stir in my chest.

Our parents never do things like that to me. They never give me ultimatums. Never threaten me. Instead, both of them, but especially Sofia, treat me like I'm one wrong word away from becoming a serial killer.

Though to be fair, I wouldn't actually mind becoming a serial killer. Seeing the fear and pain in people's eyes right before I kill them would fuel me. But people don't pay you to be a serial killer. They pay you to be a hitman. And the end result is basically the same. So my parents really don't have to worry that I will drop out of Blackwater to take up the unpaid mantle of a serial killer instead.

"No, we can do it now," Rico replies.

Silence falls over the elegant dining room. Candlelight dances over the cream-colored wallpaper and the oil paintings depicting landscape scenes from Italy as we all turn to face Rico at the table.

Given everything that went down with Isabella and Mr. Morelli, I have a feeling that I know what's coming. But I keep my mouth shut as Rico draws in a deep breath.

"On Monday, I will be reclaiming my position as heir to

the Morelli empire." Regret flickers briefly in his eyes as he glances between me and Jace. "Which means that I will be dropping out of Blackwater."

"Yeah, I figured as much." Jace flashes him a bright smile. "I'm happy for you. That it's all finally over."

Relief floods Rico's features.

When his eyes slide back to me, I hold his gaze and give him a slow nod, telling him that I agree and that I support his decision.

"Wouldn't it be better to finish out the year?" our father says. "Having a complete education is—"

"Jonathan," Sofia interrupts, and shakes her head at him from across the table.

He raises a hand in surrender, and then turns to Rico. "I suppose this means that you will be moving back to the Morelli compound too."

"Yes," he confirms.

Sadness blows across his features for a second before he smiles and gives Rico a firm nod. "Well, I'm happy for the six years we've had. And my sister would be happy to see you finally back where you belong."

Elsa Hunter, Jonathan's sister, was Rico's mother. So technically Rico is our cousin, but he has always been our brother in every way that counts. Even before he moved in with us six years ago.

"Don't say that," our mother sniffles from the other side of the table. "You're making it sound like we will never see him again."

"Oh, you're not getting rid of me that easily." Rico winks at her. "In fact, I bet I'll come over so much that you'll start to get tired of me."

"I could never get tired of you."

I'm itching to slide out a knife and twirl it in my hand, but I suppress the impulse and instead just watch them banter back and forth like that. Rico acts more like their son than I ever have.

But I supposed the distance between me and our parents comes from both sides. I don't care the way I should. And they... they see me as defective. They have never told me that, of course. And I know that they never will. But just like everyone else, they wear their emotions like colorful banners on their features. They think that there is something wrong with me. And they're right.

The worst part is that I have no logical reason for it.

Eli's sanity snapped years ago, making him a bit unhinged, but at least he has an actual reason for it. I was just born like this.

I don't really mind it, since I actually like who I am. But sometimes I just wish that my parents would stop treating me as if they're afraid that my mind will break completely if they say or do the wrong thing.

"Will you be alright, though?" Rico suddenly asks, drawing my attention back to the conversation at hand.

Since I had tuned them out and missed that part of the conversation, I just raise my eyebrows in a nonchalant expression.

"At Blackwater?" Rico clarifies. "Will you be okay in the war against the Petrovs? If I drop out, you're down to two while there are four of them."

Five, I correct in my head. There are five of them. People always seem to overlook Alina, not counting her as a threat. I think that's a gigantic fucking mistake. She is the most dangerous person I have ever met. Because she has somehow managed to get inside my head.

"We'll be fine," I answer with a casual shrug.

"Are you sure? Because—"

"I have leverage," I interrupt.

At that, everyone raises their eyebrows at me. Eli shoots me an approving smirk from next to me while Jace narrows his eyes in suspicion.

"What kind of leverage?" Rico asks.

"The kind that would make them back off if I used it against them."

I keep my answer deliberately vague so that they won't find out that it's the video of Mikhail from weeks ago. Because if Jace finds out that I am in fact already using my only leverage in order to protect him, he would become insufferable. It's better if he doesn't know about my deal with the Petrovs to make him and Rico untouchable.

At the head of the table, Jonathan chuckles. "That's my boy."

Turning, I give him a smile and a nod.

But I feel nothing.

Logically, I know that I should love my parents. Everyone with parents who are, all things considered, as decent as mine, should love their mom and dad. But I don't.

I don't hate them either. And I would of course protect them if someone tried to hurt them or kill them. They're my blood, after all.

But I just don't feel anything for them.

When I was younger, I thought that it was because I was incapable of caring about anyone. But I realized quickly that that wasn't true.

It's true that I don't love my parents, and I don't care at all about other random people in the world.

The only people that I love are my brothers.

And the sheer magnitude of just how much I love them terrifies me.

I would die for them.

I would slaughter entire cities to protect them.

I would wade through rivers of blood and burn this whole world to the ground if it meant keeping them safe.

Just feeling like that about Eli, Rico, and Jace is terrifying enough.

And now, I've started to have these flickers of emotion about Alina as well. I got angry that her classmates had pranked her and stolen her clothes. And I gave her my own shirt because I couldn't stand the thought of her walking naked across campus for everyone to see.

It's absurd.

I don't care about Alina.

Caring about my brothers is all the emotional strain that I can bear. Because once again... I. Don't. Do. Feelings.

So the fact that Alina has somehow managed to draw flickers of emotion from my cold, nonexistent heart scares the fucking shit out of me.

And *that* makes her the most dangerous person I have ever met.

15

ALINA

"It has been four days now," Maksim says, and thumps his fist on our kitchen table in emphasis. "I'm telling you, he's not coming back."

"I still think it's a trap," Anton mutters.

"How can it be a trap? It has literally been confirmed by Federico Morelli himself. Rico has dropped out of Blackwater."

Konstantin grins at his twin and adds, "Which means that there are now only two of them."

At the head of the table, Mikhail nods slowly while plans swirl in his eyes. "And four of us."

Five, I think. But I don't say it.

Instead, I stand up from the table and start gathering up our empty plates. They clink as I put them into a pile before stacking all of our used silverware in the middle of the topmost plate.

Outside the window, red and purple streaks line the heavens as the sun disappears beyond the horizon. It paints our pale kitchen walls with the same hue, adding a splash of color to the otherwise predominantly white room. I glance out at the darkening sky while I start rinsing the plates.

It has been four days since Rico unexpectedly dropped out of school. Kaden has been tormenting me as usual, as if nothing has changed, but my brothers and cousins have been in an uproar about it. At first, they thought that it was some kind of ruse. But like Maksim said, Rico's position as the heir to the Morelli empire has been announced by the patriarch Federico Morelli himself, so it must be true. And we all saw his things being boxed up and moved out of the Hunters' house the other day.

Maksim drums his hands excitedly on the edge of the table while giving Mikhail a pleading look. "Please, please, please, let's attack them."

My heart jerks in my chest, and I glance up from where I'm loading the plates into the dishwasher to instead study Mikhail's face. He taps his fingers on the tabletop while a considering look blows across his features.

"Come on, it's the perfect opportunity to both get revenge and get the upper hand," Maksim pushes.

"He's right," Konstantin adds with a nod. "We need to get revenge for what that asshole did to Anton last week."

The bruises on Anton's cheek have already faded, but he still looks embarrassed whenever someone brings up Kaden's surprise visit to our house. As if he's mortified that he let Kaden get the best of him like that in his own home.

Anger flickers in Mikhail's blue eyes at the reminder. "Yes, we do indeed."

"Plus, we still need to get that video he has of you," Maksim continues. "If all four of us launch a surprise attack on the two of them now, we'll win for sure." A vicious smile curls his lips. "And then we can make them fucking crawl."

My heart patters in my chest as I close the dishwasher and walk back to the table to grab the empty pots.

"Yes." Mikhail keeps drumming his fingers on the pale tabletop while a matching grin spreads across his face as he nods at Maksim. "Remember how furious Kaden got when you almost broke Jace's arm? If we corner Jace, we can make Kaden delete the video... and we can get some leverage of our own."

The twins nod excitedly while replying in unison, "Exactly."

To Mikhail's right, Anton tilts his head to the side and then nods too as if conceding the point.

Worry snakes through my chest. Coming to a halt next to my chair, I abandon my efforts to clear the table and instead meet Mikhail's gaze.

"I think this is a bad idea," I say, keeping my voice soft.

"How can this possibly be a bad idea?" Konstantin blurts out before Mikhail can say anything. "We outnumber them two to one."

"He's right, Alina," Mikhail says. "If we launch a surprise attack now, we *will* win. And then we will leverage Jace and Kaden against each other, and make both of them crawl and lick our fucking boots. And once I have a video of the two of them groveling at our feet, the war is won."

"I think you're underestimating them."

All four of them chuckle and snort derisively.

"Oh please," Maksim says. "There's no way they can win against all four of us when they don't even know that we're coming."

"That's not what I meant," I reply. Curling my fingers over the back of my chair, I grip the pale wood hard in an effort to stave off the annoyance that ripples through me at the way they're just brushing me off. "I think you're underestimating what a pair of vindictive psychos they are. Even if you win and make them crawl and grovel and all that, they will come for revenge."

"We'll have a video of it as leverage," Mikhail says, giving me a patient look that makes me feel like a silly girl who doesn't know what she's talking about.

I grip the back of the chair harder. "Video or not, they will retaliate. And when they do, you will get hurt. Seriously hurt."

Mikhail's expression softens, and he gives me a smile that makes me want to hurl the chair across the room.

"Look, I know that you're worried," he says, still speaking as if to a particularly slow student. "But we know what we're doing."

"Do you?" I challenge.

A hint of frustration flits across his face, and he takes a deep breath before fixing me with a firm stare. "Alina, this isn't your area of expertise. It's ours. Simply enrolling at Blackwater does not make you a qualified assassin. The world we live in and the world you live in is not the same." He blows out a sigh. "So, yes, we know what we're doing."

Clamping my mouth shut, I swallow down the wave of emotions that are suddenly clogging my throat. I don't trust myself to speak just yet, so I simply give him a nod and then grab the pots before walking back to the sink.

It takes all of my self-control not to slam the pots down in anger and hurt.

Just because I'm not a badass assassin doesn't mean that I don't have anything to contribute. But it doesn't matter how smart I am. My brothers, my cousins, my father, my whole bloody family, take one look at me and then write me off. Because I'm short and slim and breakable, they think I'm defective. Not good enough to carry on the legacy of the Petrov name. It's infuriating.

I take out all of those frustrations on the pots as I scrub them while my brothers and cousins start planning their stupid surprise attack that will get them killed.

Good. Why should I care if they get themselves killed? Then I can finally say, *I told you so.*

"Tonight," Anton says. "We should do it tonight."

My stomach lurches as panic crackles through my body. Because no matter how angry I am at my family members right now, I don't actually want them to get themselves killed.

"I agree," Mikhail says. Bracing his palms on the table, he pushes up from the chair. "Let's get ready."

Dropping the pot back into the sink, I turn towards the table as chairs scrape against the floor when the other three stand up as well.

"Please," I say, meeting Mikhail's gaze with pleading eyes. "Don't. This will end badly. I know it will."

His features soften again, and he walks towards me while Anton and the twins start towards the door. My heart pounds painfully in my chest as Mikhail slides an arm around my back and then leans down to kiss the top of my head.

"We'll be fine," he says. "I promise."

I resist the urge to grab his shirt and keep him here by force. Because this *will* end badly. If they threaten Jace, or make him or Kaden crawl and grovel, then Kaden will kill them regardless of what leverage they think they have. I know he will.

Dread pulses through me as Mikhail gives me one last smile and then walks away as well. Upstairs, I can hear the others already opening closets and getting ready.

Shit. I need to do something. But what?

What could I possibly do to make sure that the Hunters won't kill my brothers in retaliation for this attack?

An idea flashes through my mind.

Blinking, I stare at the darkening sky outside the window while my mind processes the possible consequences of such a decision. It feels like a betrayal. A massive betrayal. And if my family ever found out, they would never forgive me.

But it will keep them alive. And that's all that matters.

Sliding out my phone, I pull up Kaden's number and send him a text.

Fear and betrayal whirl inside my chest. But this was the right thing to do. My brothers and cousins will never be able to walk away unharmed from this war.

So I will take Kaden down in my own way.

My phone vibrates on my desk. Setting down the knife I was sharpening, I pick it up and glance at the screen. Surprise flits through me when I see Alina's name on it.

She has never texted me before. Our entire chat history contains only three messages. All of them are from me, ordering her to be somewhere at a certain time. And since she showed up those three times, I know that it is indeed her number. But why is she texting me now?

Unlocking my phone, I open the app and read her message.

I raise my eyebrows in genuine surprise as I stare at her text for another few seconds. I'm surprised both by the contents of the message and the tone of it.

Alina Petrov: *My brothers and cousins are attacking your house in the next ten minutes. Send them home to me without any permanent injuries. You owe me now.*

Suspicion swirls through me. Is this a trap?

After setting down my phone, I pull up my laptop and log in to check the audio files from the bug I planted in the Petrovs' kitchen. I normally go through it the day after, so I haven't listened to anything from today.

Grabbing the headphones that I keep permanently connected to the laptop, I put them on as I scroll through the files.

If they're attacking in ten minutes, they must be heading out now. Which means that the bug should at least pick up the sounds of them getting ready to leave. I start the audio from ten minutes ago since I don't have time to listen to all of it.

My eyebrows climb higher when the file even contains the actual conversation where they decided on this attack.

So, Alina was telling the truth. But why would she warn me?

However, her motives will have to wait.

Yanking off the headphones, I slam the laptop shut and hurry over to my bedroom door before throwing it open.

"JACE!" I bellow. "Get ready, we're about to have company. The Petrovs are attacking sometime in the next ten minutes."

There is a clattering sound from somewhere downstairs. Then Jace is pounding up the steps.

"How many?" he calls as he jogs past my door and towards his own.

"Four," I reply, and then pull back into my room.

After changing into better clothes, I quickly arm myself with knives and then hurry down to the front door. I reach for my boots down there on the floor right at the same time as Jace thunders down the stairs behind me. He grabs his boots and starts putting them on while I lace mine up as well.

"No permanent injuries," I say.

Jace snorts. "Of course not. What do you think I am? An amateur? They won't be able to touch me."

"I know that. I meant, don't inflict any permanent injuries on them."

He pauses with his left boot halfway to his foot and stares at me as if I just told him that he's not allowed to eat the treat that I had already placed before him. "Why the hell not?"

Figures move in the shadows outside.

"I'll explain later," I snap as I straighten and hurry away from the door. "Just do as I said."

Jace shoves his foot into the final boot. "Fine."

While I desperately want to break every bone in Mikhail Petrov's fucking body for daring to attack us in our own house, I always pay my debts. And Alina is right. I do owe her for this. If she hadn't texted me, we would've been caught unprepared. And with four against two, and surprise on their side, this night might have turned out very differently for us. So if she says *no permanent injuries*, then fine, no permanent injuries.

Casting a glance over my shoulder, I make sure that Jace has laced up both of his boots and grabbed his bat before I take up position by the back door. He gives me a nod and then moves into place by the front door.

Another minute passes.

Then a faint clicking sound comes from the other side of the back door. I hold up a hand to Jace, telling him to wait.

The person on the other side continues picking the lock. We left the front door unlocked when we got back this afternoon, so there is no need for them to pick that one. But they apparently want to enter at the same time because the shadows by the front door remain in place while the person on the other side of the house finishes picking the lock.

At last, a louder click sounds.

I watch the dark slab of wood. So far, no one at Blackwater has been stupid enough to attack us in our own house. But the Petrovs have grown bold now that they outnumber us. Maybe we should invest in some better locks.

The handle is slowly pushed downwards. One glance over my shoulder informs me that the same thing is happening by the front door. I give Jace the go-ahead.

The moment that the handle is all the way down, Jace and I kick our respective doors open.

Cries of surprise and pain come from the other side as the doors slam right into our intruders, making them stumble back from the force.

I dart across the threshold and out onto the lawn while Mikhail and Konstantin struggle to straighten and to figure out what just happened. My boot finds Mikhail's side before he can.

A huff rips from his chest as I kick him hard enough to make him stagger sideways. Since he is the most skilled one out of the two, I need to neutralize him first.

However, the moment I go in for another strike at Mikhail, Konstantin lunges for me. I duck underneath his hand and drive my fist into his stomach. Air explodes from his lungs, but Mikhail is already recovering.

I yank up my forearm to block Mikhail's hit right before it can connect with the side of my face. From my left, Konstantin surges forward again.

Shoving Mikhail's arm away, I spin and slip out a knife. Light from the lamps inside stream out through our windows and glint in the metal blade as it flashes through the air.

Konstantin sucks in a hiss and yanks his arm back as the

knife nicks his skin. It buys me some breathing room on his side, but Mikhail is already attacking again.

In my head, I curse Alina's inconvenient demand for no permanent injuries. This fight would be a lot easier if I didn't have to hold back.

Yells and thuds come from somewhere on my right, and I'm vaguely aware of the fact that Jace and the other two Petrovs have somehow ended up on this side of the house as well. I don't waste time looking to make sure that Jace is still standing. I know he is. And besides, I can't take my eyes of my own opponents.

I leap sideways as Mikhail tries to tackle me, but Konstantin is already moving too. A jolt vibrates through my bones as his shin slams into the side of my ribs, stopping my evasive move. Mikhail swings around again and strikes towards my throat. I yank my arm up and slam my elbow into his forearm, redirecting the blow.

Pain pulses in his eyes but he recovers quickly and kicks towards my hip. I dodge backwards only to smack into Konstantin. His arms wrap around me, trying to get a hold of my arms from behind. I ram my elbow backwards right as Mikhail's fist connects with my jaw.

Fucking hell.

My fingers tighten around my knife.

Drawing my arm in a wide arc, I force Mikhail to jump back to avoid getting skewered. But the second that I focus on him, Konstantin tries to grab me again.

I clench my jaw in anger and once again curse Alina and her ridiculous demand.

Since I can't let Konstantin get a solid grip on me, I throw two quick knives towards Mikhail, just close enough to make him pause and duck, while I spin around and slam my fist into Konstantin's side.

He staggers back, but Mikhail is already charging me from behind again.

"Alright!" Jace calls from somewhere across the lawn. "I think that's enough exercise for today."

While whipping around so that I don't have any fucking Petrovs behind my back, I cast a quick look towards my little brother.

Stunned shock pulses through me.

Mikhail and Konstantin also jerk back in surprise when they see him.

Lazy arrogance bleeds from every inch of Jace's muscular body as he stands there on the grass, pointing a gun at Anton and Maksim. Both of them have their hands raised slightly, and they have backed up several steps.

"Now, unless you want to spend the rest of the night mowing the lawn for us," Jace continues, and flicks his wrist to make a nonchalant shooing motion with the gun. "Can I suggest you get the fuck out of our yard?"

The other three Petrovs cast uncertain glances between Mikhail and Jace. Mikhail grinds his teeth in annoyance.

For a few seconds, he just remains motionless like that, glaring at Jace as if considering whether they can still win even though Jace can now put a bullet in his head before he even takes the first step.

Then he lets out something between a breath and a snarl, and clicks his tongue.

"Let's go," he snaps at the rest of his useless family.

I let out a mocking chuckle.

Fury flickers in his eyes as he drags his gaze to me while his younger family members back away across the grass.

"Watch your back, Hunter," he growls at me.

I just let a vicious smile curl my lips. "Says the dog running away with his tail between his legs."

Mikhail snarls something in Russian and then spits on the ground before my feet.

With that cold smile still on my lips, I slide out a throwing knife and raise my arm, aiming it towards Anton.

Panic crackles across Mikhail's face, and he quickly leaps to the side so that he is blocking my throw with his own body. I keep the knife ready to throw and raise my eyebrows in silent challenge.

He grinds his teeth again, but then starts backing away as well.

I remain where I am, watching them while Jace strolls up to me. He stops next to me, still holding the gun.

For a little while, we just stand there side by side, watching the Petrovs flee. Once the annoying Russians have at last disappeared, I sheath my knives and give Jace a sideways glance while arching an eyebrow.

"Where the hell did you get the gun?" I ask.

He shrugs and slips it into the back of his pants before starting towards the back door. "It's Rico's. He left it behind when he moved out. In case of emergencies."

Tearing my gaze from the now empty lawn, I quickly retrieve the knives I threw earlier before I follow my crazy little brother back into the house. "Then why didn't you use it from the beginning?"

Jace is silent for a while before replying, "I needed the fight."

I glance at him as I walk across the threshold and close the door behind us. I'm not sure where his bat is, but there's some blood on his knuckles so I'm assuming that he discarded it in favor of his fists. My gaze drifts up to his face, taking in the massive bruise forming on his jaw.

A hint of guilt swirls in Jace's eyes as he flicks a quick look at me. "You alright?"

I suddenly realize that I never responded when he told me he drew out this confrontation because he needed the fight, which probably made Jace think that I'm pissed about it. I'm not. If he needed the fight, then that's all the justification I need.

"Yeah," I reply, and then jerk my chin towards his jaw. "Put some ice on that."

Both relief and embarrassment blow across his face, and he reaches up to draw a hand over the bruise. "It's fine. It's not that bad and—"

Burying my fists in his shirt, I slam him up against the wall.

He blinks at me in shock but does nothing to push me back. Which means that he still feels guilty that he dragged me into a fight when he could've ended it before it even started. *Fucking hell.*

Keeping my voice hard, I growl, "Unless you want me to give you a matching bruise on the other side of your jaw, put some fucking ice on it. Am I making myself clear?"

"Alright," he replies, raising his hands in mock surrender. "Jeez. Calm down."

But there is a smile on his face now, and the light is back in his eyes. He understands what it is that I'm saying without actually saying it.

Releasing my grip on his shirt, I let out a chuckle and take a step back. Jace makes a show of dramatically brushing his hands down his shirt to straighten out the wrinkles while giving me a look of mock affront.

I raise my arm and stab a hand towards the kitchen. "Ice. Now."

Then I stalk away and walk up to my room to see if I can catch the Petrovs moping about their loss on the bug I planted in their kitchen.

17

ALINA

Before I can even raise my hand to knock, the door is shoved open. My stomach lurches as rough hands grab me by the collar and yank me inside. The front door bangs shut behind me, and then I'm shoved up against it so hard that air escapes my lungs in a huff.

Blinking, I find myself staring up into the merciless face of Jace Hunter.

There's blood on his knuckles, a giant bruise on his jaw, and violence rolls off his broad shoulders like waves.

"You have some fucking balls showing up here right now, Petrov," he growls, threats pulsing from every word.

Raising my chin, I just stare back at him defiantly.

Footsteps echo from the stairs behind his back. I slide my gaze towards the sound and find Kaden striding down the steps.

Jace tightens his grip on my shirt. "Did you hear me?"

I keep my chin raised, partly because I need to do so in order to actually see the top half of the stairs from over Jace's annoyingly tall shoulder, and simply level an expectant look at Kaden.

A smirk blows across the psycho's face as he watches me and Jace, as if he finds the situation faintly amusing.

"Well, aren't you going to tell him?" I challenge, still keeping my eyes locked on Kaden.

Or I try to keep them on him at least. When he reaches the bottom of the stairs, my view of him is blocked by Jace's massive body for a while. Then he comes into view again as he reaches his brother's side and comes to a halt there next to him.

My pulse thrums at the sheer power and dominance that they exude as they stand there side by side, staring me down. Trapped against the door, with Jace's bloodstained hands still buried in my shirt, and both he and Kaden cornering me, I can't help but question if this really was such a good idea after all.

"Tell me what?" Jace demands, finally tearing his hard stare from me and glancing at Kaden.

Kaden's dark eyes remain on me.

The silence stretches on.

I have a feeling that he is looking for signs of weakness. Waiting to see if I will start shifting my weight nervously or drop my gaze. So I make sure to keep that defiant expression on my face and that cocky tilt of my chin as I simply stare back at him in silence.

Kaden lets out a soft huff of amusement.

"She's the one who tipped us off," he says at last.

Surprise flits across Jace's features, and he blinks at his brother before sliding his gaze back to me and narrowing his eyes. "You ratted out your brothers?" He cocks his head, and when he speaks, there is clear suspicion in his voice. "Now why would you do that?"

Breaking Kaden's stare, I shift my attention to Jace and shoot him a pointed look. "I didn't *rat them out*. I made a strategic decision."

"Oh? Do enlighten us."

"I tipped you off because if they had taken you by surprise, they would've won."

Both Kaden and Jace snort as if that's ridiculous.

"Right," I mock, rolling my eyes. "Keep telling yourselves that they wouldn't, if it helps you sleep at night. But four against two, and with surprise on their side, you know they would've won."

Jace scoffs, but I can tell that he knows that I'm right. "If their win was so certain, then why did you tip us off?"

"*Because* they would have won." I hold his gaze. "And then you would've retaliated. Brutally."

Jace tips his head to the side and nods, silently confirming it.

"But now they didn't win. Because I tipped you off." I shift my gaze back to Kaden. "Which means that you owe me now."

He flicks a nonchalant glance up and down my body. "So you keep saying."

I hold his gaze with hard eyes for a few seconds before shifting it back to Jace and doing the same. My voice is unflinching and full of authority as I declare, "No retaliation."

Jace's grip tightens on the fabric of my shirt as he grinds out, "If you think I'm going to let their attack slide, you—"

"I didn't realize that the Hunters don't pay their debts," I cut him off, flicking a contemptuous look up and down his body.

Anger flashes in Jace's eyes, but I swear there is some shame in there too.

Keeping my chin raised, I look expectantly between him and Kaden. A muscle feathers in Jace's jaw, and there is obvious frustration on his features. Kaden, however, is watching me with his head cocked, looking as if he's almost a bit... impressed. It makes heat spread through my body.

At last, Jace drags his gaze to Kaden, and raises his eyebrows in silent question. The psycho just shrugs.

"Fine," Jace forces out as he shifts his attention back to me. "We won't retaliate for this attack."

"Good."

"But *only* for this attack. If they come after us again, it's open season."

"Naturally."

He holds my gaze in silence for another few seconds. Then he nods and, at long last, releases my collar. I brush my hands down my shirt, smoothing the fabric again, while Jace takes a step back.

"And I have another deal." Looking up from my shirt, I meet Kaden's gaze. "For you."

Amusement blows across his sharp features, and he raises his eyebrows expectantly.

"Privately," I say.

A smile curls his lips. Then he jerks his chin at me and starts back towards the stairs.

Jace remains standing deliberately in my way, so I have to carefully edge around his muscular body in order to follow Kaden. He turns along with my movements, keeping his sharp eyes on me and watching my every move as if I'm a venomous viper that has just slithered into his house.

Once I have finally gotten out from between his body and

the door, I hurry to catch up with Kaden, who has already reached the stairs.

"Ice," Kaden calls over his shoulder.

Confusion ripples through me, but then I realize that he is speaking to Jace, because the youngest Hunter grumbles under his breath.

"Yeah, yeah," he mutters, and starts towards the kitchen. "I know."

Leaving Jace to do whatever it is that he's supposed to do with the ice, I run up the steps so that I reach the hallway upstairs right after Kaden does. His long legs and his head start had made me fall behind.

Only dark wood panels watch us impassively as we walk down the corridor until we reach Kaden's room. Pulling open the door, he motions for me to step inside.

To anyone else, it might look like he was being a gentleman, holding the door open for me and letting me walk inside first. But I know it for what it really is. A move designed to make me worried.

After I walk inside, he could just close the door and lock it, trapping me in there. Or he could put a knife to my throat from behind my unprotected back when he walks in behind me. Or outright stab me in the back.

Straightening my spine, I ignore all of those possibilities and instead nonchalantly slide my hands into my pockets as I stroll across the threshold.

Kaden's room looks exactly like it did the last time I was here. Dark wooden floor and walls, furniture in the same material, the large bed with the strange metal frame attached on top of the wooden one, and every single part of it obsessively neat and organized.

After sweeping my gaze over the entire space, I decide on

the desk and start towards it. Pulling my hands out of my pockets, I stop by the desk, turn around, and then pull myself up so that I'm sitting on top of it.

A hint of surprise flits across Kaden's dangerously handsome face.

I flash him a smirk.

He watches me in silence for a second, as if debating whether or not to yank me off his pristine desk. But in the end, he just closes his bedroom door and then strides closer to me where I'm sitting.

Crossing his arms over his muscular chest, he stares me down.

"You said you had a proposal for me." He drags his gaze over my body before meeting my eyes again. A sly smile plays over his lips. "Let's hear it then."

My heart pounds in my chest as I reply, "We let out this aggressive tension between us once and for all."

Silence falls over the room as Kaden just watches me with an unreadable expression on that ice sculpture face of his. My heart hammers so loudly against my ribs that I'm certain he can hear it.

"What does that mean?" Kaden asks at last.

"You know what it means."

"Spell it out."

I draw in shallow breaths, feeling like my heart is going to jump out of my chest. From two steps away, Kaden watches me with a dark intensity that only makes it worse. I lick my lips. Nonchalantly leaning back on my hands, I curl my fingers around the edge of the desk in the space between it and the wall while I spread my legs ever so slightly.

"We fuck each other."

My stomach flips and my pulse thunders the moment that

the words have left my mouth. For a few seconds, Kaden says nothing. Which certainly isn't helping the wild thrashing in my chest.

Then he scoffs, and flicks a disgusted look over my body. "As if I would ever fuck a Petrov."

Embarrassment sears through me, making my cheeks burn. Which is, of course, exactly what the psycho wanted. And I know that. So instead of falling for his insult, I sit up straight again and shoot him a pointed look back.

"Don't think I haven't seen the way you look at me," I challenge, holding his gaze. "The way you study every inch of my face when I orgasm. The way your gaze drinks in every curve of my body. You want to fuck me just as badly as I..." I stop myself before I can finish the sentence.

Because while it's true that I did come here on a mission, I can't deny the fact that I actually *want* to fuck Kaden too. All those times that he has made me come with a vibrator or a rope or by some other impersonal method, I've kept wondering what it would be like to actually sleep with him. For real. To feel his hands on my naked skin. To have his lethal body pin me to a mattress. To know what it truly feels like to be fucked by someone like Kaden Hunter.

"As badly as you... what?" Kaden picks up, because of course he's not going to let that slide.

"As badly as I want to fuck you," I admit, averting my gaze while another wave of heat surges into my cheeks.

Kaden moves closer. Placing his strong hands on my thighs, he spreads my legs wide and then steps in between them so that he is standing only a breath away. His absolutely intoxicating scent wraps around my senses, making my heart thunder and my skin heat.

After sliding his hands a little higher up my thighs, enough

162

to send a throbbing pulse through my clit, he removes them. My heart stutters as he instead draws one hand up my throat and then takes my chin between his thumb and forefinger, tilting my head back up. There is a smug smirk on his lips when I at last meet his gaze again.

"You want to fuck me that badly, huh?" he taunts.

I try to slap his hand away from my chin, but it doesn't move an inch. Amusement dances in his eyes.

"You want to fuck me just as badly," I retort. "Don't try to pretend otherwise." I fix him with a stare pulsing with challenge. "So let's just do it and get it over with."

"We're enemies," he points out.

"Enemies with benefits tonight, then."

He chuckles.

"One angry violent fuck," I propose.

"And then what?"

"Then we walk away."

He raises a dark eyebrow.

"I'm not involved in this war you have with my brothers," I say. "So you and I get all of this tension between us out of the way tonight, and then we go our separate ways."

"Tension?" he taunts.

Releasing my chin, he leans down and slants his lips over mine. His breaths caress my mouth and dance over my skin. My spine tingles, and I desperately try to remember how to breathe.

He smirks against my mouth, just a fraction away from brushing his lips against mine. "What tension?"

I grab the front of his black shirt and yank his mouth down to mine.

Our lips clash in a violent kiss. I bite his bottom lip hard, and he responds by forcing his tongue into my mouth and sliding his hand into my hair. Gathering up my long ponytail in one hand, he starts winding it around his fist until he has a firm grip on my hair and full control over my head.

He pulls down, using his grip on my hair to force me to tilt my head back farther.

Then he *dominates* my mouth.

There is no other word for it.

Lightning flickers through my brain and I forget how to breathe as his demanding lips and tongue force me into submission. I tighten my grip on his shirt, holding him pressed against me as he continues stealing my sanity and the very air from my lungs. My pussy throbs with need at the fury and control in this simple kiss.

I gasp into his mouth as a sense of vertigo crashes into me.

If this is how the psycho *kisses*, then what the hell is it going to feel like when he *fucks* me?

Wrapping my legs around his waist, I pull his body harder against mine until his cock is pressed against my pussy. Desperate need pulses through me when I feel that massive hard bulge through the fabric of our clothes.

Kaden slides his arm underneath my ass, and I lock my ankles together behind his back as he lifts me up from the desk as if I weigh nothing. I release his shirt and knit my fingers together behind his neck instead as he turns around and walks us towards the bed while still continuing to effortlessly dominate my mouth.

My stomach lurches as he practically throws me down onto his bed.

The mattress bounces and his black sheets crinkle as I land on it. Blinking against the disorienting loss of his mouth and nearness of his body, I suck in a shuddering breath and scramble to untangle myself from my own limbs.

"Take off your shirt." The command splits the air like a blade.

A dark thrill races up my spine as my fingers fumble with the hem of my shirt. Then I pull it over my head and toss it to the floor. I wasn't wearing a bra underneath it, so my nipples immediately harden at the exposure.

Kaden's eyes darken as he zeroes in on them.

My heart pounds in my chest.

I start in surprise as he suddenly yanks up a hand and gives my chest a hard shove. I slam back first onto the soft mattress.

Before I can recover, strong hands appear around my ankles. I let out a yelp as Kaden yanks me towards him until my legs are hanging off the side of the bed. Raising my head, I find him unbuttoning my pants.

Heat pools at my core as he curls his fingers over the edge of both my pants and panties, and then yanks them down. My skin prickles as my final remaining garments join my shirt on the floor.

Completely naked, I stare up at Kaden.

He stands there between my spread legs, looming over me like a beautiful devil ready to punish a wicked sinner. The ache between my legs intensifies, and I find myself panting. God, I want him to fuck me. Hard.

"Why aren't you taking your clothes off?" I manage to press out while my heart does strange things in my chest.

"Why would I do that?" A cruel smile curls his lips. "I told you, I don't fuck Petrovs."

Anger shoots through me like a lightning strike. Oh hell no, he's not going to kiss me like that and strip me naked like this and then leave me hanging.

"I hate you so fucking much," I snarl at him.

He leans down over me, his expression dark and dangerous. "What did you say?"

My heart beats wildly in my chest, and I crawl backwards across the bed to put some distance between us. I don't make it far. He moves like a damn viper.

One second, he is standing beside the bed. The next, he's on top of it. I try to scramble up towards the headboard, but he grabs my thighs and yanks me down until he's straddling my hips. He stares down at me expectantly, waiting for an answer. I buck my hips and try to push him off me, but he is as immovable as a mountain.

"I said, I hate you so fucking much," I snap when it becomes apparent that I'm completely trapped.

"Good." He leans down over me, bringing his face closer to mine. That cold sadistic cruelty that I think he lives off shines in his eyes as he locks them on me. "I am going to make you and your entire family crawl at my feet and beg me for permission to surrender."

I shove hard against his shoulders, but I'm so physically outmatched against him that I can't even manage to push him back one single inch. So instead, I grab the collar of his shirt hard. "If you come after me again, you will be the one begging to surrender."

My heart jumps as he slides out a knife from his thigh holster. He spins it once in his hand before abruptly moving it to my throat. He presses the flat of the blade underneath my chin, forcing me to close my mouth and to keep it like that. One arch of his eyebrow is enough for me to release my grip on his shirt and spread my arms wide on the mattress.

A smirk dances over Kaden's lips as he watches me. "You're very cocky for someone so completely at my mercy."

Adrenaline and dangerous desire flood my system as

Kaden draws the knife down my throat. My heart pounds against my ribs. I suck in short, jagged breaths as he gently trails the sharp point down to my collarbones. When he reaches the spot between them, he pauses.

His eyes are filled with wicked promises as he levels a commanding stare on me. "You're going to have to stay very still now."

I don't even dare to breathe as he brushes the knife down the center of my chest while his eyes stay locked on mine.

Electricity flickers through my skin and every nerve inside my body is on high alert.

With his eyes still firmly on mine, he traces the curve of my breast with his knife.

Dark desire flares through me.

A terrible throbbing sensation pulses through my clit as Kaden slowly circles my tit, drawing closer and closer to my nipple. I suck in rapid breaths. My heart hammers against my ribs, and my thighs clench. The knife moves closer. I stare, transfixed, at the blade closing in on my hard and aching nipple.

A gasp rips from me as Kaden gives my nipple a tiny prick.

Both a hint of pain and insane pleasure flood my body, and I squirm against the mattress.

Kaden's other hand shoots out and grabs my jaw hard.

"What the fuck did I say about moving?" he growls.

Before I can reply, he slams the knife down on his bedside table and then yanks open the small drawer. I blink, trying to reorient myself. After the intense feeling of him tracing a knife over my skin, it's difficult. And when I finally get my mind to work again, Kaden has already made his move.

"No, wait," I blurt out as he finishes locking my wrists to

the metal frame on his headboard with a pair of leather handcuffs.

With my arms spread and my hands trapped above my head, I kick my legs weakly as Kaden shifts around so that he is facing the other way. He just grabs my ankles one at a time, spreads my legs wide, and then locks them to the frame at the foot of the bed.

"Oh, come on," I mutter, and yank against my restraints.

But he has spread my arms and legs so wide that I can't even move an inch now.

Kaden turns around and then sits so that he is straddling my left thigh before reaching to grab his knife again. "I warned you not to move."

"You try staying still when someone traces a knife around your nipple," I grumble and scowl up at him.

With a knowing smile lurking at the corner of his lips, he moves the knife to my other tit and starts circling that as well. A shiver of pleasure ripples through me, and I have to bite back a moan.

"You *like* this." It's more of a statement than a question, and his tone is full of smugness.

"No," I retort, trying to put as much conviction into my voice as possible.

His dark brown eyes gleam as he starts drawing the knife down over my ribs. "Then why are your eyes flickering with pleasure right now."

Heat sears my cheeks. What is he, a mind reader? How the hell could he read my emotions that easily?

"Just admit it…" He brushes the blade over my stomach and then traces the curve of my hip. A wide smile spreads across his lips when a shudder racks my frame. "You're a kinky little thing who likes knife play."

"You're wrong." But the words come out sounding choked and breathless.

"Am I?" A low purring sound comes from the back of his throat. "Hmm. Then I'll make you a deal."

Tension pulses inside me and my pussy aches as Kaden slides his knife along the line where my panties should be. I drag in uneven breaths. My mind is telling me that this is wrong. That this is dangerous and insane. But I can't help it. I'm so fucking turned on by this whole situation.

I'm turned on by the way he draws his knife over my skin like a caress. By the knowledge that I'm shackled to the bed and unable to protect myself. By the fact that I'm completely naked while Kaden is still fully dressed. And by his dominating presence above me.

The power he holds over me, the danger he presents, the knowledge that he could kill me right now but chooses not to, and the fact that he treats me as if he isn't afraid to break me, makes my whole body vibrate with need.

"If the blade doesn't come back wet, I'll untie you," Kaden says.

My mind is overcrowded with jumbled thoughts and emotions. What is he talking about?

Oh, the deal.

Wait, what deal?

I lift my head and open my mouth to ask precisely that. But before any sound can make it out of my mouth, something cold and hard is pressed between my legs.

A jolt shoots through me.

Sucking in a gasp, I stare up at Kaden as he presses the flat of his blade between my legs, right against my pussy. A wicked smile shines on his face as he looks back at me.

"But if the blade is wet when I remove it," he continues, his smile shifting into a smirk, "you will admit that you have a knife kink."

I swallow, my heart pounding in my chest.

Kaden stares me down, daring me to protest, for another few seconds before he removes the blade he is pressing against my pussy. Victory pulses across his face. Twirling the knife in his hand, he shows it to me.

Wetness coats the flat of the blade.

I close my eyes, mortified.

A smug chuckle rolls from Kaden's chest. "Well then, I'm waiting."

Clamping my jaw shut, I just open my eyes and glare up at him in stubborn silence. Hell will freeze over before I ever admit to this damn psycho that I have a knife kink.

Amusement flits across his face.

Then he spins the knife and angles it.

My heart lurches and my mouth drops open as he cocks his head and licks my arousal off the blade.

Fire surges through me, making my clit throb, as I stare up at him.

But Kaden just brings the blade back down as if that wasn't the hottest fucking thing I've ever seen. Lightning crackles through my veins as he traces the inside of my thigh, moving closer to my aching pussy.

"Admit it," he commands.

I squeeze my eyes shut and curl my fingers into fists.

The blade scrapes lightly along the edge of my pussy.

A whimper escapes my lips as lust burns through me.

My heart thuds so hard in my chest that I swear I can hear it echo throughout the dark wooden room.

Then the thin point of the blade disappears.

A moment later, something hard and round and thick is pressed directly against my entrance.

I snap my eyes open. Lifting my head, I stare down my body to find Kaden holding the knife by the blade instead. My heart lurches as I realize that he is pressing the rounded hilt against my pussy.

"Kaden," I breathe.

His gaze sears into me. "Yes, little doe?"

I open my mouth to speak, but my words are cut off by a gasp as Kaden pushes the top of the hilt inside me.

A jolt shoots through me as it enters.

The top of the hilt is rounded like a ball, and sinks effortlessly into my soaked pussy.

I stare at Kaden, my mouth gaping as shock and pleasure and absolute insanity whirl through me like a storm.

Unflinching power rolls off his broad shoulders as he holds my gaze.

Then he pushes the hilt farther in.

I jerk against my restraints as the raised ridges in the hilt send more pulses flashing through my body like lightning strikes as they scrape against my inner walls.

Kaden pushes it in deeper.

A moan spills from my lips, followed by a desperate whimper, as the uneven hilt creates mind-numbing friction with every excruciating inch. Throwing my head from side to side, I yank against the handcuffs and the manacles binding my ankles.

"Admit it," Kaden orders again.

I flex my fingers, clenching and unclenching my hands, but keep my mouth firmly shut.

Kaden starts slowly drawing the knife back.

Pleasure courses through me as those ridges on the hilt

move inside me again. Squeezing my eyes shut, I try desperately to suppress the moans that tear from the depths of my soul.

He moves the knife until only that ball at the very top of the hilt is still inside me.

Then he pushes it in again. Faster this time.

I suck in jagged breaths as he pulls out the hilt and then shoves it deeper again. And again. The friction intensifies with every thrust, and tension builds inside me like a thrumming storm.

My heart thrashes in my chest and I squirm in my restraints as Kaden fucks me mercilessly with the hilt of his knife.

It's the most electrifying thing I have ever experienced. I can feel every ridge on that hilt as it is thrust inside me. Can feel Kaden's hard cock press against my thigh where he's straddling me. Can feel his intense gaze sear into my skin as he watches me, noting every flicker of emotion and every needy whimper.

Pent-up release vibrates inside me.

It feels as if my body is going to shatter from the tension and the pleasure and the desperation and the sheer insane knowledge that Kaden Hunter, the worst psycho this university has ever seen, is currently fucking me with a knife… and that I *like* it.

"Say it," Kaden commands again.

The mind-numbing friction builds as he keeps thrusting the hilt inside with firm and demanding moves. Pitiful whines drip from my lips.

My brain is going to fucking melt.

"Say it."

He shoves the hilt deeper.

And release explodes through my body.

My eyes fly open and I gasp into the ceiling as pleasure crashes through me like a sweeping wave. I squirm harder as Kaden continues fucking me with the hilt while my whole body trembles from the force of the orgasm.

Tied to Kaden's bed, I moan and whimper and beg for mercy. Because God above, this is the most incredible feeling I've ever experienced. Every time I think Kaden has reached the limit of what he can make my body feel, reached the limit of the emotions he can draw from me and the reactions he can wring from my body, he just cuts through that limit like it's nothing.

I suck in deep breaths as Kaden at last pulls out the hilt completely.

The emptiness it leaves in its wake is so jarring that I don't even notice Kaden moving until he is straddling my hips again.

My chest heaves as I lie there, utterly spent, and stare up at the merciless and ruthlessly beautiful man above me.

He wraps his hand around my jaw, holding my chin in a commanding grip. "Say it."

And he has apparently fucked all the defiance out of me, because I just look up at him in complete surrender and admit, "I have a knife kink."

The smile that spreads across his stunning face makes my heart flip.

18

KADEN

Bright sunlight streams down from the clear blue sky and bathes the small patio on the other side of the street with light. I stand in the shadows between two houses, watching as four women talk and laugh while they sit there on the patio, soaking in the sunshine. Or rather, I watch *one* particular woman.

Alina's gray eyes glitter and her long blonde hair ripples as she throws her head back and laughs at something that Carla said.

My chest tightens.

Fuck, she is extraordinary. Not only is she smart and beautiful, she's also so much stronger than I expected. The way she stood up to Jace the other day and demanded that we honor our debt by not retaliating was so unexpected, and so hot, that I have barely been able to think about anything else since.

Well, that and what she looked like when I fucked her with my knife.

My cock hardens just at the memory of it, and I have to adjust myself while my damn cock throbs with need for her.

I love watching pleasure flood her features. Love hearing her moan and whimper and beg. Love seeing her body tremble from the orgasm. And I crave it all like a fucking addict.

That night, I told her that I would never fuck a Petrov.

But I wanted to.

By God and all of hell, I wanted to fuck Alina so badly that I felt like I was suffocating every second that I was straddling her in my bed, still fully clothed. I wanted to fuck her so desperately that I was willing to forget that she is an enemy. Forget that I'm planning to ruin her.

Desperate.

I was *desperate* to fuck her.

And I am never desperate.

Clenching my jaw, I squeeze my hand into a fist as I watch Alina and the others continue to chat outside Carla's house.

My obsession with Alina is getting dangerous.

Not only is she messing with my head, she is messing with the very core of my being. I never get off on watching pleasure flood someone's features. I get off on fear, pain, and tears. But the more time I spend drawing orgasms from Alina's perfect body, the more I crave that incredible light that bursts behind her eyes when she comes.

And now I'm here, lurking in the shadows and watching her like a fucking stalker.

This has to stop.

I have to stop shifting back and forth across the line between bullying her and giving her mind-blowing orgasms. I need to go back to simply humiliating her. The way it should be.

My heart skips a beat when Alina stands up.

Gritting my teeth, I glare down at my chest and the barely functioning organ inside that somehow seems to sputter to life every time Alina Petrov does fucking anything.

After saying something else, Alina gives the other three girls a wave and walks across the lawn and towards the street.

I slink back between the two houses and then follow her as she starts walking through the residential area. Since I know that she is most likely heading back to her house, I move until I reach a narrow passage between two long apartment buildings. I wait for Alina to reach the halfway point. Then I take a step out and position myself right between the buildings, blocking her exit.

She jerks back in shock. Surprise then gives way to annoyance, and then to panic when she realizes how confined and private this space is.

Her gaze darts towards a passageway a few steps ahead of her that leads to the right.

I take a step forward.

She bolts towards the passageway.

Just like I wanted her to.

A smug laugh escapes my chest as I quickly close the distance to the passageway that she ran into. I reach it before Alina can come sprinting back out of it.

Her big gray eyes widen as I stride into the narrow space. She screeches to a halt and casts a glance over her shoulder. There is a tall wooden fence there, blocking her way.

With a sadistic smile on my mouth, I advance on her.

She swallows as she backs away. But her back hits the wooden fence after only a few steps. Worry blows across her face as she casts a quick look up towards the top of the solid fence. I could definitely reach it and climb over it, but she is far too short for that. She seems to realize that too because her gaze quickly returns to me.

"Kaden," she says. It's something between a greeting, a question, and a plea.

"Alina," I reply.

Another kind of emotion flits across her face for a second. I narrow my eyes. Was that…? Is she disappointed that I didn't call her *little doe*? My non-functioning heart does that strange thing again where it beats erratically for a moment.

Anger courses through me as I curse myself. Humiliation and fear. That's what I'm here for. Nothing else.

"I need to get home," she says, flicking a glance towards the exit behind me. Then she starts moving as if to skirt around me. "My brothers are—"

I yank out two throwing knives and hurl them into the wall right next to her head.

She yelps, jerking back and pressing herself against the fence.

"Did I say that you could move?" I demand.

Fear washes over her beautiful features. Good. Fear is what I came to instill in this troublesome fucking Russian.

Her wide eyes are locked on mine. Then her gaze darts up towards one of the knives now buried in the wood right next to her.

Disbelief clangs through me. I just threw a fucking knife at her head, don't tell me that she's going to—

She yanks out the knife.

For a moment, all I can do is stare at her.

She *did*.

Even though fear still flickers in her eyes, she holds the knife out before her with a steady hand.

My entire soul is suddenly flooded with an overwhelming

urge to rip her clothes off and fuck her against the wall while she holds that knife to my throat.

I shake my head. Focus, God damn it.

Staring her down, I make my voice low and menacing as I demand, "Do you remember what I told you I do to people who touch my knives without permission?"

She snaps her gaze to her hand, and her eyes go wide as fucking dinner plates as she realizes what she has done by pulling the blade out of the fence. True fear and panic crash over her features. Whipping her gaze back to me, she drops the knife as if it had burned her.

"Please," she whispers.

I advance on her. She tries to back farther away, but the fence is stopping her retreat. A whimper slips past her lips as I reach her.

For a few seconds, I just stand there, towering over her while she tries desperately to shrink into the fence.

Then I crouch down and pick up the knife she dropped. After standing up, I wipe the blade on my pants and then slide it back into its sheath.

I raise my hand.

Alina squeezes her eyes shut.

But all I do is to wrap my fingers around the other throwing knife and yank it out of the fence. It comes free with a faint *pop*.

"Look at me," I order.

After dragging in a steadying breath, she opens her eyes. Her gaze darts between my face and the knife still in my hand. Then her eyes find mine and she keeps them there.

"We agreed to walk away," she says, her voice coming out surprisingly steady.

I cock my head, studying her. The fear is draining from

her features with every second. Fascinating. I wonder what it was that convinced her that I'm not actually going to kill her for pulling the knife out of the fence.

"No, *you* said that we should walk away," I correct her. "I never agreed to anything."

She purses her lips in an adorable show of annoyance and disapproval.

"And besides, you said one angry violent fuck, and then we walk away." I draw my free hand over her collarbones, watching with satisfaction as a shiver rolls through her small body, before I trail my fingers up her throat. "And I never fucked you."

She clicks her tongue and jerks her chin away before I can grab it. "Asshole."

Letting my hand drop from her throat, I level a sharp look on her. "What was that?" I raise my other hand and spin the knife so that the hilt is facing upwards before I flick a pointed look down at her body. "Did you want me to do something to your asshole?"

Her mouth drops open, and her stunned gaze darts between my face and the hilt of the blade.

I give her a warning look. "Answer me, little doe."

She drops her gaze to my boots and shakes her head. "No. I'm sorry."

A smug chuckle rolls off my tongue, and I drink in the sight of her submissive posture. "Thought so."

I let the silence stretch, waiting to see if she will dare to raise her head again without permission. She doesn't. As usual, she doesn't fight battles that she can't win. Smart. Very smart. And a tactic that will keep her alive in this violent, blood-soaked world of ours.

Lifting my free hand again, I trace two fingers down the

center of her chest while I twirl the knife in my other hand. Her pulse quickens along with her breathing, but she doesn't look up.

I draw my fingers around the curve of her tit, noting that she's not wearing a bra underneath her shirt today either. Alina bites her bottom lip, but keeps her eyes on my boots.

My fingers circle around her nipple until she's dragging in unsteady breaths. If I touched her cunt right now, I'm certain that I would find it soaked. But I don't. Because I'm here to humiliate her.

So instead, I pinch her nipple between my thumb and forefinger.

A whimper spills from Alina's lips.

I roll the hard peak between my fingers until she's squirming against the wooden fence. Then I pull towards me. Her tit stretches until I release her nipple. But I keep the grip on her shirt.

Pulling the fabric out so that it forms a little tent, I raise the knife in my other hand and then cut off the top of it.

At last, Alina snaps her gaze up from the ground.

Shock pulses across her features as she stares down at her shirt. It now has a large hole in it. A hole that her tit now spills out of.

Her cheeks flush a bright shade of red.

While my cock throbs, I grab her other nipple. Her gaze shoots up to mine, and a pleading look fills her eyes. But she will find no mercy here.

Pulling the fabric of her shirt towards me, I cut off the top of the little tent that forms so that there is a hole on that side as well.

Mortification floods Alina's features.

My cock strains against my pants as I watch her stand

there, her perfect tits spilling out of the two holes in her shirt. I know how degrading this must be for her. Having her tits exposed in this way is more humiliating than if I had simply cut off her entire shirt.

I reach up with my free hand again and roll her now bare nipple between my fingers.

Pleasure flickers in her eyes, fighting against the humiliation.

I keep teasing her hard nipple, rolling it and pinching it and stimulating it until her knees tremble and a shuddering moan escapes her lips.

She looks up at me with big pleading eyes. "Kaden. Please."

"Please, what?"

Another shudder of pleasure racks her delicate frame, and she splays her hand against the wooden fence to keep from toppling over.

I continue toying with her nipple while I wait for her to answer. And I genuinely don't know what she is planning to say.

Please stop.

Or, *please make me come.*

Alina squirms, pressing the back of her head hard against the solid wood behind her. Her chest heaves.

I raise my eyebrows expectantly, still waiting for an answer.

War rages behind her eyes, as if she herself can't actually decide whether to ask me to stop or to beg me not to.

She opens her mouth.

Anticipation crackles through me, because I'm suddenly desperate to hear what she has decided on.

But then she abruptly snaps her mouth shut again and clenches her jaw.

Weirdly disappointed, I release her nipple and take a step back.

She blinks, looking disoriented at the very sudden stop to my torture. I let a cold smirk slide home on my lips, and then flick a mocking look down at her exposed tits.

Red creeps back into her cheeks, and she crosses her arms over her chest to hide them.

"Did I tell you that you could cover yourself up?" I snap, still feeling frustrated that I never found out what she was going to beg me for.

She glares defiantly at me for a second, but then lets her arms drop back down by her sides again. With that glorious humiliation once again washing over her features, she averts her gaze.

"Why are you doing this to me?" she asks, her voice small and defeated.

And hell damn it, but I'm half a fucking second away from yanking off my own shirt and giving it to her. Just like I did in that locker room the other week. But I can't. Because I'm supposed to be humiliating her.

So instead, I give her a hard look and reply, "Because you owed me a shirt."

Then I turn around and stalk away.

19

ALINA

By the time Friday evening rolls around, I'm exhausted and more than a little frustrated. I barely made it back to our house and into my room without anyone seeing what Kaden had done to my shirt. I had to keep my arms crossed over my chest the entire way, and pray that my brothers wouldn't stop me when I walked through the door. And that damn psycho hasn't let up since. Every day, he finds some new way to torment me.

It's annoying as hell. Especially when my logical mind and my treacherous body also seem to react in two completely different ways to the torture that Kaden subjects me too. But I can handle it. I can endure a lot more than most people assume. And besides, it's only temporary anyway. Sooner or later, I'm going to get what I need. And then I'm going to fucking ruin him.

My phone vibrates on my nightstand.

Setting down the hairbrush I was running through my wet hair, I walk over to check it. My pulse flutters nervously as I wonder whether it's going to be from Kaden or if I'm safe for the night.

A bright smile spreads across my face when I unlock my phone to find a text from Carla. She and the other girls from her house, along with some other women from our class, are going out tonight, and she's asking if I want to come too. I quickly reply that I'd love to. She tells me that they'll be picking me up in half an hour, so I hurry back into my bathroom and start blow drying my hair.

After changing into a short dark blue dress and putting on some makeup, I rush down the stairs.

Anton must have heard my rapid footsteps on the stairs, because he appears in the doorway to the living room before I can even grab my shoes.

"Wait," he says, sounding a bit confused. "I thought you said you were going to take a shower and then relax in bed. Where are you going now?"

"Out," I reply, putting on a pair of high heels that I never get to wear on campus.

Mikhail materializes next to Anton. Crossing his arms, he fixes me with a stern look. "Out? Where? With who?"

"Carla and the other girls," I reply, stifling an annoyed sigh and an eye roll. "We're going into the city to dance."

"And drink," he says. It's not a question.

"Possibly," I admit. It looks like he's about to open his mouth to tell me that I can't go, so I quickly charge on. "There is literally nothing to worry about. I'm going out with like ten other girls. We're just going to dance and have some fun."

Anton glances over at Mikhail questioningly. Our older brother draws his pale brows down in a show of disapproval, but he hasn't flat out told me no either.

Outside on the street, a car honks cheerfully a couple of times.

"They're here," I say, and grab my purse from the coat hook before slinging the thin black strap over my shoulder. "I'll be back before six."

Mikhail jerks back in surprise and blinks at me. "Six? Six *in the morning*?"

But I've already thrown the front door open and hurried outside. Spinning around, I smile and give my scowling brother a little wave.

"Call us if you need anything," Anton calls after me as I jog down the small path towards the street.

Carla twists around in the passenger seat and gives me a brilliant glittering grin when I slide into the backseat next to the other two. Our designated driver for the night winks at me in the rearview mirror.

"Ready?" Carla asks.

I grin back at her. "Ready."

Loud music pulses through the massive nightclub and strobing lights illuminate the sea of jumping and dancing people that fill the high-ceilinged room. I lost Carla and most of the others somewhere in the crowd about half an hour ago, but I'm too drunk and happy to care.

This is exactly what I needed.

After spending weeks constantly on edge in case Kaden shows up to torment me, while also fending off Jane and Leslie's verbal blows every single day, I needed a night to just let loose and have fun.

I down my fourth shot for the night, feeling the alcohol

burn its way down my throat, and then put the small glass back on the counter. Fuzzy warmth already buzzes inside my head, and I giggle at the sensation. Behind the bar, the bartender lets out a soft chuckle while pouring another drink for someone else. I flash him a grin before spinning around and heading back to the dance floor.

My steps are unsteady and my feet ache from hours of dancing in these heels, but the more I drink, the less I feel it.

People jump and dance around me as I'm swallowed by the rippling sea of drunk people. I spot one of the girls I arrived with a short distance away, and raise my hand to wave at her. She waves back, but the crowd is too thick to get through so I stay where I am.

Throwing my head back, I let my hair ripple down behind me as I raise my arms and dance. The beat of the music fuses with the beat of my heart, making me feel like I'm one with the music. I savor the feeling. Savor the rhythmic pounding of the bass, the flashing lights above, the press of bodies around me, the scent of perfume in the air, the drunken haze in my mind, and the joy that radiates through the room. Because I know that soon, this will all be gone.

Even if my father lets me stay at Blackwater this entire year, or even for all three years, my time here will eventually end. And then I will be expected to marry some rich and well-connected man in order to ensure that our family secures those lucrative contracts. My freedom will be over, and I will once more become a prize that some foppish man wins only to put on his shelf.

My heart clenches. And suddenly, the dancing crowd that is pressing in around me makes me feel claustrophobic. I suck in a deep breath and spin around, desperately searching for an exit. I need some air.

Across the room, I can see a neon sign pointing to a back door.

With my heart pounding in my chest, I start shoving my way towards it.

I don't want a life like that. I don't want to be married off and put on a shelf. I want someone who sees me for who I am. Someone who notices my strengths. Someone who appreciates them. Someone who doesn't treat me like I'm made of glass.

As much as I hate the way Kaden humiliates me, I also love that he treats me like a real opponent. He never holds back. Never dismisses me as insignificant. He treats me the exact same way that he treats my brothers. Like a dangerous enemy. No one has ever seen me like that before.

Fresh air at last washes over me as I shove open the back door and stumble out into the darkened alley on the other side of the threshold. I drag in a deep breath to steady myself and to try to get the sense of claustrophobia out of my system.

A few other people are smoking close to the door, and they cast me strange looks.

I give them an embarrassed smile and then move farther away. Both because I can't stand the smell of cigarettes when I'm drunk, and because I just need some space.

Only red brick walls watch me as I move a little deeper into the darkened alley. Discarded beer bottles clink and roll on the ground when I accidentally kick them as I stagger past. Throwing out a hand, I brace myself on the wall. The feeling of the rough surface underneath my palm grounds me, and I turn so that I'm leaning my back against the wall. Tilting my chin up, I rest the back of my head against the cool bricks and close my eyes for a little while.

My mind spins from the alcohol and the churning thoughts that whirl through my head.

If only my father saw me the way Kaden does. As someone to be reckoned with. But he never will. Since I'm too *breakable* to become a good assassin, he is going to marry me off. For the good of the family.

I thump the back of my head against the wall in annoyance.

There is no escaping my fate, I know that. I will be married off. I just wish that it could be to someone like Kaden.

But not Kaden himself, obviously.

Because that would be ridiculous and insane and—

"Alina?"

Dread crashes over me like a cold ocean wave.

With my heart pounding in my chest, I desperately pray that I misheard as I open my eyes.

But God is not merciful today, because I do indeed open my eyes to find Eric Wilson standing there right in front of me.

My former fiancé looks down at me with a smile on his narrow face. He looks almost exactly the same as he did the day that I broke off our engagement. The same as he does every day. Blond hair slicked back in a style that is supposed to make him look rich and trendy, but in reality only makes him look slimy. Beige chinos and an impeccable dress shirt, a wristwatch that costs more than my car, and that casually arrogant look in his blue eyes that comes from knowing that daddy's money solves all problems.

"It is you," he says, as if he couldn't ascertain that it was truly me until I opened my eyes.

"Yep," I reply, feeling my head still spinning with alcohol. "Sure is."

"What are you doing out on a Friday night alone?"

"I'm not alone."

He gives me a mildly pitying look, as if he doesn't believe me. "Anyway, it's good to see you."

"Yeah." I straighten from the wall and glance towards the back door farther down, hoping to catch the eye of one of the smokers, but they have already gone back inside. My pulse patters as I shift my gaze back to Eric. "Look, I should go back inside before they—"

"Don't give me that," he interrupts, sounding frustrated. His mouth tightens in annoyance as he fixes me with a hard stare. "You know that we need to talk."

"There is nothing else to say. Our engagement is over. I'm sorry but—"

"Do you have any idea the scandal you caused when you broke it off like that?" Indignant rage flickers in his eyes. "At every social event I went to after that, it was all people could talk about."

Swallowing, I glance towards the door again while I try to edge away from the wall. "I'm sorry. It was not my intention."

"Good. Then let's resume our engagement."

I snap my gaze back to him, raising my eyebrows and staring at him incredulously. "What?"

His eyebrows are raised as well, and he looks down at me as if I'm a child that he needs to explain something very fundamental to. "It was clearly a mistake. A decision made out of nervousness and insecurity." He gives me one of those patient and highly patronizing smiles. "I know that you're worried that you won't fit into my world. But I will help you. I will train you until you can move through our social circles without embarrassing yourself."

For a few seconds, all I can do is stare at him in disbelief. Train me? Like a fucking pet?

Shaking my head, I take a step to the side in order to try to get away from the wall that I'm trapped against. "Look, it was nice seeing you again. But I really need to get back now."

His hand shoots out.

A jolt pulses through me as he grabs my forearm, halting my escape. Then his other hand appears on my other arm, holding me in place and keeping me from moving. I stare up at him, feeling his fingers dig into my skin.

"Don't you walk away from me, Alina," he warns. "I've been waiting weeks to talk to you and—"

"You have five seconds to take your hands off my girl," a dark voice snaps. "Before I fucking cut them off."

My heart flips.

Whipping my head to the side, I stare in shock at the figure who has appeared next to us.

Kaden Hunter is standing there looking like the devil himself. His severe features are dark with threats, and barely restrained violence radiates from his muscular body as he flexes his fingers on the knife in his hand. Those dark eyes of his are so cold that I swear the temperature plummets several degrees as he stares Eric down with an air of absolute power pulsing from his lethal frame.

"One," Kaden says, threats dripping from that single word.

But my treacherous heart is still doing jerky somersaults in my chest from his previous statement. *My girl.* That's what he said. *You have five seconds to take your hands off my girl.*

Genuine confusion lines Eric's face as he turns to glance at Kaden. Then he looks him up and down, and a sneer full of superiority twists his lips. As if he assessed Kaden and found him wanting.

That reaction stuns me more than Kaden's sudden appearance. How could anyone look at Kaden and write him off as inferior? The man is perfection incarnate. Not only does he literally tower over Eric Wilson, he is so far above him in every way that I would need a microscope to find my rich former fiancé if I compared them side by side.

"Take a walk, pal," Eric says, giving Kaden a dismissive once-over. But he does take his hands off my arms. "This doesn't concern you."

"I will only say this once, so listen carefully," Kaden says, as if Eric hadn't spoken. The streetlights farther away cast unforgiving shadows across his face as he stares his prey down. "If you ever put your hands on Alina again, I will cut off your fingers one by one and feed them to you."

Shock flashes across Eric's face, and he gapes at the killer before him. I'm pretty sure no one has ever spoken to him like that before.

Then indignation and anger pulse in his eyes instead, and he draws himself up to his full height and tries to look down his nose at Kaden. "Do you have any idea who my father is? If you don't apologize and leave right now, my family will bury you under a mountain of lawsuits and criminal charges."

Kaden moves like a viper.

Flashing forward, he grabs Eric's hand and kicks at the back of his knee. Within seconds, Eric is down on one knee with his arm twisted dangerously and Kaden's knife at his throat.

A cry of pain rips from Eric's lungs as Kaden twists until my former fiancé's wrist almost breaks. Eric tries to bend forward to ease the strain on his wrist, but the knife at his throat keeps him mercilessly in place. Tears of pain well up in his blue eyes.

"Please, please," he begs.

Kaden stares down at him like a god. "I truly despise having to repeat myself."

"N-no, I remember. I remember what you said."

"Then repeat it back to me."

Before he can so much as open his mouth, Kaden twists harder. A cry of pain shatters from his throat instead.

Standing there by the wall, I stare at the scene before me while my heart pounds erratically in my chest and my core pulses with forbidden emotions. I'm still drunk. Ridiculously drunk. That has to be the reason for my body's strange reaction to this unnecessarily hot power play that Kaden is orchestrating.

"Please," Eric sobs.

Ruthless power laces Kaden's tone as he orders, "Say it."

"If I ever put my hands on Alina again, you will cut off my fingers one by one and feed them to me," Eric finally manages to press out.

"Good. Now, apologize."

He looks up at Kaden with pleading blue eyes. "I'm sorry. I'm—"

Another scream rips through the air as Kaden twists his wrist harder again.

"To *her*, you fucking moron," Kaden snaps.

Tears of pain trickle down Eric's cheeks, which are now red from embarrassment or agony or both, and he sniffles before shifting his gaze to me. "I'm sorry, Alina."

"Surely you can do better than that," Kaden says as he begins twisting again.

"No," I blurt out, speaking for the first time since my own

personal psycho and unexpected savior showed up. "It's fine. I accept the apology."

"It was barely an apology." Fury burns like cold flames in his eyes as he looks down at Eric before shifting his attention back to me. "He should be fucking groveling for your forgiveness for daring to—"

"Kaden." I hold his gaze with pleading eyes. "Please."

If he actually hurts Eric in any permanent way, it's my family who will suffer the wrath of the Wilsons. And I don't want that.

Kaden looks down at his victim again, as if considering whether or not to twist that final bit and break his wrist anyway. But then he simply clicks his tongue and releases him instead.

While I'm busy reeling from the shock that Kaden actually did as I asked, Eric scrambles to his feet and quickly backs away several steps. He's cradling his right hand against his chest, but it doesn't appear broken.

Suspicion swirls in his blue eyes as he looks from me, to Kaden's face, down to Kaden's black combat boots, up to the knife that he is nonchalantly twirling in his hand now, and then back to his face again.

"You're Kaden Hunter," Eric says at last. He sounds surprised by the realization.

A true psychopath smile curls Kaden's lips in response.

It makes Eric flinch and edge another step back. Then his gaze darts to me, and his tone turns accusatory instead. "You're forming an alliance with the Hunters instead?"

Before I can protest that I'm not engaged to Kaden, that lethal psycho slips out two throwing knives and unceremoniously raises his hand to hurl them at Eric's head.

Panic pulses across Eric's narrow face, and he stumbles

backwards before whirling around and outright sprinting away.

Next to me, Kaden lets out a mocking chuckle.

After returning both the throwing knives and his other blade to their holsters, he turns around to face me.

My stomach lurches at the look he gives me.

20

KADEN

Turning around, I fix Alina with a penetrating stare. "What the hell was that about?"

She blinks at me. Then she lifts one shoulder in a nonchalant shrug and starts forward as if to walk away. "Nothing."

I grab her by the arm, forcing her to stop and turn back to face me. "Answer me."

She shoots a pointed glare down at my hand before locking eyes with me again. "Oh, so he can't touch me but you can?"

"Yes." I tighten my grip on her arm and pull her closer to me. "Because you're not his. You're *mine*."

Emotions flit across her face, and she stares up at me with wide eyes.

Then anger burns away those other emotions in a flash.

"No!" she snaps, and gives my chest an adorable little shove that does absolutely nothing to push me back. It still doesn't stop her from doing it again as she glares up at me, completely furious. "You do not get to flip-flop between humiliating me and protecting me like this!"

Amusement ripples through me, and I arch an eyebrow at her. "Flip-flop?"

"Yes, flip-flop." Another wave of anger crashes over her beautiful face, and she gives my chest another adorable shove. "Stop smiling! I'm serious. You can't just show up like this and—"

Her words are cut off by a yelp as I quickly and efficiently crouch down, wrap my arm around the back of her thighs, and throw her over my shoulder. She just remains draped like that across my shoulder in stunned shock for a few seconds while I start walking towards the mouth of the alley. Then her mind apparently finishes processing what just happened.

"What the hell are you doing?" she snaps, squirming on my shoulder as if she has any chance at all to free herself.

"You're drunk, angry, and emotional," I reply while striding down the alley. "Let's go somewhere more private to finish this conversation."

"Finish what conversation?" She kicks her legs and hits my back with her delicate hands while growling, "You can't just throw me over your shoulder like this and kidnap me!"

"I'm not kidnapping you. I just know you don't want to walk all the way to where we're going in those high heels when your feet already hurt."

Alina falls silent.

We round the corner and continue out onto the busy street in front of the nightclub. People in fancy clothes turn to stare at us. But one look from me sends them scurrying away or averting their eyes. Warm yellow light from the streetlamps illuminates the cobblestone street, and pulsing music drifts out from the multitude of bars and nightclubs around us.

"My feet don't hurt," Alina at last retorts.

Since she can't see my face, I don't bother hiding my reaction as I smile at the petty stubbornness in her voice. But I keep my voice hard as I reply, "Don't lie to me. I could see you shifting your weight from foot to foot, trying to relieve the ache in them."

"Yes, well..." she mutters, sounding like she's scrambling for some kind of comeback. It would probably be easier for her to be a smartass if she wasn't so bloody drunk. "You try dancing in high heels an entire night."

"Or you could try wearing sensible shoes."

"I wanted to look hot."

"You're already hot."

She falls abruptly silent.

Fuck, I shouldn't have said that.

Thankfully, we reach the restaurant I was taking her to before I have to figure out what the hell I'm supposed to say to recover from that slip-up. At least she's wasted. So hopefully, she won't remember that I said that.

With Alina still draped over my shoulder, I yank open the back door and stride into the busy kitchen beyond.

Yelps of surprise echo across the brightly lit room as we become visible. It makes the owner, who goes by the name Joe, stick his head in through the doorway to see what caused the sound. His brown eyes widen when they land on me.

"Mr. Hunter," he says.

Weaving through the maze of stainless-steel counters and the rows of stoves and ovens, I stride towards him and the doorway that leads back into the restaurant. "Is the private dining room empty?"

"Uhm, yes," Joe replies and hurries out of the way. His gaze darts between me and Alina, confusion pulling at his thick dark brows. "What... uhm...?" But he trails off without finishing, as if he doesn't even know what question to ask.

"Get her water," I order as I reach him. "And something to eat that will help someone who is drunk, angry, and sad."

A soft laugh rumbles from his chest, and his eyes glitter as he nods. "Comfort food. Yeah, we can do that. Just go on through. We'll be in with some food right away."

I nod back as I walk past and continue towards the small private dining room that is located above the main restaurant area. Alina has stopped struggling on my shoulder, so I reach it without having to fight with her about it. Pushing the door open, I carry her inside and then set her down on one of the cushioned chairs by the small table for two that has been positioned by the wall. There is a larger round table here as well, but I don't want to sit that far away from her.

She shoots me a glare that is entirely ruined by the messy state of her hair and the flush in her cheeks.

My cock hardens.

Fuck, she's so hot when she's flustered and disheveled.

It takes all of my considerable self-control to simply walk around the table and sit down opposite her instead of winding that long blonde hair around my fist and kissing the annoyance out of those wicked lips.

The chair scrapes against the wooden floorboards as I pull it out. It's loud in the suddenly crackling silence. I drop down onto the chair while Alina runs her fingers through her hair to smoothen it down.

She glares at me for another few seconds before she glances around the room, taking in the rich green wallpaper and the beautiful paintings in their gilded frames that decorate the space.

"Where are we?" she asks, her gaze gliding over the

polished tables made of dark wood and the dark green curtains that frame a window looking out over the main floor of the restaurant below.

"At an Italian restaurant that apparently serves incredible food," I reply.

She arches a pale brow at me and echoes, "*Apparently?*"

I shrug. "I don't really get the obsession with food. It's just... food. But Jace loves this place. And I trust Jace."

Surprise flickers in her eyes. And I catch myself just one second too late. God damn it, I hadn't planned to share that.

However, before I can say anything else equally stupid, the door is pushed open and Joe walks in with a tray full of plates and a pitcher of water.

Alina immediately looks towards him and then breathes in deeply through her nose as the scent of food fills the air.

"Here we are," Joe says as he sets down the pitcher of water on the table between us. "Water. Important to hydrate when you're drunk." He smiles. It's one of those smiles that genuinely reach his eyes, making them glitter in the soft light. "And comfort food to heal the heart."

I watch as he sets down several plates of different pasta dishes with lots of cheese and creamy sauces. And some chocolate cake too.

"Thanks," I say once he's done. "Just put it on our tab."

"Will do." He gives us a nod and another smile while lighting the candles on our table. Then he turns to leave. "Enjoy the food."

Alina smiles back at him before he disappears out the door again. Once we're alone, she looks down at the mass of food. She bites her bottom lip, looking a little uncertain.

"Eat," I say.

That breaks the strange hesitation around her, and she

raises her gaze to level a flat look at me. "You know, you could make it sound more like an offer and less like a command."

A chuckle escapes my chest, and I flash her a wicked smile. "What would be the fun in that?"

She huffs and shoots me a pointed look, but she still picks up her knife and fork and pulls the closest pasta dish towards her. I reach towards the pitcher and fill her glass with water while she twists a truly impressive amount of pasta around her fork and brings it to her mouth. It so full that she has to open her mouth all the way to get it inside.

I grip the edge of the chair hard.

It should be fucking criminal to be that damn cute.

After finally getting all of that creamy pasta and cheese into her mouth, she starts chewing as she lowers her fork.

Light bursts behind her eyes. For second, she stops chewing and just stares at me with wide eyes. Then a moan rumbles from her throat and her eyes roll back in pleasure.

My heart does an absolutely ridiculous backflip in my chest.

"Oh my God," she says around the mouthful of food. "This is *so good*!"

My chest suddenly aches, and I can't manage a reply. But thankfully, Alina just swallows the food and then pulls another plate towards her. There is a bright smile on her face as she tries that dish as well.

It makes the tightness in my chest even worse.

Gripping the edge of the chair hard, I try to fight off the torrent of emotions that threaten to drown me every time I watch that incredible light sparkle in Alina's eyes as she eats and moans with every bite.

"You're not eating?" she asks, raising her eyebrows in question.

"No." It's the only word I can manage to press out because it feels as if steel bands are wrapped around my chest, squeezing the air out of my lungs.

She watches me curiously, and licks sauce from her bottom lip.

The bloody chair almost cracks from how hard I grip it.

Thankfully, she doesn't say anything else.

I focus on trying to breathe while she finishes eating and drinking her water.

Once she's done, I've managed to get myself under enough control to speak in full sentences again.

"Now, what the hell was that all about?" I demand.

At first, she just blinks at me in surprise and confusion. Then realization washes over her features. "Oh, that guy back in that alley."

"Yes. And don't give me some bullshit excuse about how he was some random creep. He was acting like he owns you. Why?"

"Because he did."

Rage pulses through me like a lightning strike. Bracing my forearms on the dark wooden tabletop, I lean forward and say very slowly and very clearly, "He what?"

Alina just leans back in her chair and crosses her arms over her chest.

"You're not leaving this room until you tell me who the fuck that was and what the hell you mean by, *because he did*," I warn, my voice dropping lower.

"You could try asking that without the threat baked into it, you know."

"Just answer the damn question."

"He was my fiancé," she snaps. Keeping her arms crossed, she glares at me from across the flickering candlelight.

Shock still rings inside my skull like giant bells, so I only manage to echo, "Fiancé?"

"Yes. His name is Eric Wilson, and I was engaged to him."

"Why?"

"Because my father wanted to forge an alliance with his family."

"And what about you?"

She frowns. "What *about* me?"

"What did *you* want?"

"Freedom." The response is immediate. No hesitation and no time to consider.

My heart clenches painfully at the stoic expression she keeps on her face as she stares back at me with her chin raised. There are a thousand other things that I want to say, but I can't.

So all I say is, "What happened?"

"He treated me like a glass trophy to be put on a shelf." She says it so casually, as if it's an everyday occurrence in her life. "So I begged my father to call off the engagement. And he did. Thankfully. But it won't be long until my family arranges another marriage for me."

Rage licks through my veins like fire, but I manage to keep my voice calm as I ask, "Why would they do that?"

"Because that's all I am to them." Bitterness coats her words as she spits them out. "Something to be married off to secure an alliance."

"But you're a Petrov."

She blinks, looking oddly surprised all of a sudden. It's only then that I realize that that had sounded an awful lot like a compliment. As if I consider the Petrov family to hold some kind of esteem. Which they technically do, but I will die before I ever admit that.

However, she recovers quickly and instead scoffs bitterly. "Yeah, well, haven't you heard?" With that resentment still lining her features, she uncrosses her arms and gestures down at her body. "I'm too weak and breakable to be an asset to the family."

For a few heartbeats, all I can do is stare at her.

Is that really what they make her believe? That she's weak and breakable and not an asset to their fucking esteemed Petrov family?

My fingers curl around the hilt of a knife, and I have to fight down the suddenly overwhelming urge to slaughter her entire family and bathe in their blood.

How could they ever let her believe that she is anything less than absolutely fucking perfect? That she's anything less than the most dangerous person I have ever met?

Forcing out a slow breath, I make myself release the hilt of the knife and instead lean forward across the table again. Then I lock hard eyes on Alina.

"Do you know how many people I have tormented over the years?" I ask.

She glances from side to side, looking confused by the sudden change of topic. Then she returns her gaze to me and lifts her slim shoulders in a shrug. "A lot?"

I nod. "A lot."

Letting the silence stretch, I allow her mind time to come up with an appropriately high number that I know will probably still not be anywhere near as high as it should be. Only when she shifts her weight nervously in her seat do I continue.

"Do you know how many of them are still standing?" I ask.

She bites her lip slightly and furrows her brows. Then she shakes her head.

I hold her gaze in silence for another few seconds before I reply, so that she will truly understand what I'm trying to tell her.

Her chest rises and falls with short breaths, and light from the candles dance across her beautiful face as she watches me.

I keep my eyes on her as I at last speak.

"Only you."

21

ALINA

S oft sheets brush against my skin. I moan, pressing my cheek into the pillow and draw in a deep breath. An absolutely intoxicating scent fills my lungs.

Confusion ripples through me.

Untangling my arm from the sheets, I lift my hand and rub my eyes while trying to push the sleep from my bones. I blink, staring up at a dark wooden ceiling.

Which can't be right.

Because the ceiling in my room is white.

I frown, and then jerk my head down to stare at the cover that lies draped over me. It's black. I frown deeper, feeling like my mind is trying to push through mud. Why are the bedclothes black?

"Finally," a familiar voice says from my right. A *very* familiar voice.

I snap my gaze towards it, and my heart leaps into my throat.

Kaden is sitting at a desk, sharpening a set of knives. No,

not *a* desk. He's sitting at *his* desk. In his room. Which means that the bed I'm occupying is *his* bed.

My pulse flutters as I scramble out of bed and quickly straighten on the floor next to it instead while trying my best not to look as flustered as I feel.

Amusement dances over Kaden's severe features as he watches me while still continuing to expertly sharpen his blade. He flicks a glance up and down my body, and a faint smirk curls his lips.

The heat already radiating from my cheeks gets even worse. I brush my hands down my now rumpled clothes. I'm still wearing the short blue dress that I wore to the nightclub, but Kaden has taken off my high heels and placed them by the door. I glance at them while quickly raking my fingers through my messy hair to untangle it.

Kaden chuckles softly.

The embarrassment whirling through me intensifies, and I cross my arms over my chest instead before fixing him with a glare. "What the hell did you do? Kidnap me?"

A knowing smile spreads across his lips. "If I had kidnapped you, you would be gagged, blindfolded, and shackled to my bed right now."

My heart skips a beat at the mental image that flashes through my mind.

"But you're not." He lifts his shoulders in a lazy shrug. "Hence, no kidnapping."

"Then what the hell am I doing here? Because I most certainly would never have climbed into your bed on my own."

A sly smile tilts his lips. "You already have, remember?"

I shoot him a glare. "Just answer the question."

"You fell asleep in my car on the way back."

Oh. Right. I blink as memories flood my brain. The nightclub. The amount of alcohol I consumed. The confrontation with Eric. The restaurant that Kaden took me to afterwards.

My gaze darts towards the windows. It's still dark outside, which means that it must be the middle of the night. Thank God I texted Carla that I was heading home with someone else before I got into Kaden's car. Otherwise, she would probably have sent out a search party by now. Or worse, called my brothers.

As if he can read my mind, Kaden arches a dark brow and gives me a pointed look. "What was I supposed to do? Carry you sleeping in my arms into your own house? Your brothers would've tried to kill me if I did that. And then I would've had to kill them instead. Which would've left blood and bodies all over your pristine little house. And I figured that you didn't want to spend your weekend mopping up blood and burying your family members." He shrugs again and shoots a nonchalant glance at the bed behind me. "Which is why I very generously allowed you to sleep off the alcohol in my bed instead."

"I, uhm…"

"Aren't you going to say thank you?"

For what? I almost retort. But it's more out of embarrassment than any real anger. All things considered, everything that Kaden has done for me tonight has been decent. And not just decent. Some of it has been outright kind and protective.

His words from back in the restaurant still swirl inside my mind.

Do you know how many people I have tormented over the years? Do you know how many of them are still standing? Only you.

No one has ever told me that I'm strong and resilient before. And he both looked and sounded so sincere when he said it. As if he truly did mean it.

I didn't tell him that back then, but his words speared straight into my heart. They're buried deep in there now, bolstering my soul.

And for that, he at least deserves a thank you.

So I hold his gaze and say, "Thank you."

It surprises me just how much I actually mean it.

At first, there is a smug expression on Kaden's face that immediately makes me regret that I ever thanked the bastard. But then his intense eyes study me, and he seems to recognize the sincerity in my words, because his features turn serious and almost contemplative. While holding my gaze, he gives me a slow nod.

And suddenly, this whole situation just feels far too intimate.

I'm already confused as hell about my feelings for Kaden, and this certainly isn't helping. I need to get out of here before I do something stupid.

"Yes, well," I begin, my words coming out more uncertain than I would've liked. "I should head home now."

Before he can even reply, I break eye contact and hurry towards the door.

I don't even make it three steps before he's on his feet and in my way. Staggering back a step, I narrowly manage to avoid slamming right into his muscular chest. With a scowl on my face, I glare up at him and get ready to ask what the hell he's doing. But the words die on my tongue when I see the expression on his features.

"We're not done," he says, his expression dark.

My heart slams against my ribs.

He takes a step forward.

I take a step back.

There is some kind of emotion burning in his eyes. It's so intense that I feel like that fire in his gaze sucks all the air out of the room, making it difficult to breathe.

I drag in an unsteady breath as Kaden backs me across the room. My back hits the wall with a thud.

Kaden keeps moving until he's standing so close that I can almost feel the heat from his skin. He towers over me, looming like the shadow of death while his muscular body blocks out everything else until he is all I can see. His dark and mysterious scent crowds my senses, filling my lungs and making my head spin. Everything about him overpowers me. His lethal body. His intoxicating scent. His intense eyes. This man is built for complete dominance.

My heart jerks in my chest as he braces his palms against the wall on either side of my head, caging me in with his arms.

Craning my neck, I stare up at his dangerously handsome face and meet those dark eyes of his. That strange emotion still burns like wildfire in there. But I can't figure out what it is.

"You will never let Eric Wilson, or any other man, touch you ever again," he declares. "Am I making myself clear?"

My heart flips at the dark possessiveness in his voice.

And suddenly, I realize what the fire in his eyes is.

Jealousy.

Kaden Hunter is… jealous.

The absolutely ludicrous realization makes my mouth drop open.

For a few seconds, I just gape at him. Then I blurt out, "Are you jealous?"

His eyes flash, and he clenches his jaw. "I'm not jealous."

"Yes, you are."

"No—"

An astonished laugh rips from my throat, cutting him off. Shaking my head, I stare up at him in disbelief. "Oh my God, you're jealous."

"I've already told you," he growls in my face. "I'm not jealous. Jealousy would require that I actually care about you. Which I don't."

"Uh-huh. Then why are you telling me that no other man is allowed to touch me?"

Taking one hand off the wall, he wraps it around my throat in a highly possessive and controlling move. His eyes bore into mine as he levels a commanding stare on me. "Because you're mine to do with as I please. And when I give you an order, you fucking obey. Is that clear?"

A dark thrill races down my spine, and my thighs clench. God, I want him to fuck me. I want those possessive hands all over my body and I want to finally find out if he fucks as dominantly as he does everything else.

That thought is immediately followed by anger. At myself. At him. At fucking *everything*.

"No!" I snap. Yanking up my hands, I slam them against his hard chest in anger. "You don't get to do this. You don't get to tell me who I can and can't sleep with."

He remains as unmovable as a mountain, his hand still around my throat as he retorts, "Watch me."

"Asshole." I slam my palms against his annoyingly firm chest again, which doesn't even make him flinch. "You insufferable, arrogant, domineering—"

"Watch your mouth."

"I will not be watching my fucking mouth!" I glare up at him, feeling all of my restraint snap as all the rage and frustration and terrible desire from these past weeks burn through me. "Because you cannot have it both ways. Either I fuck whoever the hell I want. Or *you* fuck me and I agree not to touch anyone else."

His eyes flash and he flexes his fingers around my throat. "I've already told you, I don't fuck Petrovs."

"Great! Then it's settled." I glare back at him in challenge. "The moment I leave this room, I'm going to call Eric Wilson and head over to his penthouse and let him fuck me all the way into next week."

Tension crackles through the room like lightning. It's so thick that I swear I can feel it vibrating in the air. Kaden's expression is darker than I have ever seen, and when he speaks, his voice is soft and low and so dangerous that ice skitters down my spine.

"You do that, and I will paint his entire fucking house with his blood."

"Then I will just call someone else," I retort. "Someone you don't know. You can't keep track of me all the time. So whenever I'm out of your sight from now on, you will know that I'm away somewhere, fucking someone else."

"Or we can just revisit the scenario where I keep you gagged, blindfolded, and shackled to my bed."

"Just admit it!" The words tear out of my throat, full of frustration and anger and desperation. "Admit that you want me."

A muscle flexes in his jaw as he grinds his teeth. Fury and jealousy, and the same frustration that I feel too, burn in his eyes as he stares me down. But he says nothing.

"You have two options," I say. "Either you fuck me. Or the next time you see me, I will be in another man's bed." I shoot him a look full of challenge. "You have ten seconds to decide."

His lips crash against mine.

My heart jumps, almost breaking out of my ribcage.

With his hand still firmly around my throat, he kisses me with such desperation that I forget how to breathe.

"You vicious, blackmailing, little menace," he growls against my lips between each furious kiss.

I gasp into his mouth as he bites my bottom lip hard.

Releasing my throat, he draws his hands down the side of my ribs while his mouth continues dominating mine. Electricity shoots through my veins. His hands reach my hips. A shudder rolls through my body at his demanding touch.

He abruptly breaks the kiss and instead uses his grip on my hips to spin me around. I suck in a sharp breath as he shoves me chest first up against the wall.

"I will ruin you," he growls as he grabs the top of my dress and starts yanking the zipper down. "I will ruin you so fucking badly that you will never be able to look at another man again without feeling my hands on your body and my cock in your cunt."

Desire burns through my veins, and the response that flashes through my mind is immediate. *And I will fucking let you.*

My skin prickles as Kaden yanks the zipper all the way down and shoves my dress down to my hips. Lightning skitters over my skin as he draws his strong hands down my ribs and then over my hips, pushing the dress down until it flutters down to land in a pool of blue fabric around my ankles.

I try to turn around, but Kaden just shoves me back up against the wall. Then his clever fingers undo the clasps on my bra. My nipples harden as he yanks it off and tosses it to the side. Now only wearing my panties, I spin around to face him.

Fire burns in his eyes as he reaches down and curls both hands over the top of my panties.

Then he rips them off.

Electricity shoots through me, and my heart slams so hard in my chest that I think my ribs are going to shatter.

"I'm going to ruin you," he warns again, his voice low and rough.

Yeah, well, he's about to find out that ruination goes both ways.

Flashing him a grin full of challenge, I step away from the wall and shove him backwards towards his bed. He lets me.

His hands grip the hem of his shirt and he yanks it over his head while I back him towards the bed.

Heat pools in my belly and my clit throbs as I stare at his half-naked body. God, he's glorious. The sharp ridges of his abs and the firm muscles of his chest make me want to run my hands all over him.

I close the distance between us and raise my hands to shove him down onto the bed behind him. But the moment I do, Kaden makes his move.

My stomach lurches as he flips us around and tosses me down on the mattress instead while he remains standing next to it.

A smirk plays over his sinful mouth as he looks down at me. I narrow my eyes at him but untangle myself from the sheets and move into a better position in the middle of the bed. Kaden watches me while he slowly unbuttons his pants and draws the zipper down.

Impatience flashes through me.

Shifting my position slightly, I spread my legs and draw

my knees up a little so that my pussy is completely exposed to Kaden where he stands beside the bed, torturing me by taking his sweet time getting undressed.

A grin full of challenge spreads across my lips as I lock eyes with him.

Then I reach down and start stroking my clit.

His pants and underwear and every single piece of clothing he was wearing hit the floor within a matter of seconds.

My eyes widen at the size of his cock.

It distracts me so much that I don't even realize what's happening before Kaden has already climbed onto the bed and shoved my hand away from my clit. Keeping my wrist in a firm grip, he forces it down to the mattress next to my head instead while he settles himself between my still spread legs.

"Have I told you that you're a manipulative little villain who is in over her fucking head?" he growls at me.

I grin up at him. "And yet, you did exactly what I wanted."

His eyes dance with amusement and wicked promises as he reaches down with his free hand and brushes his fingers over my clit.

A jolt spikes through my spine.

With that wickedness still in his eyes, he traces his fingers over my clit again before rolling it between his fingers. I suck in a jagged breath. Pleasure spreads through my soul as Kaden expertly toys with my clit.

Once I'm squirming on his dark sheets, he shifts his hand so that his thumb continues rubbing my clit while his forefinger and middle finger trace the edges of my entrance.

A moan spills from my mouth.

He pushes one finger inside. I whimper as he slides it out and then pushes it back in. Wiggling my hips, I try to increase the pleasure building inside me. Kaden adds another finger, slowly pumping them in and out while toying with my clit.

But it's not enough.

It's not nearly enough.

I want him to *fuck* me.

"Enough," I snap at him, the word ripping from me with both anger and pent-up need. "You've never treated me like I'm breakable before, so stop doing it now. I'm not a virgin and I'm on birth control, so stop playing around and just fuck me the way I know you want to fuck me."

He arches a dark brow while continuing to tease me with his fingers. "And in what way, exactly, do I want to fuck you?"

"Hard."

His eyes glint, and I know that I'm right. Kaden is not sweet and gentle. So the fact that he is taking his time playing with my clit and stretching me with his fingers tells me something that I'm not sure what to do with right now. But it doesn't matter. Because he doesn't need to do any of it. My pussy is already soaking wet. And if Kaden doesn't start fucking me within the next ten seconds, I'm going to set this whole bloody house on fire.

"You want to take me hard. You want to fuck me into submission." I hold his gaze with eyes full of challenge. "So do it."

That gleam remains in his eyes as he slowly takes his hand from my pussy and shifts his position so that his cock brushes against my entrance instead. My heart slams against my ribs.

Reaching up with my free hand, I draw my fingers over his sharp jaw. "You can ruin me." I smile and shake my head. "But you can't break me."

He thrusts into me.

I gasp up into the ceiling and yank at his grip on my other

wrist as his hard cock slides into me, stretching me with its massive size. It makes both flashes of intense pleasure and small flickers of pain shoot through my body.

Kaden pulls out, and then slams all the way into the hilt.

A moan tears from deep within my lungs.

"I know," he replies at last. Releasing my wrist, he braces his hands on the mattress instead as he leans down and steals a savage kiss from my lips. "Because you're the most unbreakable person I've ever met."

My heart skips several beats.

Pleasure pulses through me as he draws back and then thrusts inside again.

Fuck, he's perfect. He's so fucking perfect.

While staring up into those gleaming dark eyes of his, I reach up and at long last draw my hands over his sculpted chest. Another moan slips past my lips as my fingers skim across his pecs and down to his abs. His body is the perfect mixture of hard muscles and soft warm skin.

While I caress every ridge of his sharp abs, he picks up the pace. Setting a hard and fast rhythm, he pounds into me with such dominant and forceful thrusts that my body slides up and down on the sheets with every move.

I grab onto his biceps to hold myself steady.

Every thrust creates mind-numbing friction that sends sparks up my spine.

Pleasure builds inside me like a crackling storm.

Kaden's eyes stay locked on my face, studying every emotion on my features, as he fucks me exactly the way I want him to. Like I'm unbreakable.

His massive cock slams into me. Over and over again. Until the pent-up tension inside me is so unbearable that I start whimpering and throwing my head from side to side.

But that only makes him slow down, pulling me back from the edge of that coming orgasm.

With a knowing smirk on his lips and a truly villainous glint in his eyes, he picks up the pace again, railing me hard until I almost climax.

And then he slows down once more.

I dig my fingers into his muscles as a snarl of frustration rips from my throat.

He brings me to the edge two more times without letting me come.

And at that point, I'm reduced to a trembling ball of need.

I swear, the man is a master torturer.

Pitiful whimpers spill from my lips when the orgasm never comes. My entire body vibrates from the terrible tension trapped inside me. I need release.

"Please," I all but sob. Sliding my hands up his toned shoulders and over his neck, I cup his face with my hands. "Please, I'm begging you."

A sly smile tilts his lips as he stares me down while starting up a punishing rhythm once more. "Feeling fucked into submission yet?"

"Yes," I gasp out, breathless, as the pleasure starts building inside me again with every dominant thrust. "Yes. Now, please, let me come."

His eyes bore into mine. "You will never let another man touch you. Ever again."

"I will never let another man touch me," I promise. My hands slip down to rest on his firm chest as I look up at him with pleading eyes. "Now, *please*. Please."

A smile curls his lips. "I love it when you beg."

My retort is cut off by a moan as Kaden thrusts into me. Deep. Hard. Fast.

Lights flicker behind my eyes as I soar towards an orgasm.

I curl my fingers against his chest, sucking in breaths that don't seem to contain enough oxygen.

He rails me hard, fucking me like he owns me.

Tension pulses inside me like a thrashing storm.

He slams into me, hitting the perfect spot over and over again.

White lights burst before my eyes as a violent orgasm crashes into me with the force of a tidal wave.

I gasp as pleasure floods my system.

Kaden keeps fucking me through the orgasm, prolonging the sweet release that ricochets through my trembling body until it feels like my brain is going to shatter.

A deep groan tears from his chest as he comes as well.

The raw sound of that groan makes my spine tingle and more pleasure pulse through me.

When the last waves of the orgasm have faded, I feel almost shellshocked by how fucking mind-blowing it was.

Kaden remain where he is for another few seconds, his cock buried deep inside me. His chest heaves, and he looks completely stunned as he stares down at me with his mouth slightly open.

Completely transfixed by the sight, I reach up and draw my fingers along his jaw.

A shudder rolls through his powerful body.

That seems to break the spell.

He pulls his cock out and twists his body to the side.

The mattress bounces underneath me as he drops down next to me.

My heart still slams against my ribs.

Tilting my head to the side, I rest my cheek against the soft pillow and watch Kaden. He lies there on his back, staring up

218

at the dark wooden ceiling while his chest rises and falls with deep breaths.

An absolutely ridiculous impulse flashes through me. But I can't seem to stop myself. So I roll over on my side, snuggle up next to him, and then drape my arm over his chest and wrap my leg over his.

His head snaps towards me, and he stares down at me with wide eyes full of astonishment. I just wiggle closer, holding him tightly and breathing in that intoxicating scent of him.

For another few seconds, Kaden only continues staring at me as if I have lost my mind.

Then he releases a soft breath and wraps his arm around me, pulling me closer until he can rest his chin on the top of my head. Then he draws in a deep breath.

I smile against his skin.

He said that he was going to ruin me.

But maybe, just maybe, I ruined him too.

22

KADEN

She has fucking ruined me. I stare down at the slim woman nestled against my body. I'm *cuddling* Alina. I don't think I have ever cuddled anything or anyone in my entire life. And yet, I'm cuddling *her*.

My logical mind is telling me that I should kick her out of my bed. And not only that. I should throw her out of my room, say something cruel, and then humiliate her by forcing her to walk back to her house naked.

But for some reason, I can't.

Because when her warm body is pressed against mine like this and she's holding on to me as if I'm the only thing keeping her together, all I want to do is to just keep her here like this forever.

"Why is it that you've never looked at me as if I'm breakable?" she suddenly asks, her voice barely more than a whisper.

I consider lying. Or simply not answering. But there is something so vulnerable in that small, soft voice of hers. It makes my heart clench painfully.

"Because I hate it when people look at me that way," I reply instead.

She lifts her head, and I immediately miss the feeling of her warm cheek pressed against my chest. Confusion pulls at her brows as she turns those big gray eyes to me. "Why would anyone do that? I mean, look at you."

As if to demonstrate her point, she runs her hand from my collarbones, over my chest and abs, and down to my waist.

And I damn near pass out from the feeling of her hand caressing my body like that.

"You're..." She stares up at me, confusion still evident on her gorgeous face. "Perfect."

My heart does a violent flip behind my ribs.

She slides her hand back up my stomach, and I have to bite the inside of my cheek to keep a moan from escaping my mouth. Only once her hand is once more resting on my chest do I dare to breathe again.

"Who would ever look at you and think you're breakable?" she says. It sounds more like a rhetorical question, but I find myself answering anyway.

"My parents."

She blinks up at me, probably surprised by both my answer and the fact that I replied at all. Then a considering look blows across her features, and she tilts her head slightly. "Why?"

"Because they seem to think that I'm one wrong word away from becoming a serial killer." Gazing up at the dark wooden ceiling, I blow out a long breath and slide my hand down the side of her ribs until it's resting on her hip. "That my mind is one wrong word away from shattering like a fragile piece of glass. But it's not. *I'm* not. So I know that you aren't either."

She falls silent. And I don't dare to shift my gaze down to look at her, so I just continue watching the ceiling while I trace small circles on her hip with my thumb. My heart patters in my chest. I don't even know what I want her to say. I don't want her pity. And I don't want her to try to reassure me that I'm normal either. Because I'm not. I am who I am.

So what am I hoping she will say?

"Isn't a serial killer and an assassin basically the same thing, though?"

A surprised laugh rips from my chest. Tearing my gaze from the ceiling, I tilt my head back down to meet her gaze. She's watching me with raised eyebrows.

I smile.

That was the best possible thing she could've said.

While continuing to stroke her hip, I chuckle softly. "Yeah, it sure is."

She nestles closer to my body, her hand resting over my heart.

For a few seconds, only the winds blowing in the dark night outside break the silence. I swear I can feel Alina's heart beating against my body. Or maybe that's my own heart.

"Is it true?" I find myself asking.

"Is what true?"

"That your family doesn't think you're an asset?" My brows pull together in a scowl. "That they think the only way you can contribute to the family is by marrying some rich asshole that will secure an alliance for them?"

Pain and sadness flicker in her eyes. And I immediately regret asking. But she answers anyway.

"Yeah." She heaves a small sigh that makes her warm breath dance over my skin. "But you know what it's like. Legendary assassin families like yours and mine always have certain... expectations. A certain legacy that needs to be upheld."

My mind briefly drifts to Jace, but I don't say anything. I haven't even talked to him about it yet.

So all I say is, "Yeah, I guess you're right."

"So I don't blame them for thinking that way."

"I do." I stop tracing circles on her skin and instead tighten my grip on her hip defensively. "Because they're wrong."

Light blooms in her eyes, and she opens her mouth as if to respond. But then hesitation blows across her features and she just closes it again.

Clearing her throat, she takes her hand from my chest and starts moving away.

The loss of her warm body against mine is like a gut punch.

"I should go," she says, carefully climbing out of bed. "I need to get home before my brothers send out a search party."

Let them, I almost growl. But I know that she's right. We've already crossed a gigantic fucking line here tonight, so it's better if she leaves before we can go any farther.

She quickly gathers up her clothes and starts getting dressed. I put on a pair of fresh underwear and the loose pants I wear to bed as well. I doubt I will be getting much sleep after this, but I can try.

Once she's dressed, she walks over to where I placed her high heels by the door. But she doesn't put them on. She just bends down and picks them up in her hand. Then she blinks, as if she has just remembered something.

Her gaze sweeps across my room until she locates her purse, which is waiting for her on top of my dresser. With her shoes still in one hand, she slinks over to her purse and then awkwardly slings it over her shoulder with one hand. Then she moves back to the door.

There is a strange tension in the air now.

For a few seconds, we just stand there, watching each other in the crackling silence.

Her gray eyes search my face. It looks like she wants to ask me where this leaves us.

But thankfully, she doesn't. Because I have no idea either.

So in the end, she just gives me a small smile and then slips out the door without a word. I watch her go, feeling both strangely empty and full of chaotic emotions at the same time.

My heart beats erratically in my chest and my mind churns as I stand there, staring at the now empty doorway.

I fucked a Petrov.

I said I wasn't going to. I *swore* I wasn't going to. But I did.

And I not only fucked her, I *cuddled* her afterwards too. And I told her things. Things about me.

What the fuck am I doing?

I have a plan. A good plan. A plan to ruin her and to finally break that damn family. I shouldn't have crossed this line. Shouldn't have brought her here. Shouldn't have let her mess with my head like this.

Because now, I don't know where we stand anymore. I don't know what I'm supposed to do with her now. What I'm supposed to do with myself now.

The only thing I do know, without a shred of doubt, is this:

No other man will ever touch her.

23

ALINA

Even all the way through the phone, I can hear my father's disappointment. I can hear it in the tight tone of his voice. I can hear it in the way he sighs. I can even hear it in the silence when he says nothing at all. Staring up into the white ceiling of my bedroom, I hold the phone to my ear and wait for him to finish lecturing me.

"So can you imagine my embarrassment when I had to hear from one of my business associates that he saw you at a nightclub," he says.

If he only knew what else I had done that night. Going out drinking is nothing compared to the real crime I committed two days ago. If he ever found out that I fucked a Hunter, he would pull me out of Blackwater in a heartbeat and lock me up inside our family home back in the city.

"It was just a night out with the girls," I protest.

"A night out with the girls? I thought you came to Blackwater to train. Not to go out partying."

"It was *one* time."

"One time that I know of."

Clenching my jaw, I say nothing. Because he's right about that, of course.

Outside the windows, the warm midday winds chase soft white clouds across the heavens. It makes the light that hits my pale walls disappear and reappear as the clouds temporarily cover the sun before moving on again.

Dad heaves a deep sigh. "I have set up a meeting for you."

"A meeting?" I frown up at the empty ceiling. "It's Sunday. I have classes again tomorrow."

"I know. It's today."

"It's almost noon."

"It's a lunch date."

My heart jerks in my chest and I sit bolt upright on the bed. "A *date?*"

"Yes."

"But you said—"

"If you have time to go out drinking and partying, then you have time to start meeting potential alliance candidates again."

"Potential alliance candidates?" I scoff. "You mean men you want to marry me off to."

"Don't be a brat. We all have different roles when it comes to protecting this family."

"And mine is to be sold off?"

Silence falls on the other end of the line.

Squeezing my eyes shut, I grimace in regret while dread washes through me like cold water. Because I know that I just went too far.

"I'm sorry," I whisper. Opening my eyes, I keep my voice soft as I say, "It's just, you said that you would give me this year. Here at Blackwater."

I had been hoping for three years, but it looks like that won't be happening.

"And I will," Dad replies. "But there is no harm in looking for potential candidates in the meantime."

"But—"

"It's just one lunch date, Alina. Is that really too much to ask?"

Yes. But I can't say that, of course, so instead I reply, "No."

"Good. Then it's settled. He will come by and pick you up in an hour."

I stare at myself, still in my pajamas, in the mirror across the room and suppress a sigh.

Great.

To be fair, Josh ends up being a pretty decent guy. He is pretty in the way that most rich people are. Light brown hair that is styled perfectly, straight white teeth, and brown eyes that glitter in the sunlight. And as opposed to the other rich heirs I've been forced to go on dates with, he doesn't only talk about himself. However, it unfortunately still doesn't change the fact that I'm bored out of my mind fifteen minutes into our lunch date.

Seated at a table for two in a trendy lunch restaurant that mostly serves various kinds of salads, I try to keep a polite smile on my face while I alternate between eating and nodding along to whatever Josh is talking about. But it's becoming increasingly difficult to concentrate, because I constantly feel like the back of my neck is prickling.

Sweeping a discreet glance around the crowded restaurant, I half expect to find Kaden standing there, glaring at me with a dangerous look on his face. I know that it's ridiculous. He has no idea where I am. But I still can't help worrying that he will somehow magically appear out of thin air and cause a scene. After all, he was very clear that night two days ago. *No other man touches you.*

"I'm sorry," Josh suddenly says, the apologetic tone of his voice cutting through my distracted mind. "I'm probably boring you with this."

I snap my gaze back to my date. Embarrassment washes through me, and I wave my hands in the air while giving him an apologetic smile. "No, no, not at all. I was just... trying to see where the restrooms are."

"Oh." He blinks. A hint of red creeps into his cheeks. Then he points towards the back of the restaurant. "They're down there."

Placing the white linen napkin on the table, I get to my feet and flash him another smile. "I'll be right back."

He nods, still looking a bit embarrassed.

I keep the smile on my face until my back is fully to him. Then I relax my facial muscles. Brushing my hands down my cream-colored dress, I blow out a long breath and walk through the busy restaurant until I reach the restrooms. I don't really need to use it, but I need a break from our date.

The ladies' restroom is one large room with three private stalls and a long counter with three sinks below a massive mirror. All of them are empty.

After I finish taking care of my nonexistent need, I kick the stall door shut with my heel and then walk over to the sink in the middle. The sound of rushing water fills the room as I wash my hands. Once I have dried them off, I remain standing there in front of the mirror, staring at my reflection and wondering for how long I can get away with hiding in here.

Before I can come to a decision, the door to the corridor outside is yanked open. Since I can't just stand here when another woman has come to pee, I sigh and turn towards the door to leave.

My heart stops.

Standing frozen in the middle of the room, I stare at the man who just walked through the door.

Kaden Hunter.

The room seems to shrink around me at his dominating presence. His broad shoulders block the view of the now closed door behind him, and there is a lethal glint in his eyes as he stares me down.

"I thought I told you that no other man touches you," he says, his voice dripping with threats.

An ominous click sounds as Kaden locks the door behind him.

I swallow. *Fuck.*

"We're just having lunch," I reply, trying to keep both the anxiety and the strange excitement that ripples through me from my voice.

"So he's not here because he's hoping to fuck you?"

My cheeks heat at his graphic word choice. Lifting my chin, I shoot him an annoyed look and cross my arms over my chest. "No. If you must know, my dad set up this meeting."

Kaden's gaze sharpens, and a muscle feathers in his jaw. "So, he's hoping to fuck you *and* marry you."

Well, yes. But I don't think that answer will do anything to improve my current situation, so instead I throw my arms out and snap, "What was I supposed to do? Refuse to go?"

"Yes."

My heart flutters at how dead serious that answer was. However, before I can reply that I can't just disobey my father like that, Kaden takes a step closer. I instinctively take a step back, but my ass hits the edge of the marble counter behind me.

Lightning crackles through my veins as Kaden drags his gaze up and down my body while closing the distance between us.

"Looks like I need to remind you of the rules," he says.

I swallow, but my heart pounds with forbidden excitement. Turns out that this lunch date isn't as boring and uneventful as I thought it was going to be.

Kaden jerks his chin at me. "Sit on the counter."

Glancing over my shoulder, I move until I'm standing at a place between two of the sinks where the counter is flat and empty. Then I place my hands on the edge and pull myself up so that I'm sitting on it.

A thud sounds as Kaden drops a pack on the floor. I glance down at it.

"Take off your panties," he orders.

I give him a flat look. "You could've told me that before I climbed up and sat down."

He just raises his eyebrows expectantly. I roll my eyes at him. A warning look blows across his features as he narrows his eyes at me. My pulse leaps.

Maneuvering on top of the counter, I quickly lift the short flowing skirt of my dress and slide my panties off before putting them on the smooth marble next to me.

After pulling something out of his pack, Kaden straightens again and walks up to me.

"Spread your legs," he commands.

With my dress now bunched around my hips, I do as he says and spread my legs wide.

My skin prickles and my cheeks heat from both the excitement and the embarrassment of baring myself to him like that.

A smile plays over his lips as he looks down at my exposed pussy. The warmth in my cheeks intensifies, but I keep my legs spread.

Kaden moves until he is standing between my legs. His dark brown eyes lock on mine for a few seconds. Power and command pulse from his muscular frame as he stares me down.

Then he draws his fingers over my pussy.

I suck in a sharp breath at the sudden touch.

"This is mine," he declares, his merciless gaze still holding mine.

Pleasure shoots through my body as he rolls my clit between his thumb and forefinger. Gripping the edge of the counter hard, I throw my head back and drag in shuddering breaths as Kaden expertly toys with my clit. Tension builds in my body.

Then he slips a finger inside me.

I snap my gaze back to him. He just smirks at me before pulling his hand back. With that smug expression still on his damn mouth, he holds up his hand between us and makes a show of examining his finger. Since I'm already wet as a fucking waterfall, it's coated in my arousal.

Another wave of embarrassment washes through me, and I glance away.

Kaden just chuckles.

Then something strange brushes against my entrance. Jerking in surprise, I whip my gaze down and stare at the

object that Kaden now holds between my legs. It looks like…
a wireless egg vibrator.

I slowly lift my gaze to Kaden.

With his commanding stare locked on mine, he looms over
me like a god, daring me to defy him.

I don't.

Curling my fingers around the edge of the counter, I grip
it tightly as Kaden pushes the small egg vibrator inside me. It's
a strange feeling. But not unpleasant. Though I'm not about to
tell the psycho that.

Once it's in place, Kaden pulls his hand back and instead
slides out his phone.

"If you even think about filming me right now," I warn.
"I'm going to—"

My threat is cut off by a gasp as the toy starts vibrating
inside me. It's then replaced by a moan at the incredible
feeling it creates. Leaning backwards, I shift my hips and rest
the back of my head against the mirror behind me as Kaden
uses his phone to increase the vibrations.

Pleasure builds inside me.

I squirm on the counter.

But just before the tension can reach those perfect levels,
the vibrations abruptly stop. Disoriented, I blink up at
Kaden.

A cruel smile curls his lips. "You thought I would let you
come?" Leaning forward, he wraps a hand around my throat
and pulls me away from the mirror so that my face his closer
to his. "Tell me, little doe, what have you done to deserve an
orgasm?"

Frustration flashes through me, and I give his chest a
shove that doesn't even move him one inch. "Bastard."

Amusement dances in his eyes as he gives me a sharp

smile. "If you want me to make you come, I would suggest working on your manners. And your obedience."

Before I can retort, he uses his grip on my throat to pull me down from the counter. My feet hit the tiled floor with a faint thud. But Kaden doesn't release my throat. Instead, he pushes forward.

Throwing my arms out to the sides, I try to brace myself as Kaden forces me to bend backwards over the counter. My dress is still bunched around my waist, leaving my legs and pussy bare.

The edge of the counter digs into the small of my back, but I can do nothing against Kaden's strength, so I just arch my back until I'm standing with my feet on the floor while most of my back is pressed flat against the counter.

"Kaden," I say. "This is very uncomfortable."

"It will be even more uncomfortable for you if you move before I give you permission."

And with that ominous declaration, he at last releases my throat. However, I'm smart enough to take his threat seriously, so I remain where I am.

Faint metallic clinking echoes between the pale walls. But right now, my gaze is limited to the ceiling, so I can't tell what Kaden is doing.

I suck in a sharp breath as something cool and hard suddenly appears on my skin.

My heart pounds in my chest as I feel that cool metal around my waist and between my legs. Two locks click into place. I barely dare to breathe.

"You can stand up straight now," Kaden tells me.

Straightening from the counter, I stare down at the contraption that I'm now locked into.

There is a thin metal band around my waist, which is

locked in place with a small padlock. At the front of that band is another wider one, which is also locked with a padlock. The wider band runs straight down between my legs and then thins again as it runs over my ass to where it's attached to the back of the one around my waist.

Incredulity clangs inside me like giant bells.

With that disbelief probably shining from my entire face, I drag my gaze up to Kaden and gape at him. "What the hell is this?"

His eyes gleam with wickedness as he gives me a knowing smile. "It's a chastity belt."

"A *what?*"

Reaching down, he pats the flat metal band between my legs that is now blocking my pussy. "In case you get any ideas about how this date is going to end."

I just stare at him in stunned silence for a while, my eyes wide and my mouth open. "You are unbelievable."

After shoving his hand away from my now imprisoned pussy, I grab the metal bands and yank at them. But it's futile. Without unlocking the two padlocks, it's impossible to get this damn thing off me.

"You should probably go back to your date," Kaden says with a nonchalant shrug. "Before he comes looking for you."

Abandoning my efforts to pry the damn chastity belt off, I instead pull my dress back down to hide it and then shoot a venomous look at Kaden. "I'm going to fucking kill you."

He just grins wider.

With a snarl, I shove past him and stalk to the door. It takes all of my self-control not to throw the door open so hard that it bangs against the wall.

Unbelievable.

A chastity belt?

The nerve of that arrogant presumptuous fucking dictator. I am going to ruin him so badly for this alone that he will never be able to be a functioning member of society again.

When I reach the table where Josh is still sitting, I have to remember not to stomp angrily with every step. Instead, I use every smidgen of patience I possess and paint an apologetic smile on my face as I slide back into my seat.

"I'm sorry," I say with an appropriately embarrassed expression on my features. "There was quite the line to the restroom."

He just waves a hand. "Don't worry about it. It's a busy place." A laugh rolls from his chest. "And we can't control nature, so to speak."

"Indeed." Picking up my utensils again, I hurry to change the topic. "So, what were you saying earlier about—"

A jolt shoots through me.

My knife and fork clatter down on the plate as I drop them in shock.

"Are you alright?" Josh asks, blinking at me in surprise from across the table.

For a moment, I can't figure out what the hell happened.

But then it happens again.

Vibrations pulse through my pussy.

I suck in a sharp breath, and then have to bite my tongue hard to stop a moan.

Disbelief once more clangs inside my skull as I stare down into my lap.

The egg vibrator. It's still inside me. *Underneath* the chastity belt.

Raising my gaze, I scan the crowded restaurant until I find my own personal torture master.

Kaden is standing halfway across the room, nonchalantly

leaning one shoulder against the wall while holding his phone in the other. His thumb moves across the screen.

Another burst of intense vibrations pulse through me.

I jerk in my seat, gripping the edge of the table hard while clamping my jaw shut to stop a whimper of pleasure.

A truly villainous smirk spreads across Kaden's lethally handsome face.

Tightening my fingers around the edge of the table, I glare at him while the vibrations silently continue to buzz inside me.

I am going to fucking *kill* him.

24

KADEN

Wicked satisfaction swirls inside my chest as I watch Alina desperately try to keep a grip on her sanity. I'm seated at a table a short distance from theirs and at an angle where I can both see every glorious flicker of emotion on Alina's face and her entire body. There is an untouched plate of salad before me, which I had to order so that I could get a table, but the only item on the tabletop that I care about is my phone. It sits there, screen up and unlocked, with the app that controls the vibrator open at all times.

Alina keeps a polite expression on her face as she nods at something her date said, but there is a tightness in her jaw. The rich idiot seated across from her doesn't seem to notice that, though.

He motions with his hands while he continues to talk about something utterly meaningless. Alina's hands, however, are resting on the tabletop. It might look casual to everyone else, but I can see how she is squeezing them, as if bracing for something.

I don't know what she's so frustrated about. It's been three whole minutes since the last time I reminded her pussy of who controls it.

The rich dumbass stops gesturing with his hands and instead leans forward. His right hand moves towards Alina's arm.

I slide my finger over the screen.

Alina flinches as the vibrations start back up again. While clenching her jaw hard, she flicks a glance down to where her date is almost brushing his hand against her forearm. She quickly yanks her hands back and puts them in her lap instead.

Smug satisfaction ripples through me.

Sliding my finger over the screen, I turn off the vibrations again.

At their table, Alina blows out a discreet breath, the tension in her body easing slightly.

And because I am an absolute sadist and a merciless psycho, that immediately makes me turn on the vibrations again.

Alina flinches again, and her gaze snaps to me.

I just flash her a vicious smirk.

With her jaw once again tightly clenched, she returns her attention to her date while the vibrations continue. I increase the strength. Emotions flicker across her face like tiny lightning strikes, and she blinks more than normal. Drawing in a deep breath through her nose, she curls her fingers into the fabric of her skirt and grips it hard.

The guy keeps talking, completely oblivious to her struggle.

After another twenty seconds, she starts squirming in her

seat. Her hands are gripping the cream-colored fabric of her dress so hard that her knuckles have turned white. I keep the vibrations on. She presses her knees together hard underneath the table. As if that would help.

Both panic and pleasure pulse across her gorgeous face.

I almost laugh. She thinks this is bad? Oh, if she only knew what awaits her later.

At last, her stubborn resolve shatters and she slides her gaze back to me. Desperation lines her features as she looks at me with big pleading eyes, silently begging me for mercy.

My cock hardens at the sight of it.

With a smug smile on my lips, I at last turn off the vibrator.

Alina all but slumps back in her chair.

The rich dude asks something, to which Alina waves her hands as if to assure him that she's okay. He looks unconvinced but doesn't press the issue. Instead, he calls for the check.

Finally.

While he pays for their meal, I pay for mine as well, even though I didn't touch it. Then I move towards the door right as Alina and her date get to their feet.

It brings me close enough to their table to hear him say, "Since you're not feeling well, I'll bring the car around to the front door."

Alina tries to protest, but he insists.

I slip out the door and head to the parking lot behind the building too. Since I followed them here, I know which car is his, so I stride across the parking lot until I reach it. Turning back around, I lean against the side of his car and cross my arms over my chest.

He appears about a minute later.

Confusion blows across his features when he finds me standing by his car, but he continues walking towards me. His gaze flits up and down my body. The confusion stays on his face, but it's now also joined by a generous amount of worry.

I stifle a snort. I haven't even started threatening him yet.

"Can I help you?" he asks hesitantly as he reaches his car.

However, he stops a few steps away from me. As if he's afraid that I'm going to yank out one of the knives strapped to my thighs and stab him. Which, to be fair, I am very tempted to do. But whether I actually do that depends entirely on how he responds to what I'm about to tell him.

"You've just had a lunch date with Alina Petrov," I say.

He jerks back a little in surprise. Then he composes himself again and clears his throat. "What of it?"

"And you did it because your family wants an alliance with the Petrovs."

Jutting out his chin, he tries to look down his nose at me. "I am not in the habit of discussing my family's business with strangers." He gives me a contemptuous look. "I don't know who you are, and I don't care. Now, move aside before I alert security."

"Kaden Hunter."

Deafening silence falls over the parking lot. From around the corner, the sounds of voices drift through the warm midday air and a car honks a few streets over.

The rich asshole stares at me, all color gone from his face. Alarm pulses in his eyes as he flicks another glance down at the telltale knives sheathed at my thighs. Then he swallows.

"Kaden Hunter," he repeats like a moron.

Pushing off from the car, I start towards him. He

immediately scrambles backwards, but his escape is cut short when he bumps into the car behind him. I close the distance between us, trapping him against the car.

"Your family wants an alliance with the Petrovs," I say.

It's not a question, but this time he nods anyway.

"Well, if you go anywhere near Alina Petrov ever again, you will make an enemy of the Hunter family." I cock my head. "Is that what you want?"

Fear crashes over his face, and he shakes his head with quick, jerky movements.

I arch an eyebrow. "No?"

"No," he breathes, still furiously shaking his head.

"Then I suggest you keep your hands to yourself and drive Alina straight home."

"I will. I swear."

"Hmm." I drag my gaze up and down his now trembling body. "And then I would suggest you delete her contact information and forget that you ever heard the name Alina Petrov. Because if I see you in the same room as her again, I will cut your dick off and stuff it down your throat."

A whimper rips from his chest, and he presses himself harder against the car behind his back, as if he's trying to shrink into it. Amusement ripples through me when I notice him instinctively shifting his hands down to protect his no doubt less than impressive cock.

After returning my gaze to his pathetic face, I fix him with an icy stare. "Understood?"

"Y-yes. Yes, I understand."

Lifting a hand, I give his cheek a few patronizing pats. "Good boy."

He flinches, and tries to curl in on himself.

I flash him a sadistic smile that makes him whimper again, and then I turn around and stride over to my own car.

Mission accomplished. Now, all I need to do is to go back to our house and wait for Alina to show up for the rest of her punishment.

25

ALINA

Josh acted incredibly strange while driving me home, sitting as far against his car door as was physically possible. As if he didn't want to get too close to me. I can't really blame him, though. He probably thought I had some weird disease because of how I twitched and trembled every time Kaden turned on the vibrator.

Thankfully, Josh dropped me off in front of my house and then drove away immediately instead of escorting me to the door. Because I have no intention of going home.

The moment Josh is gone, I start straight for the Hunters' house.

I'm going to kill that son of a bitch. Does he have any idea how fucking difficult it was to stop myself from orgasming right there in the middle of that restaurant? That final time when he kept it on until I begged him with my eyes, I was one fucking second away from climaxing when he finally turned it off.

With fury whirling inside me, I turn down another street.

A jolt shoots through me.

"No," I gasp.

My steps falter and I stare down at my body in panic as vibrations start pulsing through my pussy again.

I'm not even halfway to their house yet!

While hurrying forward again, I try to yank against that damn chastity belt through the fabric of my dress. But I've already tried getting it off. Several times. And it's not working.

Pleasure flickers through my body as the vibrations continue. But this time, they're not strong enough to actually push me over the edge. Still, they keep pulsing. Pushing me towards an orgasm and building the tension inside my body without giving me that sweet release.

When I at last turn onto their street, I feel as if I'm going to die from the unrelenting stimulations. I'm going to shatter from the tension thrumming inside me. Like a raging storm trapped in a tiny glass bottle.

Moans and desperate whines spill from my lips.

My whole body shakes and I wobble with every step.

It feels like my mind is unraveling and my body is melting.

I need release. Or I need the vibrations to stop. I need it more than I need air.

Halfway up the path to their front door, my knees buckle.

Crashing down on the ground, I curl in on myself and just drag in shuddering breaths. The vibrations continue, fraying my sanity with every excruciating second. I lift my head and stare at the door a few steps away. Part of me is hoping that Kaden will appear there and carry me inside. But the logical part of my brain knows that Kaden is not Prince Charming. Kaden is the villain.

So I do the only thing I can do.

I use every smidgen of strength and resolve that I possess.

And crawl up to their front door.

My body trembles with the pent-up release as I raise my hand to pound it against the door.

It's opened a few seconds later by Jace, who stares down at me with raised eyebrows.

"Uhm…" he says.

Pitiful whimpers escape my throat as I crawl through the door and into their elegant wooden hallway. Kaden is nowhere to be seen.

For a few seconds, Jace just watches me from where he towers over me. Then he closes the front door while raising his voice to shout, "Dude! She's here. You might want to ease up a bit."

Only silence answers him from upstairs.

And the vibrations continue.

I curl my fingers into fists and pound one hand against the floor while the tension crackling inside me steals every ounce of willpower that remains in my body.

"Please," I sob.

God, I truly must be desperate if I'm begging Jace Hunter for help. He hates my family just as much as Kaden does.

For another moment, I just lie there on the floor, trembling and trying to keep my fraying mind together. Then Jace raises his voice again.

"Kaden!" he calls. "She literally crawled across our threshold on her hands and knees. I don't think she's going to make it up the stairs. So unless you want me to carry her up, you should probably turn that off."

The vibrations stop immediately.

I suck in a gasp.

My heart slams so hard against my ribs that, for a while, the loud pounding of it is all I can hear.

But with the vibrations at last gone, I can finally think again.

Bracing my hands on the smooth wooden floorboards, I push myself up and stagger to my feet. Jace watches me with a mildly curious expression on his face. I drag in another deep breath as I look up to meet his eyes.

"Thank you," I say, my voice coming out in a croak.

"Don't thank me," he replies, though not unkindly. "You will be on your knees crawling again soon enough."

An exhausted sigh rips from my chest. Because I fear that he might be right. I need to get this chastity belt off, and it's not coming off unless Kaden unlocks it. And given the fucking torture he has put me through today, he is not particularly happy that I went on this date with Josh. If he turns on the vibrator again and leaves it on without letting me come, I will be on my knees crawling within minutes.

Jace starts towards the doorway to their living room, but then he pauses after only a few steps. Turning around, he looks back at me again. "Piece of advice? Kneel, place your palms flat on the floor, and then press your forehead to the ground before his feet."

I blink and then frown at him in confusion.

He lifts his broad shoulders in a casual shrug. "He likes that."

Before I can think of a reply, he turns back around and disappears into the living room.

I stare after him.

Kneel and press my forehead to the floor before Kaden's feet? I don't fucking think so.

There is a bat leaning against the inside of a metal container that looks like it's made to hold umbrellas. Actually, there are *three* bats in there. And not a single umbrella. After casting a quick look towards the doorway to the living room, I wrap my fingers around the handle of the closest bat and carefully pull it out.

My heart patters in my chest, but the bat comes free without making the other two clank against each other.

While imagining the sound Kaden will make when I slam this into his fucking head, I adjust my grip on the handle and hurry up the steps to the upstairs corridor. It's empty as well, so I stalk down it until I reach the door to Kaden's room.

Not bothering to so much as knock, I simply yank open the door and storm inside with the bat raised in my right hand.

Kaden is standing in the middle of his room. As usual, it's meticulously neat and clean with the bed perfectly made and everything in its proper place.

When I opened the door, there was a dark and dangerous look on his face. But as soon as his gaze lands on the bat in my hand, I swear I can see amusement glitter in his cold eyes.

It makes me fucking furious.

Before he can even say anything, I shift the bat into a two-handed grip and swing it straight at his head.

Without breaking eye contact, Kaden simply yanks up a hand and grabs the bat midair.

I jerk back in surprise. With both hands still on the handle, I try to pull the bat free. But even though he's holding it with just one hand, the damn thing doesn't move an inch no matter how much I yank at it.

Mirth dances across his severe face again.

"Tell me, little doe," he begins with a faint smile on his lips. "Once you had bashed my head in with my brother's bat, what was your plan for finding the keys to the chastity belt? If I'm dead, I can't tell you where they are."

"You don't need to tell me where they are."

He arches a dark brow. "Oh?"

"I already know."

"Do tell."

"You're organized and meticulous, which means that you would never leave them lying around just anywhere. But you also crave absolute control and you live for power plays, so you want the keys within easy reach so that you can dangle them in front of my face. Literally. Which means that the keys are in your pocket."

The smile that spreads across his face makes my heart lurch. And not for the reason that it probably should.

Faint metallic clinking fills the room as Kaden slides his other hand into the pocket of his dark pants and pulls out a small ring with two keys on it.

His eyes glint as he dangles them in the air while that smile stays on his lips. "Clever."

I lunge for the keys.

The moment my right hand leaves the bat, Kaden yanks it out of my grip while simultaneously jerking his other hand up so that I can't reach the keys. My fingers swipe through the air right where the keys used to be a second too late.

Kaden tuts and shakes his head.

Now weaponless, I lower my arms again and instead cross them over my chest as I glare up at the annoying man before me.

"You're lucky," Kaden begins, and then tosses the bat towards the other side of the room. It hits the floor with a loud wooden clattering. "That my brother is not as particular about his bats as I am about my knives. When will you learn not to touch another man's weapons without his permission?"

"When you learn not to put a chastity belt on a woman without her permission," I snipe back.

He chuckles.

Still holding the keys out of my reach, he shakes his hand, making them jingle. "You want these?" He shoots a pointed look down at the floor before his feet. "You know what to do."

Huh. So, apparently, Jace did know what he was talking about.

Still doesn't mean I'm actually going to do it, though.

Throwing my arms out in frustration, I instead snap, "What was I supposed to do? I told you that my father set up that date. I didn't want to go on it either, but I had to because I need to follow his orders."

Kaden's expression darkens. Sliding the keys back into his pocket, he takes a step forward while locking hard eyes on me. I take a step back. He keeps advancing, backing me towards the wall.

"No," he says, his voice now low and lethal. "You don't need to follow his orders."

My heart slams against my ribs as my back suddenly hits the smooth dark wall behind me. Kaden keeps coming until he is standing so close that my chest almost brushes against his stomach when I draw in unsteady breaths. Raising his hand, he trails soft fingers along my jaw.

Then he wraps his hand around my throat and levels a stare dripping with authority on me. "The only orders you need to follow are *mine*."

A dark thrill races down my spine at the way he growls that final word. My pulse flutters underneath his strong hand as he flexes his fingers around my throat. I swallow.

"He didn't touch me," I say. "You told me that no other man can touch me. Josh never did. We only had lunch."

"It doesn't matter. You do not go on dates with other men."

Frustration flashes through me, and I shove against his chest. "You can't just keep making up rules like this and expect me to follow them!"

His hand disappears from my throat in an instant. I suck in a startled breath as it instead closes around my right wrist. Yanking against his grip, I try to pull my hand back, but Kaden simply moves it up over my head.

Cold metal presses against my skin. Then a click echoes into the otherwise dead silent room.

I snap my gaze up.

My wrist is now trapped high above my head by a set of handcuffs that had already been secured to the metal ring in the wall.

Oh great. The sarcasm flows through me. He had already prepared this little trap for me before I even walked through the door.

I struggle futilely as Kaden grabs my other wrist and locks that in above my head as well. Metallic rattling fills the room as I yank against my restraints while Kaden strolls away.

"What the hell are you doing?" I demand.

A thud sounds as he closes the door to his bedroom on the way to that damn cabinet with all of his equipment.

My eyes widen as he pulls out a massive ball gag before starting back to me.

"Kaden," I warn, pulling against the handcuffs again.

Unflinching command rolls off his broad shoulders as he strides back to me and grabs my jaw. I throw my head from side to side, but I might as well be a doll in the face of his overwhelming power.

Fury and fear and terrible lust burns through me as Kaden forces the ball gag into my mouth. Once it's in place behind my teeth, he tightens the straps around the back of my head, trapping the gag there.

"Since you refuse to tell me what I want to hear, you have lost speaking privileges," Kaden declares.

I try to curse him to hell, but only garbled noise makes it past the red silicon ball that fills my mouth.

Kaden grabs my jaw again, holding my head motionless while he locks merciless eyes on me. "The gag stays on until you're ready to beg."

Releasing my jaw, he slides his hand down my throat and then over my collarbones. Lightning skitters across my skin in its wake, and my clit throbs. With a knowing smile lurking at the corner of his lips, he slides his hands to my back. My heart jerks as he starts zipping down my dress.

The cream-colored fabric slides down my chest as the zipper loosens the dress until it's bunched around my waist. Kaden slips his hands underneath the dress and guides it over my hips, letting it fall to the floor.

My skin prickles and my nipples harden at the exposure.

It was a strapless dress, so I wasn't wearing a bra underneath. And since Kaden already took my panties back in that restroom, now that the dress is gone, I'm left standing there completely naked except for the metal chastity belt.

Heat flickers through my veins and pools at my core.

Kaden slides two fingers down the center of my chest, making a shudder course through my already high-strung body.

A smile full of dark promises graces his lips as he curls his fingers around the top of the chastity belt and pulls slightly, forcing me to arch my back.

"And *this*," he begins, giving it another tug, "and the

vibrator stay on until I'm satisfied that you will obey my orders. And *my* orders only."

I try to protest and curse him again, but the gag muffles all of my words.

He lets out a smug chuckle and then takes a step back. Slipping his hand into his pocket, he pulls out his phone.

Both excitement and dread swirl inside me, fighting like wolves. But before I can figure out which one is winning, Kaden turns on the vibrator again.

A moan tears from my chest, and my eyes roll back as pleasure once more floods my veins. Yanking against the handcuffs, I wiggle my hips as those incredible vibrations pulse through my pussy.

Tension builds, pushing me towards that sweet edge.

But right before I can crest it, Kaden turns off the vibrator.

My eyes snap open again, and I try to threaten him. But that's when I realize something else.

I'm drooling.

Because of the massive ball gag, I can't swallow the saliva that gathers in my mouth. So it just slips out over my bottom lip, slides down my chin, and drips down onto my chest.

Heat sears my cheeks.

But before I can fully process it, the vibrator starts pulsing inside me again.

Another moan escapes my chest, and I squirm against the wall as pleasure soars through me once more.

Kaden just stands there before me, watching me drool and moan and whimper as he brings me to the edge over and over again without letting me come. This is even worse than the continuous vibrations on the walk over here. Because now, he can see my face and can tell when I'm about to come, so that he can bring me all the way to the edge before denying me the release that I so desperately need.

My clit throbs with need and my whole body trembles with the pent-up tension.

And I know that it's messed up, but I'm so fucking turned on by the power that Kaden wields right now. The power that he wields as ruthlessly as his blades.

Naked and handcuffed to his wall, I can do nothing to stop him as he floods my body with pleasure and wrings every emotion out of my soul before taking it all away again. And with the ball gag filling my mouth, I can't even beg him for mercy. Can't even control my body enough to stop myself from drooling.

Because right now, Kaden controls everything. My body. My soul. My entire fucking existence. He decides whether I finally get the release I need or if my mind shatters and I die from the tension trapped inside me.

I make it to ten almost-orgasms before I break down.

Staring up at him with desperate pleading eyes, I try to beg for mercy through the gag.

He arches an eyebrow at me. "What was that?"

Even though I know he's doing it on purpose because he knows that I can't speak, I still try again. Only garbled mumbling makes it out.

"Can't hear anything." He raises his phone. "Oh, well. Let's go again then."

Metal rattles as I thrash against the handcuffs in panic. I won't survive one more time. He needs to let me come now or my mind will break.

Kaden chuckles, and thankfully lowers his phone. Hope floods my chest like a sparkling summer lake as he slides his phone back into his pocket.

"Are you ready to beg?" he demands.

I nod frantically.

With a satisfied smirk on his stupidly hot face, he reaches behind my head and unbuckles the straps there before pulling the gag out of my mouth.

My jaws ache from being forced wide open like that for so long, but I barely feel it over the relief that washes through me. After finally swallowing properly, I drag in a deep breath.

A thud sounds as Kaden tosses the gag onto his dresser. His eyes stay locked on mine, though. And he raises his eyebrows expectantly.

"Please," I blurt out, staring up at him desperately. "I'm begging you."

"Tell me what I want to hear."

"I won't let any other man touch me."

"And…?" he coaxes.

"And I won't go on any more dates that my father sets up. Please. I swear it."

He flashes forward. Wrapping his hand around my jaw, he pushes the back of my head against the wall while he leans close enough to growl his next words against my lips. "You will not go on *any* dates. Whether they're set up by your father or not. Understood?"

"Yes," I gasp. My spine tingles and my clit throbs at the ruthless command in his voice and the nearness of his lips. "Now please, *please*, take the chastity belt off."

"Beg me to fuck you," he orders, merciless power dripping from every word.

I blink up at him. "What?"

"You want me to let you come? Then beg me to fuck you."

Sudden realization pulses through me. This isn't only about the date with Josh. This is also about what happened on

Friday. I forced his hand. I gave him an ultimatum and made him break his own rule not to fuck a Petrov.

Victory bursts behind my ribcage like glittering fireworks.

I won that battle. He might have won all other times, but two days ago, I took his power away from him and made him do something that he had sworn not to do.

It takes all of my restraint not to grin.

That's why he wants—no, *needs*—me to beg now. He needs *me* to beg *him* to fuck me so that he can regain some of the power he lost.

I almost laugh with giddiness from realizing that *I* took some of Kaden's power from him. But then the reality of my situation, right here, washes over me again. I might have won two days ago, but right now, I am entirely at his mercy. If he wants me to beg, I'm not exactly in any position to refuse.

But I don't really mind. Because I actually do want him to fuck me. After all of this teasing and edging and torture with a damn vibrator, I want his cock to be the thing that finally makes me come. I want to feel him inside me, pounding into me like he can't get enough of me. Fucking me hard and dominantly and without fear of breaking me. Because then I will know that he is still just as desperate for me as I am for him.

So I hold the psycho's gaze and tell him what he wants to hear. "Please, Kaden. I'm begging you to fuck me."

Satisfaction blows across his face, and I can almost see him release a breath of relief at the way the power scales tip back in his favor. But the fact that I know about it makes those uneven power scales meaningless.

"That's right," he says. After pulling out a set of keys from his pocket, he releases my wrists from the handcuffs and then finally begins unlocking the chastity belt. "*You* beg *me* to fuck you. Nothing else."

I want to laugh, because now I know just how much I have messed with his head, but I manage to stop myself before any sound can make it out of my mouth. I'm not about to screw this up when he's finally releasing me.

Two soft clicks sound.

And then the metal bands around my body finally disappear as Kaden pulls the chastity belt off me and tosses it down on the floor.

I drag in a deep breath.

With relief pulsing through my veins, I reach down to remove that damn vibrator too. But Kaden's hand locks around my wrist, stopping me.

"I'll do it," he says.

Heaving a sigh, I let my arms drop back by my sides.

While holding my gaze, Kaden slides his hand up the inside of my thigh. A shiver rolls through me and my skin tingles at his touch. He traces his fingers around my entrance for a few seconds before gently pulling out the vibrator.

After so long, the loss of it is almost jarring.

Kaden twists and places it on his dresser before moving back so that he is standing right in front of me again. Desire burns in his eyes as he drags his gaze over my body. My chest heaves even though he's not even touching me yet.

"Say it again," he demands, returning his intense gaze to mine.

Lust sears through me as I look up at him, holding his gaze. "I'm begging you to fuck me."

He surges forward.

Sliding his hands into my hair, he tilts my head back and

kisses me like he's dying and the air in my lungs is the only thing that will save him.

My heart does a somersault at the furious desperation in his movements. In the way he curls his fingers in my hair. In the way his tongue dominates mine. In *everything*.

God above, this man was desperate for this. For *me*.

I draw my hands down his hard abs and then slip them underneath his shirt, pushing the fabric upwards. Kaden takes his hands off me only long enough to grab the shirt now bunched around his chest and yank it over his head. It flutters to the floor while he slides his hands back into my hair and claims my lips again.

He moans into my mouth as I draw my fingers over his naked skin along the top of his pants. That incredible sound makes my heart stutter.

While kissing him back with equal fury, I make quick work of his pants. Shoving the zipper down, I slip my hand underneath his boxers and free his cock.

Another guttural moan tears from his chest when my fingers wrap around his hard length.

My spine tingles and my stomach lurches.

I slide my hand up and down his thick shaft, drawing a shudder and another dark moan from him.

Astonishment pulses through me. Those moans... Such fucking incredible sounds. And I drew those from him.

As if he also realizes what he just betrayed, he drops his hands from my hair and instead grabs my thighs hard while kissing me with such rage that I can barely breathe. Air explodes from my lungs as he lifts me off the floor and slams me up against the wall.

I slide my hand up and down his cock again in retaliation

for his manhandling, and I'm rewarded with another moan that he only manages to stifle halfway through.

"Keep that up and I will handcuff you again and fuck you into the next century," he growls against my mouth.

I jerk him off again, making his lethal body tremble. "Sounds good to me."

Tightening his grip on my thighs, he angles my body while he continues to wage war on my mouth. I release his cock and lock my fingers around the back of his neck as he positions his tip against my entrance.

"Beg me again," he demands between rage-filled kisses.

"Fuck you," I growl against his mouth.

He bites my bottom lip hard. "*Beg.*"

"Please fuck me." The words rip out of my lungs like a snarl, full of fury and frustration and desperate need.

He slams into me.

Throwing my head back, I gasp into the ceiling as he draws out and thrusts back in again, sheathing himself all the way to the hilt.

Pleasure spears through my body at the feeling of his massive cock filling me completely.

I slide my hands down to his shoulders, digging my fingers into the hard muscles there while Kaden starts up a brutal pace. My back hits the smooth wall with every dominant thrust of his hips. Pleasure soars inside me.

He fucks me like I'm indestructible. Like he knows that I can take anything his lethal body and twisted mind throws at me. And the knowledge of that makes me feel lightheaded.

That terrible tension that has been trapped inside me for hours now spins and whirls and rages like a storm inside my soul. Lightning crackles through my veins as Kaden pounds into me. I careen towards an orgasm that I know will end me.

"I hate you so fucking much," I pant, raking my fingers over Kaden's muscles as he rails me mercilessly.

"Good." While still pounding into me, he leans forward and kisses the side of my neck. "Now come for me."

The moment his lips brush against that sensitive spot below my ear, release crashes through me like a bolt of electricity.

I gasp as waves of pleasure ricochet through my body.

After the hours of being denied that sweet release, the feeling is so intense that I lose track of space and time.

All that exists is him. His hands on my thighs, his lips on my neck, his pulsing cock inside me. I crave his touch, his scent, his dominant hands, the feeling of his naked skin against mine, like a drug.

Desperate groans tear from Kaden's chest and pleasure pulses across his face as release crashes over him too.

And God, it's the most incredible thing I've ever seen.

Astonishment floods my veins as I watch the pleasure and incredulity that pulse in his eyes when he comes.

When the last of the orgasm fades, we just remain like that for a while, still clinging to each other. It looks like there is a war raging behind Kaden's eyes as he watches me.

Dread pricks at my insides, because now that we're done, I'm pretty sure that he is going to throw me out of his room and tell me to go home. But after the hours of edging and then this mind-blowing orgasm, my body is so utterly spent that I don't think I'll be able to stand on my own. Let alone walk back to our house.

That storm of indecision in Kaden's eyes vanishes. He has made a decision.

But instead of throwing me out, he surprises me by carrying me into his bathroom. Shock pulses through me as he gently sets me down in his bathtub, fills it with warm water, and then washes the drool and cum off my skin. Since I'm too stunned to speak, I just sit there, staring at him.

Once I'm clean, he towels me off and then carries me to his bed.

My heart pounds erratically in my chest as he sets me down in the middle of his soft bed and then starts pulling off his pants. While I secretly do want to go again, I don't think my body can handle another round with Kaden right now.

But when he's down to only his underwear, he leaves them on and simply climbs into bed next to me.

The mattress sways underneath me as he adjusts his position until he's lying on his side. Then he wraps his arms around me and pulls me towards him until my body is flush against his. My heart slams so hard against my ribs that he must surely be able to feel it. I glance up uncertainly at his face.

He just breathes in deeply, as if savoring the scent of me, and then rests his chin on the top of my head.

Tentatively, I slide my arms around his muscular chest. A low satisfied sound comes from deep inside him, and he tightens his arms around me.

My heart flutters.

And at that moment, I let myself forget, just for a little while, that Kaden Hunter is my family's worst enemy.

26

KADEN

The sounds of gunshots echo through the air. Staring at the paper target across the room, I imagine that it's that rich idiot's face as I fire again and again.

"Alright, that's half an hour," Jace says from next to me. "My patience for broody silence ran out five minutes ago, so start talking. What's wrong?"

The rest of the firing range is empty. Fortunately. Partly, that's due to the fact that it's one of the smaller ones and it's also a late Tuesday evening. But the rest of it is because of me. The people who were already in here when Jace and I showed up took one look at the murderous expression on my face and decided to make themselves scares and live to see another day.

I fire off two more rounds. "Nothing."

"Uh-huh," he scoffs. "Then why did you come with me to the firing range instead of staying at home with your throwing knives?"

Because every time I hold a knife now, all I can think about is how I want to trace it over Alina's beautiful body and watch as she squirms and whimpers on my bed before I fuck her into oblivion.

But I would rather stab myself in the eye than admit that to Jace, so I just cut him a sideways glance. "Because you're a crap shot and you need the practice."

"Bullshit." He puffs out his chest and stabs a finger at me. "I'm the best marksman of us all, and you know it."

Since I've always favored knives, he is at least a better marksman than I am. But that is another thing I will never admit to his face. After all, I don't want to be responsible for inflating his already massive ego.

So I just snort and turn back to the target. "Whatever you need to tell yourself, little brother."

Next to me, Jace yanks up his gun and fires three consecutive shots into his target. All of them dead center.

I stifle a groan. I can practically feel his smirk from over here.

But thankfully, he doesn't say anything else. Just goes back to his target practice. I do too. Or at least, I try to.

My mind constantly keeps drifting back to Alina. To her beautiful face. To those big gray eyes that glitter when she smiles. To that brilliant mind of hers. To how right it feels to fuck her like she's already mine. To how much I fucking love cuddling with her afterwards. And most of all, to how much I hated seeing her sit at a table, eating lunch with another man. She somehow manages to draw all kinds of emotions from me when I'm not even supposed to have any of those frustrating feelings that normal people have. It's infuriating.

Fucking hell, I hate what Alina is doing to me. I used to be a cold and emotionless strategist who was always above the petty emotions of mere mortals. But now she's making me feel all kinds of things. And I need to make it stop.

"Do you ever get jealous?" The question is out of my mouth before I can stop it.

Clenching my jaw, I keep my eyes on the paper target ahead while I brace myself for Jace's reaction.

But he doesn't laugh or mock me. Doesn't do anything at all to make me feel as ridiculous as I know I sound.

Instead, he just lowers his gun and turns to face me before asking, "Of what?"

I fire two more times in an effort to relieve some of the tension thrumming inside me. It doesn't work. Forcing out a breath, I instead lower the gun and turn to meet my brother's gaze. Only genuine curiosity swirls in his brown eyes.

"All the girls you fuck..." I begin and then trail off, trying to figure out how to even explain this. Flipping on the safety of the gun, I holster it and then clear my throat before continuing. "When you see them later, talking to another guy, does it ever make you want to cut the man's hands off and nail them to his balls?"

Jace raises his eyebrows. But I think it's more due to the strangely specific punishment that I described than anything else.

Cocking his head, he considers for a while and then simply says, "No."

I resist the urge to scowl. That was not the answer I was hoping for. Flexing my fingers, I try to dispel the panic that flickers through me now that I know that Jace doesn't feel like that too.

"Why not?" I barely manage to press it out without making it sound like a demand.

He shrugs. "Because they don't matter." Bitterness suddenly flashes across his face, and he turns around and fires several times into his target. "Nothing fucking matters."

Pain twists my cold black heart. I hate seeing Jace like this. I wish he would at last start the conversation. I can make him talk from there, but I need him to start. Otherwise, he's never going to admit to anything.

But I really fucking hate seeing him like this, so I try anyway. "Jace."

Fear and anger flash across his features, which means that he must be able to tell from my tone alone where this is going. Clenching the gun hard, he slowly turns back to me. When he meets my gaze again, his eyes are hard and merciless.

"Look," I begin carefully. "If—"

"Don't."

I hold his unflinching stare and try again. "If you don't want to—"

"I swear to God, if you finish that sentence, I will fucking shoot you in the head." Rage and fear pulse in his eyes, and he flexes his fingers on the gun. "Do you understand?"

For a while, we just stand there, staring each other down in silence. I want to keep pushing. I want to drag the truth out of his stubborn mouth and make him talk until he understands what I want him to know. But I can't. No matter how much it rips my fucking heart to shreds to see my little brother like this, I can't force him to do anything until he decides that he wants to do it.

So I dip my chin. Just a fraction. Silently acknowledging that I'm not going to force him to talk about the thing that I'm not supposed to know.

A tiny breath escapes his chest and the tension bleeds out of his shoulders.

"I was just going to say," I begin, and shoot him a highly calculated look of mock annoyance. "That if you don't want to cut the guy's hands off when you see him with a girl you've fucked, then what, exactly, does that mean?"

It's a lie. That was not at all what I was going to say because I have already asked that question. I know it. And he knows it. But neither of us is going to acknowledge it.

Blowing out a long breath that is filled with even more relief that I pretend not to notice, he rolls his shoulders back and lets that carefree posture back into his body. His fingers stop squeezing the gun so hard.

"It means that she's not worth it," he replies, and lifts his now loose shoulders in a nonchalant shrug.

I narrow my eyes, forcing my mind to block out my worries about Jace and instead once again focus fully on the infuriating enigma that is my feelings for Alina. "Explain."

"Okay, look. When I fuck a girl, or multiple girls too for that matter, I'm doing it just because it's fun and to get some stress release. It's just sex. So if she then goes on to fuck five more guys after me, why would I care?" He snorts and rolls his eyes. "Not that I would ever leave a girl in such an unfulfilled state that she would be able to fuck another guy straight after a night with me. But you know what I'm saying."

No, I don't. I don't know what he's saying at all. Because I would fucking slaughter every single person on this entire campus if Alina ever left my bed and then went to fuck someone else.

I blow out a long breath, trying to suppress the sudden impulse to kill everything and everyone.

"So," I begin once I have my emotions under control again. "If you were, *hypothetically*, to get angry when you saw a girl that you've fucked out on a date with someone else, what would that mean?"

"That you care about her." His answer is immediate, and his eyes are serious as he holds my gaze.

Fuck. Fucking fuck.

He's wrong, though. I don't care about her. I don't care one fucking bit about Alina fucking Petrov.

Jace's eyes search my face, and when he speaks, his tone is careful. "If this is, *hypothetically*, about Alina—"

"It's not."

"*If* it is, then just… be careful. Remember that she's a Petrov. An enemy."

"I can handle the fucking Petrovs."

"I know. I'm just saying, if Alina is playing you…"

If Alina is playing me, then that means that she has managed to outsmart me. *Me*. No one outmaneuvers me. So if she ever managed a feat *that* impressive, I would fucking marry her on the spot. But she can never outsmart me, which means that she's not playing me.

"I know what I'm doing," I tell Jace, my voice coming out harsher than I meant it to.

He sucks his teeth, still holding my gaze. Then gives me a nod.

He knows that I'm lying. Just like I know that he is lying about being fine. I don't want to talk about it, and he doesn't want to talk about it.

So we do what we came here for.

We stand there, side by side, shooting at our targets and pretending it's our demons.

27

ALINA

It has been five days, and I still haven't been able to stop thinking about that afternoon in Kaden's bedroom. About the way he pushes me to my limits, knowing that I can take it. About how his lethal body feels pressed against mine. About how he fucks me like he owns me. And more importantly, how he moans and shudders when I touch him, as if *I* own *him* too. About how much I love cuddling with him, feeling his strong arms around me and hearing the steady beat of his heart when I rest my cheek on his chest. And the way he holds me as if I'm something precious.

It's absolutely infuriating. Because it's Kaden fucking Hunter. How can something feel so right with someone who is so wrong?

Yanking my locker open, I pull out my bag and slam it down on the bench before me in frustration.

"Now you're suddenly putting some strength into your arms?" a taunting voice comes from my left.

I ignore it, but move quickly to get dressed. Jane and Leslie haven't stolen my clothes and towel again since that first time, but they still make me wait for everyone else to shower first. And I don't care enough to fight them about it.

Kaden might have left me alone this entire week, instead focusing on tormenting my brothers, but Jane and Leslie, on the other hand, have not. Just like every day of every week, they do something or other to make me feel like a worthless waste of space. And their constant mocking comments and petty acts of cruelty have worn me down more than I want to admit.

Pulling my pants up, I manage to zip them up and button them right before the two apparently tireless mean girls appear beside me. I reach for my shirt, but Jane snatches it from the bench right before I can grab it. I'm at least wearing a bra, so I'm thankfully not entirely naked above the waist as I turn to face them.

"What do you want?" I ask, barely managing to keep the venom from my voice.

Jane, who is still holding my shirt in one hand, drags a demeaning glance up and down my body. "Look at you. We're three months into the semester, and you're still as skinny as the day we got here. Do you have some kind of disease that makes it impossible for you to actually gain muscles, or what?"

Next to her, Leslie snickers and flicks a mocking look over my body.

I suppress the instinct to cross my arms over my chest, and instead simply reply in a dead serious tone, "Yes, I do. Didn't you know? I thought the teachers had already informed everyone since it's highly contagious."

Both of them jerk back, and Jane drops my shirt as if it had burned her. Or infected her.

Quickly crouching down, I snatch it up before she can

grab it again. A smug chuckle escapes my lips as I straighten.

Realization pulses across their faces.

I flash them a smirk before pulling the shirt over my head.

However, during those few seconds that my vision is obscured by the shirt, they close the distance between us again. I've barely managed to tug the hem down before Leslie gives me a shove that sends me stumbling backwards. My back smacks into the locker behind me with a thud.

The few other girls who are still getting dressed glance our way. But none of them does anything to intervene. Because of the unspoken rule that the top students get to shower first, everyone who is still here, except for Jane and Leslie, is down at the bottom of the pecking order. Just like me. And they are apparently reluctant to become the mean girls' next target. I can't really blame them for that, though.

"Did no one ever teach you not to piss off your superiors?" Leslie demands, as both she and Jane corner me against the locker.

"Oh, they did," I reply, and then flick a dismissive look up and down their bodies. "But since I don't see any of my superiors in this particular room, I think I'm good."

Anger flashes in their eyes.

Then Jane shoots me a pointed stare. "And *this* is why no one likes you."

Logically, I know that she is probably just making that up, but hurt still stabs through my chest.

"Aww, look at that. She's hurt." Jane glances at Leslie. "Should we tell her?"

Leslie cocks her head, her blue eyes still on my face. "I don't think she can handle it if we do."

"Then we should definitely tell her."

"Agreed."

"Tell me what?" I snap while desperately wishing that I was strong enough to knock their damned heads together and simply walk away from here. But with both of them trapping me against the row of metal lockers like this, I can't leave unless they move.

"No one wants you here because you're messing it up for everyone," Jane says as if it's the most obvious thing ever that I really should already know. "No one wants to be partnered with you during sparring lessons, because it makes them fall behind in their training too since you can't keep up. And no one wants you on their team during team challenges because it's a guaranteed way to lose."

Pain twists my insides. Of all the mean things they have said to me this semester, this is by far the worst. Because I don't know how to convince myself that it isn't true.

"Not to mention the fact that you're preventing a real aspiring assassin from attending Blackwater," she continues. "You're a legacy student from the great Petrov family, so the school can't refuse you entry. Which means that they had to take a spot from someone who deserved to be here and give it to you instead."

More hurt flashes through me, and I swallow against the sudden nausea crawling up my throat.

"So why are people like Carla still nice to you even though you're just messing everything up for her and for everyone else?" Jane pushes on mercilessly. She holds my gaze in silence for a second. "Because you're a Petrov."

"Exactly," Leslie joins in. Crossing her arms, she gives me a disgusted once-over. "The only reason that Carla and the other girls, and literally anyone on campus, are nice to you is because they're scared that your family will target them if they're not. But no one actually *likes* you."

"And no one wants you here," Jane finishes.

My eyes burn and my throat has closed up, so all I manage to do is to stand there and stare back at them. Clenching my jaw hard, I try to keep myself from showing any of the emotions I truly feel.

Apparently, I'm unsuccessful, because Leslie and Jane exchange a knowing look.

"Told you she wouldn't be able to handle the truth," Leslie says with a shrug.

And with that, they turn and stride out of the locker room.

The three remaining girls in here with me glance from the now closing door and towards me. One of them opens her mouth as if to say something, but I can't handle it right now. So I just turn around and hurry around to the other side of the metal lockers. I haven't even finished getting dressed yet. My socks and shoes and my bag are still by my open locker, but I just need a moment to compose myself.

Once I reach a spot diagonally from the door, where none of the other three girls can see me, I at last let myself crumble.

Tears burn my eyes as I lean back against the wall. It only takes another few seconds for them to start falling. Pain radiates from my heart.

Pressing a hand over my mouth to muffle my sobs, I slide down the wall until I'm sitting on the floor. Tears stream down my cheeks. My chest aches.

Soft rustling sounds come from across the room where the other three girls finish getting dressed. I will miss lunch entirely if I stay here too long. But I can't face the outside world just yet. Not when my body is shaking with each painful sob that rips out of my soul.

So I sit there on the cold hard floor.

And I cry.

28

KADEN

O nce again, I can't help but wonder if my little doe is hiding from me. Practically her entire class has already exited the women's locker room, but there is still no sign of Alina. Leaning against the wall halfway down the corridor, I watch as yet another girl who isn't Alina walks out the door and disappears down the hall in the other direction.

With my arms crossed over my chest, I tap my fingers restlessly against my bicep as I wait another minute.

But my patience ran out days ago, and now I'm done waiting. Only targeting the useless men of the Petrov family isn't nearly as satisfying as messing with Alina, so her week of grace is now officially over.

Pushing off from the wall, I stalk down the hall and towards the door to the women's locker room. The restless impatience swirling in my chest urges me to just yank the door open and stalk inside. But just in case there are other women in there apart from Alina, I decide to edge the door open carefully and glance inside first.

I've only opened the door about two inches when I see her. And my heart stops.

Holding that tiny crack in the door open, I just stand there frozen on the floor and stare in shock at the sight before me.

Alina is sitting on the floor with her back against the wall diagonally from where the door is located, hidden behind a row of lockers. But she's visible from this angle. Her shoulders shake, and she's pressing a hand over her mouth. Tears stream down her cheeks.

She's... crying.

Alina Petrov is *crying*.

Despite all of the humiliation and danger I have subjected her to, she has never cried like this. Some broken sobs when she's begging me to let her come, yes. But never outright cried. Not like this.

Rage burns through me like wildfire. It's so intense that my vision fails for a second and I can't hear anything over the roaring in my ears.

Why is Alina crying?

Who made her cry?

My hands squeeze into fists.

However, before I can do something stupid like charging in there and demanding those answers from Alina so that I can set the world on fire for her, another woman approaches the door.

I release the handle and draw back so that I'm standing on the other side of the door instead.

A second later, a blonde girl with nervous brown eyes walks out the door. She only manages to take two steps before the door falls shut behind her and I become visible.

Her hand flies to her mouth as she gasps in surprise.

Fear floods her features a second later.

"I'm sorry," she blurts out.

Fury sears through me. My fingers close around the hilt of a knife as I take a threatening step towards her. "*You* made her cry?"

"What? No." She stumbles backwards until her back hits the gray concrete wall behind her. Fear and panic and confusion pulse in her eyes. "Who?"

"Alina Petrov," I grind out between gritted teeth, and then nod towards the closed door to the locker room. "She's crying in there. Are you saying that you made her cry?"

"No! God, no. I swear."

"Then why did you apologize?"

Desperation floods her features, and she looks up at me pleadingly as if begging me to tell her what the right answer is. When she only finds a murderous expression staring back at her, she stammers, "For... existing?"

I force out a controlled breath, trying to compose myself again. There is no need to murder this particular individual since it's now very clear that she is not the reason why Alina is currently sitting on the floor, bawling her eyes out.

However, the quick switch in my manners from furious and threatening to cold and lethal calm does nothing to reassure the woman in front of me. In fact, it seems to have the opposite effect, because she is now visibly trembling against the wall.

"Just tell me what happened," I demand. "In detail."

Rage slices through my chest when she explains what two of their classmates said to Alina, and I have to clench and unclench my hand repeatedly to keep the emotions from my features. Only a blank emotionless mask remains on my face as I listen to her explain the situation.

"Who?" I snap when she's done.

"Jane and Leslie," she stammers.

I don't know the names of all the first-years so I ask, "Do you have a photo of them?"

She gives me a jerky nod and quickly pulls out her phone. After scrolling for a few seconds, she holds up the screen to me. But her hand is shaking so badly that I can't even see the photo. I wrap my hand over hers, holding it still.

A whimper escapes her lips, as if she's afraid that I'm going to break her wrist.

Once the phone is finally still, I can make out the faces of the two girls in the photo. One blond and one with brown hair. Both of them blue-eyed and smiling like they think they're better than everyone else.

"Where are they now?" I ask.

She swallows. "They usually go to that little wooden screen thing outside behind the canteen building to smoke before the next class."

Nodding, I release her hand after burning the image of Jane and Leslie into my mind. Then I level a commanding stare on the woman before me.

"This conversation never happened," I declare. "Understood?"

She nods desperately. "Y-yes. Yes, understood."

Without another word, I spin on my heel and stalk down the hall.

All sorts of plans swirl through my brain as I make my way towards that wooden wind shelter behind the canteen building where Jane and Leslie should be. Most of those plans end with me bathing in their blood.

How dare they tell Alina that she's a waste of space? That no one likes her? That no one wants her here?

I want to peel the skin off their worthless bodies and cut

out their tongues for ever daring to speak such vicious lies. And they *are* lies. Not only because of how *I* feel about her. Carla and the rest of her housemates genuinely like Alina too. Which I know for a fact because I looked into them the moment I realized that Alina considered them friends.

But as I draw closer to the wind shelter, I'm forced to suppress my murderous instinct. Simply torturing them to death would not undo the damage they have caused. No matter how satisfying their screams of pain and fear would be. So this situation requires a different approach.

The smell of cigarettes reaches me the moment I round the building.

Strong winds blow across the asphalt, carrying more of the faint smoke from behind the short wooden wall that sticks out from the back of the building. Thick angry clouds cover the sky above, painting the already gray concrete walls around us with even bleaker hues. I can taste the oncoming storm in the air.

I stride around the wooden wind shelter to find two women standing there, both of them holding a cigarette in one hand. I move until I'm standing right in front of them.

They jump when they see me.

"Hunter," the blonde one says. It's both a greeting and a question.

When I don't reply, she quickly drops her cigarette on the ground and squashes it with her shoe while elbowing her friend, who does the same.

"We were just leaving." She gives me what I think is supposed to be a placating smile. "It's all yours."

"Leslie," I say.

"Yes?" the brown-haired one, who has been silent up until

now, replies hesitantly while glancing from side to side with now very nervous blue eyes.

I drag my gaze to the blonde girl next to her. "And Jane."

She nods, looking equally nervous. "Yes?"

"You made Alina Petrov cry." It's not a question.

Confusion and hesitation flit across their faces, and they exchange a glance.

I hurl a throwing knife into the wooden wall behind them. It passes so close to Jane that it clips some of her blonde strands. Both of them let out a short scream.

"Don't look at each other!" I snap, my voice cutting through the air like the crack of a whip. "Look at me."

Fear shines in their eyes as they slowly turn to face me fully.

"You made Alina Petrov cry," I repeat.

Silence falls over the wind shelter for a few seconds as they just stare back at me with wide eyes. Then they nod.

Merciless fury seeps through my veins as my hand shifts to my blades. Jane opens her mouth to say something, but I have already made my move.

Yanking throwing knife after throwing knife from my holsters, I hurl them into the wooden wall one after the other.

Terrified cries echo as the blades hit with sharp *thwacks*, burying themselves in two almost complete circles. One around Jane's head and the other around Leslie's.

Once I'm out of knives, and both of them have a ring of blades dangerously close to their heads, I at last lower my hands again.

Fear radiates from my two victims, pulsing through the space between us like a physical thing and leaving a sharp tang in the air.

The moment I stop throwing, their knees buckle and they crash down on the ground.

On their hands and knees, Leslie gasps in breaths and stares up at me with terrified eyes while Jane doubles over and actually vomits.

"Please, I'm sorry," Leslie blurts out.

I stare them both down with hard eyes. "I'm not the one you should be apologizing to."

Jane clumsily wipes her mouth with the back of her trembling hand and then straightens enough to meet my gaze. "I'm sorry."

"What the fuck did I just say?" I demand, and curl my fingers around the hilt of another knife.

"No, wait!" Jane shrieks, holding up her hands pleadingly. "Please. I'm begging you."

Normally, a situation like this would turn me on. My cock would harden and pleasure would course through me at the fear in their eyes and the way they're begging for mercy. But I feel none of that now. Only rage.

"Here's what's going to happen," I declare. "You are going to go and find Alina. Right now. And then you are going to apologize to her, *thoroughly*, and tell her that you didn't actually mean any of what you said to her in that locker room."

Both of them nod with quick jerky movements, still holding up their hands in front of themselves as if that would somehow protect them if I change my mind and decide that I want to carve their eyes out.

"And be convincing." I stare them down until a whimper slips from Leslie's lips and Jane curls in on herself. "If Alina doesn't believe you, I will kill you. And if she so much as suspects that *I* had anything to do with your sudden change in attitude, I will strap you to a fucking table and torture you for weeks before I allow you to die. Am I making myself clear?"

"Y-yes," they blurt out in unison.

"Good. Now get the fuck out of my sight before I change my mind."

They scramble to their feet immediately and practically trip over each other as they hurry to escape my wrath.

I rake my fingers through my hair, ruining my perfect styling. Forcing out a long breath between my teeth, I tilt my head back and stare up at the thick clouds in the sky.

But the storm that brews up there has nothing on the storm that already thrashes in my soul. And it's getting more and more difficult to contain it.

29

ALINA

Rolling my shoulders back, I straighten my spine and keep my chin raised as I at last step out of the women's locker room. A dull ache still lingers deep inside my heart, but I've managed to block out most of it. So what if Carla is only friends with me because I'm a Petrov? At least fake kindness is better than cruelty.

Strong winds hit me in the face as I stride out of the building. I glance up at the sky. Dark gray clouds swirl up there. There is a charge in the air and I can almost taste the rain that will hit us soon.

Since we have a theoretical class after lunch, I hurry over to my car so that I can dump my bulky duffel bag in the trunk instead of having to lug it around. Unlocking the car, I pop the trunk and toss the large bag inside.

"Alina."

I freeze. Then I glance down at the duffel bag full of sweaty clothes and wet towels, and wonder if I would have time to yank it back up and swing it around to hit them in the face. But I decide against it.

Drawing in a bracing breath through my nose, I instead simply close the trunk and then turn around to face the two mean girls who have apparently come back for round two.

Just like I expected, Jane and Leslie are standing there, looking at me.

I'm halfway to spitting out a snarky greeting when I take in the expressions on their faces. They look pale. And worried. And very apologetic.

What the hell is going on?

Composing myself, I shake off the surprise and instead cross my arms as I give them a dismissive once-over. "Back again so soon? If I didn't know better, I would think you're obsessed with me."

They exchange a look, embarrassment flickering over their faces, before meeting my gaze with remorseful eyes.

Jane clears her throat. "Look, we wanted to apologize."

I jerk back as absolute shock pulses through me, and my arms drop back down to my sides as I stare at the two of them with wide eyes. Out of all the things I had expected them to say, *that* had not been it.

"You want to *what?*" I ask, hearing the incredulity even in my own voice.

They exchange another glance. Then they meet my gaze once more and grimace apologetically.

"We want to apologize," Leslie says.

Anger burns through me, and I turn to stalk away. "If this is some kind of mind game, then I don't have time for you. I need to eat before afternoon classes."

"No, wait!" Jane blurts out, sounding panicked. Grabbing my forearm, she stops me before I can leave. "Please, it's not a game. We realized that we crossed a line earlier and we really are sorry."

I glare down at her hand on my arm until she releases me. But I don't start walking again. Instead, I cross my arms over my chest and scowl at the two of them. "After everything you've done to me this semester, after all the cruel things you've said, why would today suddenly be the thing that crossed the line?"

"Because it's not true." The answer is immediate. And when I look into Jane's blue eyes, all I can see is absolute sincerity.

Next to her, Leslie nods. "Yeah, look, we know that we've said some mean shit to you. And part of it, we truly have meant. You are fucking terrible at sparring and obstacle courses. But…" Her eyes turn desperate as she looks at me beseechingly. "What we said today was a lie. People do like you. Carla and the rest of her housemates do like you."

My heart flutters in an absolutely ridiculous way because I so desperately want that to be true. But the sceptic in me is telling me that they're just messing with me again.

Keeping my eyebrows drawn down in a scowl, I demand, "Then why did you tell me that she didn't?"

Jane heaves a frustrated sigh and rakes her fingers through her blonde hair. "Because we were jealous, okay?"

"Of what? What could I possibly have that you're jealous of?"

"Carla."

I blink at her in surprise.

She heaves another sigh, this one deeper and more exhausted than frustrated. Dropping her arms back to her sides, she gives me such a vulnerable look that I can't help but actually believe it.

"Carla is at the top of our class," Jane explains, and then slowly shakes her head as if in disbelief. "And you, who are at the bottom of the rankings, have somehow manage to become friends with her. It makes no sense. Why would she like *you* while barely giving *us* the time of day?"

"Exactly," Leslie adds.

I stare at them. The cynical side of me tries to cling to the possibility that they're just messing with me again, but the logical part of my brain knows that they're telling the truth. It's written everywhere. In their words, their tone, on their faces. They actually *are* jealous of my friendship with Carla.

"Okay," I begin. Then I narrow my eyes as suspicion whirls through me. "But it still doesn't explain why you would suddenly come back and apologize for it."

"We—" Leslie begins, but I cut her off.

"And don't try to tell me that it's because you've seen the error of your ways and suddenly want to hold hands and sing *kumbaya*."

"It's not." Leslie grimaces apologetically. "We still don't like you and we don't want to be friends with you. But, well… We realized that we had made a huge fucking mistake saying those things back in the locker room."

"How so?"

"Because it was a lie. And if Carla ever finds out that we told you lies about *her* feelings for you, we will make an enemy of Carla."

"And we really, *really*, don't want to make an enemy of Carla," Jane finishes.

The last of the skepticism and suspicion that had dug their claws into me blow away like smoke in the wind.

This I can buy.

This makes sense.

They're not messing with me. They're not apologizing because they have suddenly become good people. They're

283

doing it for selfish reasons. For self-preservation. Though to be fair, I really wouldn't want to make an enemy of Carla either.

A sparkly feeling flows through me, making me feel lighter than I have in weeks. They were lying. Carla and the others do actually like me. They're not faking it because I'm a Petrov. They *like* me.

It takes everything I have to stop a wide grin from spreading across my mouth.

Instead, I level a hard stare at the two women before me. "Alright. Apology accepted."

Relief blows across their features.

"*But,*" I press on before they can get too comfortable. "If you ever do something as stupid as to steal my clothes, or do anything at all to mess with me again, I will tell Carla what you said. Understood?"

They nod quickly.

"Yes, of course," Jane says.

"We won't mess with you again," Leslie promises.

"Good." I nod. "Then we're done here."

Without waiting for them to reply, I simply stride away.

Excitement and victory bounce around inside me, and that wide grin at last spreads across my mouth the moment my back is to my two former bullies.

Not only do I now know that Carla and the others actually like me, I have also managed, completely on my own, to blackmail Jane and Leslie into backing off. No more missing clothes. No more cruel words.

Nothing can dim the happiness sparkling inside me now.

I jerk to a halt as my eyes suddenly land on a man standing halfway between the parking lot and the canteen building.

Kaden.

He looks like a lethal storm incarnate. Barely leashed violence rolls off his broad shoulders like smoke, and his right hand is already closed around the hilt of a knife. His black hair is uncharacteristically disheveled, as if he has run his fingers through it repeatedly, and he is staring at me with eyes so intense that my heart stops for a second. It looks like he is trying to carve me open with his gaze alone and read the deepest darkest secrets of my soul.

Well, *that* might be able to dim my happiness.

I heave a short sigh. I guess my week of peace is now officially over.

No, actually, fuck that. I won't let him ruin this moment of victory for me.

Pulling out my phone, I quickly type out a text while I slowly move towards the canteen building.

Me: *No. I'm in a really good mood right now. Don't you dare ruin it.*

Kaden releases the grip on his knife and instead slides his own phone out of his pocket. He reads my text while I continue to edge forward. Closer to the canteen building. And to him.

Once he's done, he looks up again. His gaze slides to the parking lot behind me. But even if he can see Jane and Leslie there, there's no way for him to know what happened today. And I will die before I ever allow him to find out that I was bawling my eyes out on the locker room floor half an hour ago, so I just keep my face blank, not giving anything away, and simply raise my eyebrows expectantly.

He types something.

My phone vibrates.

I look down at it.

Kaden Hunter: *Fine. Then I will just collect later instead. With steep interest.*

A soft scoff escapes my throat. But I suppose that's as much kindness and mercy as I will ever get from him, so I take the win and slip my phone back into my pocket.

Only a few steps separate us now.

His eyes burn holes in my body.

My spine tingles.

Keeping my chin raised, I just walk right past him.

And he lets me.

KADEN

E very day, it gets worse. Every day, that fucking storm
of bloody emotions inside my chest gets stronger. It's
tearing at my soul. Eating me alive. Making me
unable to function.

When I saw Alina crying on the floor like that last week, it
felt as if someone had shoved a hand into my chest and ripped
my heart out, leaving only a jagged hole full of blood and
broken tendons. And when I saw her strutting away from the
parking lot with that incredible look of smug victory on her
face later, I thought my body was going to burst with pride
and joy.

And I can't fucking handle it!

I can't handle feeling this much all the time.

A *bang* echoes between the dark wooden walls as I slam
the kitchen cabinet shut.

From his place on the cream-colored couch, Jace pauses
his video game and turns around to look at me. Worry flits
across his features when his gaze meets mine.

With a snarl, I just spin back around and yank open

another cabinet. I can't even remember what it is that I'm looking for. I just know that I can't handle Jace's concern for me right now. I can't handle one more fucking emotion right now.

Since the cabinet is full of oven dishes, I just slam it shut again.

"Careful," Jace calls from the couch.

I whip around to face him. He doesn't look concerned anymore. Instead, there is an arrogant expression on his features as he raises his eyebrows expectantly.

"*You* do not get to lecture me about being careful," I growl back at him, my fingers flexing at my sides.

"Yeah, I do."

"Just back off, Jace."

Grabbing the back of the sofa, he effortlessly jumps over it to land on the floor instead. Now facing me fully, he crosses his arms over his chest and shoots me a pointed look. That damn arrogant expression remains on his features.

"It's not my fault," he nods towards the kitchen side of the room, "or the cabinets fault, that you're losing the war with the Petrovs."

Fury flashes through me like lightning strikes. Curling my hands into fists, I clench my jaw and stare him down from across the room while that terrible storm inside me grows even more violent. "Watch your mouth."

Jace scoffs. Uncrossing his arms, he strides towards me until he is right in my face. Arrogance drips from every word when he speaks. "Or what? You can't even beat the Russians, so how are you going to beat me?"

"Jace." His name leaves my mouth in a low vicious snarl. The rage tearing inside me is so loud that I can barely hear anything except the violent pounding of blood in my ears, and every word out of my mouth sounds like it was wrenched from my soul and dragged over broken glass. "Back. Off. Now."

"No." He snorts and flicks a dismissive look up and down my body. "You know what? I'm going to do the exact opposite."

The roaring inside my head drowns out everything else. I'm going to shatter. My body is going to be torn apart from the inside by the thrashing storm of emotions inside me. He needs to back off right now. Right now. He needs to back off. I need an outlet. I need an outlet. I need—

"Since you're apparently too incompetent to do it..." Jace flashes me a grin full of mocking challenge, "I'm going to step in and finish this war for you."

I slam my fist into his jaw.

His head snaps to the side.

But before I can even process what I'm doing, he whips his head back and lunges at me.

I yank my arm up, blocking his strike with my forearm. The force of the blow vibrates up my bones. But I barely notice it over the roaring that still fills my head and consumes my every thought.

Shoving his fist to the side, I kick towards his hip. He staggers backwards, slamming into the kitchen table behind him. It screeches against the floor as it's pushed back several inches by his massive form, and the chairs that were pushed in underneath it clank together as they follow.

He shoves away from the table and spins around, slamming his foot towards my side. I leap back, evading it, and then dart to the side. Jace sees me coming and twists to block my strike to his ribs. A dull ache pulses through my hand as it connects with his forearm instead.

I yank up my other arm to block. One second too late.

My head snaps to the side as his fist slams into my jaw.

Another wave of searing rage roars through me, so intense that it nearly blinds me.

Charging forward, I tackle him head on, sending him crashing down back first on the kitchen table with me on top of him. He rams a fist into the side of my ribs. My body shifts to the side, and he uses that moment to scoot backwards on the tabletop. But I grab him by the hips and yank him back to me before raising my fist to hit him in the face.

Before I can, his hand shoots up and grabs the collar of my shirt.

My stomach lurches as he yanks his arm to the side, throwing me towards the edge of the table. But he keeps his fist buried in the fabric of my shirt, so he tumbles with me as we roll over the edge of the table.

Chairs clatter as they topple over.

Then we hit the floor with a thud.

Or rather, I hit the floor with Jace on top of me.

With a shove and a thrust of my hips, I roll us over so that I'm on top of him instead. He slams a fist into the side of my ribs and flips us again.

Dark wooden floorboards and bright lights above alternate as we roll across the floor until we hit the side of the kitchen island and come to an abrupt halt. Finally on top of him completely, I raise my fist and slam it towards his jaw.

He yanks up his forearms, holding them in front of his face and blocking the blow.

I strike again.

And again.

And again.

Jace blocks every single one with his forearms, as he lies

there underneath me, looking up at me with a steady gaze. Not fighting back.

He's not fighting back.

A tiny trickle of realization ripples through me.

In terms of outright brawling, Jace is more skilled than both me and Rico. He and Eli haven't tested their skills against each other in a proper fight for a while, so the jury is still out on that one. But Jace is better than me at this. He's also broader than me and bulkier than me.

Which means that he should have gotten a lot more hits in than he has.

And he should be the one on top of me right now, punching me into oblivion.

But he's not.

Which means that he is *letting me* beat him.

That loud roaring in my head starts fading, pulling that violent storm of emotions with it as it drains away. And without that clouding my mind, I suddenly realize that I know exactly what is going on. What I have known from the very beginning of this altercation even though my brain refused to process it. Refused to see it for what it was. Because I needed this fight. I needed it so fucking badly. And *he* knew.

Stopping my assault, I quickly roll off Jace's body as I drag in deep breaths. My chest heaves. Sitting on the floor, I lean my back against the side of the kitchen island and stare out at the chaos before me.

Three chairs have toppled to the floor and the table has been pushed halfway to the couch and turned on its side.

I draw my knees up until I can brace my elbows on them. Leaning forward, I rake my fingers through my hair and blow out a long sigh.

Fuck.

On the floor, Jace shakes out his forearms and then pushes himself into a sitting position.

A thud sounds as his back hits the side of the island next to me. I raise my head from my hands and glance over at him. Two red marks from my fist blooms on his jaw. My stomach twists.

But Jace just flashes me a grin and chuckles. "Here I tell you to be careful with one cabinet, so you assault the kitchen table and all the chairs instead."

Guilt and anger crack through me like a whip.

Twisting to face him fully, I grab him by the collar and hold him hard as I growl, "Don't think I can't tell exactly what you're doing. You *deliberately* provoked this fight and then let me beat you half to death just because you knew how desperately I needed an outlet."

His warm brown eyes are full of understanding as he looks back at me, but he still tries to put on a show by letting a mocking grin spread across his lips. "Half to death? As usual, I think you're overestimating your own abilities, brother."

Giving him a flat look, I release his collar with a shove and turn back to face the messy room.

"Bastard," I mutter.

"Asshole," he retorts, and I don't need to look at him to hear the smile in his voice.

For a while, the only thing that breaks the stillness is the rain pattering on the windows. Light from the bright lamp above fills the kitchen with a warm glow. Outside, the night is dark.

Dragging in a deep breath, I tilt my head back and rest it against the smooth surface behind me. Jace sits quietly next to me, his shoulder so close that it almost brushes mine. I rake my fingers through my hair before resting my forearms on my knees again.

"Thank you," I say at last.

"Anytime," Jace replies, and once again I can hear the smile in his voice.

Silence falls over our combined kitchen and living room for another few seconds. Then Jace shatters it with a statement that stuns me.

"After all, you do it for me all the time."

Tilting my head back down, I glance at my brother from the corner of my eye while surprise still ripples through me. "You've noticed that, huh?"

"Of course I have." Still facing the kitchen table, he slides a sideways glance at me as well. "But most times when you do it, I need the fight you're offering me so badly that I don't call you on your bullshit."

We shift our gazes back to the toppled chairs.

Most people assume that Jace is too loud and chaotic to notice what's going on underneath the surface, but he's far more perceptive than people give him credit for.

I blow out a long sigh, suddenly feeling drained and exhausted now that the storm of emotions inside me has faded. "How do you do it?"

"How do I do what?"

At last, I turn to face him fully again. Because I need an answer to this question. I need it desperately.

"How do you handle feeling so much?" I ask.

He turns as well, meeting my gaze with an expression I can't quite read. "Who says I do?"

"Oh, come on. Between you, me, Eli, and Rico, you're the most normal and capable one of us all in terms of handling emotions."

He snorts. "Yeah, but to be fair, that particular bar is on the fucking floor."

I chuckle. "True."

We fall silent for a while. Turning back to the toppled chairs, I draw my fingers through my hair again and heave another sigh. Jace pushes up from the floor. For a moment, I panic, thinking that he's going to leave. But he just walks over to the freezer and grabs two ice packs. Dropping one in my lap, he sits down right next to me again and holds the other to his bruised jaw.

Soothing coldness spreads through my skin and numbs the lingering ache as I pick up the ice pack and hold it to the bruise on my own jaw.

"Seriously," I say, still staring straight ahead. "How do you do it? I saw Alina cry last week and I cared. I cared so much that I almost killed two people for it."

That makes Jace turn towards me and raise his eyebrows.

I twist my head to meet his gaze and grumble, "What? I said I *almost* killed them."

He just holds up his free hand as if in surrender.

"The point is that I cared," I continue, heaving a defeated sigh. "I cared that she was hurt. And I don't fucking care about people." Desperation ripples through me, and I hold Jace's gaze with serious eyes. "Out of the four of us, you are the one who handles shit like this the best."

"I'm not—"

"Let's do a quick summary," I interrupt him, holding up my free hand and ticking off my fingers one by one. "We have Rico, who has spent the last six years not letting anyone get close to him. Then we have Eli, who is fucking insane. But he didn't even need to work on that because Raina is a bloody lunatic too."

Jace huffs out a laugh. "You're one to talk."

"My point exactly. Out of the four of us, *I* am the most emotionally crippled one of us all. But you... You feel things all the time and you still function." I stare at him in desperation and disbelief. "How do you do it? How do you kiss and fuck and cuddle a girl and then just walk away and move on to the next one?"

A mischievous glint shines in his eyes, and a smile tugs at the corner of his lips as he echoes, "*Cuddle?*"

"It was an example. A figure of speech."

"Sure it was." He grins. But before I can locate the nearest knife and stab my infuriating little brother, he moves on and actually answers the question. "Like I said earlier, I just remind myself that they don't matter. That they're not important."

Cold fear seeps through my bones and an even stronger sense of dread pulses through me. Because the moment the words have left his lips, I know without a shred of doubt that that method will never work for me.

Because Alina matters.

Alina is important.

31

ALINA

The scent of garlic and herbs hangs over the kitchen. I stir the chicken strips and the chopped vegetables in the pan before quickly checking on the rice. Then I cast a glance up towards the clock. Everything should be ready at the same time.

A loud *bang* sounds, making me jump in surprise.

"Enough is enough!" Maksim snaps.

Twisting away from the stove, I glance back at the table where my two brothers and my two cousins are seated. All of them were drinking and chatting quietly while I was making dinner, but Maksim's patience has apparently run out now. His hand is still curled in a fist on the tabletop where he slammed it down, causing that loud bang.

"The bastard has been coming at us for months already," Maksim continues. "And shit has fucking escalated these past two weeks."

I don't need to ask to know who the term 'the bastard' refers to. Kaden. And Maksim is right. Things have escalated. For my brothers and cousins, at least.

It has been almost a week since Kaden replied with that ominous text that he was going to collect later with steep interest, and almost two weeks since I crawled into his house in a chastity belt and then left it utterly fucked and thoroughly cuddled. And Kaden hasn't done anything to mess with me since then. Not one single thing. My brothers and cousins, however, have been on the receiving end of his increasingly intense attacks.

"And we can't even retaliate properly because of that damn video he has hanging over your head like a fucking sword," Maksim finishes. Slamming his fist down onto the tabletop again, he lets out a vicious string of curses in Russian.

"Trust me, I'm aware," Mikhail replies from where he's seated at the head of the table. His blue eyes sharpen as he fixes our cousin with a pointed look. "But what do you expect me to do?"

"Attack! We attack their house in full force and break every bone in their bodies until Kaden deletes the video."

"We tried that, remember? But they somehow knew that we were coming."

Guilt twists in my stomach. Turning back to the hissing pan, I stir the chicken and vegetables again while I try to convince myself that tipping off Kaden that time had been the right thing to do.

"He's right," Konstantin says with a defeated sigh. "No matter what we do, Kaden is always three steps ahead. Every time we try something, he sees it coming and turns the tables on us."

Maksim glares at him, clearly annoyed that he sided with Mikhail instead of his own twin. "Then what do you suggest we do?"

"I don't know. But brute attacks clearly aren't working. We need to fight smarter."

"And we need to do it fast," Anton adds. "It's impacting Mikhail's grades."

Shock pulses through me and I drop the spatula in surprise. It clatters down on the counter next to the stove while I spin around to face the table again and stare at Mikhail with wide eyes.

"Your grades are slipping?" I blurt out, my heart suddenly pounding.

Mikhail, being the Petrov heir, must graduate as one of the top three. Anything less is considered unacceptable by our family.

A muscle flickers in Mikhail's jaw for a second, as if the constant pressure he's under is so intense that he physically has to brace for it. But then he just gives me a strained smile. "It's nothing for you to worry about, Alina."

Curling my fingers around the edge of the counter, I grip it hard while anger streaks through me like lightning. Of course it is something I worry about. I am a part of the Petrov family too. In fact, I should be sitting there at the table too, plotting with them. Not standing by the stove in silence.

But I know that they will never see me as anything but their fragile little sister, so I draw in a steadying breath and release my death grip on the counter before simply turning back to the frying pan.

The scent of garlic and herbs once more drifts through the air as I stir the food a bit more forcefully than necessary.

"They are, though," Anton says quietly from the table behind me. "Slipping, I mean."

Mikhail says nothing, but I can feel the tension vibrating

in the air. The tension and the *desperation*. They need that video gone. And they need Kaden neutralized.

Another wave of guilt crashes over me.

Gripping the spatula hard, I clench my jaw and try to swallow down the nausea in my stomach.

I should've done it sooner. Why have I waited this long?

But deep down, I already know the answer to that.

I got distracted. Distracted by how Kaden treats me like a real person, a real *opponent*, and not some breakable glass figurine to be put on a shelf for display purposes only. Distracted by his fascinating intellect. By his strong hands and the feeling of his lethal body against mine. By the interesting contrast between how dominantly he fucks me and how gently he cuddles me afterwards. By his scent. By the flicker of emotion I see in his eyes more and more often. By *everything* about him.

But that needs to stop.

I need to stop this now.

I've had what I need for almost two weeks.

It's time to end things between us once and for all.

32

KADEN

It's time to stop. In fact, I should've stopped weeks ago. My plan was to torment Alina while I gathered what I needed, and then ruin her completely and toss her back onto the Petrovs' doorstep. And yet, I still haven't done that. I'm still playing with her. But I need to stop that now.

Alina has become too dangerous. She has too much power over me. Her tears ripped my heart out so badly that I almost killed two students because they made her cry. And her mere existence is messing with my head so much that I lost control and beat up my own little brother because I couldn't handle the storm of emotions inside me when it should be the other way around. *I* should be the calm one who offers Jace a fight when he is losing control. Not the one who pummels *him* to the floor. Not the one who needs *his* help.

But Alina has messed with my head. She has messed with the very core of my being. And I can't let that slide any longer. It's time to play my secret card. The one that will ruin Alina and break the Petrov family.

Sliding my phone out of my pocket, I send a text to Alina.

Me: *My house. One hour.*

One minute passes. Then two.

I glare down at the phone, waiting for her to reply.

It's seven o'clock on a Friday evening, which means that she could technically be out with her friends or at some party or other. It's what Jace is doing right now, after all. But I know that she's not. I know that she's at home.

At last, her reply comes in.

Alina Petrov: *Why?*

Me: *I thought I made it clear on that rooftop months ago that you don't question my orders. When I call, you show.*

Alina Petrov: *And what happens if I don't?*

Me: *I'll head over to your house with Jace and two sniper rifles.*

Alina Petrov: *You don't have access to sniper rifles. And Jace is currently at Jacques Lefevere's party, getting wasted.*

I narrow my eyes at the screen, feeling both annoyed and impressed. God damn, that woman is observant. Why the hell does she have to be a fucking Petrov?

However, before I can reply, Alina sends another text.

Alina Petrov: *Just tell me what this is about.*

Tapping my fingers on my desk, I consider for a few seconds before settling on an answer.

Me: *We need to talk.*

No immediate response comes through. I stare at the screen in silence for about a minute while impatience flickers through me. Then a text at last pops up.

Alina Petrov: *Fine, I'll be there.*

Me: *One hour. Don't be late.*

Alina Petrov: *I heard you the first time.*

Blowing out an exasperated breath, I shake my head at her defiance and rise from my desk. At least she's coming.

Time to get ready.

Exactly one hour after I sent that first text, there is a knock on the front door. Striding down the hall, I push the handle down and swing the door open.

Alina is standing there, looking at me expectantly.

"Punctual," I comment.

"Yes," she replies. "I was actually standing out here for five minutes, waiting just so that I could knock at this particular second."

I narrow my eyes, trying to read her face, because I can't tell if she's joking or not.

A faint smile tugs at the corner of her lips.

But before I can say anything, she arches a pale brow at me and prompts, "Well? You wanted me here. I'm here. Are you going to let me in or what?"

Stifling an amused huff, I take a step to the side and twist so that I can motion for her to come inside. She strides across the threshold and into the hallway without hesitation.

The scent of waterlilies drifts through the air as she breezes past me. I inhale deeply while her back is still to me. God, I love that scent.

After closing the door, I turn back to the hallway, expecting to see Alina waiting for me. But she has already started walking towards the doorway into our combined kitchen and living room. Surprise flits through me, but I don't comment on it. Instead, I take the opportunity to study her as I follow her into the large room.

She's wearing a dark purple dress that hugs her perfect body, black flats, and even a small black purse that is draped over her shoulder. Her long blonde hair is pulled back from her face by a few thin silver pins. The rest of it cascades down her back like a pale waterfall. And when she at last stops next to the kitchen table and turns to face me, I can tell that she's wearing makeup. She definitely doesn't look like someone who was just lounging around at home.

Suspicion swirls through me, and I narrow my eyes at her as I come to a halt two steps away. "Fancy outfit for a night at home, don't you think?"

"Who says I was at home?" she challenges.

I just continue staring her down, because I know that she was.

Clicking her tongue, she rolls her eyes in disgruntled confirmation. "Yes, I was at home. But I was actually also heading to Jacques Lefevere's party right when you texted."

"You had an entire hour to change clothes before you came here."

"Why would I? I'm still heading over there as soon as we're done here."

"No, you're not."

A cocky smirk tilts her lips. "Wanna bet?"

My cock hardens, and I suddenly have to fight the overwhelming impulse to push her up against the wall and do unspeakable things to her. Forcing down the urge, I instead raise my hand and point at the chair behind her.

"Sit," I command.

Her eyes flash, but she glances over her shoulder to the chair I pointed at. It's the empty one across the table from where I was sitting when she knocked on the door. There's a glass of whiskey on the table in front of my chair. Nothing in front of hers.

She scoffs.

Then she saunters around the table, plops into my seat, and picks up my glass. With a look full of nonchalant challenge on her face, she holds my gaze as she raises the glass to her lips and drinks.

Blood rushes to my cock yet again as I stare at her. But this time, I have to fight down the impulse to bend her over the table instead and then do unspeakable things to her.

Flexing my fingers, I draw in a steadying breath as I stalk back to the liquor cabinet and retrieve another glass.

How does she always manage to do this? How can she draw these violent emotions out of my unfeeling body almost without even doing anything?

After filling my own glass, I walk back to the table and grab the back of the chair she was supposed to be sitting in. It scrapes loudly against the dark wooden floorboards as I slowly pull it out. Alina just watches me, faint amusement dancing in her eyes.

A soft thud sounds as I put the glass down on the table in front of me and then sit down. Alina removes her purse and puts it down on the chair next to her in a way that almost makes her look like a fighter who's getting ready to throw down. I suppress a chuckle.

"So," Alina begins. "We need to talk."

"Yes."

Leaning sideways, I reach for the black folder that I had placed a little farther down the table. Since it's now on *her* side of the table, the move is less smooth than I would've preferred.

She just watches me as I open the folder and pull out some sheets of paper. After snapping the folder shut again, I set it down next to me and then slide the documents across the table to her. She makes no move to take them. In fact, she barely even looks at them.

After flicking a pointed glance down at them, she meets my gaze and raises her eyebrows in a highly arrogant move.

Dark anticipation curls around my spine.

Oh, I can't fucking wait to wipe that cocky arrogance from her features. Can't wait to see her beautiful face full of shock. Her wide gray eyes flooding with fear. Can't wait to hear her soft voice tremble as she begs me for mercy.

"What's this?" she says, still holding my gaze with that cocky expression.

"These are the secrets about your family that you have shared with me."

Drawing back a little, she frowns at me. "What secrets?"

"Business secrets. Financial secrets." I hold her stare, a vicious smirk curving my lips as I finish with, "Personal secrets."

At last, she breaks eye contact and looks down at the documents before her. Paper rustles as she picks up the first one and quickly scans the text written there.

Her eyes widen.

Picking up the next document, she skims that one as well.

I watch shock and confusion pulse across her face as she reads through them all.

With a smug smile on my face, I lift my whiskey glass and take a sip while I wait for Alina to finish.

Outside the window, the night is dark but far from silent. Thumping music from Lefevere's party can faintly be heard even through the closed windows. I tap my fingers expectantly on the smooth wooden tabletop as I set down my glass again.

Finally, Alina looks up from the papers and stares at me, her eyes still wide with surprise and confusion. "How did you get this information?"

I planted a bug in your kitchen and have been listening to your idiot brothers and cousins spill your family secrets for months now. But I'm not about to actually tell her that. So instead, I lift my shoulders in a nonchalant shrug.

"Doesn't matter." My gaze sharpens as I lean forward slightly, locking merciless eyes on her. "What matters is that I'm going to tell your family that *you* gave me this information. That you betrayed them to me."

It's going to ruin her. Her family is going to believe that she either gave me all of this information as a bargaining chip to get me to stop tormenting her or that she told me willingly because I managed to seduce her. Either way, they will think that she is broken. A dangerous liability. They will hate her. And the knowledge that *I*, a Hunter, is the one who got their own sister and daughter to betray them is going to fucking break the Petrov family.

Alina blinks, looking completely stunned.

Anticipation pulses through me.

I wait for fear to flood her features.

It doesn't. I narrow my eyes. *Strange.*

Instead, she gives her head a few quick shakes as if to clear it. Then she reaches towards her purse. The sound of a zipper being pulled cuts through the otherwise dead silent room. It's followed by the rustling of paper.

What the hell is she doing?

Seated there across the table from her, I cock my head and study her intently while I try to figure out why the hell this confrontation isn't going at all the way I had planned. She should be on her knees next to my chair right now, begging me not to do this. But instead, she's getting something from her purse.

Getting what? Is it money? Does she think that she can

pay me off? She should know better than that. Not only am I already rich enough that money barely holds any value to me, she should know by now that I don't want her money. I want power. I want her fear, her humiliation, her submission, her life in my fucking hands to do with as I please.

"Since we're in the sharing mood..." she begins as she straightens again.

I watch as she places two folded-up pieces of paper on the table in front of her. After unfolding them, she runs her hands over them to smooth out the creases. A frown pulls at my brows. What *is* she doing?

Grabbing the two documents, she flicks her wrist and casually tosses the papers at me. They hit the smooth tabletop and slide a few inches before stopping right before my hands. I glance down at them before meeting her gaze again and arching an eyebrow in silent question.

A truly villainous smile that makes my heart skip a beat spreads across her lips.

"That," she begins, holding my gaze, "is a record of all the secrets about the Morelli family that you have told me. Business secrets. Financial secrets." Challenge glitters in her eyes. "Personal secrets."

For a few seconds, I can't comprehend what she's saying.

Glancing down, I stare at the topmost paper.

Utter incredulity clangs through my skull as I read sentence after sentence full of information about the Morelli family and our dealings with them. Some parts are more damning than others, but all of them are things that Alina Petrov most certainly shouldn't know.

In fact, no one outside of this house should know any of this.

My heart pounds, and there is a faint ringing at the back of my skull.

Blinking, I try to compose myself as I drag my gaze back to hers.

"Interesting collection of information," I say, trying to sound indifferent, as I flick a glance up and down her body before meeting her gaze again. "How did you acquire it?"

A knowing smile slides home on her lips. "The same way you acquired yours, I presume."

I just raise my eyebrows in silent question.

She lifts one shoulder in a casual shrug and leans back in her seat. "I bugged your house."

Shock and alarm crackle through me. And it takes all of my considerable self-control to keep it from showing on my face. She bugged our house? When? How?

"Your bedroom, actually," she continues, that nonchalant expression still on her features.

Everything inside me twists and pulses with panic. She bugged my bedroom? *My* bedroom. Then that means that all of the information she has on these papers comes directly from me. From my conversations with Jace in my room or in the hallway outside, depending on where she placed the bug. And from my phone calls with my father and Eli and Rico. Fucking hell. The blame for this can't even be put on both me and Jace. This is all on me.

Disbelief still clangs through me, both because she managed to even plant a bug without me seeing it and because we had the exact same idea. Bug and blackmail with stolen information. But I can't let Alina see just how much she has managed to both stun and rattle me with this move, so I lean back in my chair as nonchalantly as I can and pick up my glass.

"My bedroom, huh?" I flash her a taunting smile as I raise the glass towards my lips. "Hear anything else interesting in there while you were eavesdropping?"

"I did, actually. Given your god status on campus, I kind of expected to hear you fucking droves of gorgeous women."

Smirking, I say nothing and instead just give her a quick rise and fall of my eyebrows before taking a sip from my whiskey.

"So imagine my surprise when all I heard was you jerking yourself off and moaning my name."

I choke on my drink.

Coughing, I try to get the whiskey out of my windpipe while alarm spears through me. Shit. I haven't done that, have I? Have I moaned her name? Out loud? Fuck. I don't know. I sure have been jerking off to images of her in my head. But I haven't actually moaned her name out loud. Have I?

While setting my glass down on the table again, I scramble to get my wits back while Alina smirks at me from across the table. I clear my throat again, getting the last drops of whiskey out. Fuck, that didn't make me sound nearly as in control as I would've preferred.

"Cute," I comment drily.

She flicks her hair behind her shoulder and gives me a calculated smile dripping with fake sweetness. "I know."

"Careful now, little doe." I narrow my eyes, fixing her with a threatening look. "Are you sure you've thought this through properly?"

"Of course I have. I would never go into a meeting like this unprepared. After all, you can't blackmail someone without actual leverage. And that, right there in front of you, is proof that you have been selling out the Morelli family to me."

"Blackmail, huh?"

"Yes. Because here's the deal. In exchange for keeping that information to myself, I want two things. First of all, you will delete the video of Mikhail groveling. From any and all devices and cloud backup storage spaces. And after that, you will leave my brothers and cousins alone. No more messing with them. No more tormenting them. No more ruining their education here."

"You drive a hard bargain." I cock my head, watching her intently. "But you're forgetting one thing."

"Oh?"

"If you release this," I tap the topmost paper in front of me before pointing to the stack of documents in front of her, "I release that."

Given how shocked she looked when she realized that I had had the exact same plan as her and bugged her house too, I don't think this particular problem was part of her little blackmail scheme. Which means that even though it was an incredibly impressive play, she still can't win.

I watch her face, waiting for that realization to flood her features.

Once again, she doesn't react the way I expect her to.

Instead of realizing that her threat is neutralized by mine, she grins at me as if she understands something that I don't.

Her gray eyes hold no fear. No hesitation. Only cold calculation.

It makes both dread and an insane thrill spike through my spine.

"Yes," she says at last. Then she transforms her features into the perfect mask of an innocent little girl with big doe eyes. "But I'm just a weak, naïve, little girl who was taken advantage of."

I blink at the abrupt change as she quickly lets the

expression fade and instead flashes me a smile dripping with threats and challenge.

"My family will be angry, yes. But it will pass." Her eyes gleam as she stares me down from across the table. "But what do you think the mafia king Federico Morelli will do to *you* when he finds out that you have jeopardized the safety of his family?"

For a while, all I can do is to stare at her while shock and incredulity and utter admiration whirl through me like a raging storm. Because she's right. If I leak my information, her family will be angry. But like she said, she will probably still get away with a disappointed lecture and some months of angry silent treatment.

But if she ever leaked her information, if Mr. Morelli found out that Alina had gotten that information from me, involuntarily or otherwise, I would be ruined. Completely and utterly ruined. After what happened with Rico's parents, Mr. Morelli considers the security of his family *the* most important thing in the world. He would never trust me again if he knew that the fucking Petrov family had obtained some of his secrets because of me, and my career would end before it even began. Hell, it might even fuck with Jace's future too since his voice is no doubt on those audio recordings as well.

Seated there at the kitchen table, I stare at the ruthless little Russian in front of me.

My heart pounds like a battle drum in my chest.

Clarity, like nothing I have ever felt before, cleaves through the storm of emotions in my chest like a lightning strike. It fills my entire soul until all those confusing emotions fade, leaving only that one realization behind. I sit there, staring at Alina.

She's smart. Ruthless. A cold, calculating schemer. Just like me.

And she has managed to outmaneuver me.

Alina Petrov has managed to outsmart me.

I'm going to fucking marry this girl.

33

ALINA

The expression on his face is not at all what I thought it was going to be. I had hoped for fear. Hoped that I would finally see the great Kaden Hunter stare at me with fear in his eyes. But I had expected fury. I had expected to see rage roar in his eyes as he stared at me in anger that someone like me dared to blackmail someone like him.

What I hadn't expected, or even considered within the realm of possibility, was that he would stare at me in open admiration.

My heart stops. And then starts beating erratically, thrumming like a startled bird that is flapping around inside my ribcage, as I stare at Kaden from across the table.

He is looking at me as if he truly sees me. As if he sees an equal when he looks at me. Sees *his* equal. A formidable opponent who has impressed him.

In all my life, no one has ever looked at me like that before.

The clever thing I had been about to say evaporates from my head, because I'm struck by a sudden realization. It's so clear that I can almost hear it ringing like small bells in my head.

If I were to marry Kaden, he would never treat me the way everyone else does. He would never treat me like a glass trophy to be put on a shelf for display. He wouldn't try to shield me from this violent blood-soaked world of ours. Instead, he would ask me to plot and scheme *with* him.

Wood scrapes against wood as Kaden slowly pushes his chair back from the table and stands up.

Giving my head a quick shake, I try to clear it as I hurry to my feet as well.

Both admiration and hunger burn in Kaden's normally so cold eyes as he rounds the table with slow calculated steps. I meet him halfway, coming to a halt before him at the head of the table. He twists, using his tall and muscular body to make me turn until I'm standing with the back of my thighs against the edge of the table instead and Kaden in front of me. Since I barely reach his collarbones, I have to crane my neck to meet his gaze when he's standing this close.

That incredible scent of his envelops me as he leans forward.

The move forces me to bend backwards over the table slightly.

Kaden braces his palms on the smooth wooden tabletop on either side of me, caging me in. His eyes dance with light and a smile ghosts across his lips as he locks eyes with me.

My heart pounds in my chest.

"You have some serious balls threatening a man in his own house," he says.

I smirk up at him. "We could always go outside so that I can threaten you on the lawn too, if you prefer."

A low chuckle escapes his chest.

He straightens, allowing me to do the same. But he keeps those gleaming eyes locked on mine as he slides out a knife from his thigh holster.

My pulse jumps and a thrill races down my spine as Kaden gently draws his blade over my collarbones. I curl my fingers over the edge of the table, trying to suppress a shudder of pleasure as the cold metal scrapes over my heated skin. My clit throbs as Kaden draws the knife up my throat, slowly and intimately like a caress, before placing it underneath my chin.

"Impressive," Kaden says, his dark voice almost a purr. "Very impressive. But you forgot one thing."

I arch an eyebrow at him. "Oh?"

Using the flat of the blade, he tilts my chin up, making me expose my throat to him. His eyes glint as he holds my gaze. "If I kill you right here, you won't be able to leak those documents."

"Wrong." I chuckle, and shoot him a knowing look. "You see, I took a page from your book. If I don't walk out of this house, those documents will be automatically forwarded to my entire family, as well as Federico Morelli's secretary."

He fixes me with a pointed look. "If you release yours, I release mine."

"And if you release yours, I release mine."

"Mutually assured destruction."

"Yes."

Emotions swirl in his eyes as he looks back at me. Respect. Admiration. Longing. And desperate need.

Then he smiles.

And my heart skips a beat.

"You sly, calculating little villain," he says, that wicked smile full of approval still on his mouth.

I grin back at him. "You ruthless, scheming psychopath."

His eyes dance with glittering light.

I grab the collar of his shirt and yank his mouth down to mine.

Still keeping the knife against my throat, he slides his other hand along my jaw and into my hair while he kisses me like he has waited his entire life for it. For this. For me.

Wrapping my fingers around his wrist, I push his knife hand back until the blade is resting against his own throat instead. Challenge lights up in his eyes. I match it.

"Strip," I command.

A devilish smile curls his lips.

I release his wrist and then watch with smug satisfaction as he slips the knife back into his holster and then grabs the hem of his shirt and yanks it off. Heat floods my veins and pools inside me as his firm chest and sharp abs come on full display. The muscles in his toned forearms flex as he tosses the shirt to the floor.

Moving away from the table, I place my hands against his warm chest and back him towards the kitchen island behind him. He lets me. I close the distance between us as he comes to a halt against the smooth side of the island. Fiery lust burns in his eyes as he watches me.

I keep my gaze on his as I draw my hands down the side of his ribs. Then I lean forward and kiss his chest.

A low guttural sound rolls from deep within his soul.

While sliding my fingers around to his back and then along the top of his pants, I kiss my way down his chest.

His eyes flutter.

I trace my tongue along the ridges of his abs.

He grips the edge of the island hard, and another moan rips from his lungs.

Drawing my fingers around his waist, I inch closer to the

front of his pants while I continue to brush my lips over his warm skin. A shudder rolls through his body as I start undoing the button on his pants. He grips the edge of the counter harder. I trace his abs with my tongue while I slide the zipper down slowly. He drags in deep breaths.

After curling my fingers over the edge of both his pants and underwear, I start pushing them down his legs. His hard cock springs free as the fabric disappears. My heart skips a beat at the sight of it, and my hands stop moving. Kaden uses that moment to remove his knife holsters and fully step out of his garments, leaving him completely naked.

My pussy throbs at the sight of his sculpted body laid bare before me.

Biting my lip, I slide my hands to his hips and lower myself to my knees.

Another shiver courses through his body.

I trace my tongue around his tip.

He sucks in a sharp breath and clenches his jaw while his fingers are gripping the edge of the counter so hard that his knuckles have turned white.

The sight makes sparkly warmth bubble through me.

Kaden Hunter is always in control. Always cold. Always composed. And yet, with just a flick of my tongue or a brush of my hand, I can make him come completely undone. I can make him lose control. And the knowledge of that is enough to make me feel drunk on power.

Leaning forward, I take his hard cock into my mouth.

A whimper spills from his lips.

I smile around his cock, and then take him deeper before drawing back again.

Towering over me, he holds on to that counter desperately while his chest heaves.

Emotions flit across his face like streaks of lightning as I suck and lick and worship his cock.

Then some kind of realization pulses across his face, and he releases the edge of the island and instead wraps a hand around my throat. With gentle movements, he pushes me back until his cock is out of my mouth.

"No," he says, and shakes his head at me while a knowing smile spreads across his lips. "You do not kneel after the massive fucking power play you hit me with tonight."

I frown in confusion as he uses his grip on my throat to pull me to my feet.

His eyes gleam as he holds my gaze. "Tonight, I kneel for you."

My heart flips at the dark promise of his words and the fire in his eyes.

"Take off your dress," he orders as he starts backing me towards the table.

Reaching up behind me, I slide the zipper down. The purple fabric brushes against my skin as I push it down to my hips and then guide it over my curves. It falls to the floor, leaving me in only my panties, as Kaden moves us the final bit to the table.

Once we reach it, he releases my throat and sweeps his arm over the tabletop. Our blackmail material goes tumbling over the edge, fluttering through the air in a rain of paper. Then he slides his arm underneath my ass and lifts me onto the tabletop. I wrap my arms around his neck and pull his mouth down to mine as he steps up between my spread legs.

He spears his fingers into my hair, kissing me hard and fast enough to steal the breath from my lungs. My heart patters in my chest.

After dominating my mouth for another few seconds, Kaden pulls back.

I gasp in a desperate breath.

With my mind still spinning, I barely notice Kaden retrieve something from the floor before he is back between my thighs again.

There is a wicked glint in his eyes and a sly smile on his lips as he plants a hand against my chest and pushes me down. I bend backwards until my back is flat on the tabletop while my legs still dangle over the side.

Kaden leans forward, bracing one hand on the table next to my heaving chest. Then he raises his other hand.

Light glints off the blade he's holding.

Anticipation rushes through my body.

I draw in a sharp breath as Kaden places the knife against my ribs. Then I keep perfectly still. His intense dark eyes are locked on mine as he slowly traces the tip of the blade down my ribs.

My clit throbs as he uses the knife to caress my hip bone.

Desire spreads through my body, rippling like warm waves underneath my skin.

Kaden lifts his other hand from the table and instead grabs my hip.

A villainous smile tilts his lips.

Then he slides the knife underneath the thin fabric of my panties.

And cuts them off my body.

I gasp as the sound of ripping fabric fills the air.

Kaden tightens his grip on my hip as he uses the blade to gently move the shredded panties completely off my body.

My heart pounds in my chest.

After he's done, he gives my pussy a firm tap with the flat

of the blade. I suck in another gasp. Smug laughter rumbles from Kaden's chest.

Then he spins the knife in his hand and sets it down on the tabletop next to me.

His eyes find mine again. And the suddenly dead serious expression in them makes me push myself up on my elbows so that I can see him better.

"Memorize this moment, little doe," he says.

My heart leaps and then pounds harder at the seriousness of his tone. I hold his gaze, hesitantly asking, "Why?"

"Because this is the moment the war ends. With my surrender."

I suck in a breath as Kaden lowers himself to his knees before me. My heart pounds in my chest. At the sight. At his words. At the sheer magnitude of what he just told me.

Pleasure skitters across my skin as he draws his hands up my legs, spreading them wide. Then he leans forward and takes my clit into his mouth.

Lightning crackles through my body.

I throw my head back, my body hitting the tabletop and my back arching as pleasure shoots through my veins like bolts of electricity.

My fingers curl and I squirm on the table as Kaden rolls my clit between his lips and then nips at it with his teeth before swirling his tongue around it in teasing strokes.

He tightens his grip on my thighs, keeping my legs spread wide as he works his lips and tongue with expert precision.

I drag in shuddering breaths as pleasure builds inside me.

Whimpers spill from my lips as he flicks my clit with his tongue before tracing it down to my entrance. I gasp, pounding my fist on the table as he pushes his tongue inside me.

My pulse thrums in my ears, and my heart is slamming so hard against my ribs that I swear I can feel it vibrate through the table.

A moan shatters from my lungs as Kaden worships my pussy.

I slide my hands into his hair, feeling the soft strands between my fingers as I grip it hard. He answers by licking and sucking and nipping at me until I'm trembling on the tabletop before him.

Pent-up need pulses inside me.

His tongue moves around my clit, going faster. Harder.

The edge draws closer.

Gripping his hair hard, I stare up into the ceiling, gasping in breaths as the muscles in my thighs and stomach tighten.

Just a little more. Just a little—

Release crackles through my veins.

My clit pulses between Kaden's lips as he continues sucking and licking it while the orgasm crashes through me. My legs shake underneath his strong hands as he keeps them spread wide for his wicked mouth.

Throwing my head from side to side, I moan and whimper incoherently as flashes of pleasure shoot through me, filling my soul.

When the final pulses fade, Kaden at last takes his mouth from my pussy.

"Oh my God," I gasp up into the ceiling, my chest heaving and my soul feeling like it has just floated out of my body.

Kaden kisses the inside of my thigh. "Yes, you are."

Warmth flickers through my soul, and another small whimper escapes me.

"Do you want me to stay on my knees for another round?"

he asks, his voice low and his lips brushing against my sensitive skin.

"No." I suck in a couple of deep breaths, trying to calm my racing heart. Then I push myself up on my elbows so that I can meet his gaze. A grin spreads across my lips. "I want you to bend me over this table and fuck me like you own me. No, actually, not only that. I want you to fuck me like you *know* that you own me."

A dark laugh rumbles from his chest. Still bracing his hands on my thighs, he rises to his feet again so that his powerful body is towering over mine.

There is a devilish glint in his eyes as he slides his hands up to my hips. "Always."

My stomach lurches as he yanks me forward. I suck in a breath as my ass slides over the edge of the table and my feet hit the floor once more. I'm still wobbly from the orgasm, so his hands on my hips is the only thing keeping me upright.

Holding me steady, he leans down and claims my lips with a possessive kiss. I melt into his touch. He kisses his way down my throat before abruptly drawing back and instead spinning me around so that I'm facing the table.

I blink, my head so utterly scrambled by the orgasm and his touch and his kisses that all I can do is to just follow his lead.

He guides my hips to the edge of the table and then plants a hand between my shoulder blades. I place my palms on the dark wood as he bends me over the tabletop until my tits are pressed against the hard surface.

Then his hand disappears from my back. The one on my hip remains, though. I rest my cheek against the smooth surface, letting it cool my flushed skin.

A jolt shoots through me as the point of a knife suddenly appears at the back of my neck.

I let out a shuddering moan as Kaden starts tracing a blade down along my spine. Dark desire flits through my soul.

Once he reaches the end of my spine, he traces the knife along the curve of my ass. I squirm against the table. Kaden tightens his fingers around my hip, holding me immobile.

My heart pounds as he slides the blade down my leg and towards the inside of my thigh. Every nerve in my body is on high alert. I fucking love this. The danger. The knowledge that one flick of his wrist could end me. The knowledge that he has complete power and control over me in this moment, and that I know that he will only ever use it to give me pleasure.

Using the flat of the blade, he taps the inside of my thigh expectantly.

I spread my legs wider for him.

Once I have obeyed and widened my stance, he leans over me and kisses my spine. My toes curl and my heart flutters.

Straightening again, he shifts his hand and instead places the flat of the blade against my pussy.

I suck in a sharp breath at the sudden coldness.

My clit throbs harder.

With slow but commanding moves, he raises his hand, using the blade between my legs to force me up onto my toes.

My heart slams against my ribs.

Arching my back, I rise up until I'm standing on my toes. It gives him full access to my pussy.

Once I have reached his preferred position, he removes the knife from between my legs and sets it down on the table.

A jolt shoots through me as he slides his fingers over my

entrance, checking if I'm wet and ready again. As if he doesn't already know exactly how much his knife play turns me on.

He lets out a satisfied chuckle when his fingers come back soaking wet.

"You really do have a knife kink, don't you?" he muses.

But my response is cut off by a moan as he draws his hard cock through my wetness and then positions it at my entrance.

"Don't worry," he says, gripping my hips with both hands. "We'll have all of eternity to explore that, and all other kinks as well, together."

Then he thrusts his hips.

I groan in pleasure as he sheaths himself inside me.

With a firm grip on my hips, he slides out and then slams back in again.

Pleasure flickers through me at the incredible friction.

He keeps his hold on me as he starts up a hard pace.

Bracing my forearms on the tabletop, I curl my fingers into fists and squeeze my eyes shut as my body rocks back and forth with the commanding movements. Pleasure pulses through me with each dominant thrust.

God, he really is fucking me like he owns me and knows it.

His pace shifts again, becoming even more savage.

I gasp out a moan and press my forehead to the table as I soar towards another orgasm. My hips slam against the edge of the table as Kaden fucks me hard enough to make the heavy table scrape against the floor with every thrust.

Releasing my right hip, he instead reaches up and grabs my hair.

Pent-up need whirls through me as Kaden pounds into me while winding my hair around his fist until he has full control of my head movements. With a firm pull, he makes me raise my forehead from the table and instead crane my neck back.

He keeps me like that, my head tilted back and my throat exposed, as he slams into me with ruthless power.

"Kaden," I moan as the pleasure inside me builds quickly.

My small body trembles on the table beneath him as he rails me just the way I want him to. Possessively. Dominantly. Like he knows that I can take whatever he dishes out. Because I can. And he is the only one who has ever been able to see it.

The table slides a good two inches forward as Kaden pounds into me.

He lets out a growl and releases his grip on my hair. I let my forehead sink back onto the cool tabletop while he grabs the table and holds it in place as he continues fucking me. My cheeks are flushed and every nerve in my body feels like it's filled with crackling electricity. I gasp in desperate breaths as every thrust of his hips sends me careening towards another orgasm. Lights flicker behind my eyes.

A breathless scream shatters from deep inside my chest as his cock hits the perfect spot and release slams into my trembling body.

My pussy tightens around his cock as he keeps fucking me through the orgasm.

I feel like I'm melting from the rush of pleasure and the overload of sensations as Kaden prolongs my orgasm while chasing his own.

When release crashes over him as well, I think my heart is going to give out, because the moan that tears from him is so raw that I can feel it in my very bones.

His fingers tighten around my hips as he spills himself inside me.

Then everything goes still.

For a while, our heaving breaths are the only thing that can be heard inside the now messy kitchen. That, and the faint thumping music from the party farther down the street.

Kaden leans down and kisses my spine.

Goosebumps spread across my skin and another wave of pleasure washes through me.

Then he pulls out and takes a step back.

I don't think my legs can support me right now, so I just remain lying there, slumped over the table while my heart continues pounding in my chest.

A yelp slips past my lips as Kaden suddenly slides his arms behind my legs and back and picks me up. I blink, trying to clear my foggy brain, while wrapping my arms around his neck on pure instinct.

"Where are we going?" I manage to press out as he starts carrying me out of the kitchen.

His answering smile would've made the devil himself proud. "To my room." He gives me a knowing look. "I think we need some more toys for round three."

34

KADEN

The faint scent of waterlilies fills my lungs as I
breathe in deeply and wrap my arms tighter around
Alina's small body. She nestles closer to me while a
satisfied moan escapes her luscious lips. My heart skips a beat
at the sound. Tilting my chin down, I kiss the top of her head.

As much as I love fucking her until she's trembling and
begging and moaning my name, I think I love this more. This
quiet moment afterwards when I can just hold her in my arms
and feel her heartbeat against my chest and her warm body
against me and know that she is mine. Completely and utterly
mine.

I tighten my arms around her.

Mine.

Alina taps my chest.

Clearing my throat a bit sheepishly, I realize that I'm
probably strangling her, so I relax my grip slightly and instead
roll over on my back. She draws in a deep breath and shifts so
that she has one arm draped over me while she's resting her
cheek on my chest.

"Let's save that for next time," she says, amusement clear in her voice.

I glance down at her, arching an eyebrow. "Save what?"

"Choking. I want to try it, but I don't think my body can handle one more orgasm right now. So let's save it for next time."

My chest shakes as a surprised laugh rumbles out of me. "Deal."

Reaching up, I push a few loose strands of hair out of her face and hook them behind her ear. Her eyes flutter as my fingers brush her skin. I watch those gray eyes of hers glitter as she smiles. God, she's beautiful.

"And if we want to relive this night," she begins, mischief suddenly dancing across her features, "all we need to do is to just listen to the audio."

I narrow my eyes at her. "That's right. Because you have a bug somewhere in here."

While still resting a possessive hand on Alina's hip, I sweep my gaze over my room. Various sex toys and other pieces of equipment are now scattered around the room, which is something that stresses me out. I don't like it when my surroundings are messy. My room is always clean and neatly organized. Which begs the question, how the hell has she managed to hide a listening device in here?

"Indeed I have," she replies, looking entirely too smug.

"And where, exactly, is it?"

Challenge glints in her eyes. "Why should I tell you that?"

Quickly rolling over, I straddle her and pin her hands to the mattress over her head. She blinks up at me, looking stunned. Then that smirk creeps back onto her features. I lean down, slanting my lips over hers.

"Because if you don't," I breathe against her mouth, "I will handcuff you to the headboard again and give you an hour of edging and ten more orgasms before I finally allow you to beg for my permission to tell me where your little listening device is located."

A ripple goes through her body, and I can feel her pressing her thighs together between my legs. Tilting her chin up, she kisses me and then bites my bottom lip before kissing me again.

"Now who's the sly, calculating little villain?" she whispers against my lips.

I kiss her back. "Still you." Biting her bottom lip in return, I grind my hips against hers. "Now, are you going to fess up? Or should we go again?"

She moans into my mouth before letting her head drop back down on the pillow. Heaving a sigh in surrender, she shoots a look towards the desk by the wall.

"It's underneath the desk," she finally admits. "Under the edge at the back, in the gap between the wall and the desk."

I raise my eyebrows in genuine surprise. "When the hell did you have time, or opportunity, to plant it there?"

"You remember that night when I came here after my brothers and cousins attacked your house?"

"Yes."

"And how I walked over and sat down on top of the desk and told you that we should just fuck and get our frustrations out?"

My eyes widen. "That's when you planted it? You've been planning this for that long?"

"Of course."

"How did I not see you plant it?"

"Because you were too distracted by how I spread my legs

and by my suggestion that we should fuck. Which was of course exactly why I did it."

Suspicion swirls through me, and I narrow my eyes at her. "You didn't come here because you wanted me to fuck you? You came to plant the bug."

"Precisely."

Grinding my hips against hers again, I shoot her a pointed stare. "Admit it. Even though it was a secondary goal, you *were* hoping that I would fuck you too."

She just looks up at me with fake innocence.

I roll my hips again.

She yanks against my grip on her wrists and squirms underneath me before finally admitting, "Alright, yes."

A laugh escapes my lungs. Releasing her, I roll back over and drop down on the mattress next to her again. "God, you're even more ruthless than I gave you credit for."

She lets out a smug chuckle and snuggles closer to me again. "Thank you."

For a while, we just stay like that. Lying there in my bed with my now messy black sheets around us, holding each other and savoring the moment. Alina rests her hand on my chest, and after a while, she starts tracing small circles on it.

"How are we going to keep this a secret?" she asks quietly.

Lifting my head, I meet her gaze and arch an eyebrow. "Who says we are?"

She rolls her eyes and pushes herself up on her elbows so that she can look at me head on. There is a serious expression on her face now. "You're a Hunter."

"And you're a Petrov."

"Exactly."

I just raise my eyebrows again in silent question.

She sighs and squirms slightly, looking miserable. "We're enemies. We're not supposed to be together."

"According to who?"

"To everyone. To the rules of... well, everything."

"Fuck the rules."

She blinks at me.

Holding her gaze, I repeat, "Fuck the rules. You're mine now. So people can either get onboard or get the fuck out."

Light floods her eyes, and she draws in a shuddering breath, as if she's happy that I don't want to keep her, keep *us*, a secret. As if I would ever keep Alina a dirty little secret. Fuck no. She will be standing proudly in the light. Right next to me.

With a smile quickly spreading across her lips, she nods and echoes, "Fuck the rules."

"That's right." I kiss her forehead and then sit up, climbing off the bed. "In fact, let's make it official right now."

"Now?" she squeaks.

She scrambles after me, getting caught in the tangled sheets while I stride over to the dresser and pull out some fresh clothes.

"Now?" she repeats once she has finally gotten out of bed. "What do you mean, *now*?"

"We're going over to your house to tell your annoying brothers that we're together now. That way, they and your father will stop trying to set you up on any more ridiculous dates with rich assholes."

She stops, her mouth slightly open as if she had been about to protest. Then she tips her head to the side, considering.

I pull out a pair of boxers and put them on while she finishes thinking this through.

"You're right," she says at last. Meeting my gaze, she gives me a firm nod. "Let's do it tonight. But maybe we should take a shower first?"

A wicked grin spreads across my lips as I stride back to her. Sliding my fingers into her hair, I tilt her head back and claim her mouth with a possessive kiss.

"No," I say, grinning against her lips. "I want my cock still covered in your wetness when I lay my claim on you in front of your brothers."

~

Once we have gotten dressed, and Alina has taken a shower, we make our way across the darkened residential area and towards her house. Loud music from Lefevere's party still thumps through the warm night air.

Alina is once more wearing that stunning purple dress that she had planned to wear to the party. But since I cut her panties off with my knife, she is now without underwear. She might have showered to get my cum off her before we meet her brothers, but the fact that she has no panties on makes up for that.

Dread and worry flicker in Alina's eyes as we at last reach her house and come to a halt in front of the door.

"Just try not to…" she begins and then glances around as if searching for the right word. Eventually, she finishes with, "Hurt anyone."

Amusement ripples through me, but I motion down towards my body, which is devoid of weapons. At Alina's request, I left all of my knives at home.

She lets out a huff and shoots me a knowing look. "As if you need your knives to be deadly."

I just flash her one of those smiles that my brothers call a *psychopath smile.*

Rolling her eyes, she gives my chest a shove in annoyance. But it seems to have the desired effect, because most of her nervousness disappears as she then draws in a deep breath and squares her shoulders.

Then she at last pushes down the handle and opens the front door.

The sound of voices immediately drifts down the hallway. I follow Alina as she walks across the threshold. After closing the front door behind us, we move down the hall and towards the doorway that leads into their kitchen.

Warm light spills out across the threshold, and the sound of an intense discussion gets stronger. I can hear all four Petrov men as we close the distance to the doorway.

Amusement pulses through me when I focus on what they're saying and realize that they're discussing ways to take me down.

This should be fun.

Alina shoots me a pleading look, to which I reply with an innocent shrug, and then we're walking across the threshold and into the kitchen.

Warm light from the lamps in the ceiling illuminates the pale room and glints against the stainless steel of the kitchen appliances. A few empty bottles of alcohol cover some of the otherwise spotless marble countertops, but most of the bottles are still on the table.

I study it.

Mikhail sits at the head of the table, with Anton to his right and Maksim to his left. Konstantin sits on Maksim's other side. All four of them are fully engrossed in their discussion, and most of them have their eyebrows drawn in frustration.

Alina clears her throat.

"You're back," Anton says, as he and the others start turning their heads towards the doorway. "Was the party—"

Shock pulses across their faces, and all four of them shoot up from their seats.

"Get the fuck away from her," Mikhail snaps as he shoves his chair aside and lunges for me.

But he has obviously been drinking quite heavily because I easily sidestep his clumsy attack.

"No, wait!" Alina calls as her cousins descend on me as well.

Ramming an elbow into Maksim's stomach, I duck under Konstantin's fist and then straighten in time to block Anton's kick to my side.

"Stop!" Alina yells again. "He's with—"

"I'm going to fucking kill you if you've touched her," Mikhail snarls as he surges forward.

I slam my palm into his forearm, redirecting the blow, while flashing him a smirk. "Oh I've done more than touch her."

Rage hot enough to burn the world down roars through his eyes, and he swings blindly at me again. Behind me, Alina has put herself between me and the other three.

As Mikhail's fist speeds past me, I grab his wrist and then twist his arm.

He lets out a cry as I force his arm up behind him, making him press his cheek against the counter beside us. I snatch up one of the empty bottles and slam it against the edge of the sink.

Glass shatters, the sound of it echoing through the room.

Alina, who was waving her arms around and trying to explain to the others that I'm not here to attack them, whips around to stare at us.

"Damn, you're pathetic," I tell Mikhail as I lift the bottle.

He growls something presumably vicious in Russian while yanking against my hold on his wrist and trying to get his cheek off the counter.

I bring the now broken bottle up to his face.

He stills.

"Good," I say, holding the jagged edges close to his eye. "Now, can you calm yourself down enough to have an actual conversation? Or should I finish what Eli started last year and finally take your eye?"

"Kaden," Alina snaps, her voice full of authority.

Twisting my head, I find her standing there two steps away with her eyebrows raised, giving me a look that I can only interpret as, *what the fuck did I just tell you?*

"He started it," I point out.

A frustrated breath rips from her lungs, and she rolls her eyes in annoyance. Then she levels that pointed stare on me again. "Just put the bottle down." Her gaze shifts to her brother. "Mikhail, stop trying to kill him. He's here to talk. *We* are here to talk."

Clinking noises fill the dead silent kitchen as I toss the broken bottle into the sink and then release my hold on Mikhail's arm.

He immediately shoots up from the counter and rolls his shoulder. Twisting towards me, he bares his teeth while rage flashes in his eyes.

"We?" Anton suddenly says, breaking the tense silence. "What do you mean, *we* are here to talk?"

Surprise and confusion pulse across Mikhail's face too as

he at last turns to Alina. The twins stand on Anton's right, staring at her as well.

For a few seconds, only the faint thumping of music from outside the windows breaks the stillness.

Then Alina raises her chin and declares, "Kaden and I are dating."

I swear I can feel the shockwave that pulses through the room.

All eyes turn to me as the four annoying Russians just gape at me in stunned disbelief. Then four simultaneous voices tear through the stillness like gunshots.

"The fuck you are!" Mikhail screams, whipping back towards Alina.

"You can't be serious!" Maksim blurts out while his twin says, "You're joking, right?"

Anton shakes his head while staring at her. "Please tell me this is a joke."

With her chin still raised, Alina walks over so that she is standing right next to me. Defiance burns in her eyes as she stares down her brothers and cousins while pointedly sliding her hand into mine.

I flex my fingers around her hand while flashing the four angry men in front of us a smug smirk.

Rage crackles across Mikhail's face again. Lurching forward, he tries to grab her arm and yank her hand out of mine. I'm just about to shove him away when Alina raises her other hand, stopping him.

"Yes, I am serious," she says, locking hard eyes on the twins. Then she shifts her gaze to her brothers. "Kaden and I are dating."

Disbelief and anger pulse across Mikhail's face as he yanks

up his arm and stabs a hand at me while staring at Alina. "He's a *Hunter*!"

"I know."

With that fury still flashing in his eyes, he switches to Russian and starts speaking quickly and angrily.

Alina draws her eyebrows down, her scowl deepening with each sentence.

"Is that really what you think of me?" she replies in English. "That I'm so fucking clueless and naïve that I would let someone play me that blatantly?"

"He's using you!" Mikhail all but screams while stabbing his hand in my direction again. "Can't you see that?"

Slipping my hand out of Alina's, I take a step forward, putting myself between the two of them.

"Be very careful with the tone you use when you speak to her," I warn, my voice dropping low and deadly. "If you don't stop screaming in her face and insulting her intelligence, I'm going to grab that bottle and finish what I started."

He jerks back a little, looking startled.

Then he clears his throat awkwardly and takes a step back, as if just now realizing that he was in fact screaming in his sister's face.

After raking his fingers through his hair to push the blond strands out of his face, he turns towards me and pins me with a hostile stare. "I want you out of my fucking house. Right now. I won't let you use her."

"You think I'm using her?" I let out a humorless laugh. "How about this, then? A show of good faith."

The twins scramble out of the way as I stride over to the edge of the kitchen island. Positioning themselves on Anton's other side, they frown at me as I reach a hand underneath the edge. Mikhail moves around me so that he can see what I'm doing as well.

Shock pulses across all of their faces as I pull off the small black listening device that I stuck there the last time I was in this kitchen.

"Here," I say, tossing it to Mikhail. "Show of good faith."

"You bugged our house?" he growls, catching the device and glaring between it and me.

"That's how you always knew when we were coming," Anton blurts out.

"Yeah." I shrug. "But now that's gone."

Mikhail narrows his eyes at me. "I still won't let you touch her."

"It's not up to you," Alina snaps.

We all turn back to face her.

She's standing with her spine straight and her hands on her hips, staring us all down with hard eyes.

"It is not your call," Alina says, enunciating every word. "It's mine."

"But you—" Anton tries to protest, his worried gray eyes flicking between her and me.

"My life. My decision," she interrupts. Determination burns in her eyes as she sweeps that hard stare over all four of her family members. "You do not get to decide who I can and can't date. I decide that. And I choose him."

Emotions pulse through my chest at the possessiveness in her voice, and I suddenly feel like my heart is going to burst.

Anton's gaze softens, but the twins glance towards Mikhail to check how they should react. The eldest Petrov holds Alina's determined stare for another few seconds before blowing out a long breath and turning to me.

"Then what does this mean for us?" he asks.

"It means that the war is over," I reply. "*I* might think you're an annoying asshole who needs to learn his place, but Alina loves you for some reason. So I will stop fucking with you."

Crossing his arms over his chest, he sucks his teeth and considers in silence for a while. Then a note of challenge bleeds back into his stupid face.

"And you'll delete the video of me," he declares.

I just snort dismissively.

"I'm serious, you fucking bastard," he growls. "If you're not just playing her, then prove it. Delete the video."

Sliding my hand into my pocket, I pull out my phone.

He narrows his eyes and taunts, "You won't do it. It's the best piece of leverage you've ever had over me. There's no way you'll delete it. Not for anything. And certainly not for her."

While smothering the urge to stab him in the face, I click into my cloud storage files and scroll until I get to the video.

"See?" Mikhail continues, looking at Alina and motioning towards me. "He's just going to threaten to post it now. He's not—"

Holding up the screen so that he can see it, I delete the video.

He blinks.

"You..." he stares at the screen as I swipe through to show that it's really gone. "You..."

Alina moves so that she is standing next to me again. Her warm hand slips into mine, and she gives it a little squeeze. There is a smile on her lips, and it's so fucking beautiful that my heart almost stops.

Pulling myself together, I lock the screen and put my

phone back into my pocket. Then I fix Mikhail with an arrogant stare and raise my eyebrows pointedly.

"Anything else?" I demand.

"I, uhm…" He glances at his brother and cousins, who look just as stunned as he does.

"Excellent," I say when no other reply seems to be forthcoming. With my hand still in Alina's, I pull her with me towards the doorway. "Then let's head to that party you wanted to go to."

Confusion pulls at her brows as she follows me out into the corridor, leaving her stunned family behind. "Why?"

I flash her a sly smile. "So that I can tell everyone on campus the most important thing that they will ever learn at this university."

"And what's that?"

"That you're mine. And off fucking limits."

35

ALINA

Happiness sparkles through me like tiny bubbles. I feel lighter than air. In fact, I can't even remember the last time that I could breathe this easily. It's as if the whole world has opened up and my future is finally mine again.

With a smile on my face, I practically jump out of bed even though I went out drinking with Carla and the other girls last night. But I don't feel hungover. I feel like I could climb mountains.

It has been a week since Kaden and I announced our relationship, and my brothers and cousins have spent every day since then trying to talk me out of it. But that's all they can do. Talk. Plead. Try to persuade me. And none of it has any effect on me.

Kaden makes me feel strong and powerful in a way that no one ever has. He sees me. The real me. There is also another incredible thing, which I have discovered this past week, that he does. Or rather doesn't do. He doesn't smother me. He's not trying to keep me locked up the way my father always has. Last night, I went out with Carla and the others alone, without him, and I didn't need to fight with him for it or try to convince him to let me do it. I simply told him and he accepted it.

That is what I have always wanted from a relationship. Someone who sees me. Someone who understands that I am my own person. Someone who treats me as an equal.

The fact that that person ended up being a Hunter still baffles me, though.

And it infuriates my brothers. I know that I will have to field more of their attempts to sway me the moment I leave my bedroom. But for now, nothing can spoil my good mood.

After taking a shower, I get dressed and run a brush through my wet hair while checking my phone.

There is a text from Kaden. It came in at around half past three last night, which was when I was still dancing and drinking with my friends. I frown, wondering why he would text me in the middle of the night.

Setting down the hairbrush, I unlock the screen and open the app.

Kaden Hunter: *I bet you two orgasms that sober you is going to blush at this text that drunk you just sent me.*

My heart leaps, and I quickly scroll up to read the text that I sent him two minutes before he wrote that reply. I certainly don't remember drunk texting him, but I clearly did, because my message is right there.

Heat flushes my cheeks as I read through the sentences where I give him a very kinky and very graphic description of what I'm going to do to him the next time I see him.

Clearing my throat, I press the back of my hand against

my cheek in a useless attempt to cool the heat now radiating from my face. God above, drunk me is apparently a lot more creative than sober me.

I drop my hand from my cheek and send a text back.

Me: *Sober me did indeed blush. Drunk me and sober me still regret nothing.*

His response is immediate.

Kaden Hunter: *Good. Never apologize for who you are.*

Me: *So... does that mean I get the two orgasms you bet me?*

Kaden Hunter: *Obviously. But I'm going to make you beg me for them. Thoroughly.*

A thrill races down my spine and a wide grin spreads across my mouth. After sending a quick reply telling him to give it his best shot, I at last leave my bedroom and head down towards the kitchen. I'm practically skipping down the steps and through the corridor.

But the moment I walk into the kitchen, my happiness dims and I feel like I've stepped into a sullen rain cloud.

Mikhail, Anton, and the twins all stand there around the island, watching me the moment I walk across the threshold. There is both concern and worry on Anton's face, while Maksim and Konstantin only look determined. Mikhail's face is an unreadable mask, and he has his arms crossed over his chest.

Dread washes through me, and I glance from side to side. "What?"

"We're going to have a family meeting," Mikhail announces.

A groan slips out of me before I can stop it. "About what?"

"You know what."

While blowing out an annoyed sigh, I slip past them and

shove two pieces of bread into the toaster with more force than necessary. The machine lets out a terrified *ding* as I angrily slam down the tiny lever.

Turning back around, I cross my arms over my chest as well and glare at all four of them. "We don't need to have a family meeting, because there is nothing to discuss. *I* have made a decision about *my* life. That's it. How you feel about it makes no difference."

Mikhail holds my gaze with hard eyes. "You're still a Petrov."

"And—" I begin, but Anton cuts me off.

"Dad is already waiting for us back at the house." Concern still etches his brows and he gives me a pleading look. "Mom too. Please, Alina. You know how Dad gets. This conversation needs to happen at some point, so isn't it better to just get it over with?"

I open my mouth, ready to argue. But the problem is that he's right. Dad is not going to just let this go without a fight, so this confrontation is going to happen whether I want it to or not. So I might as well just get it over with.

"Fine." I heave a deep sigh. "Just let me eat my toast first."

My dad is the most imposing person I have ever met. Even though he is actually an inch or two shorter than Kaden, I have always felt as if his presence just fills the whole room the moment he walks into it.

His brown hair lies slicked back in a severe way so that it won't obstruct his vision. I inherited his gray eyes, but his somehow still seem vastly different from mine. There is a hardness in them that makes most people take a step back when he locks his stare on them.

My mother is the opposite. She's short and slim, with big blue eyes and flowing blonde hair. I inherited both her hair color and her petite frame. And just like people do when they see me, they immediately write her off as harmless when she walks into a room. To be fair, they're mostly right. She's not an assassin. In fact, she and Dad married as part of a business deal much like what they're trying to set me up with. While I'm pretty sure they have grown to love each other, their marriage was an arranged one for strategic benefits.

And I will be dead before I let them trap *me* into one of those as well.

"We have already been over this," Dad says, and slams his palm down on the dining room table hard enough to make the cutlery rattle. "You are not getting involved with a Hunter."

Setting down my knife and fork, I meet his hard stare. "And I have already told you that it's not your decision to make."

"You're *my* daughter!"

"I'm still my own person."

"You—" he stops abruptly when Mom places a hand on his forearm.

He glances over at her, and she shakes her head softly. The discussion has grown more heated in the past ten minutes, and she has apparently had enough yelling across the table now. To be fair, she is sitting in the spot between me and Dad, so she gets the worst of it.

As usual, Dad is seated at the head of our grand dining room table. Mikhail sits on his right and Mom on his left, with me on Mom's other side and Anton on Mikhail's. After that, the twins are seated on our other side, facing each other across the table. The rest of the chairs are empty since my uncle stepped out for some air.

Midday sunlight streams in through the windows and illuminates the white-painted furniture and the silver-framed paintings on the walls. Since it's so bright outside, the silver chandelier above the table is unlit. As are the other candleholders along the table.

After another long look from Mom, Dad draws in a deep breath as if to compose himself, and leans back in his chair again. I take a bracing breath as well.

We've been at this for hours already, which is why Mom decided that we should take a break for lunch. But lunch just turned into a continuation of the argument.

I glance out at the bright midday sun outside, suddenly very glad that I had the presence of mind to text Kaden while we were still in the car. The moment we walked inside the house, Dad took all of our phones and sat us down for this family meeting. That was hours ago. And given that we still haven't gotten anywhere in our argument, this is probably going to take all day. But Kaden now knows that I'm at my family's house, so he won't panic and start torturing people on campus to get my location when he suddenly can't find me.

"We're just worried about you," Dad at last says, his voice now a bit calmer, after another deep breath.

Picking up my fork, I poke at a tomato on my plate while uncomfortable emotions make my insides twist. "You don't need to worry about me. I can take care of myself."

"Not against the Hunters."

"You trust *them*," I begin, using my fork to point at Mikhail and Anton, "to take care of themselves against the Hunters. Why not me?"

His gray eyes soften slightly. "Because you're not like them. You're you. Now, I'm not saying that that's a bad thing. But your brothers, and your cousins too for that matter, have been trained for this world their entire lives. They can hold their own against a family like the Hunters. But you… You just don't know what it is that you're getting yourself into with this decision."

Tears burn behind my eyes at the rejection, but I refuse to let them fall. Instead, I set down my fork again and raise my chin. "You think Kaden is only with me to take advantage of me."

"Yes."

Another burst of pain hits me behind the ribs, but I ignore it. "Even after Mikhail told you that he removed a listening device that he had planted and deleted a compromising video as a show of good faith."

"Yes." Sympathy, and a hint of pity, floods his features as he holds my gaze. "Because you don't know the Hunters like I do. Kaden Hunter is a calculating little psychopath who is always thinking fifteen steps ahead. He's playing the long game. That show of good faith was a calculated move. Just like dating you is a calculated move."

When he's done speaking, he looks at me as if he's waiting for me to start worrying and fidgeting and doubt Kaden's feelings for me. But I don't. I know exactly who Kaden is. I already know that he is a calculating little psychopath who is always thinking fifteen steps ahead. After all, it's one of the things that I like about him. And I know that he often plays the long game. But I also know how he looks at me. How he speaks to me. How he treats me. And most of all, I know how he feels about me. It's right there on his face, clear as day, every time he looks at me. And there is no faking that.

Holding my father's gaze, I simply reply, "I know exactly who Kaden is."

Frustration flashes across his face, and he slams his palm down on the table again. Glasses and silverware rattle from the force of it, and Anton quickly throws out a hand to stop a tiny spoon from tumbling off the edge of the table. The twins exchange a quick look. Mikhail just looks between me and Dad, while Mom sighs and drinks deeply from her glass of wine.

"Stop being so damn stubborn for one second and listen to me!" Dad snaps, leveling me with a look that would've made grown men tremble in their boots. "The Hunters cannot be trusted."

"I—" I begin, but he immediately cuts me off.

"You are a twenty-year-old girl with no real life experience." His glare sears all the way through my soul. "You will listen to what I tell you."

My cheeks burn with both fury and embarrassment. Crossing my arms, I just stare back at him in silence.

"The Hunters cannot be trusted," he repeats. Slowly this time. As if to make sure I truly understand. His gray eyes are hard as granite as he stares me down from across the table. "You might think that Kaden Hunter cares about you, but I assure you that he doesn't. He will discard you the moment that you become an inconvenience for him."

Deafening silence descends on the white and silver dining room. Tears burn behind my eyes again, and my throat is closing up. I swallow and try to keep a stoic expression on my face as I raise my chin.

"You're wrong," I reply, somehow managing to keep my voice steady.

Dad draws a hand over his face and heaves a disappointed sigh as he slumps back in his chair. Shaking his head, he picks up his glass and drinks deeply from it.

"Fine," he says. "If you don't believe me, then I guess I'll just have to show you instead."

36

KADEN

Hands grab at me. I jerk awake, striking out and trying to roll away before I even know what's happening. My fist hits something soft, and a grunt sounds. But in the darkness of my bedroom, I can barely see anything except for a mass of looming shadows around my bed.

I lunge for the knife on my bedside table. But before I can reach it, several hands grab my legs and yank me away. My stomach lurches as I slide right off the bed. Hitting the floor with a thud, I kick out hard with my legs while once more trying to roll to the side.

"JACE!" I bellow. "Attackers—"

A boot slams into my stomach.

Air escapes my lungs in a huff, cutting off the rest of my warning.

I try to scramble away from the mass of hands that reach towards me. Fucking hell, how many people are there? They surround me like a fucking wall. And I'm only wearing the soft black pants that I sleep in. No protection. And no knives.

"Your useless brother isn't here," a familiar voice suddenly says. A *very* familiar voice. "He's at a party, drunk out of his mind, four streets away."

While kicking out at the nearest pair of legs, I grind my teeth and try to glare up at the person who spoke even though I can't tell which one of the dark figures is him. Mikhail Petrov. How the fuck did he and his stupid brother and cousins even get into our house without me hearing it?

A grunt sounds as my kick lands, and I twist up onto my knees. But right before I can push to my feet, a boot smacks into my jaw. My head snaps to the side from the force of the kick, and I topple sideways.

Hands immediately appear around my arms, wrenching them behind my back. I buck and fight with everything I have, but two people put their boots on my back while two more bend my arms up behind me. One person plants a boot on the back of my neck, forcing me to keep my head down on the ground, while another one fucking sits down on my legs.

Which means that there are six attackers.

But there are only four Petrovs on campus.

So who the fuck are the other two?

Cold metal presses against my skin as someone snaps a pair of handcuffs shut around my wrists. I growl, yanking against their hold on me. But with six against one, and with me unarmed and half-naked, there is no getting out from underneath this.

"Do it," another voice says.

This one, I don't immediately recognize. This voice sounds less angry. More in control. And also… older. I think I've heard it before, but for some reason, it doesn't seem to belong at Blackwater.

Suspicion flares through me.

But before I can follow that thought all the way to the end, someone jabs a needle into the side of my neck.

And the world goes black.

There is a dull pounding at the back of my skull. And a throbbing pain somewhere behind my left eye. Nausea rolls through my stomach.

I blink, trying to fight through the fog in my head.

"Finally," someone says.

After another few seconds, my brain registers the voice as belonging to Maksim Petrov.

Confusion floods my system. Why is he…?

Then the muddled soup in my brain clears, and memories crash back in.

My bedroom.

The attackers.

Anger sears through me.

I've been kidnapped by the fucking Petrovs.

Blinking, I try to clear my unfocused vision quickly in order to take stock of my surroundings. I lift my hands to rub my eyes. Or rather, I try to. My forearms don't move since they have apparently been tied to the arms of a metal chair. I stare down my bare chest and down over my black sleep pants to find that my ankles have been shackled to the legs of the chair as well, and the whole bloody thing appears to be bolted to the fucking floor.

The sound of a door being opened pulls my attention from the chair and up towards the rest of the room.

It's some kind of windowless basement with concrete walls and floor, which could mean that we're still at

Blackwater. Though I don't recognize this particular room, and I've scouted out most locations. In addition to the chair I'm currently occupying, there are a couple of tables by the walls, one of which Maksim is leaning against.

I shift my gaze to the three people who walk in through the gray metal door on the other side of the room. Mikhail, Anton, and Konstantin.

If my vision wasn't still swimming slightly, I would've rolled my eyes. Instead, I settle for arching a pointed brow as I lock eyes with the eldest Petrov.

"I show you mercy and end the war that you were losing, and this is how you repay me?" I comment, and then tut as if Mikhail is nothing more than a disobedient child. "My, my, I knew the male side of the Petrov family was untrustworthy and dishonorable, but this is a new low. Even for you."

"If I were you, I would be very careful not to insult my family right now," a new voice says.

No, not a new voice. It's the same voice that spoke right before I blacked out from whatever they injected me with.

Tearing my gaze from the four idiots who are approaching me, I shift it back to the still open doorway to find two more people walking across the threshold.

I suppress the impulse to raise my eyebrows.

Now *this* is a surprise.

Ivan Petrov, the head of the Petrov family and Alina, Mikhail, and Anton's father, stalks into the room along with his brother, who is Maksim and Konstantin's father. And if they're here, it means that we're not a Blackwater anymore. If I had to guess, I would say that I'm currently being held at the Petrov family house in the city. Which admittedly complicates things a bit.

My gaze shifts discreetly around the room again, but there is no sign of Alina. Which worries me.

However, I don't dare to show any of that on my face because Mikhail and the other three have almost reached me now. The metal door bangs shut behind Ivan and his brother as they stride forward to take the two empty places in the middle of the half circle that their children have formed in front of me.

Shifting my gaze back to Mikhail, I flash him a mocking smile. "So this is how you managed to get into our house. You called your daddy for help."

He backhands me across the face.

But I saw the strike coming, so I managed to brace myself and prevent my head from snapping to the side. That seems to infuriate Mikhail even more, and he raises his fist again. I just keep that mocking smile on my mouth.

"Enough," Ivan says as he and his brother come to a halt in the middle of the semi-circle.

Mikhail and Anton stand on his right, and the twins on the other side. I slide a nonchalant glance over all six of them while discreetly testing my restraints again. The shackles don't even give an inch.

This is going to be an interesting... night? Morning? Afternoon? Since there are no windows, I can't tell how much time has passed while I was unconscious. But surely Jace will realize that I've been taken sooner or later. Hopefully sooner.

"We've brought you here to deliver a message," Ivan continues, locking hard gray eyes on me.

"Most people would've just called or texted." I lift my shoulders in an arrogant shrug. "But since I'm already here, go ahead."

A muscle flickers in his jaw, and irritation flashes across his face. I almost chuckle. God, he's as easy to rile as his sons.

"Stay," Ivan begins, his voice dripping with threats. "The fuck. Away. From Alina."

I make a show of looking around the room. "Yes, where is my little doe?"

His fist cracks into my jaw. This time, I didn't have enough time to brace myself, so my head snaps to the side from the force of the strike while pain pulses through my bones.

"She's not your little *anything*," Ivan growls above me.

Slowly turning my head back, I give him a true psychopath smile that actually makes his brother flinch. "Are you sure about that?"

"She's upstairs, sleeping," Mikhail suddenly says before his father can hit me again. He flicks a disgusted look up and down my body. "Blissfully unaware that there's a rat in our basement."

Ivan straightens and glances at his son. Mikhail just looks back at him in silence for a second before returning his attention to me. Ivan clears his throat. Lowering his raised fist, he seems to compose himself again. I just sit there, watching them with a disinterested look on my face.

"Since you are apparently as dumb as the rest of your family, I will say this again." Ivan levels a commanding stare on me. "Stay away from Alina."

I hold his gaze and simply reply, "No."

His eyes narrow, and he clenches his right hand as if he has to physically stop himself from hitting me again. "It wasn't a suggestion. You are going to break up with Alina. And then you are going to spend the rest of your life making sure that you are at least thirty feet away from her at all times."

"Ah," I say. Victory pulses through me, and I let that show

in the wide grin that slides home on my mouth. "So you've tried to get *Alina* to break up with *me*, but she has refused. So now, you're trying to get me to end it instead."

The rage that blows across his hard features is confirmation enough.

Incredible warmth suddenly pulses through me. Alina's family has been trying to make her break things off with me, but she has refused. Even in the face of all that pressure, she still refused.

"Yes," he admits. Leaning down, he braces his hands on my restrained arms and gets right into my face. "But do you know what the difference is between you and Alina? She is my daughter, and I cannot and will not hurt her." His fingers tighten on my arms, digging into the muscles. "You, on the other hand…"

The other five Petrovs grin at me in wicked anticipation from behind his back. I stifle the urge to roll my eyes. Well, this is going to be fucking annoying.

Ivan takes his hands off my arms and instead reaches behind his back. A hint of worry flickers through me when he pulls out two guns. With one in each hand, he moves them forward and then places the muzzle of each gun against my knees. I watch them for a second before returning my gaze to Ivan.

His gray eyes are as hard and merciless as stone as he stares down at me. "You are going to stay away from Alina."

Sitting there, strapped to the fucking chair, I look up at him with equally hard eyes. "No."

He pushes the guns harder against my knees. "Stay away from Alina or I'll blow your kneecaps."

I just continue holding his gaze. "No."

His fingers tighten on the triggers. "The moment I fire

these guns, your kneecaps will shatter like glass and your career will be over. Your future will be over."

"Alina is my future."

"You won't be able to walk."

"I can still crawl to her."

A muscle feathers in his jaw, and he cocks his head as he edges his fingers farther down on the triggers. "Last chance. Stay away from Alina."

Keeping my chin raised, I stare back at him. "No."

He pulls the triggers.

My heart pounds and every nerve in my body feels like it's on fire. But I manage to just sit there and stare up at Ivan fucking Petrov with impassive eyes as two clicks echo through the room.

No bangs. No gunshots. No blood and bones and pain. Only two clicks. Which means that he pulled the triggers, but the guns weren't loaded.

Genuine surprise flashes across his face for a second. Since his wide eyes are staring at me and not at the guns, I'm assuming that he's not surprised about the fact that the guns weren't loaded, but rather at the fact that I chose to let him pull the triggers instead of just agreeing to leave Alina.

My heart is still hammering against my ribs and my pulse is pounding in my ears, because I had no idea that the guns weren't loaded. But I meant what I said. I will be dead before I ever let Alina go.

Ivan gives his head a quick shake as if to clear it, and then straightens. Shifting the guns in his hands, he ejects the empty magazines and slams in ones that actually have bullets in them. Behind him, the other five Petrovs watch me with expressions that vary from confusion to surprise to wariness. I keep the nonchalant mask on my face as I look back at them.

Once Ivan is finished, he turns to me again.

However, before he can do anything else, the metal door on the other side of the room bursts open.

I snap my gaze to it.

My heart lurches.

Ivan and the other Petrovs whip around while raising their guns at the eight people who pour across the threshold. Cold metal appears against my temple as Ivan presses one of his guns to my head, but I barely feel it over the satisfaction and relief that pulse through my soul.

Thank you, Jace.

Jace, Rico, Eli, my father, and four of Rico's guards from the Morelli compound fan out across the floor, guns and sniper rifles raised and pointed at the stunned Petrov men.

While keeping his gun trained on our enemies, Jace flicks a quick glance up and down my body. Guilt and regret flit across his face. Next to him, Rico is staring at Anton as if he now wishes that he had followed through on his threat and broken his arm a few weeks ago. But Eli... Eli is the worst.

Fucking hell, I have never seen anything like it on his face before.

Hellfire burns in his golden eyes, and the scar that cuts through his brow and down to his cheek seems to stand out even more against those flames. Holding a sniper rifle trained on Mikhail's head, he looks about one second away from painting this entire house with blood and then burning the world down.

I know that my brothers care about me, of course. We've never tried to deny the bond that exists between the four of us. But it isn't until this very moment that I realize that they might actually love me to the same terrifying degree that I love them. The thought makes my head spin.

"You've crossed a line now, Petrov," my father grinds out between gritted teeth where he stands in the middle, aiming his gun straight at Ivan.

"How the fuck did they get in here?" Konstantin hisses under his breath.

"We locked Alina in the control room so that she could watch this, remember?" Maksim whispers back. "She must've unlocked the doors for them from in there."

Surprise flits through me. Alina is watching this?

"Your son crossed a line when he put his fucking hands on my daughter," Ivan snarls back in response to my father's statement.

"And if he was raping her, I would've shot him myself. But he isn't. He put his hands on your daughter because *she* wants him to. Now, put your fucking guns down and give me back my son, or we'll kill everyone in this room." He jerks his chin towards where the red dot from Eli's sniper rifle still hovers at the center of Mikhail's forehead. "Starting with your heir."

A ripple goes through the room. Anton and the twins flick a glance towards Ivan, waiting for orders. But Mikhail only keeps his eyes on Eli, who looks to be one wrong word away from pulling that trigger regardless of what our fathers decide. Fury and insanity burn in his eyes like the deepest pits of hell. Given how little impulse control he has, I'm surprised that he hasn't already opened fire.

Another few seconds pass.

The tension in the room is so potent that I can almost see it vibrating in the air.

Then a low snarl rips from Ivan's throat and he yanks his gun away from my temple.

"Untie him," he snaps to the others.

While the twins holster their guns and start releasing me,

the others remain staring at my family, their weapons still raised. Well, everyone except for Ivan, who sounds like he is cursing us all to hell under his breath.

Once I'm free, I make a show of rolling my ankles and wrists before pushing up from the chair. Turning around, I face Ivan again. A taunting smile tilts my lips.

"This wasn't exactly how I had planned to meet my future father-in-law," I say, and then lift my shoulders in a casual shrug. "But I suppose a little animosity was to be expected given the number of times I have humiliated your sons at Blackwater."

Rage flares in his eyes, and he flexes his hand on his gun while gritting his teeth. It looks like he's about to yank it up and shoot me in the head. I open my mouth to give him one more push. But before I can say anything, Rico speaks up.

"Kaden."

If it had been my father warning me, I would've ignored him. But it's not. It's Rico. So I just huff out a laugh and flash the leader of the Petrov family a vicious smile.

Then I turn around and saunter away with the rest of my family.

37

ALINA

Ten hours later, anger still courses through me like molten fire. It's so intense that I can barely hear myself think over the loud pounding in my ears as I stalk across Blackwater's residential area and towards Kaden and Jace's house.

Since it's a Sunday evening, the streets are full of people going about their business. Some heading home to get a good night's sleep before classes start again tomorrow morning, and others heading out to train. Normally, people don't move out of the way when they see me coming. But one look at my face, and everyone I meet on the sidewalk shifts to the side to let me pass.

God, I can't believe that my family actually kidnapped Kaden!

Lingering fear and panic pulse through me, mixing with the anger, as the image of my father putting his guns to Kaden's knees flashes through my mind again. I screamed so loudly in that control room that I almost shattered the monitors. And when he pulled the triggers, my heart stopped.

Even though there turned out to be no bullets in his guns, I don't think I will ever forgive my father for that.

Strong winds blow in from the distant forest and whirl between the buildings, bringing with them the scent of pine trees and warm stone. I draw in a deep breath in an effort to calm the raging fury inside as I close the final distance to the Hunters' house.

After Kaden and his family left our house this morning, he sent me a text informing me that they had gone back to their own home in the city, which I was able to read once my own family finally had released me from the control room and given me back my phone. While he spent the rest of the day trying to get his family to stand down instead of declaring open war on mine, I had simply informed my family that if they ever did something like that again, they would never see me again. Then I took my mother's car without permission and drove back to Blackwater alone.

Ten minutes ago, Kaden finally texted me to tell me that he had managed to get his family to stand down, and that he and Jace are back at Blackwater as well.

My heart patters nervously as I walk the final distance up to their door and knock on it. I know that Kaden won't hurt me. But after the absolute shit show this morning, I'm not so sure about Jace. Hopefully, he won't be the one opening the door.

As if misfortune itself had heard me, the door is pushed open to reveal Jace. His brown eyes are hard and his massive body blocks the entire doorframe as he crosses his toned arms over his chest and looks down at me. The muscles in his chest and arms strain against the white t-shirt he's wearing.

I swallow and just look up at him, not quite sure what to say. A simple *hi* seems woefully inadequate.

"You here to kidnap my brother again?" he asks.

"No," I reply, shifting my weight self-consciously while holding his gaze. "I swear, I didn't know that they were going to kidnap him. Once I found out, I tried to call for help but they locked me in the control room."

He is silent for a while. My heart slams against my ribs. I feel like I'm standing before a merciless god who is weighing my soul.

"You're the one who unlocked the doors for us, aren't you?" he asks at last. "From the control room."

"Yes."

"How did you know that we weren't going to kill your family the moment we walked into the room?"

"I didn't."

He falls silent again, watching me with unreadable eyes. Then he nods slowly and uncrosses his arms.

Taking a step to the side, he jerks his chin at me. "Come on in."

Relief flutters through me, and I step across the threshold and into the dark wooden hallway beyond.

Leaning out, Jace grabs the door handle and pulls the door shut behind me while calling, "Kaden! Alina's here." He turns to me. "Want a drink?"

"To be honest, I could use more than one."

"Same." He lets out a huff of amusement. But then something that looks an awful lot like guilt blows across his features, and he repeats in a dead voice, "Same."

Confusion pulls at my brows, but before I can ask what that was all about, he starts towards the kitchen and motions for me to follow. From upstairs, the sound of a door being opened and closed drifts through the otherwise silent house.

I follow Jace into the kitchen while slow footsteps start towards the stairs above.

Glasses clink as Jace pulls some out of a cabinet and sets them down on the kitchen island. Then he uncorks a bottle of whiskey and fills the two glasses with more liquid than would be considered decent. He slides one of them towards me right as Kaden walks into the room.

Ignoring the glass, I spin around and face Kaden. My mouth is already open, an apology about to spill out, when I take in the state of him.

Jerking back in shock, I blink and can only stare at him for a few seconds.

There is a massive bruise on his jaw from where my father hit him. But more than that, he looks pale and unsteady.

"What's wrong?" I blurt out, fear slicing through me.

But he just closes the distance between us and wraps his arms around me. Pulling me to him, he holds me tightly and kisses the top of my head. A long sigh escapes his chest.

With my arms around his muscular body, I hold on to him as if my life depends on it. My heart thumps hard in my chest, beating against his. And for a few seconds, I just stand like that, holding him and reminding myself that he's here. That we're here. That he's okay.

But given the state of him, he is apparently not okay.

Tilting my head up, I meet his gaze. "Why are you so pale?"

He just shakes his head. "It's nothing."

"It's because he's been puking his guts up half of the day," Jace supplies from behind my back. "Side effect from whatever it was that they drugged him with. Fucking hell, I should've—"

"How many times do I have to tell you," Kaden snaps,

interrupting him. Seriousness pulses across his face as he holds his brother's gaze with hard eyes. "It was not your fault."

Releasing Kaden, I turn around to find Jace pacing the floor like a caged wolf. Half of the whiskey in his glass is already gone.

Guilt and regret swirl in Jace's eyes as he looks at his brother. "I should've been here."

"You're my brother," Kaden replies. "Not my babysitter."

"I still should've—"

"Don't make me fucking repeat myself." He shoots a pointed look down at the glass in Jace's hand. "And ease up on the fucking drinking. I'm the only one who's allowed to puke my guts up in this house today."

The muscles in Jace's arms shift as he flexes his fingers in frustration. Then he slams the half-full glass down on the island and stalks towards the doorway. After giving Kaden one more look full of pain and regret, he disappears into the hallway. A few seconds later, his footsteps echo from the stairs, heading up.

Kaden heaves a deep sigh and rakes his fingers through his hair. Shaking his head, he walks over to the sink and grabs another glass before filling it up with water. After draining the whole thing, he refills it and then turns to me.

"I'm sorry," I whisper before he can get a single word out.

He draws his dark brows down and levels a commanding stare on me. "Don't apologize for something you didn't do."

"But it was *my* insane family that did it."

His mouth quirks in a half-smile as he nods towards the spot where Jace disappeared. "And mine is any saner?"

A laugh escapes my throat. It's full of relief and guilt and desperation and joy all in one.

This whole day, I've been so high-strung that it feels as if my very soul is vibrating with pent-up tension.

Keeping one hand on the island for support, I stagger around it on legs that are suddenly wobbling. Kaden immediately sets his glass down and comes to meet me. I slam into his chest, barely able to stop my momentum once I had started moving. Wrapping my arms around him, I hold him tightly while my whole body shakes.

He slides his arms around my trembling body, holding me tightly, and bends down to rest his cheek on the top of my head.

"You would have let them cripple you," I press out in a choked sob.

"You would've been worth it."

My restraint shatters. The floodgates burst open and all the emotions that I've been bottling up just start pouring out of me. Clinging to Kaden like a life raft in a terrible storm, I cry into his chest so hard that my body shakes.

He just stands there, holding me tightly and stroking a hand over my hair while I bawl my eyes out.

Once my tears have poured all of those emotions out of my body, I suck in a ragged breath to compose myself. But I feel so completely drained that I don't dare let go of Kaden. If I do, I will simply crumple to the ground.

"I'm sorry," I whisper against his chest, suddenly feeling embarrassed about my breakdown.

He continues stroking my hair with gentle movements. "Don't be."

"I'm not usually this weak."

"Crying does not make you weak. It just means that you have been strong for too long."

A sob rips from deep within my soul.

He holds me closer. "You never have to pretend with me. You never have to worry about looking weak or breakable. I already know how strong you are. So if you need to cry, cry. And if you need to break down, break down. I will help you pick up the pieces afterwards."

My heart swells with relief and gratitude. How could I ever have believed that Kaden was cold and emotionless? He reads emotions better than anyone I have ever met, and he knew exactly what I needed to hear right now.

I tighten my arms around him. Pressing my cheek to his chest, I listen to the steady beat of his heart. The sound of it makes a warm sense of calm spread through my exhausted body.

"Can we go away somewhere next weekend?" I ask, still holding on to him. "Just you and me. I need to get away from all of this craziness for a few days and just breathe."

"Of course we can. But are you sure your family will let you travel to some unknown place with their most hated enemy?"

"My family doesn't *let me* do anything anymore. From now on, I do whatever the hell I want."

His chest shakes as he chuckles. Then he leans down and kisses the top of my head. "That's my girl."

espite Alina's declaration, her brothers and cousins still spent the entire week trying to talk her out of it. But when Friday afternoon rolled around and I came to pick her up in my car, they had no choice but to let her go. Not before shooting me threatening looks from behind her back, though.

A faint smirk blows across my lips as I lie there in the large comfortable bed, resting my hand on Alina's hip while she sleeps next to me. If they only knew what I spent all of last night doing to their little sister, then they would be storming our hotel room and shooting more than just threatening looks at me.

I glance down at the gorgeous woman lying pressed against my side. Her arm is draped over my chest, and she has one leg wrapped over mine as well. Blonde hair spills out across the white sheets, looking like a rippling waterfall. With every deep breath, her chest rises and falls against the side of my ribs. I study her face. Her lips are parted the tiniest bit, and by God and all of hell, I just want to reach out and trace my fingers over those perfect lips. But I manage to restrain myself. After last night, she no doubt needs the rest.

So instead, I tilt my head to the side and gaze out the window.

Rain pours down from the dark gray heavens. Just like it did last night. I scowl at the area outside the window.

I take us to a beautiful gothic mansion by the seaside, and it ends up raining as if it's a bloody monsoon.

Hopefully, it will ease up today. Or tomorrow at least. Though to be honest, I wouldn't mind spending all weekend locked up in this room with Alina. And given her enthusiasm last night, I don't think she would mind either.

Movement outside the window catches my eye.

At first, my whole body goes on high alert since I can't help but think that it might be her brothers who have come back for round two. Or round two hundred and two. Or whatever number of attacks we're currently at.

But as I stare out the window, the man who walked out into the garden outside is joined by a woman. He grabs her by the hands and pulls her to his chest. She laughs as she embraces him.

Rain pours down on them, soaking them both.

But they just laugh and tilt their faces up to the sky and start dancing in the rain.

My heart twists painfully.

"What's wrong?"

I blink in surprise, and then draw in a breath to steady myself before shifting my gaze back to Alina. She's awake now, watching me with big curious eyes.

"Nothing," I say, trying to brush aside the uncomfortable feelings that surged through my chest.

She fixes me with a commanding stare. "Don't give me that."

Heaving a defeated sigh, I rake my fingers through my hair and then nod towards the window. The couple outside is still laughing and dancing in the rain and being utterly fucking adorable.

"I will never be able to give you that," I say, suddenly not daring to meet Alina's gaze.

"Soaked clothes and a cold?" she teases, amusement in her voice.

"Cute, spontaneous couple things." I swallow, tracing circles on her bare hip but still not daring to meet her eyes. "I will never be able to give you that. Because I'm not wired that way."

Her fingers brush against my cheek. Taking my jaw in a gentle grip, she turns my head back so that I meet her gaze again.

"I don't want that." Her eyes are serious as she holds my gaze. "I want *you*."

I give her a look. "I'm a cold and ruthless sadist with psychopath traits who is barely capable of feeling emotions the way normal people do."

"I know."

Holding her gaze, I shake my head slowly, trying to get her to understand what she's getting herself into. "I don't care about anyone else. The rest of the world could literally burn down outside my window and I wouldn't care. The only people I love are my brothers and you."

She blinks, and light pulses in her eyes. With her eyebrows raised, she pushes up on her elbows so that she can meet my gaze head on as she hesitantly asks, "You love me?"

A laugh full of exasperation and disbelief rolls from my

throat, and I raise my eyebrows at her. "I let your father put guns to both of my knees and pull the triggers rather than tell him that I would stay away from you. And you're still wondering whether I love you or not?"

She slaps my chest with the back of her hand and then climbs up and swings a leg over my body so that she's straddling me. I place my hands on her hips, looking up at her.

"Of course I love you, little doe," I say, my voice becoming soft in a way that it only does with her. "I love you so much that it terrifies me."

"I thought you didn't get scared."

"How could I not? When you're the most dangerous person I've ever met."

The brilliant smile that spreads across her beautiful face is enough to make my heart skip several beats.

Bracing her hands on my chest, she leans down and steals a kiss from my lips.

"I love you too," she whispers against my mouth between kisses. "Not in spite of who you are. *Because of* who you are."

That cold black heart in my chest pounds so hard that I'm sure she can hear it. I never thought it possible that I would feel this way about anyone. Or that anyone could possibly feel this way about me.

But Alina changed everything.

She sees all the cold, unfeeling psycho parts of me, and she loves me anyway.

Her words echo through my mind again.

No, not *anyway*. She loves me *because of* it. Because of who I am.

"I will never dance in the rain," I say as one last attempt to make her understand what she's getting herself into by choosing me.

But she just sits up straighter and flashes me a knowing smile. "I know. But that doesn't mean that we can't dance anyway."

Rolling off me, she climbs out of bed and reaches for her clothes. I push myself up on one elbow and raise an eyebrow at her in silent question. She laughs and jerks her chin.

"Come on," she says. Then a mischievous glint shines in her eyes. "And bring some knives."

Surprise and confusion still pulse through me, but I do as she says. After getting dressed, I strap on my knife holsters and then follow her out the door.

My confusion only deepens when she leads me to the deserted ballroom on the other side of the mansion. I scan the large empty room, noting the golden candelabras and the frescos in the ceiling, before I shift my gaze back to Alina and once more raise my eyebrows in question.

"Teach me how to evade someone in a knife fight," she says, and falls into a defense stance. "That will be our dancing."

For a few seconds, I just stare at her in silence while surprise finishes ringing through my head. Then I say, "No."

She draws back, looking stunned. And embarrassed. And a little hurt.

I use that opportunity to close the distance between us and slide out two knives.

"I will not teach you how to evade someone in a knife fight." A sly smile curls my lips as I come to a halt before her. "I will teach you how to fight with knives."

Spinning the blades in my hands, I hold them up, offering them to her hilt first.

Shock pulses across her features. Her mouth drops open a little, but no sound makes it out, as she stares between my face and the blades I'm offering her.

"No one touches your knives," she manages to press out at last.

"Exactly. No one except my brothers." I hold her gaze with serious eyes. "And you."

She sucks in a small breath.

My heart flips at the tiny sound of shock and the emotions that flood her eyes.

Reaching forward hesitantly, she curls her fingers around the hilts.

Once she has a firm grip on them, I release the blades.

She looks down at them and then flexes her fingers on the hilts.

Heat washes through my body and fills my soul with pulsing fire as I watch Alina straighten and roll her shoulders back as she falls into an attack position. Because the sight of my blades in her hands is the hottest fucking thing I have ever seen.

God, she's perfect.

And she is mine.

ALINA

After our activities last night and the knife fight lessons in the ballroom, my muscles are sore and my body is exhausted. But my heart has never been happier. This is what I want for my future. Him. Us. This feeling of being invincible. Untouchable. Like we can do whatever we want, and to hell with everyone else's opinions.

"What's that little smirk for?"

I blink, coming back to reality, and look up from my plate to find Kaden watching me from across the table.

The grand dining room around us is packed with people, their cheerful chatter floating through the warm air like a soft blanket. Hundreds of candles are burning in the gothic chandeliers in the ceiling, bathing the large room with warm light and glinting in the pristine silverware.

Composing myself, I flash Kaden an even wider smirk. "I was just thinking about our future."

"Oh?" He raises his eyebrows. "And what does that entail?"

"Doing whatever the hell we want, and God help anyone who tries to stop us."

His dark eyes glitter and a smile spreads across his lips as well. "Keep talking like that and you'll find yourself with my ring on your finger and my last name before the year is over."

Surprise flits through me. "You want to marry me?"

"Of course I do." He frowns at me as if that should've been obvious. "Why wouldn't I?"

I clear my throat a bit self-consciously. "Well, I thought, since you've said it yourself that you don't really do the cute couple things... I just thought that maybe..." I trail off, not sure how to finish.

"You're mine."

A ripple courses through me at the dark possessiveness in his voice. Swallowing, I hold his intense gaze as he locks serious eyes on me.

"You are mine," he repeats, enunciating every word. "And I want the whole fucking world to know that. So you will have my ring on your finger. It's not a matter of if. It's when." Mischief sparkles in his eyes and a sly smile curves his lips as he gives me a knowing look. "And besides, I want to tie you to me in every possible way so that you can never escape me."

A laugh bubbles from my chest, and warmth fills my soul. Matching his grin, I give him a quick rise and fall of my eyebrows. "Careful now. If you do that, I might just ruin you."

"You already have." Standing up from his chair, he leans right across our table and wraps his hand around my throat before claiming my mouth in a possessive kiss. "And I wouldn't have it any other way."

My heart swells so much that it's practically bursting with light. I smile against Kaden's lips as he steals one more kiss before releasing me and sitting down again.

At the table next to us, a man in a dark blue shirt openly stares at us.

Kaden turns his head towards him.

Since the staff at this mansion expressed concerns about the highly visible blades that Kaden was wearing, he now carries his knives in a holster underneath his suit jacket instead of around his thighs.

With his gaze locked on the man who is still gaping at us, Kaden slips a hand underneath his suit jacket and slides out a knife. Fire pools in my belly as he effortlessly twirls the blade in his hand.

One of his signature psychopath smiles slides across his lips as he spins the knife again while holding the man's gaze. "If you cannot keep your eyes on the ground, I can always cut them out and put them there for you."

Silverware rattles as the man jerks back so fast that he slams his knee into the table leg. With fear pulsing across his face, he scrambles out of his seat and hurries towards the double doors on the other side of the room. I watch him yank open one of the intricately carved oak doors and beat a hasty retreat.

Arching an eyebrow, I slide my gaze back to Kaden while I'm trying to stifle both a laugh and a sigh of exasperation.

He just lifts his broad shoulders in a casual shrug and slides the knife back underneath his suit jacket before picking up his wine glass.

At last, the laugh wins out. Shaking my head, I chuckle under my breath and then reach for my own glass as well. But before I can pick it up, a man approaches our table. I brush my hands down over my blue silk dress, getting ready to apologize to the manager of the restaurant.

But the man who stops at our table is not the manager.

For a few seconds, I can't process what's going on.

What the hell is *he* doing here?

Eric Wilson, my former fiancé, looks down at us from where he is now standing just a step away. As usual, he is impeccably dressed, his blond hair is slicked back, and there is a hint of casual arrogance in his blue eyes. He fits right in at a mansion type hotel like this, which is probably why I didn't spot him until he walked right up to us. I frown, studying his face. Annoyance and displeasure line his features.

"I won't let you do this," he announces.

Kaden slides his cold eyes to Eric, and the temperature in the room plummets so severely that I'm surprised my breath doesn't cloud before my face when I speak.

"No one *lets me* do anything," I reply, raising my chin and leveling a hard look on Eric. "Least of all you."

But Eric just shakes his head and looks at me as if I'm a stupid little girl who doesn't understand how the world works.

"You heard her," Kaden growls from across the table. "Now, leave before I cut that disrespectful tongue out of your fucking mouth."

"You can't be serious!" Eric blurts out, his eyes still only focused on me, as he throws out an arm and stabs a hand in Kaden's direction. "You can't possibly want to marry *that*."

"Do not speak about him that way," I warn, my voice turning low and vicious.

"He's a psychopath! He can't make you happy. Because he doesn't even know what happiness is, for God's sake!"

"Just because *you* can't make any woman happy doesn't mean that everyone else is equally incapable," I retort.

A frustrated sigh rips from his chest, and he spears his fingers through his hair. Then he draws in a deep breath as if to compose himself and lets his hands drop back down by his sides before fixing me with a serious stare.

"Come with me, Alina," he says, sounding almost like he's pleading now. "I swear I will give you anything you want. I can give you more than this psychopath ever could."

Arching an eyebrow, I drag my gaze up and down his body in a highly dismissive way. "I have seen what you have to offer, and I was left thoroughly underwhelmed."

Color rises in his cheeks as he flushes with what looks like both anger and embarrassment.

Kaden lets out a low chuckle under his breath and shoots me an approving look that warms my soul.

After clearing his throat, Eric brushes his hands down his beige dress shirt and straightens his spine.

"Well," he sniffs. "I did try to do this the civilized way."

Suspicion blooms inside me as he pulls out his phone. But all he does is to send a short text. Then he puts it back into his pocket and meets my gaze again.

"I really did try, Alina," he says, and the genuine regret in his tone sends a flare of panic up my spine. "But I guess this is how it has to be."

"What are you—"

The double doors burst open.

Kaden and I shoot to our feet as men in combat clothes swarm into the dining room. The other guests scream and scramble away.

"Everyone out!" one of the men bellows. "By order of the Hunter family."

I jerk back in shock and glance towards Kaden.

He has already stripped out of his suit jacket and is now only wearing the white dress shirt underneath with the knife holsters that crisscross his chest.

"These are not my family's people," he says, low enough for only me to hear, as he yanks out two knives and presses them into my hands. "Remember what I showed you. If anyone gets close, go straight for the kill and don't hesitate."

I nod, taking the knives. Dread and panic roll through my stomach as I turn my gaze back to the rest of the room.

The other guests, as well as the staff, have already fled. Only Eric and the horde of men are left. My former fiancé has backed away and taken up position two steps in front of the small army we're now facing.

"What the hell is this, Eric?" I demand, trying to hide the fear thrashing inside me with rage. "This seems like a bit of an overreaction just because you got dumped."

"As usual, you fail to see the bigger picture," he replies in a patronizing tone before his gaze hardens. "This isn't just about our engagement. It's about yours. You cannot form an alliance with the Hunters."

"Keep him talking," Kaden murmurs under his breath.

The men dressed in black before us spread out, moving between the messy tables as if to flank us. Kaden shifts beside me, his calculating gaze sweeping over the room as if he is waiting for them to get into a specific position.

"My family, and the rest of the families in our elite circle of society," Eric continues, his voice now taking on a haughty note, "have been able to keep your families in check by playing you against each other. Which is why we can't allow you to form an alliance."

"Why not?" I ask, doing as Kaden said and trying to keep him talking.

"Because it would make you too powerful, of course." He shakes his head, and genuine regret once more floods his features. "But as soon as your family learns that you were killed in an attack ordered by the Hunter family, which all of the guests heard clear as day before they fled, it will start a blood feud."

My heart jerks in my chest. *Killed?* They're here to *kill* me?

"Which means that there will be no alliance and no all-powerful assassin family coalition to threaten us," he finishes. "So that, dear Alina, is why I tried to be civilized and persuade you to—"

Kaden hurls his throwing knives.

KADEN

etal glints in the light of a thousand candles as four throwing knives shoot through the air. The men advancing on us try to jerk back when they realize what's happening, but they're too late. The blades bury themselves in four throats. Choked gurgling noises erupt throughout the grand dining room. Then the four men collapse to the shining hardwood floor and all hell breaks loose.

I yank out a pair of fighting knives instead as the rest of the men rush forward.

I knew that I would only get one surprise attack, so I had to make the most of it, which is why I waited until they were in a position where I could hit four people at the same time. It still doesn't exactly even the odds, but four dead within seconds should at least make some of the others wary of getting too close.

Throwing out my arm, I shove Alina back several steps behind me as the first pair of attackers reach us.

Cold fury burns through me like ice.

They're here to kill Alina. *Kill* her. Because it would upset the power balance if our families joined. I am going to fucking slaughter them all.

Ducking under the first fist, I spin the blade in my hand and ram it into the man's chest. A huff rips from his throat, but I'm already moving again. While yanking the knife out of his chest, I twist and kick at the other guy. He is forced to abandon his strike and instead jump back to avoid getting his knee bashed in.

Two more guys join the others, trying to get around me to reach Alina.

Rage crackles through me.

Whipping around, I slash one blade across one man's arm while ramming the other into the second guy's leg. They scream in pain. But the surviving man from the first wave has already recovered and lunges for me again. And two more advance from the other side.

If they had been assassins, *real* assassins, we would already be dead. But no one in our world would ever be stupid enough to accept a contract to kill a Petrov or a Hunter, so these men are just common thugs with no elite training and no access to real weapons. But there are just so fucking many of them.

Blood sprays across my face as I slice through someone's carotid artery before I duck underneath a strike and ram my blade into someone else's gut.

Pain pulses through my arm.

I yank my hand back and whip my gaze around, realizing that some of the men before me have now picked up steak knives from the tables around them.

In the sea of black, something beige suddenly moves to my

left. I whip around, dodging a kick to my hip from one of the thugs while also catching sight of that beige smudge.

Eric, in his beige dress shirt, tries to sneak past behind his little army and grab Alina. But she slashes her knives through the air, just like I showed her, forcing him to jump back.

I yank out one of my two remaining throwing knives and hurl it at him.

A cry of pain echoes through the air as the blade sinks into his leg, and he crashes down on the ground. I hurl my final throwing knife into his other leg. Blood leaks onto the hardwood floor, and he tries to crawl away. But his legs are no longer working properly. *Good.* Because I will be saving him for last.

Fire sears through my skin as a knife suddenly slices across my ribs. I growl, turning back to the main battle that I was forced to ignore for a few seconds. But a few seconds was all they needed.

A mass of black-clad thugs charges me.

Blocking out everything else, I focus solely on them.

Strategies form inside my mind.

And I execute them.

Twist. Duck. Stab. Spin. Slice.

Too many people are attacking at the same time for me to be able to block all their strikes, so I have to choose which attacks to block and which to let through.

Red stains spread across my white dress shirt as those steak knives open up several wounds on my body, and my bones ache from the punches and kicks that slam into me. But since I choose carefully which attacks that I let through, none of the injuries are life-threatening. And none of the attackers get through to Alina.

Clenching my jaw, I keep my mind thinking ten steps

ahead to make sure that no attacker ever crosses the unseen line that I have drawn where I'm standing as I fight to protect Alina.

Blood runs down my arms, turning my hands so slick that I have to sacrifice a few precious seconds to twist my blades and wipe the blood from my palms so that I can regain a steadier grip.

But I keep fighting. And the men before me keep dropping.

Spinning and twisting and slashing, I throw all of the rage and fury and my terrible fear for Alina's safety into my attacks. Blood sprays and screams shatter as I tear through the men like the winds of death.

When the final black-clad man at last drops to the floor, my body is so high on adrenaline and panic that I can barely comprehend what is happening or where I am anymore. A mass of bodies litters the previously spotless hardwood floor. Some of them are moving and groaning in agony. Some are not.

I suck in shallow breaths, my chest heaving and my heart pounding, as I whip my gaze around the room. Eric is trying to crawl away towards the door. And Alina…

I snap my head around.

Relief crashes over me like a tidal wave when I find her still standing behind me with her knives in her hands. She opens her mouth to say something. But right then, noise echoes through the room.

The doors crash open again. I whip back around to see another wave of black-clad men pour across the threshold.

Terror surges through me like cold water as I notice the guns in their hands.

Fuck. How are we supposed to win this now?

"Get on the ground!" someone shouts. "On the fucking ground! Now!"

I throw myself to the left so that I'm blocking Alina completely with my body and raise my knives again. I have no more throwing knives, so unless they get close enough for me to strike, I can't attack them. But if they want to get Alina, they will be forced to come within striking distance. Or shoot through me.

Red dots appear on my now blood-soaked shirt as five rifles are trained on my chest.

"I said get down on the fucking ground!" the same voice bellows.

Blood pulses from my wounds and slides down my skin, and my entire body is screaming with exhaustion. But I remain exactly where I am.

"Kaden," Alina suddenly says from behind me, "It's—"

"On your knees," a familiar voice interrupts. "Now!"

Relief crashes through me.

I never thought that the sight of those particular faces would draw such an emotion from me, but right now, they're the second-best group of people who could have possibly walked through the door.

"Dad," Alina calls.

I suck in a shuddering breath as every man in the entire fucking Petrov family stalks into the room with their guns and rifles raised. The other men who entered before them fan out, checking the people on the ground for weapons.

But Ivan Petrov doesn't look at his daughter. His hard gray eyes are locked on me. As is his gun. "I said, on your knees."

My immediate instinct is to refuse. But there are about fifteen weapons aimed at me, and I can tell by the expression on the Petrovs' faces that they will actually kill me if I do anything other than exactly what they tell me to. And besides, no one in this room is a threat to Alina. At least no one who is still standing.

So I hold Ivan's gaze and slowly lower myself to my knees.

His people spread out quickly through the room while he continues to advance on me. Mikhail and Anton walk beside him, aiming two rifles at my chest.

"Drop your knives," Ivan orders.

"Dad!" Alina protests from where the twins are holding her back. "It's not him!"

But I just toss my blades to the side.

"Hands on your head," Ivan says.

Raising my arms, I interlace my fingers behind my head while still holding his gaze. He and his two sons close the final distance between us. Looming above me, they stare down at me where I'm kneeling on the floor before them.

"We followed you," Ivan says. "And we've been watching you from across the street all day, just waiting for you to mess up. To do something that would give us an excuse to put you down." A vicious smile curves his lips. "And now you have."

I just stare up at him, keeping my mouth shut.

"It was Eric!" Alina screams, fury pulsing from her voice. "Not Kaden! Eric tried to have me killed. He's over *there*! So stop pointing your fucking guns at Kaden."

"Do not take that tone with me," Ivan snaps.

But he shifts his gaze to where Alina is presumably pointing. His eyes narrow on where Eric is still trying to inch towards the doors, two knives sticking out of his legs. I draw in deep breaths as another wave of exhaustion rolls over me. Fuck, I feel like my body is going to give out.

"Just ask him!" Alina continues, sounding absolutely enraged.

Mikhail and Anton glance at their father. He continues watching Eric in silence for a few seconds. A pensive expression blows across his features. Then he clicks his tongue.

"Watch him," he tells Mikhail.

Without waiting for a reply, the head of the Petrov family turns and strides towards Eric with his youngest son in tow. Mikhail shifts his position so that he is standing to my left instead, keeping his rifle aimed at my temple. God, he must love this. Having me on my knees like this. But I can't muster enough fucks to give right now. Alina is safe. That is all that matters.

Across the room, Eric screams as Ivan plants his boot on his wounded leg and shoves down. Ivan's harsh voice echoes through the candlelit room as he starts interrogating Eric.

I tune them out, because it is taking all of my willpower just to keep my arms raised and my hands behind my head. The muscles in my arms are screaming in protest and the wounds across my body throb, sending more blood sliding down my skin and soaking my white shirt.

But I remain where I am, on my knees with my fingers interlaced behind my head, in front of a large semi-circle of dead or wounded men.

After a while, Ivan and Anton start back towards me.

My head is swimming and it's taking most of my self-control to keep my arms from shaking. But I keep my eyes hard as I tilt my head back and meet Ivan's gaze again while he comes to a halt before me.

There is an unreadable expression on his face.

Then he raises his gun and presses it directly against my forehead.

"NO!" Alina screams from somewhere behind me.

I just keep holding his gaze.

He stares down at me, as if waiting for fear to flood my features. But I only feel terror when my brothers' or Alina's life is in danger, so the emotion that Ivan is waiting for never comes. If he wants to shoot me, then he's going to shoot me. It's as simple as that.

But he doesn't pull the trigger.

Instead, he watches me as if he is trying to read answers on my face. But he finds none of those on my features either. So in the end, he jerks his chin to indicate the slaughter around us.

"You did this?" he asks.

"Yes," I simply reply.

"Why?"

My answer is immediate. Because it's the most natural thing in the world. The easiest decision I have ever made. The most solemn vow I will ever make.

"Because I will protect her until the day I die."

41

ALINA

This gothic mansion hotel that we're still occupying has probably made more money in this one day than they have in the past year. After my father finally accepted that Kaden was the one who had protected me against the attack, not instigated it, he called the head of the Hunter family since both our families were affected by this attack. And together, they bought out the hotel for the next three days, called in cleaning crews to handle the dead bodies, and the still surviving thugs too, while sending the other guests away with a not-so-subtle threat to keep their fucking mouths shut. My father had Eric shipped away on his own, for him to handle personally later.

Kaden's father and brothers arrived within the hour. As did the doctors that his family keeps on payroll. None of his wounds were life-threatening, but they still needed stitching. I haven't seen him since they arrived, since the Hunters retreated to one side of the hotel while we took the other. And even though I wasn't injured, my family is still fussing over me as if I'm the one who just fought off an entire room of thugs on my own.

"I still can't believe the fucking nerve of them!" Maksim growls, and slams his hand down on the table. "We need to retaliate. Hard and fast."

"I agree," Mikhail adds from where he's leaning against the wall of the conference room that we're currently occupying. "And the retaliation needs to be so bloody and so brutal that people will whisper about it for years to come. A warning to everyone not to cross our family."

Dad nods, his expression hard. "We will."

Rain beats the row of windows behind the table, filling the room with the sound of the whirling storm outside.

"God, what if they had actually managed to kill Alina?" Anton says, shaking his head in disbelief. His gray eyes soften as he turns to me. "Are you sure you're okay?"

Sitting in one of the white wooden chairs in the neatly furnished conference room, I glance down at the blue dress that I wore to dinner and still haven't taken off. Light from the swirling metal lamps in the ceiling reflect against the silk, making the fabric shimmer. The hem of the dress is soaked with blood.

Just seeing that darker line at the edge of the skirt makes a storm of emotions whirl through me. Am I okay? No, I'm not.

Images of what happened inside that dining room flash before my eyes. Images of Kaden fighting like a demon from hell while all I could do was stand there uselessly behind him. It was the most incredible display of fighting skills I have ever seen. And I know that I would only have gotten in his way if I had tried to help. That I will always get in the way if I try to help in a fight like that. I'm not an assassin. But I'm smart. I should have seen the attack coming. I should have known that

Eric wouldn't just let me go. I should have figured out that our actions would be seen as a threat to the rich elite. Should have seen this attack coming.

I suppress a sigh.

Could've, would've, should've.

There is nothing to be done about that now. What's done is done. But I will do better next time. I can't protect Kaden the way he protects me in a fight. But I can keep him safe by making sure that our enemies never surprise us in the first place. And I will.

So I draw in a determined breath, give Anton a smile, and reply, "Yes, I'm fine."

He smiles back. By the wall on my left, I can feel Mikhail's gaze once more drifting to me, as if he constantly needs to check to make sure that I'm actually here. My brothers can be overprotective and a downright pain in the ass sometimes, but they love me. And I know that they only want to see me happy and safe.

"This should never have happened," Dad says from where he is still angrily pacing back and forth across the hardwood floor. "I should never have let you enroll at Blackwater."

"What?" I blurt out, completely baffled. Whipping my head around to face him, I raise my arms and motion at the hotel around us. "The attack didn't even happen at Blackwater."

"It doesn't matter. It's the situation in itself." Coming to a halt, he pins me with a stern look. "I should've married you off the moment you turned eighteen. Then none of this would've happened."

Staring at him, I shake my head. "You can't be serious."

"*You* are the one who isn't serious!" he snaps back, stabbing a hand at me. "In case you didn't know, I get updates from your instructors at Blackwater. And do you know what they tell me? That you're failing almost every single class that isn't purely theoretical. So what are you doing at Blackwater? You're not there to get stronger so that your future husband can't take advantage of you. You're there to party and have fun!"

I can't really argue with that one since he is in fact right.

"It's time to stop playing around at Blackwater and come home," he continues. "And instead get serious about finding a suitable alliance."

Anger courses through me, and I shove to my feet. The chair scrapes against the floor behind me and almost topples over from the force of the movement. Anton and Mikhail cast worried glances between me and Dad, as do my cousins and my uncle. Their eyes dart back and forth as if they're watching a tennis match. A tennis match where the tension in the room is so thick that it's practically crackling between the white walls.

"You want to marry me off for an alliance," I begin, staring my father straight in the eye. "Then here's one. Kaden Hunter."

The twins suck in a breath between their teeth.

Dad clenches his jaw. "You are not marrying Kaden Hunter."

"Why not? You saw what he did in that dining room. He would kill for me. He would *die* for me. No one else could keep me safe the way he can."

"He's a Hunter." Dad practically spits out the name.

"Exactly." I hold his gaze unflinchingly, keeping my voice level and not backing down. "You've been trying to marry me off for an alliance. Wouldn't an alliance with the Hunters be the best one of all? Not only will you never have to watch your back around them anymore, you will also gain a powerful ally."

Anger still pulses on his face as he opens his mouth to no doubt refuse again. But then he pauses. A considering look blows across his features as he narrows his eyes. Mikhail slides his gaze to him as well.

"Again, you saw what he did in that dining room," I continue. My heart is pattering against my ribs, but I feel like I finally have them right there on the edge. They just need one more shove in the right direction to land on my side. "He almost got himself killed protecting me and he only stood down once you walked into the room and he knew that I was safe."

Dad rubs a hand over his jaw, thinking.

"Not to mention what happened in our basement," I add. "You saw how Kaden reacted. He would have let you cripple him rather than leave me."

He sucks his teeth.

"I have Kaden wrapped around my little finger," I push. "Trust me. If I say jump, he jumps. What better leverage could you have over Jonathan Hunter than me controlling one of his sons?"

Schemes swirl in Dad's gray eyes as he stares at the dark night outside the windows while absentmindedly drumming his fingers on his arm. Everyone else in the room watches him in silence, waiting for his decision.

My relationship with Kaden isn't at all what I just made it sound like, but my father would never understand if I told him the truth. So I played the one card that I know he understands. Power and control.

At last, he tears his gaze from the stormy night outside.

My heart leaps as a proud smile spreads across his lips and he slowly turns towards me.

"My daughter." Holding my gaze, he lets out a soft breath. "I'm sorry that I haven't truly seen you until now. You are a Petrov. And as dangerous as your brothers."

My entire soul fills with sparkles.

"Because you have done the one thing than none of us ever could." Proud warmth pulses from his whole body as he looks at me. "You have neutralized the Hunters."

42

KADEN

The argument has been going for so long that the doctors have already finished stitching me up and left the building again. In fact, I'm pretty sure that even the cleaning crews are done in the dining room by now. Exasperation washes over me as I rub a hand over my face before giving my father a pointed look.

"Last time I checked, I don't need your permission to get married," I point out.

"You're not marrying a Petrov!" he retorts, throwing out his arms in frustration. "She is the reason you almost died in that dining room earlier."

The fact that he is yelling at me really is saying something about his feelings for the Petrov family, considering that he has almost never dared to deny me anything. Let alone raise his voice at me. But I don't give a shit. Alina is mine. And the sooner I can put a ring on her finger, the sooner everyone else will back the fuck off.

"Almost died?" I retort. "Give me some credit. You saw

what the room looked like when you arrived. It will take more than that to kill me."

Some of that retort is partially negated by the fact that I'm still sitting down. But after the blood loss and the exhaustion of the fight, the doctors practically threatened me into sitting still while whatever they injected me with did its job. So I have remained in my seat.

"He's right," Eli says from where he is seated next to me. "Given that aftermath, it had to have been one hell of a fight."

Warmth spreads through my chest, and I cast him a quick glance from the corner of my eye. His mouth quirks in a barely visible grin. Rico and Jace are also seated at the large table in the conference room that we're occupying. The moment the doctors told me that I needed to keep sitting down for a while, all three of my brothers immediately stopped pacing like caged wolves and casually sat down around the table with me. As if they knew how much I would hate being the only one who was sitting down like some kind of weakling. I appreciate the gesture more than I can say.

"It doesn't matter," our father says from where he is still stalking back and forth on the floor. "She's still a Petrov."

"So?" I fix him with a look full of challenge. "Eli is dating a Smith and you don't have a problem with that."

Eli nods, silently backing up my argument.

"Not to mention the kind of background the girl I'm dating comes from," Rico adds.

Jonathan blows out a breath full of frustration and exasperation as he stops and turns to face the four of us head on. "*Your* future marriage falls under Federico's jurisdiction," he points out, giving Rico a look. Then he shifts his gaze between me and Eli. "And the Smiths are different. They're trust-worthy. A stable and predictable family."

Eli chuckles under his breath and wiggles his eyebrows at the three of us.

Jace and I snort while Rico rolls his eyes.

I don't think anyone who has met Raina would describe her as *stable and predictable*. She's absolutely insane. Even more so than Eli. And that really is saying something.

"You can't trust the Petrovs," our father finishes.

Since this argument isn't getting anywhere, I decide to switch tactics. "And that's exactly why I should marry Alina. We will lose an enemy and gain an ally."

"How—"

"Think about it. If I marry Alina, she will be in my house and at my mercy for the rest of her life. And as long as I hold her safety over their heads, the Petrovs will never dare to threaten us again."

That gets his attention.

Running a hand over his jaw, he considers in silence for a few seconds.

Outside the windows, the storm continues raging. Rain pelts the glass and winds howl around the building.

At last, Jonathan looks back at me and nods. "That's an excellent point."

"I know." I arch an eyebrow at him. "Have I ever done anything without a proper plan?"

"No, I suppose you haven't." Rolling his shoulders back, he clears his throat and then starts towards the doors. "Let's get this over with then, shall we?"

Chairs scrape as we hurry to get to our feet as well. I grab the fresh shirt that Jace brought me from my room and pull it on, gently guiding it over the bandages and stitches.

Eli lets out a low whistle of approval as the three of them

wait for me to finish. Jonathan is already out the door and probably halfway down the corridor by now.

"*If I marry Alina, she will be in my house and at my mercy for the rest of her life. And as long as I hold her safety over their heads, the Petrovs will never dare to threaten us again,*" Eli mimics in my voice. "Damn, you're brutal."

"And a sneaky little liar," Rico adds with a sly smile.

"Because we all know that you're whipped as fuck," Jace finishes, flashing me a wide grin.

Eli and Rico laugh as they nod while giving me knowing looks. I narrow my eyes at them all.

"Shut up," I mutter.

They fall in beside me as I start towards the door. There is a wicked smirk on Eli's mouth as he casually throws an arm over my shoulder.

"Who would've thought that our own little Kaden would fall so hard for a girl," he says, that grin still on his face.

"And not only that," Rico adds from Eli's other side. "A girl that he wants to marry and settle down with."

"You do not get to give me shit about settling down and playing house," I retort, shooting him a pointed look.

"If you want," Jace begins before Rico can reply. "I could try to find one of those French maid costumes for you, so that you can start wearing it around the house to practice."

I narrow my eyes at my grinning little brother. "I just took down an entire room full of people. I have no problem adding three more bodies to today's kill count."

He snorts and rolls his eyes. "As if you could ever take me."

Eli and Rico just chuckle. I blow out an exasperated sigh and shake my head at all three of my very annoying brothers.

Down the hall, our father reaches the double doors to the dining room. But he waits for us to catch up before he reaches for the door handles. Eli slides his arm off my shoulders as we close the final distance, and I straighten my shirt again.

Eli, Jace, and Rico all give me a look that needs no words. I know exactly what it says. They might mess with me because it's fun, but they're happy for me. And they approve of Alina. I give them a small nod.

An impeccably clean dining room meets us as we open the doors and walk across the threshold. Our cleaning crew, combined with the Petrov one, has not only worked fast but also incredibly well. Everything is back to the way it was before.

All the tables are back in their original place, complete with silverware, plates, and glasses ready and waiting for the next guest. The gothic chandeliers in the ceiling are still burning with hundreds of candles, casting light over the hardwood floor. Not a speck of blood remains on the now once more polished surface.

I sweep my gaze across the room, immediately locating the one person that I care about in the group waiting for us.

Alina is standing next to her father at a table for four in the middle of the room. She has now changed out of the blue silk dress and is watching me with a small private smile on her beautiful face. My soul immediately warms.

Her annoying brothers and cousins are standing to the left and right of the table. All of them have their arms crossed and their eyebrows drawn down as they stare at me in disapproval. But worst of them all is Ivan Petrov himself. He glares at me and my father as if he would rather be anywhere but here right now. I flash them a cocky grin.

As we reach the other side of the table, my father and I come to a halt in front of the chairs while my brothers take up position beside us.

"So, we're apparently going to formalize an engagement contract and an alliance," my father begins, his hard eyes locked on Ivan.

"Apparently we are," Ivan replies.

Wood grinds against wood as we pull out the four chairs and sit down facing each other. Me opposite Alina and our fathers opposite each other. Since Ivan reached out about this an hour ago, they already have a contract drawn up and printed out. A copy of it is waiting on the table in front of all our seats.

"Let's get this over with," Ivan says once we're all seated.

Jonathan nods. "Lets."

I keep my eyes on Alina while we finish negotiating the contract until both our families are satisfied. I can't believe she managed to get her father to agree to this. He hates our family, and me in particular, and he was dead set on marrying her off to some rich idiot. Ultimately, I do what I want. But Alina needs her family's permission for this. Which was something that I was sure she would never get. So how the hell did she manage to convince them to go through with this?

"Are we all in agreement?" Jonathan eventually asks, only sounding slightly annoyed.

"Yes," Alina, Ivan, and I all reply.

"Great. Then let's sign."

Papers rustle as we all sign the contracts before us.

Once it's done, we all stand up. Alina is smiling so brightly that my heart almost stops. But Ivan still glares at me, so I hold out a hand across the table as if to shake his.

His lip curls in disgust as he looks down at my hand before shooting me another glare. "Don't push it."

I let out a smug chuckle as he stalks away from the table.

Mikhail shoots me a threatening look before he and Anton and the twins follow Ivan out the door.

A look that I can only interpret as 'God, give me strength' blows across my father's face as he shakes his head and then turns to leave as well. Eli and Jace flash me a grin while Rico winks at me. Then they follow Jonathan out, closing the two double doors behind them. I turn to Alina.

Mischief glitters in her eyes as she rounds the table and comes to stand in front of me. "Hello, fiancé."

"Hello, wife," I reply.

She swats my chest with the back of her hand and gives me a look. "Not yet."

"Soon."

"You need to finish your senior year at Blackwater first."

"So?" A sly smile curls my lips as I draw my fingers along her jaw. "You're still mine."

Grabbing the collar of my shirt, she pulls my face down to hers and claims my lips.

Heat pulses through my body at the possessiveness in her kiss. I slide my hands into her hair, kissing her back until she's gasping for breath.

"And you're mine," she whispers, resting her forehead against mine. "I'm sorry that I didn't see this attack coming. Next time, I will."

I slide my fingers from her hair to her jaw, tipping her chin up so that she meets my gaze again as I straighten. There is both determination and vulnerability in her eyes as she holds my gaze.

"Next time, *we* will," I correct her. "Together."

She smiles. And once more, my heart almost stops. God, I want to spend the rest of my life watching all of these incredible emotions shine on her gorgeous face. And now, I will.

Curiosity swirls inside me again, and I cock my head as I study Alina.

"How did you get your father to agree to this marriage?" I ask.

A sly smile spreads across her lips, and she flicks her long blonde hair behind her shoulder. "I told him that I have you wrapped around my little finger." Then she raises her eyebrows at me. "You?"

I laugh, and then incline my head in approval. "Same."

She laughs as well. Her warm hands trail up my arms before locking around the back of my neck, pulling me down for another kiss. This one giddy and full of promises for the future.

What she told her father was the truth, though. She does have me wrapped around her little finger. There is nothing I wouldn't do for her. No lines I wouldn't cross. And the best part is that I know she feels the same way about me.

This strong, smart, and scheming woman. How could anyone think that she is made of glass? She is made of the strongest steel.

Only a true warrior could look into this cold, emotionless heart of mine and still find something to love.

I will never put her on a shelf like a trophy or a fragile little glass figurine.

She will be right by my side.

Plotting mayhem and bloody schemes.

Forever.

EPILOGUE

ONE YEAR LATER

The church is full of people. Candles are burning along the entire aisle even though sunlight still shines in through the stained-glass windows. Wood creaks as people take their seats, and there is a pleasant murmur in the air. It would look like the perfect picture of how to celebrate unity... if it weren't for the fact that the entire crowd is clearly split in two.

On the left side of the aisle is my family and the rest of our people. Several of them are speaking quietly in Russian while casting suspicious looks at Kaden's side of the church. Some of them are, in turn, shooting equally wary glances at my family while speaking softly in Italian.

I laugh under my breath. Kaden and I have been together for a year now. They can't possibly still think that this is some kind of trap.

"The bride shouldn't be out in the church in her wedding dress like this before the ceremony starts," a casual voice says from behind me.

Straightening from the open doorway I was leaning on, I

turn around to find Kaden's father standing behind me. Jonathan Hunter is wearing an impeccable dark blue suit that complements his brown hair and blue eyes perfectly. Narrowing my eyes slightly, I flash him a knowing smile.

"That's the best thing about being the bride." I give him a quick rise and fall of my eyebrows. "My wedding. My rules."

He chuckles, and then tips his head at me as if conceding the point. Then his expression turns serious as he holds my gaze. "It's not too late to run, you know."

"Run?" I raise my eyebrows. "From what?"

"This." He flicks his wrist to indicate the wedding that's about to begin soon. "Kaden is a very complicated person. There are a lot easier partners you could choose."

"I don't want easy. I want *him*." I fix Jonathan with a sharp look and nod towards the entrance to the church while giving him a fake sweet smile. "And if witnessing this wedding is that distressing for you, you can always wait outside until it's done."

Amusement flickers in his eyes, and it looks like he's suppressing a smile as he raises his hands in surrender. "I just had to make sure."

Then he starts back towards where the rest of his sons are waiting. But right before he moves out of earshot, I swear I can hear him chuckle and whisper to himself, "She's going to be perfect."

I shake my head at his retreating back, but then blink in surprise when Jace suddenly shoots up from his seat at the front of the church and sprints between the pews. My brows crease in a frown. But then I spot the reason.

A young woman with beautiful red hair jerks back as Jace skids to a halt in front of her. I'm too far away to hear anything, but Jace crosses his arms over his broad chest and levels a disapproving stare at her.

She throws her arms up in frustration and says something while shaking her head.

Jace looks like he is trying to keep his cool as he raises his arm and points a commanding hand back towards the pew closer to the back where she had been sitting. He says something that makes irritation flash across her face, and she stabs a finger into his chest while retorting with something I still can't hear.

Mirth ripples through me as I shake my head at them. It has only been a few weeks since the two of them were forced into this kind of close proximity, and I can't wait to see how this will all play out. Especially since that wild girl has apparently made it her mission in life to drive Jace crazy. In more ways than one.

But before I can see how this latest argument ends, another altercation draws my attention.

My heart leaps into my throat as I spot my father and brothers corner Kaden the moment he steps into the church from a side door. Kaden comes to a halt, standing completely still as the three of them surround him. Dad is standing in front of him, presumably saying something. But his back is to me so I can't tell what it is.

Kaden's gaze slides over my father's shoulder and lands on me, as if he could feel my presence even across an entire room full of people. His lips quirk faintly in a tiny smirk as he meets my gaze for a few seconds before shifting his attention back to my father.

A smile dripping with challenge spreads across Kaden's mouth.

Then he reaches up and pats my dad on the arm in a highly dismissive and condescending way before simply strolling off.

I don't know whether to laugh or roll my eyes or groan in exasperation.

"If everyone could please take your seats," the priest calls, his voice echoing through the grand stone building. "The ceremony will start shortly."

The priest's gaze shifts to me, and he raises his eyebrows expectantly.

This time I do roll my eyes. But he's right. I'm technically not supposed to be standing here. So I sweep my gaze over the candlelit room one more time and then turn and slip back through the doorway and into the small waiting room close to the beginning of the main aisle.

It's warm, brightly lit with normal ceiling lamps, and furnished with pale wood. I brush my hands down my white wedding dress and then check my appearance in the mirror.

"God, you're gorgeous," a stunned voice suddenly says.

I spin around to find Kaden standing there. It looks like he just walked through the door and then forgot where he was going once he spotted me. Warmth spreads through me, heating my cheeks, both at his words and at the breathless tone of his voice.

His mouth is slightly open as he rakes his gaze up and down my body.

"I don't think you're supposed to use God's name like that in a church," I tease, drifting closer to him while trying to force my flushed cheeks to cool down.

A mischievous glint appears in Kaden's dark eyes. "Fuck, you're gorgeous." He grins at me. "Was that better?"

I laugh, coming to a halt in front of him. Tilting my head

back, I drink in the sight of him while my heart skips several beats.

The first time I saw him, I thought he looked beautiful but in a severe way. Like an ice sculpture. And he still does. With his sharp cheekbones and piercing dark eyes and straight black hair, he still looks beautiful and dangerous like a sharp shard of ice. As if simply touching him would be enough to draw blood. It's part of what drew me to him in the first place. The danger. The power. The cold control he always wields.

But now I also know the roaring wildfire that burns inside of him. To the outside world, it might look like he is completely emotionless. But I know him better. I know the real him. I know that he feels emotions even more strongly than anyone else I have ever met.

He would slaughter entire countries to keep me safe. And he would burn the world down for me if I so much as asked him. He loves me with such intensity that the universe itself would tremble before it.

And I love him with the same insane fire.

He sees me. The real me. And he loves everything that he sees. He doesn't try to shut me away. Instead, he wants me right there next to him. He makes me a better version of me. Stronger. Smarter. Even more ruthless.

Reaching up, I draw my hands along his sharp jaw. A shudder of pleasure rolls through him, as it usually does when I touch him. Even after all this time.

"I saw my father and brothers corner you out there," I begin. "What did they say?"

His dark eyes glint. "They put a gun to my spine and told me that they would make me a quadriplegic if I ever hurt you."

A half amused, half exasperated laugh rips from my chest. Letting my hand drop back down, I shake my head at my infuriating family before fixing Kaden with a knowing look. Amusement plays over my lips.

"A bit too late for that, don't you think?" I tease. "Given everything you did to me when we first met?"

He reaches up and wraps a hand around my jaw. Leaning forward, he flashes me a villainous smile and slants his lips over mine. "I have never done anything that you couldn't handle."

Heat ripples through me as he steals a kiss before releasing my jaw. Outside the door, the music starts playing. My heart lurches. It's time.

Kaden turns around to face the door while I move so that I'm standing next to him.

"Well," I begin, casting him a look from the corner of my eye. "If it makes you feel better, your father tried to convince me to call off the wedding too."

Arching an eyebrow, he glances down at me. "And what did you say?"

"I told him very politely to fuck off."

He laughs.

The sound of it goes straight into my soul, filling it with sparkling warmth.

With the most incredible light dancing in his eyes, he smiles and holds out an arm to me. "Well then. Shall we do this?"

I take his arm. "Yes."

A brilliant smile spreads across my face as Kaden and I walk down the aisle side by side.

My father is not walking me down the aisle to hand me over to Kaden. Because I'm not a possession that can be given away from one male relative to another man. No. Kaden and I walk down the aisle together. Because we are entering this marriage as equals.

Everyone shifts in their seats to watch us as we walk past the rows of wooden pews and towards the priest. Candles flicker from the faint draft it creates, making the tiny flames glitter in the gold decorations throughout the church. I smile, my hand still on Kaden's arm, as we close the final distance to the waiting priest.

Happiness bubbles inside me.

As Kaden and I come to a halt before him, the priest gives us a nod and a small smile. Then he raises his voice so that it carries across the entire church.

"We have gathered here today not only to join two people in holy matrimony," he begins. "But also to join two families. It is time to put aside your guns and become one. It is time to trust—"

A loud *bang* sounds from the back of the church.

Guns are cocked and clothes rustle as everyone shoots to their feet.

Towards the back, the fiery redhead who came here with Jace flushes a bright shade of scarlet where she's standing next to a chair she toppled over while no doubt trying to sneak away. Embarrassment pulsing on her face, she snaps her mouth shut and promptly sits down again.

I shift my gaze to the rest of the crowd.

And find a standoff.

With guns.

Lots of guns.

Everyone on my side of the aisle is on their feet and pointing weapons at the Hunters while they're scanning the church for signs of an ambush. On the other side of the aisle, all of the Hunters and the rest of their people are standing up as well, guns leveled at my family and our people as they flick their gazes around the room in search of the threat.

I burst out laughing.

Well, maybe that trust between our families that the priest was talking about needs some work.

But Kaden and I trust each other. And that is all that matters.

Once everyone notices the toppled chair and the mortified woman sitting next to it, several people from both sides of the aisle clear their throats awkwardly. My dad and Jonathan Hunter exchange a quick look, flick an apologetic glance towards me and Kaden, and then wave a hand for their respective sides to stand down.

The sound of guns being de-cocked echoes throughout the room as everyone inside the church stops leveling weapons at each other and instead sits back down.

Laughing again, I shake my head at our two insane families.

Next to me, Kaden huffs out an amused breath as well.

"Did you know that all of them were armed?" he asks quietly.

"Nope," I whisper as I turn back around to face him. "You?"

"Not a clue."

Light from the candles glitter in his eyes as he holds my gaze.

On our other side, the priest, who had taken cover during the short standoff, is straightening again and awkwardly brushing his hands down his robes.

"We should probably just kiss now before someone starts shooting," I muse, a smile tugging at my mouth.

A wide smile spreads across his lips. "Good idea."

Sliding a hand along my jaw, he threads his fingers through my hair as he leans down to claim my mouth.

Fireworks explode inside my soul as he kisses me fiercely.

His brothers let out cheers and whoops.

"Wait," the priest calls, sounding distressed. "You're not supposed to kiss yet."

While still keeping one hand in my hair and kissing me senseless, Kaden produces a knife from somewhere in his suit and levels it at the priest in a silent threat.

I laugh against his lips.

Kaden Hunter is mine. This beautiful, dangerous, knife-wielding villain is all mine. And I am his.

And God help anyone who gets in our way.

BONUS SCENE

Do you want read about Alina and Kaden's spicy wedding night? Then scan the QR code to download the exclusive bonus scene:

Made in the USA
Las Vegas, NV
24 February 2024